It felt strangely liberating to voice aloud the thought he'd tried so hard to avoid for the past two days. "At the rate I'm declining, by tomorrow I'll probably no longer be able to function as the ship's chief medical officer."

"You don't know that," Ezri said.

"I can *feel* it, Ezri." He decided that now wasn't an occasion that called for a stiff upper lip. "I believe I'm . . . *reverting.* Regressing to what I was before Adigeon Prime."

Her eyes widened with sudden understanding. "Before you were genetically enhanced."

"I can't begin to explain it," he said, nodding. "But somehow our encounter with the alien artifact has begun . . . *undoing* my genetic resequencing."

She seemed to mull that over for a moment before responding. "It sounds crazy, but it fits. Nog and I are reverting, too, if you think about it. He's become the two-legged Ferengi he used to be. I've been turned into the unjoined Trill I was before the *Destiny* brought me together with Dax. And you're becoming . . ." She trailed off.

Slow, plodding, uncoordinated, dumb *Jules Bashir.*

Jules. He had repudiated that name during his childhood, after his parents had, in effect, repudiated *him*—when they'd had his DNA illegally rewritten when he was only six years old. Whatever Jules might eventually have accomplished left to his own devices had been rendered moot from that point on, forever after consigned to the shadow-world of roads not taken. Inaccessible mirror universes.

He vividly recalled the day, three short years ago, when he had taken his parents to task over this. Facing the very real possibility of dismissal from Starfleet because of his illegal genetic alterations, he had wished that Richard and Amsha Bashir had never taken him to Adigeon Prime, that they'd instead simply allowed nature to take its course with young Jules, for better or for worse.

That errant wish now appeared to be coming true—and the brutal reality of it horrified him. He realized now that it meant the loss of abilities and talents which he had come to take for granted over the better part of three decades. The loss of what he sometimes feared were the only things that gave him value as a human being.

The loss of *self.*

STAR TREK
DEEP SPACE NINE®

MISSION: GAMMA

BOOK THREE OF FOUR

CATHEDRAL

MICHAEL A. MARTIN
and
ANDY MANGELS

Based upon STAR TREK®
created by Gene Roddenberry, and
STAR TREK: DEEP SPACE NINE
created by Rick Berman & Michael Piller

POCKET BOOKS
New York   London   Toronto   Sydney   Singapore   Cardassia Prime

An *Original* Publication of POCKET BOOKS

POCKET BOOKS, a division of Simon & Schuster, Inc.
1230 Avenue of the Americas, New York, NY 10020

This book is published by Pocket Books, a division of Simon & Schuster, Inc., under exclusive license from Paramount Pictures.

ISBN: 0-7434-4564-3

First Pocket Books printing October 2002

10 9 8 7 6 5 4 3 2 1

POCKET and colophon are registered trademarks of Simon & Schuster, Inc.

For information regarding special discounts for bulk purchases, please contact Simon & Schuster Special Sales at 1-800-456-6798 or business@simonandschuster.com

Cover art by Cliff Nielsen

Printed in the U.S.A.

*To my wife, Jennifer Dottery, whose patience
approaches the asymptotic infinite*

—M.A.M.

*For Tim Tuohy, our past editor on the
Star Trek: Deep Space Nine comics at
Marvel. Thanks for giving us an assignment
with Starfleet!*

—A.M.

ACKNOWLEDGMENTS

The authors wish to acknowledge that the poem quoted in Chapter 23 comprises the closing lines of *Through the Looking-Glass And What Alice Found There* by Lewis Carroll—a book much beloved by young Jules Bashir, as well as by many previous generations of youthful adventurers.

We also owe a debt of gratitude to our editor, Marco Palmieri, whose patient efforts made this a much better book than it otherwise would have been.

I am a part of all that I have met;
Yet all experience is an arch wherethrough
Gleams that untraveled world, whose margin fades
For ever and for ever when I move . . .

—ALFRED, LORD TENNYSON,
"ULYSSES"

CATHEDRAL

"Are we certain it was suicide?"

Lieutenant Ro Laren turned to Sergeant Shul as they stalked down the corridor, with Dr. Simon Tarses following close behind. "I'm not certain of anything yet, Shul," Ro replied. "At this point, what I know is that Councillor zh'Thane says that Thriss committed suicide in Shar's quarters."

Tarses spoke up, his brow furrowed. "Thriss seemed to be beyond the worst of her depression when she was working her last shift at the infirmary. And Counselor Matthias was optimistic about her improvement. I find it hard to believe that Thriss would have taken her own life."

"If she didn't, then we're looking at a murder investigation, Doctor," Shul said. "And I don't mean to be crass, but with everything else happening on this station, we don't need *that* to contend with, as well."

Ro grunted in agreement, then, before they got much

farther down the hall, spoke in a low voice. After all, Andorian antennae were very sensitive, and she had no clue who might be listening two junctions down the corridor. "Whatever the situation, please remember that Andorian customs are different from ours. I haven't been able to brief you before now on certain . . . aspects of their relationships, but I suspect you may have already picked up clues along the way. This will be very delicate, especially with Councillor zh'Thane involved."

Both men nodded, and they continued toward Shar's quarters. No one was there to meet them outside the door, so Ro touched the wall panel that activated the door chime. "Councillor, it's Lieutenant Ro. I have Doctor Tarses with me."

The door slid open, and it took Ro's eyes a moment to adjust to the dim light within the room. Just inside the door was zh'Thane, her usually immaculate hair slightly disheveled. From her garments, Ro guessed that she had been asleep when she had gotten the call about the tragedy.

As Ro moved to enter the room, zh'Thane held up a pale blue hand as if to stop her. "Who is this other man?"

"This is Sergeant Shul Torem," said Ro, gesturing toward her deputy. "He's well versed in Starfleet protocol pertaining to forensic investigations. And he can be trusted to be discreet."

Tarses spoke up. "Councillor, there may be a chance to save Thriss's life if you'll allow me to attend to her."

Zh'Thane swept her arm toward the interior of the room, where two figures crouched in the darkness, their arms around their legs and their heads bowed. The body of Thriss lay on the bed, perfectly still. "She seems quite beyond help, Doctor. If you can do something, please do, but do *not* violate the integrity of the body. The skin must not be broken."

Tarses nodded, then moved into the room with his tricorder in one hand and his medkit slung over a shoulder. As zh'Thane moved back a step, Ro and Shul stepped into the room, though they did not spread out.

"Can you tell me what happened, Councillor?" Ro asked.

"Dizhei came to Shar's quarters, concerned that Thriss's depression might be more consuming than she had revealed to us. She found her on the bed, already dead. She called Anichent and me to the room, and I, in turn, called you."

Shul spoke up, his voice cool and low. "Was there any sign of struggle?"

"No, Deputy," zh'Thane said. "Dizhei had tried to move her, to get her to respond. But there did not appear to be any struggle, and certainly nothing dangerous was found. Other than this." She produced a small hypospray from the folds of her robe. "She was clutching this in her hand."

His hands gloved, Shul gingerly took the device from zh'Thane and placed it into a small plastic bag he had pulled from a belt pouch. "Has anyone else touched this?" he asked as he handed the bag to Dr. Tarses, who had already opened his tricorder.

"Not to my knowledge. I pulled it from Thriss's grasp myself."

Ro looked the councillor directly in the eyes, steeling herself. Zh'Thane was already intimidating enough, and the situation was fraught with potential for giving offense. "Councillor, you have made it very clear to me that Andorian customs are not something to be shared with outside parties. However, I am unsure what the correct customs *are* in this situation. Because this happened aboard Deep Space 9, I am . . . obliged to investigate further. But I don't wish to make the situation any more painful, either for you or for Thriss's bondmates."

"I appreciate your discretion, Lieutenant," zh'Thane replied. "This is indeed a very private matter, and while I am cognizant of your need for answers, I must insist that this room—and the body of my son's bondmate— be considered off-limits to any Starfleet or station staff for the foreseeable future."

Shul began to object, but zh'Thane cut him off. "I will grant you a few minutes to gather whatever information you require, but I can assure you that this unfortunate situation is a—" Her voice caught in her throat for a moment, and she looked to the ceiling before continuing. "Faced with what she felt was an untenable situation, Thriss took her *own* life. There is no mystery to be solved. Nor has a crime been committed, other than the crime of selfishness on the part of my son, who tore apart his bond. And on the part of Thriss, who made certain that none of her bondmates could have a future together."

Zh'Thane gestured for Ro and Shul to search the room, then told the computer to raise the light level. As Shul began inspecting the area, Ro looked at the kneeling forms of Dizhei and Anichent, both of whom appeared to be quietly meditating. Their antennae curled limply before them, like wilted flowers. Their faces downcast, they held themselves as still as statues. Indigo-tinged blood was still wet from gashes furrowed into their uncovered arms, and Ro could see the same blood crusted on their fingertips.

Ro moved to the bedside where Tarses was still scanning Thriss. In a low voice, he said, "I don't think there's any hope here, Ro. Whatever killed her stopped everything cold. There's not even any residual neuro-electrical activity or muscular contractions."

"We have the hypospray that zh'Thane found in her hand. Maybe that will tell us what killed her," Ro said, sparing a glance in Tarses' direction. The doctor was preoccupied with his tricorder's display, apparently fine-tuning his scan for some particular substance.

Ro looked around the bed for any clues. There were not, as the councillor had said, any signs of struggle, other than those probably caused by the Andorians trying to rouse their partner. None of the vases and sculptures near the bed or on its headboard were broken or toppled. She lifted Thriss's hands, checking under her nails. She didn't see any dried blood; it hadn't been Thriss who clawed at her bondmates. They must have injured themselves—or perhaps each other—in their grief.

A few moments later, Dr. Tarses cleared his throat, prompting both Ro and zh'Thane to look in his direction. "It certainly appears that the substance in the hypospray was the cause of death," he said quietly. "Arithrazine."

Ro frowned. "I thought arithrazine was for treating theta-radiation exposure. Like the Europani refugees."

"It is," the doctor nodded. "But it's designed to work in concert with the radiation in the patient's system. By itself—and in large enough doses—arithrazine can cause rapid neural depolarization. And it explains the arithrazine ampules I discovered missing from the infirmary about an hour ago."

Ro was startled by a sudden motion from the kneeling mourners. She felt her body tense involuntarily, reminded of Thriss's earlier outburst of violence at Quark's bar. But neither Anichent nor Dizhei appeared to pose an imminent threat. They both appeared crushed, defeated.

"Then I trust that all your immediate questions have been answered, Lieutenant," zh'Thane said, facing Ro.

Ro noticed then that zh'Thane's own hands were clasped behind her back, perhaps to conceal the visible trail her own grief had left upon her body.

Ro nodded to Shul and Tarses, and they began to gather themselves to depart. "Certainly, Councillor. I believe we have enough information for now. Is there anything I can do to help . . . to provide for funeral or memorial arrangements?"

"No. Again, these quarters are to be considered off-limits to all station personnel." Zh'Thane gave Ro a sharp look, as if to warn her. "If I *need* to, I'll discuss the matter with Colonel Kira to make certain this requirement is honored. I will contact you regarding other arrangements as we need them."

Ro was uncomfortable with the councillor's near-threatening tone, but knew that now was not the time to debate it. "I'll make certain to discuss the matter with Colonel Kira myself, and advise my personnel of your . . . restrictions."

"We will need a stasis chamber for Thriss's body," zh'Thane said, seeming not to notice that Ro had spoken. "Please have it delivered as soon as possible. *Discreetly.*"

"Certainly." Ro eyed Tarses, who nodded almost imperceptibly as he moved toward the door with Shul.

As zh'Thane turned away from her, Ro began to make her way to the door as well. She stooped near Anichent and Dizhei, but carefully avoided coming into contact with them. They maintained their crouched positions, both of them seeming to be entirely inward-directed.

In a low voice, Ro said, "My sincere condolences on the loss of your bondm—"

Anichent lunged at her like a mad *targ,* his eyes wild, spittle flying from his mouth. The strangled growl he let out was unlike anything Ro had ever heard before, and she toppled backward, kicking out to try to get into a defensive posture.

Shul drew his phaser and leveled it at Anichent, but there was no need. Anichent froze where he stood, though his chest heaved and drool still came from his mouth. Ro backed away and stood, holding one hand up to calm Shul, and the other in front of her, palm outward, to placate Anichent.

"Please leave," zh'Thane said, her back still toward them. "As you can surely see by now, Shar's choice not to conform to his predestined bonding has destroyed not just Thriss's life. My son has also ravaged the lives of Anichent and Dizhei."

Ro and the others backed out of the room in silence. None of them spoke until they were back at the Promenade, where the bustle of life replaced the pall of death.

2

A gout of blue flame ripped through the long ship's irregular hull as it sped through space, maneuvering from
side to side in an effort to dodge further blasts from its
pursuers. The disruptor weapons on the larger craft were
mounted on gimbals, allowing them to track its smaller
prey's movements closely.

The smaller ship accelerated, the lambent internal
fires of its propulsion system becoming preternaturally
bright. Another salvo struck her laterally, slicing deep
into the hull plating amidships. Undeterred, the small
craft's pilot continued to spin and weave, evading the
next burst of energy. Moments later, another blast struck
a glancing blow, shearing off an extrusive wing element.
But the wounded vessel soldiered on, headed toward a
somewhat less empty region of space, where fragments
of cometary ice shimmered as they made their cen-
turies-long procession around this system's distant primary star.

And then, in front of the fleeing craft, yet another ship loomed. Exiting the system's Oort cloud was a large, gray, nearly flat vessel flanked by blue-illuminated engine nacelles integrated into its hull. Across its nacelles and protruding dorsal surface the designation NX-74205 was visible, thanks to several running lights.

The damaged ship swooped to give the newcomer a wide berth, only to catch yet another disruptor blast on its port side. Molecular fires danced across the hull of the now all but wrecked vessel, and crystallizing atmospheric gases rushed out as she careened forward—now on a collision course with the newly arrived ship.

A short time earlier
Ensign Thirishar ch'Thane sat alone on the floor of the darkened quarters he shared with Nog. He listened intently to the quiet, taking solace in this solitary, lightless space. Since Nog was currently on a survey mission with Lieutenant Dax and Dr. Bashir, he would probably have the room to himself for the next several hours. At least until his next duty shift began.

The only light in the room came from the holo of a laughing Thriss, which blazed down at him from the room's small desk. The image captured a few crystalline moments, endlessly replaying her soundless laugh, the carefree toss of her platinum hair. Looking at the image was sheer torture.

But he owed her a penance. Owed it to Dizhei and Anichent as well. Owed it to every Andorian who had ever dared hope for a better future.

He couldn't bring himself to look away.

So far, Shar had shared the news of Thriss's suicide only with Ezri, whom he knew he could trust not to tell anyone else. But how long would it be before Nog or others among this crew of forty began guessing at what was troubling him? Shar was already certain that his decision to sit out the shuttlecraft *Sagan*'s current survey mission had already given Nog cause to suspect that all was not right with him.

A yellow alert klaxon sounded, and a light began flashing rhythmically above the doorway.

Shar regarded the intrusive illumination contemplatively. After ordering the computer to extinguish its light and noise, he was only mildly surprised to note how little it concerned him.

And he wondered if he had finally begun to drink from the same cup of despair that had killed both Thriss and his future.

Commander Elias Vaughn sat forward in his seat, one hand absently stroking his salt-and-pepper beard. His eyes were intent on the *Defiant*'s main viewscreen, where he could see a large, bulbous ship pursuing and firing on a somewhat smaller, gracefully tapered vessel. The pitted, scarred hulls of both vessels bore mute testament to countless previous battles.

"Any luck hailing them?" Vaughn growled at Lieutenant Sam Bowers, who was running the tactical station.

"No, sir," Bowers said with a shake of the head. "I'm hailing them on all frequencies, but nothing's coming through."

"Take us in closer, Ensign Lankford," Vaughn said, nodding to the blond woman who sat at the conn. Vaughn then turned his head slightly, speaking over his shoulder toward the tactical station. "Keep all shields at the ready, Mr. Bowers. This is obviously a touchy situation, and until we can get some idea of what's happening and why, we need to see to our own protection first."

"Aye, sir," Bowers said.

The turbolift doors whooshed open, and Vaughn saw his daughter, Ensign Prynn Tenmei, tug momentarily on her tunic as she stepped out onto the bridge. They locked eyes for an instant. "Sorry to cut your lunch short, Ensign," Vaughn said, then mimed wiping his hand across his mouth.

Tenmei got the hint and subtly removed the remnants of red sauce from her lower lip as she took her post at the conn. Lankford moved aside for her, taking a secondary post at the back of the bridge.

"I wonder what this fight is about?" Vaughn said to no one in particular.

On the viewscreen, the heavily damaged alien ship flared with crackling electrical energy, then spun toward them at a dizzying speed.

"I think it's about to land in our laps," Tenmei said dryly.

"Evasive maneuvers!" Vaughn shouted. The *Defiant* lurched to the side, tossing the bridge crew along with it as the ship's inertial dampers struggled to keep the artificial gravity field stable.

A split second later, something slammed into the *Defiant,* and Vaughn heard an unmistakable rending sound coming from the port side of the navigational deflector.

"Shields holding!" Bowers yelled. "We've taken a glancing hit from the pursuing vessel."

Vaughn thought he would decide later whether or not the pursuing vessel's attack on the *Defiant* had been deliberate. "Damage?" he barked.

"The pursuer's weaponry didn't do anything to us," said Bowers.

11

Tenmei checked a conn display. "But that near collision cost us our portside targeting sensors."

"What's the status of the damaged alien ship?" Vaughn asked, turning toward the science station.

"It survived its brush with our shields and is now headed deeper into the Oort cloud, Captain," said science specialist Kurt Hunter. The eager-looking young officer quickly consulted a readout before continuing. "But it's losing power rapidly, no doubt because of all the damage its pursuer has inflicted on it. My scans show that both of these vessels have only rudimentary warp capabilities."

"Well, I can't just let the underdog die without any clue as to what this is all about," Vaughn said. "Mr. Bowers, I need to talk to somebody out there. Fast."

"Still hailing on all known Gamma Quadrant frequencies," Bowers said, putting his hand up to his earpiece. "And on most of the Alpha Quadrant frequencies as well. They don't seem to . . . Wait, I'm getting something."

Abruptly, the viewscreen image transformed from the serenity of trackless space to a vision of utter chaos. Vaughn caught a few disjointed glimpses of what appeared to be a ship's bridge manned by more than half a dozen slick-carapaced, insectile creatures. Most of them were apparently panicking, and several seemed to be yelling into the viewscreen simultaneously. Their narrow, chitin-covered heads were mounted on stick-thin bodies; the creatures scuttled about on tripod legs, some of them walking upside down on the ceilings.

"I'm trying to figure out what they're saying, Captain," Bowers said. "But the universal translator isn't having an easy time of it. All I'm getting is gibberish."

"Well, it's clear enough that they're pretty agitated," Vaughn said, feeling a surge of sympathy for the hapless insectoids. During almost eight decades as a Starfleet officer he'd survived enough shipboard disasters to feel that he understood their plight on an extremely visceral level.

"Which of the ships is this transmission coming from?"

"The one that *isn't* firing on us, Captain!" Bowers punched several buttons and braced himself. The ship rocked to the side. "Shields still holding. The aggressor ship is using some kind of disruptor weapon. Not too much of an immediate threat to us, but the smaller ship isn't so well shielded."

Vaughn leaned forward in the chair again as Tenmei touched her console, splitting the viewscreen's image into two. A smaller, inset image displayed the gibbering aliens on their manic bridge, while the rest of the screen showed the attacking ship and its prey.

"Hail the attacker again," Vaughn said.

"No response, sir," Bowers said after nearly another minute had elapsed. "I take that back—they're firing again!"

Vaughn watched as the disruptor's searing light pierced the darkness. From the positions of the multiple plasma blasts, it was clear that the aggressor had several hull-mounted weapons.

The screen flashed for a moment, and the ship rocked gently. "Shields down to ninety percent," Bowers said.

So their hitting us before was no accident, Vaughn thought. *They don't seem to want us here. Why?*

"Let's give them some encouragement to back off. Mr. Bowers, Ensign Merimark, target *only* their weapons systems. If I'm not mistaken, they're mounted on several external armatures, three dorsal, two ventral."

As the young ensign took her place behind Sam at a secondary tactical station, a grinning Bowers drew a bead on his targets. "Good eye, Captain. Targets locked."

Vaughn's eyes narrowed slightly. "Fire."

A series of blasts from the pulse phaser cannons streaked toward the attacking vessel. Within seconds, all had found their mark, and five small, tightly targeted explosions detonated on the other ship's hull. Other than those specific points, the alien vessel appeared to have suffered no damage.

"Good shooting," Vaughn said, complimenting the two tactical officers behind him. His eyes still narrowed, he began a mental countdown. *Five. Four. Three. Two. One.*

"Captain, the attackers are veering off and reversing course," Tenmei said. "Should I pursue?"

"No, Ensign. There's a ship in distress, and that has to take precedence. Besides, we still have no idea what prompted either their attack on us or their pursuit of the damaged ship."

Vaughn turned toward Bowers, who was working the controls with calm alacrity, one hand touching his earpiece. His silent frown of concentration spoke volumes to Vaughn. "Anything intelligible coming from that damaged vessel, Mr. Bowers?"

"I'm getting a lot of audio-channel chatter, sir, some of it on some pretty unusual frequencies. But the UT doesn't seem able to parse their language."

Hunter spoke up then, punching a button on his console that restored the screen image solely to that of the noisy aliens. "Captain, it looks like some of the aliens are wounded. Whether we can understand them or not, I think they could use our help."

Vaughn studied the viewscreen and could see that Hunter was indeed correct. In the background, some of the aliens were staggering, clutching appendages that were slickened with dark, viscous fluids that appeared to have leaked out of compromised exoskeletons. One hovered over a fallen comrade, clearly trying to tend to its injuries.

Vaughn punched a button on his armrest, opening a communication channel. "Nurse Richter, muster up whatever medical staff you can. You're about to have company, and some of them appear to be in a bad way. Ensign Gordimer, please have an armed security detachment report to the medical bay. Chief Chao, prepare to beam wounded parties directly there on Lieutenant Bowers's signal."

Vaughn turned back to Bowers and nodded curtly. The tactical officer began recording transporter coordinates from the crippled alien vessel. On the screen, several of the wounded aliens began to shimmer out of existence, causing even greater consternation among their spindly fellows.

"Oh, for crying out loud." Vaughn put his fingers to his forehead, wincing. "Mr. Bowers, patch a visual feed from the medical bay to the other ship so they know we're trying to *help* their crewmen and aren't just kidnapping them. And keep trying to find a way to communicate with them."

"Yes, sir," Bowers acknowledged and set immediately to work.

Vaughn turned back to the front of the bridge. "Prynn . . . Ensign Tenmei, please find out where the shuttlecraft *Sagan* is and get her crew back here on the double. Dr. Bashir certainly picked a fine time to go out on a survey mission."

Easing back into the captain's chair, Vaughn sighed heavily. He studied the screen for a moment, watching the panicked, herky-jerky movements of the aliens. The image summoned an unbidden recollection of a comical children's holovid he had seen during his youth.

"I can't raise the *Sagan*, Captain," Tenmei said, breaking his brief reverie. "In fact, I'm getting no signal from the shuttle at all."

Comedy was suddenly the furthest thing from Vaughn's mind.

3

Colonel Kira Nerys had hoped to wend her way through the Promenade without being noticed. She had only been back from visiting Bajor—and Kasidy Yates—for a short time, and she felt certain that she would find every trauma in the quadrant metaphorically stacked on her desk when she reached her office. Thus, when she heard the clipped and slightly reptilian voice calling her name, she had to muster her resolve not to ignore it.

"Colonel Kira, may I have a moment?" the Cardassian said, catching up to her.

"Certainly, Gul Macet. What do you need?" Kira felt a surge of relief at the prospect of being reprieved from her office backlog, however briefly. She smiled; it was gradually getting easier to do that around Macet, though the fact that he was a virtual double of Gul Skrain Dukat—visually, if not morally—still made any sort of exchange of pleasantries a bit tense.

"I wanted to revisit our previous discussion regarding the Cardassia–Bajor peace talks. It's been two weeks now since the negotiations stalled. Two weeks since I had to ferry Ambassador Lang back to Cardassia Prime empty-handed."

This wasn't news to Kira, though she found it hard to believe that two weeks could have passed so quickly.

Nodding, she said, "Yet you're back here, even without the ambassador."

"To do whatever I can to hasten the time when she and our other official representatives might be invited back to the bargaining table. I have waited patiently while you have—I presume—applied pressure on the Chamber of Ministers to bring this about. But how much longer must I wait, Colonel? How much longer must my *people* wait?" Macet opened his eyes wide, a nonverbal signal that, Kira had learned, was common to Cardassians who had just said something provocative and expected a response.

Kira wasn't at all surprised by Macet's question, nor by his obviously mounting impatience. Shortly after Second Minister Asarem Wadeen had taken a hard line with newly appointed Cardassian ambassador Natima Lang during the last round of peace talks—thereby causing their collapse—Macet had asked her to weigh in on the matter with First Minister Shakaar Edon, using whatever political pull she could muster.

What a joke, Kira thought. She was well aware that the problem of Bajor's intransigence extended all the way to the highest levels; culpability for the failure of the talks lay not with Asarem, but with First Minister Shakaar himself. This, of course, wasn't something she could reveal to Macet, no matter how much she had come to trust him of late.

Macet cleared his throat. "Well?"

Kira sighed, her smile collapsing as she shook her head. "I'm afraid we may have to resign ourselves to waiting a while longer."

"A while," Macet repeated, his eyes narrowing slightly.

"A very brief while, if that's any consolation."

"Ah. *After* Bajor officially enters the Federation, you mean. The talks will resume, but only after the Federation takes responsibility for them."

A hard lump formed in Kira's throat. She didn't like this any more than Macet did. "I'm afraid so," she said, her voice a hoarse whisper.

Macet was silent for a long moment. Finally, he said, "I am very disappointed to hear you say that, Colonel. Especially given your renowned influence over your world's leaders, both secular and religious."

"You're still giving me too much credit, Macet," she said, shaking her head yet again. "You know what it means for a Bajoran to be Attainted. Even the secular authorities don't have much use for someone who's been cast out of the faith."

Macet smiled as though hoping to offer encouragement. "Ah, faith. You have no shortage of that, Colonel. It is as abundant as your humility. The kind of *personal* faith you possess can move entire worlds."

Kira couldn't restrain a bitter chuckle. "Worlds are one thing. Ministers are different beasts entirely." *Especially Shakaar,* she thought.

Seeing Macet's sour expression, Kira continued. "Look, I know how much you need closure on a Bajor–Cardassia peace treaty *before* the Federation begins running Bajor's diplomatic efforts. I feel the same way."

"It's the only path that leads to an honest rapprochement," Macet said, looking thoughtful. His features took on a vaguely menacing cast as he added, "and to a *permanent* peace."

Shaking off mental images of belligerent, paranoid, future Cardassians someday returning in force to menace her homeworld, Kira nodded. "You'll get no argument from me, Macet. But the first and second ministers don't appear to see the matter with the same urgency we do. They're perfectly content to wait a few months."

Macet stared across the Promenade into the star-spangled darkness visible through the large upper-tier windows. His face slackened and his eyes grew pained. "I don't need to tell you how desperate things are back on Cardassia Prime. How many people are still homeless. How many children are still starving and disease ravaged. Those who weren't killed wholesale during the last hours of the war, that is."

Thoughts of Cardassia's suffering children brought to mind painful recollections of the late Tora Ziyal, whose recovered artworks Ambassador Lang had brought to Bajor as a gesture of peace—a gesture that Shakaar had effectively rebuffed, through Asarem. Her paintings and drawings, of exquisite beauty and poignant expressivity, had gone on display in Elim Garak's former tailor shop—where some faceless, Cardassian-hating vandal had despoiled many of them.

Macet continued: "It's ironic, really. For as long as I can remember, we Cardassians had always regarded ourselves as more advanced than you Bajorans. We had believed ourselves to be more sophisticated intellectually, culturally, politically—by any measure we could conceive. Now, after all we've been through—after the great price the Dominion War has levied against Cardassia for its sins—Bajor is exacting its revenge not through war, but through petty politics. Your ministers are not just keeping our worlds from attaining a true and lasting peace. They may also be confirming some of Cardassia's oldest and ugliest prejudices. Good day, Colonel." And before Kira could say a word, Macet strode away toward the Promenade's busy center.

He's right, she thought. As she resumed walking toward her office, a great upwelling of sadness spread through her soul. *If professional diplomats can't find common ground, then what hope is there for the rest of us?*

She was nearing the turbolift to ops when two Bajorans—an older woman and a younger man—approached her. Both were hooded, though not exactly in the style of her world's clerics or worshipers. She steeled herself for what was to come. Ever since she had released the prophecies of Ohalu onto the Bajoran civilian comnet, and had been Attainted by Vedek Yevir Linjarin, her interactions with most Bajorans had been frosty at best.

"Colonel Kira," the younger man said. "May we have a moment of your time?"

"I'm late for an appointment," Kira said, thinking ruefully of the mounds of work that awaited her. "Perhaps one of my officers can help you?"

"A moment is all we ask," the woman said. She moved her hood back on her head, as did the man, and Kira could see their ears now. Their unadorned ears. They were not wearing the earrings that signified Bajor's faith. Kira's hand involuntarily moved to her own right ear, from which her own earring had dangled before her Attainder had stripped her of the right to wear it.

"We want to thank you for revealing the truths of Ohalu to us," the man said. "The teachings of Bajor's temples have always governed our lives, but the prophe-

21

cies you disseminated answer so many more questions. You have helped us along our own spiritual path."

"The truth of the Prophets cannot be monopolized by any one group of believers," the woman said. "And the truth of the Prophets has been hidden for far too long. You have helped to reveal it. Do not mourn the loss of your standing in the Bajoran orthodoxy. Your *pagh* is obviously stronger than that."

"You have revealed to us a destiny that was obscured for far too long by those in control," the man said. "The Prophets *are* with you."

Smiling, the pair recloaked their heads and continued on their way amid the bustle of the Promenade.

Kira stared after them, unsettled. *What was* that *about?*

The blood sizzled on his forearm, burning through his black coverall into his tough skin, but Taran'atar ignored the pain. He wielded the creature's severed arm like a club, planning to use the clawed digits at its end as spear points.

Sensing that one of the giant arthropods was about to jump on him from behind, Taran'atar rolled to the side, tucking his limbs in close. In the past, he might have just stood his ground and let the alien attack him, but after fighting against forty-three adversaries from various species, he had begun to master a variety of fighting styles and strategies.

The creature landed, its splayed feet absorbing the impact of the fall on its spindly legs. Although there were variations, all of Taran'atar's current attackers were from the same alien species. Oversized arthropods, each of them had two legs and two arms, plus a lengthy curled and segmented tail. Their three-meter-tall bodies were protected by carapaces of black, organic armor.

Their heads were elongated and gourdlike, with mucus-dripping jaws from which issued a screech that would have struck terror into most humanoids.

Taran'atar had already dispatched four of them, but at least six more still crawled in the shadowy canyon, and he wasn't sure that there weren't more lurking nearby that he hadn't seen yet. He had to use additional caution because of the creatures' acidic blood; his hide was tough, but healing from extensive burns was not how he wanted to spend the next several days.

Standing, Taran'atar feinted to the right with his arm club, and as the creature dove to that side, the Jem'Hadar soldier scissored his leg out, sweeping it into the feet of one of the aliens. It toppled, off balance, and he grabbed a rock, smashing its skull in one brutal blow. Its death screech reverberated through the canyon.

Suddenly the din became overwhelming as the shadows uncurled themselves and the creatures screamed down at him. His count had been wrong. There were at least a dozen of them left, and they were angry. Skittering and bounding down the rock walls, they came at him.

Roaring his own rage, Taran'atar met their attack, forcing two of them into each other so that their snapping jaws ripped into each other's heads, green ichor spewing about the canyon. He ducked from underneath their dying bodies to find another alien in midair, about to land atop him. He thrust the arm club upward with all his strength, punching through the creature's thorax and spine, impaling it. The move may have eviscerated the beast, but its weight drove it down onto Taran'atar's hand, the blood burning through his gray scales and down to softer flesh beneath.

The creature opened its jaws, snapping at Taran'atar's face. The Jem'Hadar then saw a disconcertingly sharp set of inner jaws shoot out toward him. With both hands occupied holding the beast's scrabbling claws and ravening mouth at bay, Taran'atar had little choice. He opened his mouth wider than the width of the alien's inner jaws, and bit down on the creature's extrusion. He felt it crunch inside his teeth, and caustic ichor sprayed onto his face. He tossed the alien to the side, pulling the severed limb from its chest and spitting out the vile appendage he had just bitten off.

The other creatures prowled on the walls, skittering upside down like spiders, wary of the fearless Jem'Hadar. He let out a bellowing roar that echoed through the canyon.

"Hey, pallie!"

Taran'atar looked around for the voice that called to him. Finally he saw a man—a gray-haired human dressed in black and white—standing on one of the ledges up the canyon wall. Light spilled from behind him, and the sounds of other humans and music echoed from the light.

"Would you mind terribly keeping the noise down to a dull roar, please? You're drowning out the band. And truth to tell, you're spooking some of the high rollers."

Taran'atar was about to respond, when one of the aliens jumped him from behind, its claws raking around his chest. Reaching up, he grabbed the creature's elongated head, using its forward momentum to flip it over his head. As it hit the dirt, the Jem'Hadar smashed his hand down in a chopping motion, severing his attacker's neck and allowing its head to roll into the canyon.

Looking back up toward the human, Taran'atar saw him exiting through what appeared to be a doorway set into the illuminated area. He wasn't certain, but he thought he heard the departing human say something that sounded like, "Sheesh, and I used to think *Worf* had a problem with holosuite violence."

At times such as these the task with which Odo had entrusted him—to live among Alpha Quadrant humanoids in an effort to understand their often incomprehensible ways—seemed utterly unachievable.

4

Chief medical officer's personal log, stardate 53574.7

It's good to get off the ship from time to time, even if only to take part in a routine survey mission of a solar system's frozen hinterlands, where the most interesting sights are icy boulders and planetesimals which receive so little illumination that many of them can't actually be seen. But Chief Engineer Nog finds the region fascinating for professional reasons, as does Ezri, whose scientific curiosity—the legacy of Tobin and Jadzia—has been coming to the fore quite a bit ever since the Defiant first embarked on its current explorations of the Gamma Quadrant.

Ezri will be in charge of the mission, and she seems extraordinarily comfortable with the mantle of command that comes with being the Defiant's first officer. I have to admit that her increased con-

fidence in recent months has taken some getting used to. The Ezri Dax I fell in love with, after all, could have been a poster child for disorganization and personal chaos.

But I've concluded that I don't mind the change one bit.

The universe sang to the shuttlecraft *Sagan*.

In a manner of speaking.

If, Julian Bashir thought, one was willing to apply a rather liberal dollop of imagination to the cacophonous sounds reverberating through the cabin.

"It's beautiful," Nog said, leaning forward in the copilot's chair, smiling into the faint glow of the cometary cloud visible through the viewports. Something, gods only knew what, was causing the crystalline ices of the region's various frozen bodies to resonate like tuning forks at various shifting frequencies. Of course, those vibrations couldn't generate actual sounds in the vacuum of System GQ-12475's Oort cloud, but the *Sagan*'s sensors were capable of measuring the vibrations and rendering them in the shuttle's cabin as something audible—if not entirely enjoyable.

Unless, Julian thought, one happened to share Nog's sometimes rather outré musical tastes.

"Absolutely beautiful," the young Ferengi engineer repeated, indicating a visual display of an icy ten-kilometer-wide body that suddenly glissaded back and forth through an entire series of overtone pitches. The timbre was an eerie mating of glass harmonica and chainsaw.

From the portside seat, Lieutenant Ezri Dax fixed Nog with a good-natured scowl. " 'Beautiful' isn't the first adjective that springs to mind, Nog. I guess nine lifetimes just isn't long enough to acquire a taste for free-form splitter music."

"Free-form, yes," Nog said, wrinkling his nose. "Splitter, definitely not." It appeared that the word "splitter" had left a bad taste in his mouth.

Standing behind the cockpit seats, Bashir smiled at them both. "Sounds more like Sinnravian *drad,*" he said, keeping his expression carefully neutral.

"Exactly, Doctor." Nog grinned as he examined a sensor display. He sounded impressed. "Humans usually aren't very familiar with the atonal minimalists."

"Humans aren't blessed with the same . . . auditory endowments as Ferengi," Bashir said, not wishing to be drawn into the aesthetic debate he sensed was brewing.

"Humans usually can't stay in the same room with *drad,*" Ezri deadpanned. "But Julian is knowledgeable about *drad.* And splitter. And other diseases as well."

Nog pouted, and Julian forced down a smile. Serious work lay ahead, after all. After Shar had mysteriously opted out of this survey mission—a development that Ezri had proved oddly reticent about discussing—Nog had stepped in enthusiastically. Of course, the *Sagan*'s visit to this system's comet halo had at least one major engineering-related application: the use of cometary bodies, because of their crystal lattice structure patterns, as sites for high-bandwidth, long-range sensor relays. Nog had seemed rather excited about the prospect of using a solar system's Oort cloud bodies as natural enhancers for a small number of devices that might provide detailed scans of distant habitable planets—as well as advance warning of the presence of potentially hostile sentients—from as far off as a light-year.

The *Sagan*'s sensors had been probing the region's

field of sparsely distributed icy bodies for the better part of an hour, and had turned up several unanticipated—and so far inexplicable—waves of subspace and gravimetric distortions, which Nog and the *Sagan*'s computer had transformed into an ongoing atonal musical performance. But the point sources of these anomalous readings remained elusive. Julian was beginning to feel fidgety, not to mention redundant, in the company of an accomplished engineer and a polymath with lifetimes of potentially relevant expertise. *Serves me right for being so interested in so many things—and for letting Ezri bring me along on this mission as her good luck charm.*

The "music of the spheres" struck a particularly pungent note, rudely interrupting Bashir's reverie. "All musicological analysis aside for the moment," he said to no one in particular, "what haven't we considered yet as the possible cause of the distortion waves that have been, ah, serenading us for the past hour?"

Ezri's keen expression brought a vivid picture of Jadzia to mind. *Of course,* he thought. *She's in Jadzia's element now.* Loving someone possessed of so many facets was a lifelong process of discovery and accommodation.

"From everything we've observed so far," Ezri said, "I'd still say it's clearly an interdimensional effect."

Bashir nodded. "But centered exactly where?"

"If we had access to the *Defiant*'s sensors," she said with a shrug, "we might know that by now."

"If the *Defiant* were to come any closer," Nog said, shaking his head, "her warp field and cloaking device emissions would only drown out whatever it is we're, um, *not* finding out here."

Bashir sighed. "So we're going to be at this for another few hours, most likely."

"Looks that way, sir," Nog said. "Or maybe even longer."

Even as Nog spoke, another wave of dimensional distortion crashed against the icy comet fragments, causing several to emit a momentary, ear-splitting howl, which faded into discordant background harmonies as the computer automatically cut the volume back to a more agreeable level.

Ezri grimaced. "Kids today. Their music is just noise."

Bashir agreed silently, suddenly feeling old. *Give me one of Frenchotte's Romulan oratorios any day.*

Nog had either ignored or missed Ezri's jab. He seemed ready to applaud, as though he'd just heard one of Vic Fontaine's Las Vegas sidemen lay down a particularly adroit jazz solo.

Ezri leaned forward over the console, a worried look momentarily crossing her face. "That one peaked pretty close to our position," she said.

"But where did it come from?" Nog said as he studied a gauge on his side of the cockpit.

Then the universe abruptly stopped singing. Instead, it opened its maw as if to swallow the shuttlecraft *Sagan* whole. Or at least that was how Bashir assessed matters during the split second it took him to glance out the fore viewport and shout, "There!"

"Hard to starboard, Lieutenant," Ezri snapped in a calm, authoritative voice. Seemingly gone forever was the tentative, uncertain Ezri whom Bashir had first met more than a year ago. Nog tapped a quick command into his console and the shuttle lurched, forcing Bashir to grab the back of Ezri's seat for a moment while the inertial dampers caught up with the sudden shift in velocity.

The cabin lights flickered, went out, and were replaced a moment later by the faint glow of emergency power.

"Engines?" Dax said, her voice full of iron authority.

"We still have impulse power and thrusters," Nog said.

"Take us out to five-hundred klicks, then bring us about. I want to see this thing from a safer distance."

An eternity later—though Bashir knew that perhaps only ten seconds had actually passed—the *Sagan* was parked in a stable orbit, apparently safe from the dark leviathan that had reared up at them from out of the ether.

"What is it?" Bashir asked, his momentary surge of fear giving ground to curiosity and wonder as he looked out the viewport. Whatever it was, the object was enormous. It hung in space, a faintly glowing hulk composed of crosscut planes and angles. Even with his genetically enhanced mind, Bashir had trouble counting just how many intersecting vertices the thing possessed. As the alien structure slowly rotated in the void, each new face it presented seemed entirely different, even after it had made what must have been a complete rotation. Gold, silver, and ruby colors vied for attention on its multitextured surfaces. The object utterly defeated the eye, sometimes appearing to be a tangle of impossibly intersecting Platonic shapes, planes, and lines, other times taking on the aspect of a Gothic cathedral. It brought to mind the visually deceptive works of the ancient Terran artist M. C. Escher.

It didn't make any sense. Surely, Bashir thought, he ought to be able to keep track of this thing's architectural lines, however weirdly its alien builders may have arranged them.

"Whatever it is, it looks pretty benign from this far out," Ezri said after studying the thing in silence for a few minutes.

"I wonder why we didn't see it sooner," Bashir said.

Dax stared thoughtfully through the viewport. "Maybe the object's own subspace distortions are turning the surrounding cometary bodies into a natural cloaking device of some kind."

"Well, now that we can see the thing, what do you suppose it is?" Bashir repeated.

"The Divine Treasury?" said Nog, his eyes as wide as deflector dishes.

"I certainly hope not," Bashir said.

"Why's that?" Ezri wanted to know.

"Well, don't most Ferengi believe that the Divine Treasury is the first thing they'll see after dying?"

Nog swallowed hard. "You're right. I hereby withdraw the comment."

"Whatever it is," Ezri said as she glanced at a readout, "it's about four times bigger than a *Galaxy*-class starship—at least it is at the moment."

"I'm not sure I'm following you," Bashir said. "Are you saying that its *size* is changing?"

Ezri nodded, evidently fascinated by the numbers she saw scrolling past. "As near as I can tell, it's turning on some sort of interdimensional axis, and different amounts of its mass are peeking through into our universe at different times. It might be a four-dimensional object moving through five spatial dimensions, or it might have an even higher number of macroscopic dimensions. We're seeing just the shadow it casts in three-dimensional space. And that shadow changes as the thing rotates through higher-dimensional space. We almost flew right into its interdimensional wake."

"Well, that's certainly a relief," Bashir said.

"That we weren't accidentally swept away into the nth dimension?" Ezri asked, cocking an eyebrow in his direction.

"No."

"What then?"

He smiled. "It's one of the conceits of the genetically enhanced, I'm afraid. Unless something is out-and-out incomprehensible, we generally expect to be able to figure it out, and usually rather quickly. So it's comforting to learn that the thing is an imponderable—like the birth of the Inamuri entity we witnessed shortly after the *Defiant* entered the Gamma Quadrant."

Ezri smiled as she returned to her readouts. "I'm not letting you off the hook that easily, Julian. We'll figure out what this thing is, eventually. The incomprehensible just takes a little longer."

"Well, we don't need to know what it is to figure out what it's doing," Nog said. "From these sensor readings, it seems pretty clear that this object is the source of all the dimensional distortions wc've been picking up."

"Our cosmic concertmaster," Bashir said, staring appreciatively out the fore viewport at the ever-shifting vista that lay before them. "I wonder how long it's been out here, waiting for us to come along and discover it?"

"I've already started running analyses on the hull materials," Nog said. "I don't have anything conclusive yet, but it's old. Something like half a billion years old."

Bashir was speechless. Any civilization capable of building such an enigmatic structure had to be far more technologically advanced than the Federation. But why had they built it? And what had become of the builders?

Ezri's eyes locked with Bashir's, and he immediately recognized Jadzia's quirky *I-love-a-mystery* smile.

"Like I said, the thing doesn't look so dangerous now," she said. "Any objections to my ordering a close-up inspection?"

Since the *Defiant*'s Gamma Quadrant explorations had begun, there had been times when Bashir had thought it strange to be taking orders from a lieutenant—

who also happened to be the woman he loved, as well as Commander Vaughn's first officer. But more recently he had begun learning to sit back and enjoy the ride.

He grinned at Ezri. "You're in charge, Lieutenant."

Ezri grinned back at Bashir before turning toward Nog. "Lieutenant, let's have at it."

Nog parked the *Sagan* in a close orbit, only about fifteen kilometers from the nearest part of the continually changing alien structure. Ten minutes of exterior scans revealed that the hull materials did indeed contain a fair amount of gold, platinum, and other precious metals, along with a number of transuranic elements that Bashir had never seen before. And he still had yet to see a precise repetition of any of the weirdly morphing structure's surface features—which presumably meant that they had yet to see it make an entire revolution on its axis through higher-dimensional space. Though he wasn't a specialist in higher-dimensional topology, it was obvious to him that the artifact's surface convolutions had to be incredibly complex.

Bashir found himself pacing back and forth in the cabin behind Ezri and Nog, who busied themselves at the sensor consoles.

What's inside *the bloody thing?*

"Keep trying the deep interior scans, Nog," Ezri said. "And watch the subspace horizon line. We don't want to get close enough to that thing's dimensional wake to fall over the edge."

"Aye, sir. Compensating." Nog sounded frustrated as he touched various controls. "I just wish this thing's shifts in mass and gravity were easier to predict."

"Over the edge?" Bashir said. "I don't understand."

Ezri gestured toward one of the cockpit gauges. "I've

noticed that the object seems to be causing a very slight drain on the *Sagan*'s power. I'd bet all the *raktajino* on Qo'noS that it's because the energy is dropping off into whatever dimension the object is moving through to get here."

Bashir didn't like the sound of that. "Is it dangerous?"

"It's negligible so far," Dax said. "But we don't want to get much closer to it than this, or it might not stay that way."

"Oh," Bashir said. He was gaining a deeper appreciation of Jadzia's expertise in physics. He wondered if Ezri was aware of how easily she had stepped into her predecessor's scientific boots.

"Are the sensor beams still just bouncing off?" Ezri said.

Nog nodded. "Mostly, though I'm reading several large, empty chambers a short distance beneath the hull. I think I'm reading a residual power source of some kind deep inside, but I can't be sure. And scans for life signs are inconclusive."

Bashir suddenly stopped pacing when the idea came to him. "Why don't we just knock on the front door?" he said quietly.

Ezri turned toward Bashir and looked at him as though he had just sprouted a pair of Andorian antennae.

"Let's hail them," Bashir said by way of clarification. "Maybe somebody's still home."

After half a billion years, that may be a wee bit optimistic, he thought. Galactic civilizations tended to have life spans lasting centuries or millennia; those capable of enduring for hundreds of millions of years were rare indeed. *But, nothing ventured . . .*

After a moment's consideration, Ezri nodded toward Nog. "I can't see the harm in that. Lieutenant?"

"Opening hailing frequencies," Nog said as his fingers moved nimbly across the console. He looked relieved that no one had suggested that they beam inside to take a look around. "Sending greeting messages in all known Gamma Quadrant languages."

Thirty seconds passed in silence. A minute.

"I don't think anybody's home after all, Julian," Ezri said with a faint *I-told-you-so* smile. "Why don't you contact the *Defiant?* Tell them we're on our way back with the data we've gathered so far."

"Aye, Captain," Bashir said with a deferential nod, then crossed to a subspace transmitter console on the cabin's port side.

"Charity!" Nog's exclamation stopped Bashir in his tracks. Ezri looked at the engineer quizzically, evidently unfamiliar with that particular Ferengi vulgarity.

"Excuse me," Nog said, composing himself. "I think the doctor might have been onto something. Looks like somebody *is* home. Or some *thing.*"

Ezri's hands became a blur over her console, evoking for Bashir the stories he had heard about Tobin Dax's facility with card tricks. "The computer is downloading data. Nog, prepare to purge the system if it looks like anything dangerous."

"Ready."

"That power source you detected must be keeping a computer system on-line," Bashir said to Nog.

"Pretty sturdy hardware," Nog said, looking impressed as he watched strings of indecipherable alien characters march across one of the cockpit monitors, overlaying themselves across a false-color tactical image of the inscrutable spaceborne cathedral.

Bashir felt a tingle of apprehension, recalling a report he had read about a similar alien artifact once having seized control of the computers of Starfleet's flagship.

"How about it, Nog?" he said. "Is it dangerous?"

Nog shook his head. "Nothing executable. Looks to me like it's just a text file."

The information abruptly stopped scrolling. Nog punched in a command that shunted the information into a protected memory buffer.

"A whopping *huge* text file," Ezri said. "Nearly eighty megaquads."

"So what does it say?" Bashir said, his task at the subspace radio console all but forgotten.

Ezri's expression was a study in fascination. "It could be the sum total of everything this civilization ever learned about science, technology, art, medicine . . ."

Nog shrugged. "Or it could be a compilation of their culture's financial transactions."

Bashir considered the unfamiliar lines and curlicues still visible on the screen. Before him was something that could be the Gamma Quadrant's equivalent to the Bible or the Koran. Or an ancient municipal telephone directory.

"It could take lifetimes to puzzle it all out," Dax whispered, apparently to everyone and no one. Bashir found the idea simultaneously exhilarating and heartbreaking.

Staring half a billion years backward into time, Ezri appeared awestruck, no longer the duranium-nerved commander she had been only moments before. Her current aspect struck Bashir as almost childlike.

"Let's try running some of it through the universal translator," Bashir said, intruding as gently as possible on Ezri's scientific woolgathering. "We can probably decipher some of it by comparing it to language groups from other nearby sectors."

After a moment Ezri nodded. "What he said, Nog," she said finally, returning to apparent alertness.

An alarm klaxon abruptly shattered the moment. "Collision alert!" Nog shouted, as he manhandled the controls and threw the *Sagan* hard over to port. Bashir had a vague feeling of spinning as he lost his footing, and his head came into blunt contact with the arm of one of the aft seats.

He struggled to his knees, shaking his head to clear it, holding onto the chair arm. He looked up at the main viewport.

The alien cathedral had suddenly sprouted an appendage. Or rather, a long arm, or tower, or spire had just rotated into normal space from whatever interdimensional realm served to hide most of the object's tremendous bulk.

Though the spire couldn't have been more than a few meters wide, it was easily tens of kilometers in length. It had no doubt been concealed within the unknowable depths of interdimensional space until that moment.

And it appeared to be rotating directly toward the *Sagan* very, very quickly. Bashir felt like a fly about to be swatted.

"Nog, evasive maneuvers!" Ezri shouted, her mantle of authority fully restored.

"Power drain's suddenly gone off the scale, Captain," Nog said, slamming a fist on the console in frustration. "The helm's frozen."

"Looks like we got a little momentum off the thrusters before the power drain increased," Dax said calmly. "Maybe we'll get out of this yet."

Or maybe we'll drift right into the flyswatter's path. Bashir clambered into a seat immediately behind the cockpit and started to belt himself in. Then he stopped when the absurdity of the gesture struck him. *We're either getting out of this unscathed, or we're going to be smashed to pieces.*

He rose, crossed to the subspace transmitter, and tried to open a frequency to *Defiant.*

Only static answered him. He glanced across the cabin at Dax, who was shaking her head. "Subspace channels are jammed. Too much local interference from this thing."

"Our comm signals must be going the same place as our power," Nog said.

Into this thing's interdimensional wake, Bashir thought.

"Brace for impact!" Dax shouted.

The lights dimmed again, then went out entirely, and a brief flash of brilliance followed. Bashir felt a curious pins-and-needles sensation, as though a battalion of Mordian butterflies was performing close-order drill maneuvers on his skin. Darkness returned, and seconds stretched lethargically into nearly half a minute.

Once again, the emergency circuits cast their dim, ruddy glow throughout the cabin. The forward viewport revealed the alien cathedral hanging serenely in the void, its spire no longer visible, its overall shape morphed into even wilder congeries of planes and angles.

Dax heaved a loud sigh. "Our residual momentum must have carried us clear. Couldn't have missed us by much, though."

Bashir couldn't help but vent some relief of his own. "Thank you, Sir Isaac Newton."

"Ship's status, Nog?" Dax said.

"Most of our instruments are still down, but our power appears to be returning as we drift away from the object's wake. We've already got some impulse power and at least a little bit of helm control. And the subspace channels are starting to clear up, too."

For a moment, Bashir felt dizzy. He assumed either the inertial dampers or the gravity plating must have taken some damage.

"What just happened to us?" he said.

"My best guess is we passed right through the edge of the thing's dimensional wake," Nog said. "It's a miracle we weren't pulled into wherever it's keeping most of its mass."

Bashir had trouble tearing his gaze away from the starboard viewport and the weirdly graceful object that slowly turned in the distance. *A miracle indeed. That something like this even exists is something of a miracle, I'd say.*

For a moment he thought it was a pity that he didn't believe in miracles.

A burst of static issued from the cockpit comm speakers, then resolved itself into a human voice. *". . . mei, come in, Sagan. This is Ensign Tenmei. Sagan, do you read?"*

"Go ahead, Ensign," Dax said, frowning. It was immediately obvious that something was wrong aboard the *Defiant.*

"I'm afraid we're in need of Dr. Bashir's services, Lieutenant," said Tenmei.

"Is someone injured?" Bashir said over Ezri's shoulder, the alien artifact suddenly forgotten.

"We have wounded aboard, but they're not ours." It was Commander Vaughn's voice, deep and resonant. *"They're guests, and some of them are in pretty rough shape."*

Bashir wasn't relieved very much by Vaughn's qualification. Injured people were injured people, and he was a doctor. "Acknowledged, Captain," he said as he watched Nog launch a subspace beacon.

Good idea. We're going to need to find our way back here when we have more time.

Dax took the sluggish helm and gently applied power to the impulse engines. "We're on our way, sir."

"Too bad the *Defiant*'s not carrying an EMH," Dax said to Bashir as they got under way.

"I far prefer flesh-and-blood help in my medical bay," Bashir said. Strangely, he felt no urge to explain about the mutually antipathetic relationship he shared with Dr. Lewis Zimmerman, the inventor of the emergency medical holograms that were found on so many Starfleet ships these days. In fact, he found that he was no longer in the mood for conversation of any sort. As the alien cathedral dropped rapidly out of sight, he gathered his energies for the triage situation that he presumed lay ahead.

But the alien cathedral's ever-changing shadow still moved very slowly across the backdrop of his thoughts.

5

Mirroring Yevir's mood, the dusky sky was darkening, slowly eliding from lavender to a deep rose. The air crackled with the cool of late winter and the scent of *nerak* blossoms, a tantalizing hint of the coming spring. Ashalla's city streetlights were already aglow, illuminating the paths of the many Bajorans who bustled to their shrines and homes.

An older woman stopped Vedek Yevir and began speaking to him. Her grandson was planning to marry next month, and she wanted to know if he would ask the Prophets to bless the union. Smiling, Yevir promised that he would do so at the main Ashalla temple on the following day. Shedding tears of gratitude, the woman thanked him and backed away.

Yevir noticed that other passersby on the concourse had in turn noticed him. Most of them nodded and smiled as they passed him, and he recognized most of their faces. He couldn't help but wonder how many of them had read the accursed so-called prophecies of Ohalu—and how far the poison that Colonel Kira had released four months earlier had spread through the very heart of Bajor's capital city. *How many of these people hope that I will become kai? How many of them would prefer Vedek Solis instead?*

His guts braiding themselves into knots of anxiety, Yevir continued walking, passing the bakery where he often bought pastries on his way to his office. The proprietor gave him a respectful wave. Yevir knew that the man would soon make his way to the evening temple services; he was exceedingly faithful. Still, it seemed odd that he hadn't yet closed his shop for the evening, so close to the sounding of the first temple bells.

Ahead, Yevir saw several people gathered around the plaza's public holovid kiosk. He stepped up to listen, in time to hear a newscaster discussing the day's events with a political commentator.

"*. . . the end of the second week since the peace talks stalled between Bajor's representatives and Cardassia,*" said the newscaster. "*Do you see any progress in the initiative to resume the talks?*"

Yevir recognized the commentator as Minister Belwan Ligin, an old-line conservative who had lost most of his family during the Occupation. Despite this, he had always struck Yevir as remarkably fair and evenhanded in his judgments about the Cardassians. "*I don't believe that any direct progress has been made, but certainly Minister Asarem and the others are going to begin feeling real pressure soon. With Bajor's entry into the Federation imminent, it seems to me that a viable peace agreement would be in both peoples' best interests. But*

Asarem has proven to be quite astute in the past when dealing with potential crises, so perhaps . . ."

Yevir walked away from the kiosk, shifting his bag over his shoulder. Perhaps he ought to schedule a meeting with Asarem, or even First Minister Shakaar Edon, to discuss how best to get the talks restarted. Either of them would probably welcome a fresh perspective on the matter. Surely they could be persuaded that reaching a mutually favorable denouement now—before the Federation relieved Bajor of all such responsibilities—was the only way to create a lasting peace with Cardassia. And it certainly wouldn't hurt his chances of becoming the next kai if he were to help broker such a resolution.

But how?

As he entered the four-story, stackstone-fronted building that housed his offices, Yevir saw many of the lower-level staff members preparing to leave for the evening. He greeted each of them by name, wishing them all an uplifting temple service. Yevir's assistant stood up from behind a desk as he rounded the corner toward his office.

"Vedek Yevir. How blessed to see you," Harana Flin said, and he knew she meant it. Harana indicated a young woman who sat in a corner chair. "She's been waiting to see you for some time now. I told her I wasn't sure when you would return this evening, but she insisted on staying."

"It's all right, Flin," Yevir said, using the woman's familiar name. He placed a hand on her shoulder and smiled gently at her. "I will be happy to see her. Thank you for your diligence. Now you'd best hurry or you'll miss first bells."

Harana gathered a wrap around her shoulders and let herself out as Yevir turned toward the waiting woman. She was very pretty, with high cheekbones and delicately oval eyes. Her hair was braided, encircling the top of her head in the *helep* style he knew was popular among the university crowd in Musilla Province these days. She was dressed in light blue robes that flattered her pale skin, and she held a young child whom she was clearly suckling beneath the robes.

"Hello, child," Yevir said, smiling. "Won't you come into my office?" He stepped ahead of her, opening the door. He expected her to be shy, in the manner of most supplicants who came calling. But she walked confidently, her head held high.

He entered the office after her, and as she sat on a chaise nearby, he set his shoulder bag on the desktop. He pulled out several books, placing them on top of a pile of documents that he kept neatly stacked in his work area. Next, he withdrew the small gold-and-amber jevonite figurine that Kasidy Yates, the wife of the Emissary, had given him more than two weeks earlier. He set the translucent statue at the top of the stack before turning his attention back to his visitor.

"You seem familiar, child. Have we met before?"

The young woman stared at him for a moment, though he could glean nothing of her thoughts from her eyes. She smiled slightly as she spoke, expressing neither shyness nor shame. "No, Vedek Yevir, we have not met. At least not officially. But you may know my face from the files that the Vedek Assembly very likely keeps on people like me."

What an odd thing to say. Yevir's curiosity was piqued. "I'm not sure I understand."

"My name is Mika. Cerin Mika. I was once a member of the Pah-wraith cult."

Yevir nodded, at last recognizing her more fully. "Yes, I remember you now." Cerin Mika—or simply

Mika, as she had told interviewers she preferred to be addressed—had been one of the few dozen cultists who had resided briefly on Empok Nor, during Gul Dukat's tenure as their leader. Dukat had impregnated her, and after she had given birth to his child, had nearly succeeded in murdering her. If not for the intervention of Kira Nerys, Mika's child would never have known its mother.

In the year and a half since that time, Mika had become a minor celebrity, as well as a figure of some controversy. The Bajoran people had been quick to forgive the woman, blaming Dukat for victimizing yet another innocent, spiritually minded Bajoran. Despite Dukat's betrayal—or perhaps because her babe was half Bajoran and half Cardassian—Mika and her husband, Benyan, had become vocal advocates for peace between Bajor and Cardassia. They spoke publicly, and recently had begun lobbying certain ministers on a fairly regular basis.

"What can I do for you?" Yevir asked, though he was already fairly certain he knew what was on her mind.

"I will come straight to the point," she said, reaching within her robes to detach the child from her breast. "I am the niece of Vedek Solis Tendren."

Yevir's brow furrowed as he realized that she had reasons other than a common doctrinal outlook to support Yevir's chief rival for the kaiship. Vedek Solis had made it clear that he sought Bajor's top religious leadership position—and that he did so at the behest of a newly formed sect which taught that Ohalu's heresies were the True Way of the Prophets.

As intrigued as he was suspicious, Yevir said, "I must confess that I'm at something of a loss as to what I can do for you."

Her smile persisted. "It may well be that I can do

something for *you,* Vedek Yevir. I trust you're aware of the details of my past association with the Pah-wraith sect. It wasn't the first time I'd explored alternative religions."

"And I trust that your experiences with Gul Dukat have taught you the error of your ways."

She laughed at that, a pleasant, crystalline sound. "I have never been completely . . . satisfied with the orthodox teachings of Bajor, despite my uncle's best efforts to put me 'back on the right path.' My sojourn with Dukat hasn't changed that."

Yevir shook his head slowly. "Forgive me, child. But I can't help but think that Dukat's attempt on your life couldn't have been a clearer sign from the Prophets that it was a mistake for you to stray from Their wisdom. Unless, of course, you no longer believe in it."

It was Mika's turn to shake her head. "I *have* faith, Vedek Yevir. Faith in something *beyond* me and my life. Faith that there's something larger out there. But I've become less certain than ever that this something has anything to do with the so-called Prophets."

Mika's sudden irreverence grated on Yevir, though he'd certainly heard such talk many times before. During the dark days of the Cardassian Occupation, and sometimes afterward during his stint in the Bajoran Militia, he'd sometimes heard battle-scarred veterans and anguished civilians question the beneficence of the Prophets. It was to be expected. Now that he served his people as an instrument of the Prophets' plan for Bajor, Yevir saw it as his sacred obligation to help all such suffering souls come to understand that the Prophets were the true source of all hope. He owed it to all whose *pagh* was in tumult, to all who stumbled in darkness.

Even those who were bent on turning a dangerously heretical vedek into Bajor's next kai.

Mika continued, "A few months ago, my husband and I were made aware of the transmission of the prophecies of Ohalu onto the comnet. We read them and started talking to others who had read them as well."

Yevir tried to keep his upper lip from curling in distaste, without perfect success. "It's a shame that Ohalu's heresies have replaced the true Words of the Prophets in the minds of so many misguided souls."

"Ohalu's writings didn't *replace* the teachings we all grew up with. They merely *supplemented* them. They—"

"That isn't so, child," Yevir interrupted her. "Ohalu argues that the Prophets are not our spiritual guides, but are instead merely powerful, enigmatic beings whom we mistakenly worship. His so-called 'prophecies' undermine the very basis of our society. Without our divine Prophets, what are we? Where did we come from? Where will we go?"

She looked at him pointedly. "Since you and several of the other vedeks have already publicly supported the questioning of the old ways, I'm surprised to find your attitude toward Ohalu so inflexible. You *have* read his work, haven't you?"

He replied with a curt nod, then said, "Yes, though it pained me to see the verities of the Prophets twisted so."

"Then you must know how many of Ohalu's prophecies have come true," she said resolutely. "The words he wrote millennia ago have become *our* reality. It is not some vague future he foresaw, but our lives, our *present*."

Mika had placed her finger directly on a raw nerve. Yevir had already sought—to little avail—the guidance of several Orbs on one burning question: *Why are so many of Ohalu's accursed prophecies so accurate?*

He knew well that Bajor's major orthodox religious writings abounded with prophecies, some vague and general, others more specific. But many legitimate prophecies had to be justified, interpreted, *clarified,* to bring them into line with current events. Why did it seem that *none* of Ohalu's prophecies required such clarification? Ohalu's predictions had so far proven to be uncannily accurate. But if the heretical prophecies were true as a whole, then everything the Bajoran religion was built upon stood revealed as a lie; the Prophets could not, therefore, be Bajor's protectors, but rather were merely an alien species who studied his people like so many bugs under glass, and occasionally deigned to aid them.

Yevir could not reconcile this. In his heart, he *knew* the Prophets. The Emissary had touched him with Their power. And Yevir's mission, his future, his every aspiration and ambition, was based upon his own steadfast, unwavering, unquestioning belief in the Prophets and Their plan.

He gathered his thoughts carefully before answering Mika. "You've been taught by Solis. And Dukat. And the Prophets only know how many others. So you must know better than most that prophecies may be interpreted in *many* ways, especially by those eager to bend those prophecies to their own agendas. Gray can be made to resemble black or white, depending on the elements that surround it. So too can heresies seem to offer solace, especially in times of turmoil."

Her smile bore a trace of sardonic humor. "Why do you immediately say that the gray is black, instead of white? Have you truly opened your heart and mind to the *possibilities* Ohalu offers Bajor? Yes, our world is in turmoil. It is going through a rebirth, transitioning from

49

the Occupation to freedom, from war to peace, from an independent world to a member of an interstellar coalition. . . . Isn't it possible that the faith of the Bajoran people needs to experience a similar rebirth as well?"

"The Bajoran people need their faith in the invariant will of the Prophets," Yevir said, allowing some steel into his voice. "Particularly in times such as these." Not for the first time, he wondered if the Emissary had placed him on the path to becoming kai merely to have him preside over his flock's disintegration. The thought was a lance that pierced the depths of his soul.

"You may be right," Mika said. "Placing our faith in all-powerful beings who want to take care of us is tempting indeed. It absolves our people of personal responsibility. Everything we do, or whatever is done *to* us, is the will of the Prophets. And for those who deny Them, there is nothing but shame and censure."

"The Truth of the Prophets cannot be denied, child." Yevir recalled the screams of a mortally wounded resistance fighter, a young woman who'd died in his arms some fifteen years ago. With her last breath she had cursed the Prophets, whom she'd accused of having abandoned her, her family, and Bajor. He closed his eyes, trying to banish the horror of the memory. "The Truth of the Prophets cannot be denied," he repeated, embracing the words like a lifeline.

But Mika wasn't going to let him off so easily. "Where were the Prophets during the Occupation?" she said, her tone growing accusatory. "Why have they not aided us in the rebuilding of our world? Why have those who claim to most strongly represent the will of the Prophets been unable to establish a lasting peace with the Cardassians?"

Feeling a frustration he'd not experienced since the Occupation beginning to steep within his soul, Yevir

turned his back to her, his hands clenching and unclenching out of her view. He swallowed his distress and
mounting rage quickly—*Let the Prophets' love flow
through me*—and turned back to her. "Is this why you
came to see me today? To spout the polemical blas-
phemies of Ohalu?"

"No," she said, her eyes clear and placid. "I am not
here to convince you to bless the Ohalavaru."

Yevir recalled having heard that name bandied about
in derogatory fashion by some of his fellow vedeks. The
translation of the ancient High Bajoran word struck him
as ironic. " 'Ohalu's truthseekers'?"

"Yes. That is the name of our sect." She paused, holding her hand palm outward in a placating gesture. "As I
said, I'm not here to debate theologies, or even to convince you to respect our faith. But I have come to you to
ask for your help."

Yevir sat down in his chair, looking past the jevonite
statue at the woman. "With what?"

"I believe—*we* believe that Colonel Kira Nerys has
been done a great injustice by the Vedek Assembly. In
your own address to the Bajoran people, you said that
we needed to reevaluate the old ways and seek new
answers to old questions. To keep our minds open.
Kira is guilty of nothing but allowing the Bajoran people the chance to question their faith. To decide on
their own which answers they will accept . . . whether
those answers come from the Prophets or from themselves."

Yevir was sorely tempted to interrupt her again, but
forced himself to sit quietly and allow her to continue.
"As you may recall, it was Kira who saved my life, my
husband's life, and the life of my child. And all the
others who had followed Gul Dukat to Empok Nor.

51

Afterward she provided us with more knowledge—and helped us all reevaluate our decisions of faith. *Now* she has merely done the same thing for Bajor as a whole."

"Comparing your decision to abandon the Pah-wraiths to the questioning of the Prophets *isn't* likely to win me over," Yevir said, unable to keep the frost from his tone.

"One learns only by asking questions," Mika said, almost serene. Yevir recognized the words as one of Solis's most oft-quoted aphorisms. "One only grows by seeking answers. Some of those who have read the prophecies of Ohalu have rejected them; Ohalu's answers did not suit them, and their faith in the Prophets became *stronger* as a result. But others have found that they want to continue their spiritual explorations." She paused for a moment, appearing to search for the right words. "Even the Emissary questioned openly who and what the Prophets are, and what Their role in Bajor's past, present, and future really might be."

Wearying of the debate, Yevir rubbed his forefinger and thumb over his nose ridge, closing his eyes for a moment. Finally, he said, "I will *not* rescind Kira's Attainder. Whether or not the questions Ohalu poses are valid is not a factor in the Assembly's decision. And Kira's decision to disseminate Ohalu's heresies without regard to their effect on Bajor's religious community—especially now—is unforgivable."

Mika frowned. "You must hate her very much, Vedek Yevir. I am disappointed."

"No, child," he said. Ever since Kira's act of betrayal, Yevir had searched his soul carefully for such unworthy motivations. He had found none. Indeed, he had agonized over the Attainder decision. "Though I can understand how it might appear that way. I know the Attainder must be personally devastating to her."

"Then surely you can find it in your heart to forgive her."

"Actions such as hers are beyond my authority to forgive. Kira has taken it upon herself to affect Bajor's spiritual well-being—without training, without warning, and without official sanction. To be blunt, this makes her simply too dangerous to keep within the faith."

He expected Mika to react angrily to his plainspoken argument, as the Emissary's wife had done when he had rebuffed her attempt to discuss lifting Kira's Attainder. But instead, Mika merely seemed more resolute. "I understand," she said. "I had to try. Still, there are others in the Assembly who may be less . . . inflexible about their Attainder votes." She stood, readying herself and her sleeping child to leave. "Vedek Yevir, I hope that one day the Prophets will lead you to the forgiveness of Kira, and to Ohalu's truth."

Before he could react, Mika's child began to fuss, pushing a small hand out of the robes in which it had been wrapped. The hand was chubby and slightly gray in color, its skin rough and leathery. From where Yevir sat, an absurd juxtaposition of the jevonite figure with the child made the baby's arm appear to be growing out of the statue's side.

Yevir stood bolt upright. "May I see your child, Mika?"

Mika's eyes narrowed in response to his swift action, but she obliged him by stepping closer and sweeping the robes away from the child's sleep-crinkled face. Yevir could see that the boy seemed larger than before, a toddler who looked to be about a year old, rather than an infant.

Yevir stepped to the side of his desk and reached

out to touch the boy's face. His skin had the same grayish cast as his limbs, as well as another, somewhat unexpected trait. On the slumbering boy's nose was a fully developed set of Bajoran ridges, while his brow and forehead were framed by the raised scales of a Cardassian. An elevated oval on his forehead held a depression in its center, in the shape of an elegantly crafted spoon. The boy's eyes, which had just opened, were of a crystalline black and seemed to watch the vedek with an intensity that matched Yevir's own.

The vedek's hand traced the ridges on the child's forehead, and the boy grasped his finger, chattering happily. Yevir found himself smiling in wonder. Looking up, he saw that Mika was smiling as well.

The child is at peace. He has erased the tension we both felt, bridged our two worlds.

Yevir's mind raced. He stepped back, gesturing toward the door. "Thank you, Mika. Your son is beautiful. I will consider your words. If you will consider *mine* as well."

As the young woman turned to leave, she said, "I consider the words of many, Vedek Yevir. Wisdom and freedom can be fully gained only by opening one's mind."

She was quoting her uncle again. He smiled. "Walk with the Prophets."

"And you," she said. And then she was gone.

Yevir sat down behind his desk and immediately reached for the gold-hued jevonite statue. The figurine had come from the ongoing excavations at B'hala, brought to the Emissary's wife by one of the prylars working at the site. Yevir wasn't sure why he felt so strongly connected to the artifact. The figure was peculiar, bearing little resemblance to the more primitive art found elsewhere at the dig. It was a humanoid shape swathed in robes. Its eyes, though mere carvings, still managed to appear as though they watched anything in view. Its nose was ridged like a Bajoran's, but its forehead also bore raised, scaly scar patterns. Its neck was long and gracefully sloping, held up in pride and unbowed by adversity. When Yevir had first laid eyes on the figure, he had wondered if it represented some millennia-dead Bajoran martyr or holy man, whose facial disfigurements bore testament to the trials he had endured in the name of the Prophets. But almost immediately he saw that it held a deeper, subtler meaning.

Using the same hand with which he had touched Mika's child, Yevir now caressed the face of the small statue, and he became utterly certain, at last, what the object represented—the melding of a Bajoran and a Cardassian. The blending of the Bajoran nose ridge with the forehead scales of a Cardassian was unmistakable. And why hadn't he noticed the subtle ridges running down both sides of the figure's neck before? The statue was obviously the image of a mixed-heritage child like Mika's, though it was carved millennia before the two planets could possibly have produced such a union. Before, in fact, either people had met or even known of one another's existence.

Like the hybrid child he had just touched—and like Tora Ziyal, whose memory the Cardassians had resurrected in their overtures of peace—the statue represented a commingling of related species.

It is a symbol of unity.

Hope surged within Yevir's breast, and his earlier feelings of despair vanished like mist over the fire caves.

Replacing them were a cacophony of thoughts and plans, an epiphany of what he must now do.

He tapped at his comm panel, then remembered that Flin had gone for the day. That was fine. What he had to do was perhaps better done alone. Yevir called the spaceport most regularly used by the Vedek Assembly; although it mainly transported civilians, a few of its ships were always at the preferential disposal of the clergy. Using the after-hours automated system, he booked passage to Deep Space 9 on the next available transport, three hours hence.

Finished with the first step, Yevir reviewed his mental checklist of the probable whereabouts of his closest Vedek Assembly colleagues. Vedeks Eran and Scio would be in services now, ministering to the faithful. Kyli and Bellis would most likely already be in private meditation. That left Vedeks Frelan and Sinchante as the two among his inmost circle whom he was likeliest to reach on the first attempt. Yevir keyed both names into his comm panel, and swiveled to face the screen. He reached out with his other hand to touch the jevonite statue on his desk.

Both women answered on the split screen within moments of one another, and Yevir could see that each appeared to be alone in her respective chambers. Incense burned in braziers beside ornate prayer mandalas in both rooms, in honor of the evening temple services, from which the busiest and highest ranking vedeks were understandably excused. It occurred to Yevir only then that he had gotten so sidetracked by his encounter with Mika that he had completely neglected his own evening prayer rites.

"Something has happened," he said after exchanging perfunctory pleasantries with his two old friends. "I have been seized by a notion so . . . *radical* that I can scarcely defend my thinking. And yet, I am experiencing a clarity of mind that tells me this notion can only be the truth."

As both women simultaneously raised their eyebrows, Yevir began to outline his plan.

6

Ezri was gratified to note that none of the shuttlecraft *Sagan*'s critical systems had sustained mortal damage during the encounter with the enigmatic alien artifact. But because the little vessel was limited to impulse power during the trip back from the depths of System GQ-12475's Oort cloud, the return flight to the *Defiant* took nearly forty minutes. While they were en route, Commander Vaughn supplied a quick briefing about the *Defiant*'s intervention in the fight between the two local space vessels, as well as a summary of the gravest injuries sustained by the crew of the less well armed— and currently crippled—ship. With the help of several hastily dragooned corpsmen, Nurse Krissten Richter was struggling to keep up with the very worst trauma cases.

Ezri hoped that Krissten wasn't fighting a losing battle. Although she was better than competent, Julian's assistant was only a medical technician, after all, not a doctor. Julian's obvious anxiety was perfectly understandable.

As the *Defiant* hove into view on the screen, so did the battered alien vessel that was keeping station about two hundred meters off her port bow. Ezri forced down any outward show of apprehension as she noted the black rents in the other ship's pitted hull, obviously the result of an unhappy encounter with a concentrated phaser or disruptor barrage. Most of the internal lights were dark, and only the exterior running lights allowed her to see the lines of the long, irregularly shaped hull.

Relinquishing the piloting chores to Nog, Ezri glanced up at Julian, who stood directly behind her flight chair, his expression anxious as he studied the alien ship. She took his hand and gave it a gentle squeeze as Nog put the *Sagan* on its final approach to the docking bay built into the *Defiant*'s ventral hull.

Julian returned the squeeze, though his expression remained grim. Ezri could tell at once that he was already in "triage mode."

"Bashir to *Defiant*. Please beam me directly to the medical bay."

The clear tenor voice of junior engineer Jason Senkowski responded, *"Acknowledged."*

Ezri released Julian's hand so he could take a step back. Noting that Nog's attention seemed occupied, she mouthed a silent "I love you" to Julian just before the shimmering transporter beam took him. A moment later, the *Sagan* floated upward into the narrow shuttlebay in the *Defiant*'s belly and was maglocked into its parked position as the docking-bay door silently rolled closed beneath it.

Ezri's stomach suddenly lurched up into her chest.

For an absurd moment, she thought that the Dax symbiont was trying to escape from her body.

She became aware of Nog's concerned stare. "Are you all right, Ezri?"

She opened her mouth to speak, and heard herself release an unflattering and uncharacteristic burp instead. *I haven't yarked on an instrument panel in over eighteen months. Why the hell should I be getting spacesick now?*

She assayed a weak smile as she started shutting down systems and putting her console into "safe" mode. "I'm fine. Lunch must not have agreed with me."

"I warned you," Nog said with a grin. "You should have had the tube grubs." The thought made Ezri feel as green as the skutfish that plied the floors of Trill's purple oceans.

Nog had obviously noticed. "Maybe I'd better run some diagnostics on the *Sagan*'s food replicators."

Ezri's stomach heaved again. "I'd rather not discuss food at the moment, Nog. Let's just finish locking down this shuttle. And we have to get that alien document transferred to the bridge."

Nodding, Nog thumbed a comm panel and called Lieutenant Bowers.

"Bridge. Bowers here."

"Sam," Nog said as he began scratching at his leg. "I've just started uploading a pretty big file to your station."

"I see it," Bowers said. *"It's coming through now. What is it?"*

"Text. *Alien* text, and we're going to need a translation and a cross-linguistic analysis of the thing."

Now it was Ezri's turn to stare at Nog. He hadn't stopped scratching his leg.

His *left* leg, she realized with some surprise. *The biosynthetic one.*

"That's one big document, all right," Bowers said

with a whistle. *"There's megaquads and megaquads here."* Ezri heard Bowers crack a joke featuring the phrase "billions and billions," an expression which apparently had been mistakenly attributed to the *Sagan's* human namesake. She wished she felt like laughing, but decided instead that she'd settle for not feeling nauseated.

"Thanks, Sam. Nog out." The engineer continued scratching his leg.

Ezri's own distress melted away, at least somewhat, as she allowed herself to segue into her "concerned counselor" mode. Though she had spent three months on the command track, none of her nurturing instincts had dulled. Besides, focusing on something other than her own lurching insides seemed like a good idea just now.

"Phantom limb still bothering you?" she asked. She knew all too well that Nog didn't appreciate any tiptoeing around the subject of his biosynthetic limb. It was usually best just to be up-front about such things, at least with Nog.

"No, not really," he said, only now seeming aware of what he had been doing. "I usually don't think much about it. I mean, it was a lot worse during the first few months after AR-558, but it still happens from time to time. The itching, I mean."

Ezri furrowed her brow as the obvious solution came to mind. "I wonder . . ." She trailed off, lost in thought.

"Wonder what?"

"Nog, do you mind if I put my counselor hat back on for a moment?"

He bared his sharpened teeth good-naturedly. "Bearing in mind, of course, that free advice is seldom cheap."

"No charge, I promise. But I wonder if your old psychosomatic symptoms might have begun flaring up again lately because of delayed stress."

Nog looked skeptical. "From AR-558? Sure, that battle was hell, and it cost me a leg, but—"

"I don't think this is only about AR-558," she said, shaking her head. "At least not directly. I think it's really about Taran'atar."

Nog looked blank. "I don't follow you."

"Ever since Taran'atar came aboard DS9, you've been forced to share space with a Jem'Hadar soldier."

"Oh. And it was Jem'Hadar who shot my leg off at AR-558."

Ezri winced at that image. "Sounds like you've already done the math."

"I've thought about it," Nog said, his mouth a grim slash. "And I've concluded that the less I have to see of *any* Jem'Hadar soldier, the better I like it."

Ezri was taken aback by Nog's vehemence. "Why?"

The young Ferengi appeared to consider carefully just how much he wanted to reveal before replying. Ezri was about to try to change the subject to something less threatening when he said, "Right before we left for the Gamma Quadrant, I had a little run-in with Taran'atar that convinced me I've been right about him all along."

Ezri's counselor instincts went into overdrive once again. "What do you mean?"

"I mean that all Jem'Hadar are cold-hearted killers, and nothing can change that. Not even a direct order from Odo." Nog turned away, apparently concentrating intensely on an instrument panel.

They finished stowing the *Sagan* in silence. After Ezri advised Commander Vaughn that they were coming up to the bridge to make a preliminary report about the alien artifact, she and Nog disembarked into the narrow shuttlebay, entered the adjoining corridor, and made their way to the turbolift.

"Bridge," Nog said, his voice hushed.

"Taran'atar isn't responsible for what happened to you at AR-558," Ezri said, trying to keep her tones even and nonjudgmental.

"No. But he won't let me forget it, either. Just by being on the station. That's one of the reasons I was so glad to come on this mission—no unnecessary reminders."

Ouch, Ezri thought. *I deserve that for trying to play counselor as well as first officer.* Still, she hated to leave emotional loose ends hanging. Aloud, she said, "I don't want to see you let an old resentment like this fester. It won't do you any good in the long term."

Just as the turbolift reached the bridge, Nog told the computer to halt it. She noticed that sweat had broken out on his hairless brow. "Ezri, I appreciate your help, but I'm fine. I can put up with having a Jem'Hadar on the station because I'm trained to follow orders. But nobody can order me to like it. Or to forgive the Jem'Hadar for taking my leg."

Ezri nodded and told the computer to release the turbolift doors, which whooshed open a moment later. Stonily silent, Nog preceded her onto the bridge.

No, I can't order you to forgive anyone, Nog. Only you can do that.

The twelve aliens Commander Vaughn had beamed to the medical bay had suffered injuries ranging from third-degree burns to fractures to blunt-force trauma to punctures. The two who were conscious spoke a few words that the universal translator evidently found as unintelligible as Bashir did. Their long, willowy forms, awkwardly arranged on the too-short biobeds, were equally alien, their black, chitinous exoskeletons reminding him of a cross between hardwood saplings and giant versions of the crustaceans his father sometimes caught on Invernia II. Their almost perfectly round heads bore black-whiskered faces that were oddly evocative of both praying mantises and sea lions.

And there was something very familiar—weirdly comforting, in fact—about their deep, dark eyes.

As Bashir, Ensign Krissten Richter, and a pair of corpsmen tended to the messy details of improvisational trauma surgery, all of them elbow-deep in alien gore, Bashir quietly entered the mental room in which he stored his childhood memories and took his first patient down from a high shelf at the back of a little-visited closet. The first surgical procedure he had ever performed had been sewing up the torn leg of Kukalaka, his favorite plush bear, at the age of five.

Seeing the eyes of his childhood companion writ large on these alien faces tempted him to dub his patients "Kukalakans."

Nurse Juarez's temporary absence had never been felt more accutely. But Edgardo was still on bed rest in his quarters, waiting for his leg to finish healing after an EVA mishap two days ago.

Three of the aliens had expired during the time it took the *Sagan* to return, and it had since taken nearly thirty minutes of extremely messy surgery before Bashir felt confident that no more of them were in imminent danger. Eight of the aliens were now curled up on biobeds or on the floor. Although they were all unconscious and weak, they appeared stable for the moment, and comfortable enough in the *Defiant*'s class-M atmospheric mix.

Bashir wiped his gloved hands across the front of his amber- and umber-splattered surgical smock. Just as he was about to order Ensign Richter to transport the healthiest five of the lot back to the alien ship, the vital signs of the ninth creature took an abrupt turn for the worse.

The being lying on the biobed before Bashir would have stood nearly two and a half meters in height—were it capable of standing. Below its elongated, bulbous head were two upper limbs; farther down jutted three equally long lower extremities—none of which seemed sturdy enough to bear the being's weight. But at the moment Bashir was far more concerned with the thick yellow ichor that had once again begun bubbling up through the brutal diagonal tear in the creature's blue-black abdomen. The first round of protoplaser suturing on the wound had evidently not held.

Bashir placed the dermal regenerator on a higher setting and quickly stanched the worst of the bleeding. Satisfied that his makeshift suturing job would remain in place this time, Bashir slowly moved his tricorder across the creature's belly to scan for evidence of internal bleeding. But it was damned difficult to interpret tricorder readings on creatures one had never before encountered, or even read about.

Bashir glanced up at Richter, who looked on with concern etched into her sharp features. One of the corpsmen, the youthful-looking Lieutenant John Candlewood, watched impassively for a moment before moving on to check the vital signs of some of the other unconscious aliens.

Krissten appeared to need a little encouragement. "You and the corpsmen did some fine work here, Krissten," Bashir said.

Tears welled up in the young med-tech's large, blue-green eyes. "Not fine enough for three of them."

Bashir spoke in a tone he usually reserved for his most grievously ill patients. "Some patients are beyond saving, Krissten. Even the ones we know how to treat."

Closing her eyes, she nodded slowly. *No one ever gets used to death,* he thought. *And nobody ever should.*

Bashir glanced down at the tricorder display. One of the creature's large thoracic vascular channels was leaking fluid into its body cavity. A humanoid with an internal injury like that would probably have bled to death within a minute or two.

"I'm going to have to go in there again and patch up that blood vessel," Bashir said. *Assuming that it* is *a blood vessel,* he thought as he picked up a laser exo-scalpel from the instrument tray beside the biobed.

"Initiating sterile field," Krissten said, her training evidently overcoming her emotional distress.

Bashir's brow furrowed as the field's faint blue glow arced across the alien's wounded thorax. Four minutes later, Bashir had neatly cauterized the ruptured vessel without disturbing any of the surrounding—and still mysterious—organs and tissues. It appeared he had succeeded in stopping the creature's internal bleeding.

So why was the alien's breathing suddenly becoming so labored?

Krissten was clearly troubled by the same thing. "I don't understand why he's starting to have respiratory trouble now," she said with a shake of her head. "If our atmosphere were poisonous to them, we would have known about it the moment they came aboard."

The creature opened its eyes, gasped, and released a string of guttural sounds that could have been coughing or an attempt at speech. The only thing Bashir knew for

certain was that the medical bay's universal translator
hadn't placed them in the latter category.

The alien fixed both of its glistening, plum-sized
black eyes on Bashir and reached weakly in his direction with one spindly arm. The creature's three opposing
digits trembled as they clenched and unclenched. Krissten took a cautious step backward. But Bashir saw no
threat in the alien's gesture; he took it instead as a plea
for help. The creature's quivering, willowy limb brought
to mind the time he had spent with Ensign Melora Paz-
lar, whose thin Elaysian bones were probably just as
frail because of her homeworld's low gravity.

Of course. Why didn't I think of that earlier?

The weak alien lowered its trembling arm and let out
a painful-sounding wheeze. Bashir tapped his combadge. "Bashir to Nog."

"Nog here, Doctor. What can I do for you?"

"Can you get me a reading on the artificial gravity
levels aboard the alien ship?" Bashir smiled at the perplexed look on Krissten's face.

Nog's voice was infused with the enthusiasm of a busy
engineer hard at work at his craft. *"I can do better than
that, Doctor. Shar and I are already aboard helping them
pick up the pieces of their engine room. And the gravity
here is one of the biggest nuisances we have to deal with."*

"How so?"

*"Well, if you try to walk too fast, you end up falling
on your butt in slow motion. I'd say the local gravity is
set at about point-one-five of standard."*

Bashir recalled having seen the ancient 2-D images of
Apollo astronauts "bunnyhopping" across the lunar surface in their bulky environmental suits, and sometimes
toppling over, tortoise-like, after having taken a bad
step. And there were the Russian cosmonauts who'd had

to be carried from their capsules on stretchers after returning to Earth from months-long zero-gee orbital missions.

"Thank you, Nog. Bashir out." He nodded to Candlewood, who had been following the exchange intently and immediately took the hint.

"Adjusting the local artificial-gravity environment to Earth-Lunar standard, sir," Candlewood said as his fingers moved briskly over a wall console.

Bashir felt immediately lighter, and the wheezing alien at once began breathing more easily and deeply. The unconscious patients also seemed to have been invigorated by the change, as their respiratory muscles suddenly found themselves with considerably less work to do. Bashir imagined he saw a look of gratitude in the unfathomable oil-drop eyes of the creature who lay before him. He offered it a reassuring smile, though he was well aware that his countenance was probably as inscrutable to the alien as the alien's was to him.

Bashir turned his gaze toward Krissten, who was gripping the edge of the surgical table with white knuckles. "Have you had any low-gee training, Ensign?" Bashir said.

"Not for years and years," she said, still clutching the table like a rock-climber who had just watched a buddy plummet into an abyss. Krissten did not seem reassured by Candlewood's deft, deliberate steps as he went off corpsman duty and exited the medical bay. "Kol is a fan of zero-gee recreation. Not me."

Bashir smiled, recalling a low-gee hoverball tournament he had once played against Krissten's girlfriend, Deputy Etana Kol, who had won two out of three of those matches. He suppressed a sudden urge to show off his genetically enhanced reflexes.

"Just move carefully and slowly," he said. "I'll help you stow the surgical equipment."

He reached for the exoscalpel that he had placed on the instrument tray and lifted it. He scowled when he noticed that it was still activated. *Could have sliced my thumb off if I'd picked the damned thing up wrong. How could I have forgot to turn it off?*

He moved his thumb toward the "off" toggle.

For a moment Bashir's hand seemed to defy him, and he lost his grip on the instrument. It felt as though his hand had been slickened with tetralubisol. *Damned gravity.*

He bobbled the device, grabbing at the still-active exoscalpel as it fell—and succeeded only in batting it toward his patient. Krissten yelped as she, too, grabbed for the instrument, bumping Bashir and knocking him down in the process.

The alien on the biobed screamed as the exoscalpel sunk hilt-deep into its chest, precisely where a human's heart would have been.

"Doctor, it was as much my fault as yours," Krissten said after they had repaired the damage and had once again stabilized the patient. Luckily, the exoscalpel had not hit anything vital.

Bashir stood silently beside his again-unconscious patient, the crisis past, the surgical gowns already doffed and in the matter recycler. The healthiest five aliens were already back aboard their own ship. Bashir rubbed his hands together. But no matter how hard he scrubbed, they didn't feel quite clean.

Finally he said, "Thank you, Ensign. But you weren't the one who forgot to deactivate the exoscalpel."

She wasn't ready to let it go. "You're not used to lunar gravity, Julian."

"It shouldn't have been a problem for me," he said with an emphatic shake of the head.

Krissten's face was a study in concern. "An accident like that could have happened to anyone, under the circumstances."

Not to anyone with my talents. Not to anyone with my genetically engineered reflexes and stamina.

Not to me.

It occurred to him for the first time that something substantive might really be wrong with him. He recalled the vertiginous, seconds-long eternity during which the shuttlecraft *Sagan* had collided with the giant alien artifact's interdimensional wake. The shuttle had been tossed about on the quantum foam like a cork on some wine-dark cosmic sea. Could the encounter have caused the *Sagan*'s crew to suffer unpredictable deleterious effects?

But why *this* effect? It made no sense. And neither Ezri nor Nog had complained of any symptoms. Perhaps he was jumping at shadows.

He forced a weak smile. "Maybe you're right, Krissten. Thank you."

Behind Bashir, the medical bay door hissed open to admit someone.

"I prescribe rest for the entire medical staff," Krissten said, smiling back at him. "Then we can forget that any of this ever happened."

If only it were that easy.

Bashir thanked the ensign, then turned to the doorway.

Ezri stood on the threshold. He wondered for a disjointed instant just how much she had overheard.

"I was curious about the last of our patients," she said as she entered. Then she scowled and gripped the door-jamb tightly. "And what the hell's going on with the gravity in here?"

Bashir gave her a quick explanation of the environmental needs of his alien patients, as well as an update on their steadily improving condition.

"Do you think these people might be able to shed some light on that alien structure we ran into out there?" she said. "Commander Vaughn is getting pretty curious."

Bashir smiled wryly at her understatement. Vaughn had stopped by earlier, during the busiest part of the surgical procedures. He'd obviously been beside himself with questions about the two groups of aliens, their conflict, and the weird structure that the *Sagan* had encountered out in the Oort cloud—questions that he'd had no opportunity to ask.

"There's no way to know what they can tell us," Bashir said, "until we figure out how to talk to them."

"Good point. Until then, can you spare some time to help me brief Commander Vaughn and the rest of the senior staff about our survey mission?"

Bashir glanced back at Krissten, who nodded affirmatively. Her wan smile reminded him of how fidgety she always became during staff briefings. She was obviously content to stay here and watch over the last four convalescing aliens, letting the officers sit shuffling padds around a mess hall conference table. She evidently liked formal meetings a good deal less than she did the lowered gravity.

"I'll call you immediately if anyone's condition changes, Doctor," Krissten said, making an effort to appear casual while clinging to the side of one of the biobeds as though her very life depended on it.

"All right," Bashir said. Smiling, he turned to Ezri. "After you, fearless leader. Let's regale everyone with our tales of derring-do from the far frontier."

* * *

Because of the alien ship's low gravity and dim, amber-colored illumination, Nog moved about with extreme care. Junior engineers Permenter and Senkowski seemed completely involved in their attempt to mime basic engineering concepts to the tall, thin pentaped who seemed to be in charge of the engine room.

Nog was glad that Shar had come along as well. Although the Andorian science officer was still more tight-lipped than usual, Nog hoped that getting engaged in the repairs to the alien ship would help draw him out, encourage him to discuss whatever had been bothering him.

Nog noticed that Shar, who was absently holding a hyperspanner, was looking in his direction. Shar's antennae twitched in evident curiosity.

"Are you unwell, Nog?" Shar said.

"I'm fine," Nog lied. In fact, he felt anything *but* fine. The itch he'd first begun to notice while parking the *Sagan* had continued unabated and seemed to be intensifying. Until maybe forty minutes ago, Nog had been willing to consider Ezri's suggestion that the itching might have been psychosomatic, something related to his acknowledged aversion to being forced against his better judgment to share space aboard DS9 with Taran'atar. But now it felt as though hundreds of carnivorous Hupyrian beetle larvae were building a hive in his biosynthetic leg. How could the cause of this be something in his head?

He promised himself that he'd run, not walk, to the *Defiant*'s medical bay just as soon as he was certain that this wreck of a warp core wasn't going to blow up in everyone's face. Until then, he'd cope with the discomfort. Concentrate past it. Suck it up.

Deal with it, Cadet! Deal with it!

He recalled his earliest Academy days. New plebe cadets couldn't afford to display any sign of weakness.

Especially not Ferengi *cadets.* For some reason he couldn't fathom, reminding himself that his lowly cadet days now lay more than two years behind him was doing precious little to bolster his confidence.

Nog came out of his reverie when he noticed that Shar was still looking at him expectantly. He was thankful that Permenter and Senkowski were still preoccupied with their instrument calibrations. Nog tried to put on his best *tongo* face for Shar, though he didn't want to appear as evasive as his friend always did whenever he was asked a direct question about his family. Concentrating on that helped distract him from the mounting agony in his leg.

Until he saw the alien ship's chief engineer extend two of its impossibly slender lower limbs toward one of the countless handholds that covered every bulkhead, loft itself spiderlike toward the ceiling, and fetch several of its tools and instruments with its remaining three appendages.

Watching a creature whose movements so resembled those of a Talarian hook spider made it very difficult not to think about legs, itching or otherwise.

Shar still stared at Nog, his antennae fairly vibrating with unasked questions.

Nog knelt long enough to fetch an EPS pattern tracer from his open toolkit. He focused past the pain in his left leg as he rose.

"I'm fine, Shar. Really. Now let's finish getting this engine room shipshape so we can get back to the *Defiant.*"

The alien structure turned slowly end over end, hovering in midair about a meter above the longest table in the mess hall. Commander Vaughn sat at the head of the

73

table, his fingers steepled before him as he watched the object's ever-changing profile.

How long has it been drifting all alone out there? Vaughn thought, his soul filled to bursting with an almost religious ecstasy at the sight of this marvelous, inscrutable thing. *How many aeons have come and gone since its builders turned to dust?*

Seated across the table from Vaughn, Ezri Dax absently scratched at her abdomen. Then she gestured toward the hologram that dominated the *Defiant*'s ad hoc briefing room as she finished relating the tale of the *Sagan*'s near collision with the ancient object. Dr. Bashir sat beside her, listening attentively. The four remaining chairs were occupied by Lieutenant Sam Bowers, Ensign Prynn Tenmei, and science specialists Cassini and T'rb.

Vaughn looked around the room. Bashir, T'rb, and Cassini began reading the sensor reports that now scrolled across everyone's padds. But Bowers—whose specialty was tactical and security rather than science—seemed completely entranced by the image of the artifact. Tenmei appeared utterly absorbed by it as well.

Vaughn smiled to himself. *Maybe the apple really doesn't fall far from the tree after all.*

Vaughn watched as the artifact turned, shrank almost to invisibility, then grew a series of outsize flanges and sprouted structures resembling the flying buttresses of a medieval cathedral. Then, as ephemeral as a ring of smoke, the thing's shape changed utterly yet again, adopting an austere, Platonic solid aspect.

"I don't suppose anybody will mind if the tactical officer asks a really obvious and dumb question at this point," Bowers said. "But how does this thing change its form? I've never heard of any type of architecture capable of doing *that*."

"Strictly speaking, Lieutenant," Bashir said, "it isn't really changing its form at all."

"Come again?" Bowers said, looking perplexed.

"Imagine you're on a boat floating on an ocean," Bashir said in a professorial tone. "Floating nearby is an iceberg. All you can see of the iceberg is the little bit that's peeking out of the water. The bulk of it is hidden by the water."

"All right," Bowers said, clearly expecting more.

Bashir obliged him. "Now imagine that the iceberg is slowly rotating on an axis that's deep under the water. You'll continue to see just a fraction of the ice at any one time—but always a different portion of the whole."

"And," Cassini added, "if you row your boat too close to the spinning berg, you'll be caught in its undertow and get dragged under the water with it. That's what appears to have nearly happened to the *Sagan*."

"Metaphorically speaking," T'rb added, rubbing at the vertical line that bisected his sky-blue forehead.

"So what *is* the thing?" said Ensign Tenmei.

"It could be anything," Bashir said with a shrug. "A space colony. An observatory. A retail establishment."

"A police station," Bowers said.

"An interdimensional ski lodge," Tenmei said with a tiny smirk.

"A hospital," Dax said quietly. "Or a church."

"Whatever it is," Bowers said, "could it be related to the fight between our alien guests and the folks who attacked them?"

"Until we crack the language barrier," T'rb said, "the reasons for that conflict will pretty much be anybody's guess."

Bowers scowled. "Maybe not. It would help if some of our engineering detachment could snoop around a bit aboard the damaged ship. See if they can find what they're doing way out on the fringes of this system."

"Unfortunately," Vaughn said, "the aliens seem to be supervising every move our people make over there. It looks like interviewing our patients may be our only hope for figuring out the aliens—and the artifact."

Vaughn noticed the wry smile that had appeared on the doctor's face at Ezri's suggestion that the artifact might be a church of some sort. "Regarding the alien object," Bashir continued, looking in Ezri's direction as he spoke, "all we really know is that an intelligent and perhaps extinct species built it more than five hundred million years ago for some purpose which remains obscure. We also know that this structure possesses certain higher-dimensional characteristics that we don't fully understand. We really don't have any other information—except for the alien text file we downloaded from one of the thing's internal computers."

Vaughn smiled back at Bashir. From Vaughn's perspective, the doctor was a mere pup. Vaughn knew that in his century-long life, he'd very likely forgotten more than even a genetically enhanced thirty-five-year-old could have learned. But Vaughn was often impressed by how painstakingly empirical Bashir could be in the pursuit of knowledge. And he was occasionally amused by the young doctor's apparent obliviousness to all matters mystical. He recalled the Orb experience that had led to his taking command of this ship—and to this mission. Yes, mortal beings had built the alien artifact; this was not the work of enigmatic gods or supernatural spirits.

But knowing those facts made the thing no less wonderful or awe-inspiring to Vaughn.

Aloud, he said, "That alien text file has got to be the key to discovering the artifact's origin and purpose." He fixed his gaze on the *Defiant*'s security chief. "Mr. Bowers? Lieutenant Nog placed the text file in your care. Please give us a report."

Bowers touched a control on his padd, and the holographic image of the alien artifact was replaced by scrolling lines of swooping, unreadable characters. "For starters," Bowers said, "the file is *huge*. More than eighty megaquads, which is about a third of our computer core's overall storage capacity."

"That fact alone is going to put a real strain on our number-crunching—or, in this case, text-crunching—resources," said Cassini.

"It's too bad we have to tie up so much of the computer core," Tenmei said, "with a document we can't even read."

"You mean we can't read it *yet*," T'rb said, apparently very sure of his abilities. "Cassini and I have already started running a cross-comparison between this text and samples of written language groups we've downloaded from adjacent sectors of Gamma Quadrant space."

Cassini sounded equally confident. "It might take a while, but if we've ever flown anywhere near the Gamma Quadrant's equivalent of the Rosetta stone, we'll crack this thing. It's just a matter of time."

"Perhaps then we'll also be able to converse with Dr. Bashir's new patients," Vaughn said.

Bowers leaned back wearily in his chair. "That would be a relief, sir. It's damned difficult to work out repair schedules and visits to the aliens in the medical bay when all you have is the one or two concepts the universal translator can recognize. Everything else comes down to hand gestures and interpretive dance."

"We can't assume that the language the Kuka—that the aliens speak," Bashir said, "is in any way related to the ancient text."

It's not like Julian to stammer like that, Vaughn thought, scowling. Glancing at Ezri, he thought he noticed something different about her as well. She seemed to be getting rather pale. And was one of her eyelids beginning to droop?

Stroking his neatly trimmed beard, Vaughn said to Bashir, "I want to know more about this interdimensional wake the *Sagan* encountered near the artifact. Specifically: Could it have had any harmful effect on the shuttle's crew?"

Bashir paused for a moment before answering. "It's possible, sir. But I'll need to run some tests before I can say for certain."

"I *have* run some tests," said Tenmei. Vaughn and Bashir both favored her with a blank look. "On the *Sagan* itself, I mean. The *Sagan* is in close to optimal condition. Except for a peculiar quantum resonance pattern, that is."

"Meaning what?" Vaughn said.

Tenmei shook her head and shrugged. "I wish I knew."

Vaughn abruptly put aside every reverent thought he'd had about the alien artifact thus far. He didn't like the direction this was taking one bit.

Vaughn looked at Ezri again. This time he had no doubt—she was indeed looking pale. Why hadn't Julian noticed? "Lieutenant, how long have you been feeling ill?"

Ezri sighed wearily, evidently deciding it was best to come clean. "It happened . . . I think it started during the flight back from the alien artifact."

"I see." Vaughn was fully aware that this fact might or might not be significant. Shifting his gaze to Bashir, he said, "Has anyone else from the *Sagan*'s crew experienced any symptoms?"

The doctor suddenly looked uncomfortable, as

though he wanted to be parsecs from the mess hall. He appeared to be groping for words.

That wasn't like him at all.

"Doctor?"

"I . . . believe I may have experienced a lapse in concentration while tending to our alien patients," he said finally. "I'm not at all certain what to make of it. If anything."

Vaughn felt his cheeks flush with anger. He glared first at Bashir, then at Ezri. "And you were both planning on reporting these difficulties exactly *when?*"

Bashir stiffened at that. "With respect, sir, at the time neither of us was aware that there *was* a problem. I'm still not entirely convinced there is one now."

Vaughn moved his hand through the air as though to wave the question of timeliness away. "All right. But what about Nog? How has he been feeling?"

"I'll contact him," Bashir said. "He's still making repairs to the alien vessel."

At that moment, Dax cried out and collapsed across the conference table, clutching her belly and screaming in pain.

Ignoring the pain raging in his leg, Nog watched as the alien EPS conduits finally lit up in the correct sequence. Power had begun flowing into the proper channels. And, more importantly, nothing had exploded.

Permenter heaved a theatrical sigh of relief, then displayed an *I-told-you-it-was-going-to-work* grin to the still sheepish-looking Senkowski. Even Shar wore a triumphant smile, which Nog knew was a carefully constructed affectation on the Andorian's part, for the benefit of the humans around him. Even the alien engineer looked pleased, his chitinous mandibles moving from side to side to display what might have been happiness or gratitude.

"Release the magnetic bottles now, Shar," Nog said. After Shar touched the appropriate controls, Nog could feel the rumble in the deckplates that signaled the resumption of a controlled matter-antimatter reaction. Now that warp power was partially restored, the rest of the repairs would go forward much more easily. Force fields could be erected strategically throughout the ship, buttressing the collapsed sections and reinforcing the crude patching that had already been applied to some of the exterior hull breaches.

But I won't have to supervise the rest of it directly, Nog thought, now eager to get to the *Defiant*'s medical bay so that Dr. Bashir could examine his leg.

The deckplates continued throbbing, with increasing intensity.

The throbbing sensation moved up from the deckplates and into Nog's left leg, which suddenly felt as though it had been thrust directly into an unshielded antimatter pile. Nog screamed and watched the bulkheads trade places in slow motion. Deck became wall. Bulkhead became ceiling. His back pressed up—or down?—against something cold and unyielding.

He looked up, straight into the impenetrable eyes of the alien engineer. Beside the alien stood Shar, his image pulled and twisted as by a crazily warped mirror.

"*Defiant,* emergency beam-out!" he heard Shar shout as darkness engulfed him.

7

Two weeks, Ro thought as she leaned back in the chair behind the security office desk. Unbidden, a muscle in her upper back began rhythmically clenching and unclenching itself. Rolling her shoulders to work out the kink, she tossed the padd containing the incident report—the *unfinished* incident report—onto the desk.

Two weeks, and I'm still mopping up after Thriss.

The door chime rang. Ro looked through the glass to see who was trying to monopolize her time *now.* But the moment she saw who it was, she relaxed and ordered the computer to open the door.

"Didn't expect to find you still in your office so late, Ro," said Lieutenant Commander Phillipa Matthias, leaning tentatively through the doorway. "Got a minute?"

Ro smiled. She genuinely liked the station's new counselor, not simply because she was friendly toward her—not to mention solicitous of her sometimes prickly moods—but also because she spoke plainly and directly.

Starfleet counselors were rarely so refreshingly free of professional psychobabble as was Matthias.

Ro also knew that she could rely on Phillipa not to waste her time. "A minute?" she said as she rose from behind her desk and stretched. "I've got as many as you need. Tell me: Have the Andorians agreed to talk to you?"

Phillipa bit her lip, looking uncharacteristically uncomfortable. "Well, doctor-patient confidentiality would have constrained what I could tell you. *If* Dizhei and Anichent had decided to open up to me. But they haven't. Frankly, I'm not a bit surprised. Andorians aren't known for being overly fond of the counseling trade."

"I wonder why."

"It's the antennae."

"Come again?"

"Those antennae are a wonderful means of nonverbal communication. Sometimes unintentionally so. That's why Andorians are lousy at keeping their poker hands a secret, but absolutely terrific at judging other people's emotional states. They probably realize it, too, which explains why they aren't keen on having counselors around. Especially when they're this raw emotionally."

Ro felt another slow, pounding, warp-core-breach of a headache coming on. She understood, and sympathized with, the anguish Anichent and Dizhei were experiencing. She recalled all too well the desolation she had felt after a Jem'Hadar minefield claimed the life of Jalik, a fellow Maquis fighter. And there had been her father's grisly death at the hands of Cardassian torturers, which she had witnessed at the tender age of seven. But she also knew that it was possible to survive such horrors. Despite all the death and cruelty she had witnessed during her brief span, Ro had never felt so completely paralyzed as those two young Andorians seemed to be.

After so many interminable days of mourning, couldn't one of them find the emotional wherewithal to give her a somewhat coherent statement regarding Thriss's death? Even in the face of personal tragedy, official reports still had to be filed.

Life had to go on for the surviving members of Shar's bondgroup.

"Have they let Dr. Tarses speak with them?" Ro said. "Or changed their minds about letting him perform an autopsy?"

Phillipa shook her head. "They let Simon in tonight, just before he went off-shift. He visited on the pretext of checking on the stasis chamber they've borrowed from the infirmary. But that's *all* they'd let him do. For me, they wouldn't even open up the door to their quarters."

Shar's quarters, Ro thought. The rooms where the despondent Thriss had taken her own life. Where two of her soul mates still maintained a vigil, two long weeks later.

"Do you feel they're dangerous?" Ro said at length, recalling how Anichent had charged at her, lunacy shining in his cold gray eyes.

"Anyone that overwrought always has the potential to be dangerous, at least to himself. But when the person in question is an Andorian, that makes things even more volatile."

"In other words, I'd better maintain the guards I posted outside Shar's quarters."

Phillipa nodded, but looked apprehensive. "As long as they stay out in the corridor, and a few doors away. Like I said, those antennae can be pretty sensitive, especially to the EM fields produced by phasers. That said, my sense is that they're likely to refrain from any further, ah, demonstrative behaviors."

"What makes you say that?"

"Because they have each other. And grief shared is grief halved."

Ro wanted to believe that. But she understood only too well the impulse to spread grief around, the way *nerak* flowers scattered themselves on the wind beside the River Glyrhond.

"Maybe I should make another stab at talking with them," she said, recovering her padd and walking toward the security office door with it. Phillipa followed her out into the corridor, her brow scored with consternation.

"I don't think that's such a great idea, Ro."

Ro stopped in front of the turbolift just as its doors opened. "You just finished explaining that they wouldn't talk to you because you've got too much empathy."

Ro stepped inside, treading on Phillipa's response as she moved. "That's an accusation nobody's ever made about me."

The turbolift doors quietly closed on Phillipa's wordless *you'll-be-sorry* expression.

Standing in the habitat ring, Ro looked down the corridor to her left. Four doors away, Corporal Hava stood at parade rest, his hand near the butt of his phaser. Ro turned her head to the right, where Sergeant Shul Torem stood quietly an equal distance away in the opposite direction. Somehow, the grizzled veteran managed to appear both relaxed and vigilant.

Clutching a padd tightly in her right hand, Ro was uncomfortably aware of her own weapon's conspicuous absence as she pressed the door chime before her.

"Go away."

It was Dizhei's voice. Though the gray duranium door muffled it considerably, Ro could hear the underlying rawness.

"Go away. Whoever you are."

"It's Lieutenant Ro," Ro said, relieved that Anichent hadn't been the one to answer the door. "I'm here on official business."

A long beat passed before Dizhei spoke again. She sounded calmer now, though she seemed to be trying very hard to rein in her emotions. "Please, Lieutenant. We do not desire any visitors right now. Anichent and I will contact you. Later. When we are ready. After Shar returns."

Ro was quickly growing tired of conversing through a metal door. "Shar isn't due back from the Gamma Quadrant for several more weeks. I understand your grief, Dizhei. And you already know that I respect your people's funerary customs. But I have regulations to follow and reports to file. Certain things need to be resolved, sooner rather than later."

The heavy gray door stood as mute and inert as a Sh'dama-era stone monolith.

After nearly half a minute, Ro broke the silence. "How does Anichent feel about speaking with me? I'll only need a few minutes of his time."

More silence. Ro's spine suddenly felt as though it had been dipped in liquid nitrogen as a thought occurred to her: What if Anichent wasn't merely being reclusive?

Perhaps he *couldn't* come to the door.

"Dizhei? Open the door now. Please. I really need to speak with Anichent."

Nothing.

Ro gestured toward both guards, who responded by quietly drawing their weapons. She hated that things were coming to this. But she had to know what was going on behind that metal slab.

Tapping her combadge, Ro said, "Computer, security

override at the personal quarters of Ensign Thirishar ch'Thane. Authorization Ro-Gamma-Seven-Four."

The door slid aside and Ro entered the room, holding herself bowstring-taut. Hava and Shul followed a few paces behind her.

The air was moist, and hot as summertime in Musilla Province. The darkness of the small main room was broken by the flames that danced atop a pair of tall, pungent-smelling candles. Countless bejeweled pinpoints adorned the emptiness beyond the large oval window. Between the candles, at the room's spinward edge, stood a bier surrounded by the faint bluish glow of a large stasis chamber. Thriss's corpse, clad in a simple white gown, lay in state atop the bier, per Andorian custom. The pale cerulean light that bathed the body gave it an oddly lifelike aspect, as though Thriss were merely sleeping and might be awakened by an errant footfall or a creaking deckplate.

In spite of herself, Ro made a special effort to be silent as she stepped toward the two figures who knelt before the bier. She stood for a long moment behind them, allowing her eyes to adjust to the wan candlelight and the room's fluttering, crepuscular shadows.

She watched Anichent and Dizhei in profile, observing that they both seemed to be in a deep meditative state. They looked tired and gaunt, their nondescript Andorian prayer robes draped over their bodies like sails. Ro couldn't determine whether they had continued cutting their flesh, as they had begun doing immediately after Thriss's death. Their eyes were closed, their limp antennae draped back across disheveled white hair. Neither of them acknowledged her presence. Ro couldn't tell whether they were indeed sharing their grief, or if each was trapped in some solitary emotional purgatory.

Thanks to a briefing Phillipa had given her, Ro felt she

knew at least the basics of Andorian biology and funerary customs. Because their species' reproduction depended upon all four members of a bond, the death of any one of them was a terrible blow to the survivors—and often produced some extreme grieving rituals. Obviously, neither Dizhei nor Anichent seemed able either to let go of their lost love or to go on with their lives. They wouldn't prepare Thriss's body for interment or even allow a proper autopsy. Before any of those things could happen, all three surviving members of their sundered marriage quad had to assemble in shared grief beside Thriss's body. Therefore, they were determined to await Shar's return, consuming only water—and interacting with no one—until that day.

No matter how far off that day might be.

If not for their tangled white manes, blue skin, and antennae, Dizhei and Anichent might have been a pair of Bajoran religious acolytes, beseeching the Prophets for guidance. Ro had always felt somewhat detached from—not to mention bemused by—the fervent religious beliefs of many of her fellow Bajorans. Her father's murder at the hands of Bajor's Cardassian oppressors had taught her that piety and a concussion grenade nearly always got better results than did piety alone.

The self-abnegation on display before her stirred up some of the conflicted feelings the Bajoran faith frequently roused within her. And even though she knew that it was useless to judge another culture's practices against those of her own, the sight roused an even deeper, more fundamental sentiment.

It made her angry.

She brought her padd down against the top of a low table, hard. In the silence of the room, the noise sounded like a thunderclap.

Dizhei started as though she'd been dealt a physical

blow. She turned toward Ro, glowering. Ro could hear Shul and Hava moving in behind her, ready to react. But Dizhei did not rise to her feet.

"Is this intrusion a sample of what we can expect from Bajor after it enters the Federation?" Dizhei said, fairly hissing the words. Gone was the veneer of amiability Ro had noted when the Andorian first came aboard the station several weeks ago.

Ro picked up her padd, ignoring the comment. "I apologize for barging in, Dizhei. But I had reason to suspect that Anichent might be in danger."

Dizhei laughed, a harsh sound that contained no humor. "Because we Andorians are such a violently emotional lot, no doubt."

"I never said that," Ro said. She clutched the padd in a death grip.

Dizhei's gaze softened as she seemed to consider her next words carefully before uttering them. "You didn't have to, Lieutenant. We both know it's true."

Anichent lifted his head then, as though it were supporting an enormous weight. Still kneeling, he gazed up at Ro, who felt her legs and shoulders tensing in an involuntary fight-or-flight reaction. Her pulse quickened, and she heard a sharp intake of breath from Hava, who now stood beside her.

"She saw it so clearly," Anichent whispered, the despondence behind his words almost palpable. "More clearly than any of the rest of us ever could have."

Ro knew that he could only be referring to Thriss. "What did she see?"

Before Anichent could respond, Dizhei cut him off with a harsh Andorii monosyllable. Anichent lowered his head and closed his eyes once again, as though lost in prayer or meditation.

Dizhei fixed her eyes on Ro's. "Your men can lower their weapons," she said quietly. "Anichent can barely move, let alone attack you."

"Stay alert," Ro told Shul, who grunted an acknowledgment. To Dizhei she said, "I really hate to be indelicate, but without an autopsy, station regulations require me to log an official statement from Thriss's closest available family members. Councillor zh'Thane doesn't qualify, but as members of Thriss's bondgroup, either of you does. I'm sorry, but this is the only way I can officially close the matter. It'll take maybe ten minutes. Then we'll be gone, and won't bother you anymore."

Dizhei looked incredulous and angry. "Surely you have more important things to do with your time right now than to harass us."

"As a matter of fact, I do," Ro said, feeling her own pique beginning to rise with the inevitability of gravity. "This station is going to be swarming with Federation and Bajoran VIPs over the next few days. I've got to stage-manage the Federation signing ceremony, and it's going to be a security nightmare as it is. I can't afford to have a case like this still open and unresolved here with all of that going on."

"I see," Dizhei said, her ice-blue eyes narrowing, her antennae moving forward as though searching for something to impale.

Tamping down her anger, Ro raised a hand in supplication. "Look. I know this is a terrible time for you. But surely two weeks has been time enough—"

"Time," Anichent said in a voice rough enough to strike sparks, his speech slurring as he raised his head again. "What is time when there is no future?"

Ro approached Anichent more closely, watching as the candlelight flickered in his gray eyes. Gone was the upbeat, sharp-witted intellectual she'd observed weeks ago. *This* Anichent was a mere husk. A vacant, hollowed-out revenant.

"You've drugged him," Ro said to Dizhei. It wasn't a question.

Dizhei nodded. "To save his life."

"We've got to get him to the infirmary."

"No. I know the Andorian pharmacopoeia better than your Dr. Tarses does. Anichent is far safer here. Where I can watch over him."

All at once, Ro understood. Anichent *would* be safer in a place where he wasn't likely to come out of his drug trance at an inopportune time. In a place where he couldn't succumb to the temptation to throw himself willfully into death's jaws. A semantically twisted phrase she'd encountered once during a Starfleet Academy history course sprang to her mind.

Police-assisted suicide.

The remainder of Ro's anger dissipated as she considered the likely source of the Andorian people's violence. It wasn't innate, as with the Jem'Hadar. Or indoctrinated, as with the Klingons. Instead, it was born of pain.

I understand pain.

"Stand down," Ro said to the guards. "Dismissed." Hava didn't need to be told twice, but Shul required a moment's persuasion before he, too, departed.

"Do you truly believe that you understand now?" Dizhei said after she and Ro were essentially alone. Anichent had retreated once again into his drugged stupor.

Dizhei rose to her feet and approached Ro, who managed to keep from flinching, but steeled herself against the possibility of another violent outburst.

Ro nodded cautiously. "He's lost hope."

Dizhei responded with a barely perceptible shake of the head. She spoke softly, as though fearing that the oblivious Anichent might overhear. "No. It's more profound than even that, Lieutenant. He believes that hope itself no longer exists. That Thriss's death is merely an augury for our entire species."

"There's always hope," Ro said, without convincing even herself.

"Looming extinction has a way of snuffing out hope," Dizhei said.

My son has also ravaged the lives of Anichent and Dizhei, zh'Thane had said. Ro recalled the councillor's explanation of how Andorian marriage quads were groomed for their unions from childhood, and how few years the young adult bondmates had to produce offspring. It came to her then that the odds of Dizhei and Anichent finding a replacement for Thriss might be remote—perhaps impossibly so.

She saw it so clearly, Anichent had said. Ro knew that utter, bleak despair was what Thriss must have seen. Not just for herself, but for her entire world.

And here I am, barging in and interrogating them about her. Good job, Laren. Ro felt as though she'd just kicked a helpless Drathan puppy lig.

Dizhei resumed speaking. "Anichent truly believes that we are dying as a species because of our complicated reproductive processes. I tell you this only because I know that Shar considers you a good friend. He trusts you."

Ro felt the warning sting of tears in her eyes, but held them back by sheer force of will.

"It's mutual," Ro said. "We have a number of things in common." *We're both outsiders who don't share our secrets with very many others. And especially not our fears.*

Dizhei's antennae slackened once again. She studied Ro in silence, obviously waiting for her to make the next move.

"Do you believe that Anichent is right?" Ro said softly.

Dizhei closed her eyes and sighed, composing her thoughts before speaking. "There are times when I'm not at all certain that he's wrong. But I can't afford to let myself think that way often. If I do, then the rest of us will be lost, along with whatever tiny chance remains of finding another bondmate to replace Thriss in time to produce a child."

Dizhei straightened as though buoyed by her own words. Her bearing suddenly became almost regal. This is how Charivretha zh'Thane must have looked thirty years ago, Ro thought.

"I will watch over Thriss until Shar returns, as our customs demand. And I will do the same for Anichent, to keep him from following her over the precipice. Even if doing so occupies every moment of every day until Shar returns. Even if it kills *me*."

Ro considered the despair that had stalked so many of her friends and loved ones. Few, if any, of her intimates had ever had such sound reasons for despondence as bond-sundered Andorians. These were people for whom complex reproductive biology was the single defining attribute of their lives. After suddenly losing that capability, how could one *not* succumb to hopelessness? Ro felt an uncharacteristic but irresistible urge to get a drink. Or perhaps several.

"Now, about that report you wanted," Dizhei said, her antennae probing forward as though sniffing the air.

Ro shut down her padd and lowered it. A bead of

sweat traced a leisurely path between her shoulder blades.

"It will wait," she said, suddenly overwhelmed by the enormity of Dizhei's burden—and by Anichent's hopelessness. Routine police work now seemed utterly trivial by comparison. "Please forget I asked. And forgive me."

Ro hastily excused herself, then stepped back into the cool corridor before Dizhei could see the tears she could no longer restrain.

Halfway through her third glass of spring wine, Ro felt considerably calmer.

"Whoa there," said Treir, who sat across the table in Ro's dimly lit booth. She eyed the two empty wineglasses significantly. "Maybe you'd better consider slowing down to sublight speed, Lieutenant."

"I'm off duty at the moment," Ro said, swirling her wine. This vintage was a little drier than she was used to, but still serviceable. "And sometimes the best way to handle your troubles is to drown them."

The Orion woman offered a wry smile, her teeth a dazzling white against her jade-green skin, much of which was displayed by the strategically placed gaps in her designer dabo girl costume. She raised her warp core breach, a beverage Ro had never been able to distinguish from industrial solvent, in a toast. Although Treir's drinking vessel dwarfed Ro's, in the viridian-skinned woman's large but graceful hands it was proportionally the same size.

"To the drowning of troubles," Treir said, and they both drank. "Or at least to taking them out for a nice, brisk swim. Let's see, now. Which troubles are in most urgent need of drowning? There's the Andorians that have taken up residence in Ensign ch'Thane's quarters.

And the signing ceremonies for Bajor's entry into the Federation."

Ro offered a wan smile as she raised her glass to her lips. "You should talk to Lieutenant Commander Matthias about apprenticing in the counseling business."

Ro reflected on how much their relationship had changed since she and Quark had rescued Treir from the employ of the Orion pirate Malic a few months back. There was obviously a great deal more to Treir than her brassy exterior had initially led Ro to believe.

Treir glanced quickly over her shoulder, then returned her attention to Ro, to whom she spoke in a conspiratorial whisper. "Oh, and don't forget the single most horrific item on the entire dreary list of troubles to be drowned—there's still the matter of that second date my boss somehow tricked you into."

Ro nearly spit her wine across the table. Lately she'd been so wrapped up in station business that she'd completely forgotten.

"I heard that!" The voice belonged to Quark, though it took Ro a moment to zero in on his exact whereabouts. Then she saw that the owner and proprietor of DS9's principle hospitality establishment was standing three booths away, beside the small group of Terrellians whose drinks he had just delivered.

A moment later, he stood next to Ro's table, scowling at Treir and gesturing accusingly at the drink in the statuesque green woman's hand.

"Is *this* what I'm paying you for?"

"Check the schedule again, Quark," Treir said, nonchalantly sloshing what little remained of her warp core breach. "I'm off duty. And when I'm off duty, I sometimes moonlight as Lieutenant Ro's bodyguard." She threw Ro a wordless *I-can-make-him-leave-you-alone* glance.

"Hello, Quark," Ro said, involuntarily warming to his presence.

Quark's rejoinder to Treir appeared to die before reaching his lips. "I hope we're still on for tomorrow night," he said to Ro with an anticipatory smile. "We'll have Holosuite Three all to ourselves, starting at 2100 hours."

Ro noticed Treir staring at her. *No-really-I-can-make-him-go-away-if-you-say-the-word,* she seemed to be saying.

Ro smiled back at Quark, and it felt like the first time she'd done anything other than scowl in weeks. "We're still on, Quark. I haven't forgotten."

Shaking her head in incomprehension, Treir excused herself and departed, evidently having seen and heard quite enough. *Let her think whatever she wants,* Ro thought, amused.

"You know, I'm really beginning to look forward to this," Ro said, more than a little surprised to discover that she actually meant it. "I think I could really use the diversion."

Quark looked surprised for a moment, then quickly recovered his best *tongo* face. "You chose the program last time. So tomorrow night, *I* get to pick, just like we agreed."

"I remember," she said. Then she let her smile collapse in order to make her next point with absolute crystal clarity. "Now *you'd* better remember: Don't even think about running one of your *Vulcan Love Slave* holonovels, or else it's going to be an extremely short evening."

He looked wounded, his hands raised in a *don't shoot!* gesture. "I wouldn't *dream* of doing anything like that."

"And no programs that require me to dress like Treir."

She'd had to do that once already, in the line of duty, and that was once too many.

Quark was making quite a show of agreeing with her. "That's fine with me. That sort of apparel wouldn't be appropriate for Las Vegas anyway."

"Las Vegas?" She didn't recognize the name. "Is that a Gamma Quadrant planet?"

"It's a city on twentieth-century Earth," Quark said, cheerfully baring his snaggly teeth. "Courtesy of Dr. Bashir. Full of bright lights, indescribable sounds, and inhaled carcinogenic vapors. Harmless *holographic* carcinogenic vapors, of course."

"Sounds like a Cardassian labor camp," Ro said with a frown. "Except for the part about the holograms."

"I suppose my description hasn't done the place justice. Actually—"

Ro's combadge chose that moment to speak up. *"Kira to Ro. I've got a situation on my hands, Lieutenant."*

The sound of Kira's voice neutralized the spring wine as authoritatively as a bucket of cold water. "Ro here, Colonel. Please tell me nobody's hurt or dead this time."

"It's nothing quite that serious. At least, not yet. But I still need to see you in my office right away."

"On my way." Ro stood up and excused herself. "Tomorrow night, 2100 hours."

"Wear a nice evening gown," she heard Quark say as she walked quickly away from the booth. "Something semiformal and off the shoulder would be nice. With sequins!"

As she moved toward the bar on her way to the Promenade, she practically collided with Morn, who had chosen precisely the wrong moment to step down from his perch. Ro felt like an astronomer bearing witness to the formation of an antimatter quasar; the sight of Morn disconnected from his barstool had to be at least that rare.

Smiling politely, she picked her way quickly past the massive Lurian before he had a chance to draw her into yet another one of his interminable family anecdotes.

Moments later, she strode from the ops turbolift and into the station commander's office.

Kira rose from behind her desk. "It's Gul Macet," she said in response to Ro's unspoken question. "He's asked for immediate departure clearance for his ship. And he won't explain why, or when he intends to return."

Ro frowned. "The *Trager* was supposed to stay at the station for at least the next few days. Macet told me he'd placed his ship at the disposal of the Cardassian delegates still on the station doing the low-echelon stuff."

"Yes, the people who have diplomatic meetings about whether and when Bajor and Cardassia will *have* more diplomatic meetings," Kira said, nodding. "My instinct is to tell Macet to just sit tight and wait his turn."

Ro mulled that over for a moment. With the current levels of station traffic, that would bump back the *Trager*'s departure by at least six hours. Why was Macet in such a hurry?

"Has he given you any reason to suspect anything other than an innocent internal scheduling mix-up?" Ro said.

Kira's smile was small and rueful. "Besides his looking so much like Gul Dukat that it's virtually impossible to think about him objectively?"

"Besides that." Ro knew that Kira's point, though made flippantly, was entirely valid. How could any Bajoran who'd endured the casual brutalities of the Cardassian Occupation keep a level head around a man who wore the face of Bajor's most hated oppressor?

But Ro also knew that there were larger issues to consider, namely Bajor's relationship with Cardassia during that world's postwar reconstruction—and the Federation's evaluation of the Bajoran government's actions before formally accepting Bajor as a member.

An event that now loomed only days away.

Kira's furrowed brow told Ro that the colonel was busy weighing those very same issues.

Ro followed Kira from the office and down the steps into ops, where Ensign Selzner stood beside a communications console. She was clearly awaiting Kira's instructions as to how to handle Macet.

"Hail the *Trager*, Ensign," Kira said before turning back to Ro. "Trust has to start somewhere. Even at the risk of misplacing it."

Absurdly, Kira's comment reminded Ro of her upcoming date with Quark.

"Thank you, Colonel," Macet said, doing his best to smile in an ingratiating manner. "You've just made my life immeasurably easier. Macet out."

Kira's image vanished from the viewer on the *Trager*'s cramped bridge. Macet's smile likewise disappeared.

Macet turned his command chair toward the Bajoran man who stood less than two meters away, just out of range of the viewer's visual pickup. "I am loath to do anything that might serve to undermine Colonel Kira's trust. You have no idea how difficult it was to gain whatever small measure of it I may have squandered just now."

"I understand," Vedek Yevir said. "Neither trust nor true faith comes easily to Colonel Kira."

"Yet you still insist on the necessity of all this . . . subterfuge," Macet said as he stroked the tufts of hair on both sides of his chin and considered what Yevir was asking of him.

"I assure you, it's *entirely* necessary." Yevir's face was overcome with a passionate intensity that Macet had rarely seen before. "I regret these deceptions every bit as much as you do. And I assure you, if our pilgrimage fails, I alone will assume the responsibility before your superiors as well as my own."

Macet smiled, more than a little reassured. *He's a step away from the kaiship. He has more friends and influence in the Vedek Assembly than anyone else alive. Other than perhaps First Minister Shakaar, there are no superiors he's obliged to answer to.*

"All right," Macet said. "But there are considerations here that are far more important than either of our personal reputations. And I'm still not certain what I can do to assist, other than providing transportation."

"Oh, there's a great deal you can do, Gul Macet, with the right help. Things that politicians and diplomats won't or can't do. And when the politicians and diplomats fail to do the right thing, then we must seek the help we need from others."

Macet could no longer hold back the obvious question: "Who?"

"Get the ship under way," Yevir said, his smile growing even more beatific. "And I will explain everything during the voyage."

8

Bashir gathered up Ezri's limp form and carried her toward the medical bay at a full-out run. Bowers ran alongside, using his combadge to alert Ensign Richter to the emergency as they sprinted through the corridor and into the turbolift.

Moments later, Richter and Bowers were helping Bashir place Ezri's feverish, perspiring body onto the table in the operating room adjacent to the main medical bay. Bashir dismissed Bowers with a curt nod. He was grateful for this room's Earth-normal gravity as he unlimbered his medical tricorder and ran its scanner quickly across Ezri's torso.

The readings were grim.

"What is it, Doctor?" said Krissten as she entered the chamber.

"Her isoboramine levels are falling steadily."

As Krissten studied her own medical tricorder, a puzzled frown creased her face. "I've never seen anything like this before. Is her symbiont in immediate danger?"

"It certainly will be in another hour or two, if nothing changes in the meantime."

"What could have caused this?"

Afraid that he already knew the answer, Bashir chose to dodge the question for the moment. "Trill physiology can be tricky, Krissten. Run a full battery of deep-tissue scans. We'll laser-biopsy as necessary."

"Aye, sir," she said, then calmly set about her tasks. If there was one thing Krissten Richter had proved repeatedly over the past four years, it was that he could rely on her to keep her wits about her during a crisis.

Ezri's eyes opened and she let out a long, forlorn wail. The sound pierced Bashir's soul to its core. Above the biobed, a monitor confirmed that she was experiencing intense neurological trauma. Her nervous system was on fire, and he had no clue yet as to why.

"Get me the delta wave inducer," Bashir said. "I want her unconscious."

He pressed the wafer-thin device against Ezri's temple, and she immediately relaxed. Her eyes closed and she grew quiet.

Please come back to me, Ezri, he thought as he lifted an exoscalpel from the instrument tray. He found himself staring at it as though he'd never seen it before. His hand felt unsteady, and recollections of his earlier near disaster with the instrument did nothing to calm him.

Don't blame yourself, Julian, she had told him long ago, on a similar occasion. Back when she had been Jadzia Dax, and Verad Kalon had forced him to remove the symbiont from her body. Jadzia's voice, weak and fading, spoke from his private citadel of memory: *Don't blame yourself, Julian. You did everything you could.*

101

He forced himself to place that unhappy memory back on the high mental shelf to which he normally relegated such thoughts. He concentrated instead on trying to recall the particulars of every disease agent that might cause a spontaneous separation of host and symbiont. If one of these turned out to be the cause of Ezri's condition, then a cure might already exist.

Hope buoyed him as he quickly adjusted his tricorder to look for particular genera of viruses and retroviruses.

Bashir's combadge chirped before he'd completed a single pass with the device. *"This is Merimark in the transporter room, Doctor."*

Damn! "Can it wait, Ensign?"

"'Fraid not, sir. Incoming medical emergency on the alien ship. I'm beaming possible wounded parties directly to the medical bay."

"Acknowledged. Who's coming?"

"It's Nog and Shar, sir."

When it rains, it pours, Bashir thought as he watched a pair of figures shimmer into view in the main medical bay chamber.

Bashir glanced toward Nog, who was propping himself up on his elbows, trying to get comfortable on the biobed. From his position, he couldn't see the nearby bed on which Ezri lay unconscious.

Just as well, Bashir thought.

"I can't believe this is happening," Nog said, possibly for the hundredth time. He gritted his teeth as Lieutenant Candlewood checked the dressings on the stump of his left leg and made a quick tricorder scan of the rapidly healing—though still raw—wound that lay beneath.

Nog's voice was flat and devoid of emotion. "I really can't believe this is happening."

Neither could Bashir. But the subject of Nog's incredulity wasn't his primary concern at the moment.

Ezri is.

She lay on the biobed between Nog's and the one located in the medical bay's farthest corner, on which the last of the convalescing aliens slumbered. Ezri's breathing was ragged and shallow, and her pallor had increased hourly while she had drifted in an out of consciousness, confused and terrified during her few brief intervals of wakefulness. At least she was asleep at the moment, Bashir thought, without the need for the delta wave inducer. He was thankful for that one small mercy.

Krissten stood on the far side of Ezri's biobed. "Dr. Bashir," she whispered. "You've been . . . *hovering* for hours. Why don't you get some rest? I'll call you the next time she comes to."

The medical bay doors hissed open before he could reply. Rubbing a weary eye with the palm of his hand, he turned toward the sound.

Commander Vaughn strode deliberately into the room, his craggy features solemn. Shar was at his side, his expression even more unreadable than usual, if that was possible.

Vaughn was first to speak. "Trying to communicate with the aliens has kept us a bit busy for the past few hours, Doctor. Sorry I haven't had a chance to get down here before now."

Bashir felt slightly muddled for a moment. Aliens? Then a glance at the long, spindly figure curled awkwardly on the third biobed brought him to alertness.

"Yes, of course, the aliens," Bashir said at length. Now that he had released all of them except one, gravity in the medical bay had been adjusted back to its customary one gee, except for the immediate vicinity of the corner biobed. Krissten had made no secret of her delight at the return of Earth-normal gravity.

"Has anyone managed to translate their, uh, language yet?" Bashir asked.

Shar's white dreadlocks, stark against his sky-blue skin, twirled slightly as he shook his head. "It's hard to tell. But with Lieutenant Bowers and Crewmen T'rb and Cassini assisting me, I think we will manage it eventually. The alien text you downloaded may prove helpful in that regard after all."

"Any change down here?" Vaughn said, looking in Ezri's direction.

Bashir gazed at Nog and decided that any discussion of Ezri's prognosis ought not to occur within range of the chief engineer's sensitive ears. There was nothing to be gained by stressing him with bad news. Bashir gestured toward his office as Shar excused himself to speak with Nog.

"Give me the bad news first, Doctor," Vaughn said, once the office door had closed discreetly behind him and Bashir.

"Ezri's slipping away from us," Bashir said. *From me.* He felt exhaustion suddenly gaining on him, with despair coming up hard on its heels. He sank heavily into the chair behind his desk.

"How?" Vaughn said, standing on the other side of the desk.

"There's massive peritoneal inflammation in and around the symbiont pouch. As well as progressive neurotransmitter and endocrine imbalances, including toxic levels of thorocrine production."

"Bottom line?"

"Ezri's body is rejecting the symbiont. It's happening very slowly, but there's no denying it. And apparently no stopping it either. Her neurotransmitter production has fallen to critical levels, and her body is even rejecting direct isoboramine injections."

"Isoboramine?" Vaughn said.

"It's a neurotransmitter unique to Trills. Without a sufficient isoboramine concentration, the neural link between host and symbiont collapses, and the symbiont has to be removed in order to keep it alive."

"Any clue as to what's causing it?" Vaughn said, folding his arms.

Bashir shook his head. "All I can tell at this point is what's probably *not* causing it. I can find no trace of any unusual virus or prion anywhere in her body. I tried a course of metraprovoline, lethozine, and metrazene, which will knock certain retroviruses out cold, even if we'd failed to detect them. No response. And I got the same results with the full spectrum of general antirejection drugs, the sort we ordinarily use on organ transplant patients. Neurogenics, for stimulating neurotransmitter production and uptake, have also proved to be a dead end. I even tried bethanamine."

"Another neurotransmitter?"

"An inhibitor, actually. Bethanamine is a little-known Trill drug set which has been used occasionally to safely separate symbiont from host. But it failed to work on Ezri, for no reason I can fathom. In fact, nothing I've tried as yet has made very much difference at all. It's as though her body is a computer running a program that can't be altered once it's started."

"Could the *Sagan*'s encounter with the alien artifact have anything to do with this?"

"I still can't say for certain. All I know for sure is that Ezri's isoboramine levels are still falling and the critical neuro-umbilical pathways between her and Dax are degrading. Net result: Her body is continuing to reject the symbiont. And I can't stop it." Bashir slammed his fist on the desk in frustration and then lapsed into silence.

From the back corridors of his memory, he heard the words of encouragement he had spoken to Jadzia after Verad had briefly taken possession of the Dax symbiont. *You're not going to die. Do you hear me? I'm not going to let you die.* He tried not to dwell on his ultimate failure to deliver on his promise to Jadzia, a mere four years later. Or the fact that another such failure now appeared all but inevitable.

Vaughn's impatient prodding brought him out of his reverie. "I said, 'What's next?' Surely you're not giving up, Doctor."

Bashir shook his head, though he already felt utterly and completely defeated. "The symbiont appears to be exhibiting signs of incipient ischemic necrosis. As Ezri's body continues to weaken, the symbiont is losing more and more of its vascular support. I'm afraid I'm running out of options."

What I need is a miracle.

Vaughn seemed to turn that information over in his mind for several moments before speaking again. "How long does she have?"

"At the rate she's producing rejection toxins, she might last a few more hours at the outside. That goes for the Dax symbiont, too, unless we remove it."

Vaughn clearly was not ready to concede defeat. "All right. There are no other Trills on board, so transplanting the Dax symbiont is out of the question. Unless . . ."

"Sir?"

"What about placing her in stasis, symbiont and all?"

"A stasis field wouldn't slow down the ongoing neural collapse. It might even hasten it."

"All right." Bashir could still hear a note of hope in Vaughn's voice. "Trill symbionts have been implanted in humans from time to time, correct?"

Bashir nodded cautiously. "But only on a *very* temporary basis. Even if we'd started heading for Trill yesterday at maximum warp, the journey would still take weeks too long. And no Trill–human symbiosis could last long enough to keep the symbiont alive long enough."

"Couldn't we transfer the symbiont briefly into a series of different human hosts?"

"The hosts could probably tolerate that. But there's no way the symbiont could. A series of marginal transplants like that would place far too much strain on it, without allowing for a sufficient refractory period. If the Dax symbiont is going to have any chance at all, it has to be returned to the Caves of Mak'ala on Trill, or the nearest equivalent, within a few hours of its removal from the host."

Vaughn appeared to grasp the ramifications immediately. "And if the symbiont continues to weaken, you're going to have to remove it from Ezri sooner rather than later."

Bashir nodded. He felt hollow inside.

"So regardless of whether or not the Dax symbiont survives . . ." Vaughn trailed off.

"Barring a miracle, Ezri is going to die." Bashir felt detached from himself as he spoke the words. *There. I've finally said it out loud.*

"You mentioned 'the equivalent' of the Caves of Mak'ala," Vaughn said, stroking his beard, plainly still considering every conceivable alternative.

"Merimark and Leishman are already busy constructing a portable symbiont pool like the one I rigged to carry the Dax symbiont after Jadzia's death last year.

But there are still no guarantees. The symbiont has already become dangerously weak."

Vaughn looked somber. "So you have a decision to make."

Bashir found that he was having trouble maintaining his train of thought. He took a moment to compose himself before speaking. Perhaps fatigue was catching up with him. How long had he been awake?

"I can hold out for a miraculous last-minute cure for both Ezri and Dax," he said. "Or I can give the symbiont a fighting chance at having another life."

A life I'll probably play no part in. For the first time, Bashir understood at a gut level how hard the earliest days of his relationship with Ezri must have been on Worf, the late Jadzia's husband.

"At the expense of Ezri's life," Vaughn said. But Bashir could detect no reproach in the commander's tone. Vaughn's vivid blue eyes took on a faraway aspect that spoke eloquently of other times, other deaths, other unwilling but unavoidable surrenders to decay and entropy.

Vaughn placed a gentle, fatherly hand on Bashir's shoulder. "I'm truly sorry, Julian."

"So am I." His words sounded banal in his own ears, but he could think of nothing better to say.

"How is Nog?" Vaughn said after a moment's silence.

The doctor managed to summon a weak smile, actually grateful for the change of topic. It was a relief to put aside, however briefly, the crushing weight of the decision he carried on his shoulders.

"Let me show you," Bashir said, leading Vaughn back into the main medical bay chamber and to Nog's biobed. Shar stood beside the young engineer, who was sitting up and reading something on a padd. Vaughn failed to completely conceal his surprise when he noticed what lay on the low table beside the bed.

It was Nog's left leg, severed at the knee.

"Hello, Captain," Nog said, making as though to rise from the bed, then evidently realizing that the maneuver hadn't been one of his best-considered ones. He gestured with his head toward the orphaned limb on the table, at which Shar was staring abstractedly.

"Sorry about this, sir. Shar has just brought me up to date on the repairs still going on aboard the alien ship."

Vaughn appeared to be trying hard not to stare at Nog's disarticulated leg, but was not entirely successful. "Between Shar, Senkowski, and Permenter, everything's well in hand over there. You've already done most of the heavy lifting yourself."

Shar nodded affirmatively to Nog. "I expect the alien vessel to be ready to get under way within a day or so."

"You just rest and do whatever Dr. Bashir tells you," Vaughn said to Nog. "Got it, Lieutenant?"

Nog looked sheepish as he handed the padd to Shar. Bashir caught a glimpse of technical schematics on its display screen just before it disappeared behind Shar's back.

Bashir pointed to the leg. "Nog, may I?"

"Go ahead, Doc. Just bring it back when you're through with it. I find it sort of comforting to have the thing around, now that it looks like I might not be needing it again."

Bashir held the limb before him to allow Vaughn to examine it. Vaughn took it and turned it over and over. He appeared puzzled. Shar, however, who had brought Nog and his severed leg to the medical bay, seemed to be taking this in stride.

"What happened?"

"Nog's body has apparently rejected it," Bashir said,

then allowed his words to sink in for a moment. Vaughn's raised eyebrow made it plain that he, too, understood that bodily rejection was emerging as a common theme here. "And that's not the end of it, either."

"Son," Vaughn said, handing the leg back to Nog. "What did you mean when you said that you 'might not be needing it again'?"

Nog grinned as he lifted the coverlet that had been draped across his lap and slowly unwound the dressing from the stump of his left leg. As the bandages fell neatly away, Bashir looked at both Vaughn and Shar to gauge their reactions. Shar's eyes widened slightly, his antennae probing unsubtly forward. Vaughn's jaw fell like a nickel-iron meteor.

Bashir quickly examined the tiny, perfectly formed leg sprouting from Nog's stump. It had grown by several centimeters during just the last hour.

Bashir wasn't certain how much time had passed before the nonplussed Vaughn finally found his words. "Can you . . . explain this, Doctor?"

"At the moment, I'm simply at a loss," Bashir said, shaking his head. "Even his burned femoral motor nerves are regenerating."

"I'd be sorely tempted to call *this* a miracle," Vaughn said, his gaze locking firmly with Bashir's. "And wherever we find one miracle, we might do well to keep searching for others." He was clearly talking about Ezri.

"I wish I could afford to believe in miracles, Captain," Bashir said, biting his words off. "Unfortunately, I have to make do with the real world."

The medical bay doors hissed open again. Merimark and Leishman entered, using antigravs to carry a meter-wide, half-meter-deep oblong container. The pair set the object down gently beside Ezri's biobed.

"One medical transport pod suitable for a Trill symbiont," Merimark said as she glanced uneasily at the unconscious Ezri. "Ready for activation when you give the order." Bashir recalled that Kaitlin Merimark had become one of Ezri's closest friends among the *Defiant*'s current crew complement. It couldn't be easy for her to see Ezri in her current condition.

"Thank you, Ensign," Bashir said, then turned to Vaughn. "I'll make a thorough investigation into Nog's condition as soon as possible. But at the moment I'm afraid I've more pressing matters to attend to."

Vaughn looked grave. "I take it you've come to a decision." *About Ezri* went unsaid, though the words hung in the air like smoke over the Gettysburg battlefield.

"Yes. The only decision possible."

"I understand," Vaughn said. "Come on, Shar. Let's get back to work." Shar, his facial muscles suddenly unusually tense, nodded silently. Bashir wondered how much Shar knew about Ezri's condition. He wished he had time to brief everyone beforehand about what was about to happen, and to allow Ezri to say her own farewells to one and all. But he no longer had that kind of time. He'd squandered that time with his repeated, fruitless attempts to save Ezri and the symbiont both.

Feeling miserable, Bashir watched Vaughn and Shar exit the medical bay.

He told himself that Ezri wouldn't have wanted any maudlin good-byes. She'd have another life soon, once they returned Dax to the Trill homeworld after the conclusion of the Gamma Quadrant mission. She'd have plenty of time then to catch up with auld acquaintances, he thought.

" ' 'Tis not too late to seek a newer world,' " Bashir said quietly to no one. Then he noticed Nog's quizzical stare.

"What's going on, Doc?"

Bashir realized that he had been protecting Nog from the truth about Ezri. He sighed, collected his thoughts, and said, "Nog, you deserve to know what's really about to happen to Ezri."

The only decision possible.

For perhaps the first time in his life, Bashir really, truly wished he were dead. "Ensign Richter," he said. "Please prepare Ezri for surgery." Then he turned back to Nog and started to explain, as gently as possible, that Ezri was going to die very soon.

The woman I love is going to die.

In preparation for the procedure, Ezri was moved back into the small surgical bay, where she slowly drifted back to consciousness. Her eyes opened and she smiled. Despite her pallor and fever, the smile made her as radiant as Bashir had ever seen her.

And it's the last time. The last time I will ever see that smile.

His heart pounded, auricles and ventricles transformed to hammers and anvils. Doing his best to manage his roiling emotions, Bashir explained to her what was about to happen. She listened attentively and took the news with considerably more grace than Nog had. Or Merimark. Or even Krissten, for that matter.

But Ezri's equanimity rattled him at first. He had to remind himself that Dax had already experienced host death eight times before.

"I understand, Julian. I love you. And I trust you to do whatever you have to do . . . to save Dax."

Once again, he heard Jadzia's voice, echoing up from a well six years deep: *Don't blame yourself, Julian. You did all you could.*

He desperately wished he could believe those words.

"Julian."

"Yes?"

"I don't want to be conscious when you . . . cut the cord. Not like Curzon. That was different."

Bashir knew that Curzon's symbiont had been surgically removed as well. But that had been done at the end of a very long, very satisfying life.

"I understand," Bashir whispered, his words catching in his throat.

"I don't want to be . . . *emptied,* like the time Verad took the symbiont . . ." She trailed off. Bashir noticed for the first time that her face was wet.

Julian, Jadzia confessed in the back corridors of his mind. *I'm scared.*

"I understand," he repeated. He felt a single fat tear roll down his cheek. Another one jostled for position behind it. He squeezed her hand gently. She squeezed back, hard. He bent down and brushed his lips against hers, then straightened and released her hand.

"I'm ready, Julian," she said at length.

Blinking away his tears, he donned his surgical mask and lifted an exoscalpel from the tray beside the operating table. At his nod, Krissten carefully attached the delta wave inducer to Ezri's temple.

"Ensign Juarez is standing by to activate the artificial environment container," Krissten said in a subdued voice. After learning about Ezri's condition, Edgardo demanded to be allowed back on duty, insisting his leg had healed sufficiently.

Ezri mouthed a silent *I love you* to Bashir, then smiled.

"Good-bye, Ezri," he said.

Her lips curled into a faint smile. Then oblivion took her.

Responding to Bashir's nod, Krissten activated the sterile field. He gripped the exoscalpel tightly in his gloved hand, grateful that the instrument showed no signs of slipping this time. Krissten silently opened the front of Ezri's surgical gown, exposing Ezri's abdominal pouch. Very gently, he moved the exoscalpel's tip across her abdomen, leaving a slender crimson line in the instrument's wake. A moment later, the body of the symbiont began to emerge, its brown, lumpy skin glistening under the room's bright lights.

The symbiont inched forward, fairly oozing into his hand. After it had emerged entirely from Ezri's body, Bashir cradled it gingerly. The eyeless, limbless creature's helpless emergence reminded him of a cesarean section he had once performed; he had to remind himself this "baby" carried within it a store of experience and knowledge at least an order of magnitude greater than his own.

"This is going to be a somewhat unusual procedure," Bashir told Krissten as he raised the symbiont slightly higher, studying the superficial patches of necrotic tissue that had already begun to appear along the moist, amber-colored umbilicus still connected to Ezri's abdominal pouch. "There's already been so much neural depolarization along the entire neuro-umbilical trunk that the nerve bundles will have to be cut in a specific order to minimize the risk of neuroleptic shock for the symbiont."

"Understood," Krissten said, her voice muffled slightly by her surgical mask.

"Neurocortical separator, please."

She took his exoscalpel and replaced it with the requested implement. Gently hefting the symbiont in his left hand, he touched the tip of the compact, gleaming cylinder to a point about six centimeters down the length of the umbilical cord.

Ezri's body jerked reflexively as the separator sank its tiny polyduranium probe into the cord. "Note that I have just severed the gross motor pathway nerve bundle," Bashir said, his voice sounding flat and tinny in his own ears. He felt detached from his actions, as though he were a first-year med student watching with his classmates while a faculty member performed surgery in a Starfleet Medical operating theater.

He knew that he couldn't proceed without that kind of detachment.

"The separator is now locking onto the fine motor bundles," Bashir said, pressing on. Ezri's fingers spasmed as the second nerve-fiber bundle separated. He withdrew the separator and closed his eyes for a moment.

I'm killing her. Just as surely as if I'd tossed her out an airlock.

"Symbiont vital signs are weak but holding steady," said Krissten. "No sign of neuroleptic shock."

Forcing his self-recriminations aside, Bashir opened his eyes and focused on the umbilicus with renewed concentration. Next, he severed the monopolar neurons that coordinated autonomic neurophysiological exchanges between Ezri's and Dax's nervous systems. Then he cut the redundant autonomic glial-cell pathways. He paused for a moment to recall the correct order: major, minor, and ancillary nodes. Yes, that was right.

Nearly done. God, let this be finished before I turn this thing on myself.

Next, the separator's laser bit into the RDNAL organelle, a construct that consisted of a long tube buried in the very core of the umbilical's complex bundles of nerve fibers. Moving nimbly, Bashir sealed the organelle on Ezri's end of the umbilicus, which fell onto her abdomen like so much discarded ODN cable.

Jadzia's voice haunted him once again. *I've never felt so empty.* He forced himself to ignore the memories—to ignore Ezri, who lay before him not quite dead, not quite alive, yet still gone forever.

"Note," he said, "that the symbiont is now completely free of the host's body. There's been no change in the symbiont's vitals."

Krissten turned toward Nurse Juarez standing quietly by the door. "Edgardo, please ready the container." Juarez approached the table, prepared to take the symbiont to the oblong receptacle which lay in the far corner of the room.

"Krissten, please prepare a hypo with twenty cc's of isoboramine. I'm going to inject it directly into the symbiont's end of the umbilicus."

Krissten hesitated for a moment, then fetched the hypo and placed it in Bashir's hand. She held the symbiont for him while he gently applied it to the tip of the umbilicus and pressed the plunger home. Bashir felt a wave of relief sweep over him as Krissten carefully handed the symbiont to Juarez, who in turn carried it toward the open, liquid-filled container in the corner.

Krissten turned back to Bashir, a question in her eyes.

"Yes?" Bashir said as he allowed his gaze to wander back to Ezri. He watched the gentle rise and fall of her chest, listened to the gentle sussuration of her breathing.

"We tried this drug before," Krissten said. "But it had no effect. Why the second injection?"

Bashir gave his head a weary shake. "That was *iso*boramine, Krissten. This time I used boramine, which should stave off the symbiont's growing necrosis and prevent delayed neuroleptic shock while it's confined to the artificial environment."

"*No,* Doctor."

Bashir had never heard Krissten flatly contradict him before. He looked toward her and saw that her eyes had become immense. She appeared near panic.

"Excuse me, Ensign?" he tried to keep the irritation out of his voice, but didn't succeed completely.

"Doctor, that injection wasn't boramine. It was *iso*boramine."

Bashir felt as though he'd been slapped across the face. "What?"

"That hypo contained thirty cc's of isoboramine, sir. As *you* ordered."

A realization colder than the winds of Trill's Tenaran ice cliffs suddenly ran up his spine. Boramine. Isoboramine. Somehow, he had confused them. The two substances had similar names, obviously. But they differed from one another as much as oxygen did from fluorine.

And he knew that the consequences of mistaking one for the other could be every bit as serious.

Bashir watched as Juarez knelt beside the symbiont's medical transport pod and prepared to place Dax inside its life-giving purple liquid bath. Juarez stopped in mid-motion, frowning.

He looked helplessly at Bashir and Krissten. "It's . . . *squirming*."

"My God," Bashir said, rushing to the nurse's side with a medical tricorder. He made a quick scan. "It's an isoboramine overdose. The symbiont is going into neuroleptic shock."

"I thought Trill symbiosis *depended* on isoboramine," Juarez said.

"It does," Bashir said, still incredulous over the magnitude of his error. "But the symbionts can't tolerate it in large doses."

"Is there an antidote?" Krissten asked.

117

Bashir gently took the creature from Juarez and cradled it in his arms. The symbiont convulsed in his hands as though about to burst. His mind raced to find an answer to Krissten's question. Why was it becoming so hard to think?

"Yes," he said after a moment's hesitation. "Fortunately, there is a counteragent."

Krissten grabbed another hypo and stood attentively, awaiting his orders. It was only after the moment began to stretch that Bashir realized that this time he wouldn't need to drop a scalpel to endanger a patient's life.

All it would take was a lapse of memory.

"Doctor?" Krissten was beginning to sound panicked.

His head began to pound, as though he were in the throes of severe *raktajino* withdrawal. He closed his eyes very tightly, willing the throbbing pain to pass.

"Give me a moment to concentrate," he said, trying hard not to display his own rising alarm. The small, helpless bundle that contained the essence of the woman he loved continued to heave and shudder in his arms. He could feel intuitively that it was beginning to die.

"Doctor?" said Krissten, now clearly worried.

Bashir ignored her. He thought instead about the miracle to which Vaughn had attributed Nog's new leg. And the cathedral-like alien structure that had clearly caused the miracle.

What better place than a cathedral to go looking for miracles?

And in his mind, he was no longer in the medical bay. No longer aboard the *Defiant*. No longer even in the Gamma Quadrant. His mind's eye opened as he slipped into the stretched null-time of memory. Before him stood four great, russet-colored buttressed arches topped by a thirty-meter dome. The silvery structure gleamed under a clear desert sky, resplendent in the late-afternoon sun.

Shortly after his parents had taken him to Adigeon Prime for genetic resequencing, Bashir had discovered that he'd needed to find ways to cope with the torrential flood of information his agile mind had begun absorbing and retaining. At the age of eight, Bashir read a biography of Leonardo da Vinci, from which he had learned an appealing and useful mnemonic trick. Using the same care he had lavished on some of humanity's greatest masterpieces, Leonardo had constructed a vast, detailed cathedral entirely within his formidable mind. Every vestibule, gallery, staircase, foyer, and chamber was carefully catalogued in the polymath artist's memory, every sculpture and painting placed just so, every bookshelf, book, and page painstakingly arranged, indexed, and preserved for virtually instantaneous access.

All Leonardo had had to do to retrieve any specific fact he'd previously placed within his "memory cathedral" was to close his eyes, stride the great basilica's wide corridors, and enter whichever carefully catalogued vault contained what he sought.

Young Julian Bashir had chosen a much simpler, though still impressive, design for his own mnemonic citadel—that of the Hagia Sophia, Istanbul's great sixth-century cathedral. In all the years since, he'd never been tempted to move his personal treasury of memory into a larger, more complex structure, probably because of his father's preference for the gaudier Baroque- and Rococo-period architectural styles of a millennium later.

In the self-contained universe of his own mind, Bashir bounded up the Hagia Sophia's stone steps and ran through the arched doorway, through the vestibule, and into the wide aisle surrounding the central basilica.

Of course, it had been years since he'd had to resort to using this mnemonic trick so directly; he'd long ago learned to place his memorization skills on a kind of intellectual auto-pilot, until his subconscious information retrieval had become virtually error-free, almost an autonomic function, like breathing.

He turned right and found the staircase he'd installed at the age of ten, the year he had first begun seriously organizing pharmacological information in his cathedral-of-the-mind. As he ascended, he noticed that the fifth step made an echoing squeak as he put his weight on it, just as he remembered. He recalled how he'd deliberately installed several such things throughout the building, as mnemonic self-tests. He smiled as he continued upward.

In a few moments he'd remember how to save Dax's life.

A heavy oaken door stood before him at the top of the staircase. He pushed on it, but it was evidently locked from the inside.

He frowned. It should not have been locked.

He pounded on the door with his fists.

The door abruptly vanished, and he tumbled forward into a large, curving room that conformed to the Hagia Sophia's exterior shape. The place was stacked to the ceiling with massive-looking wooden bookshelves. Waning sunlight streamed in through the gauzy drapes.

A dark-haired woman in a Starfleet uniform stepped into view from behind one of the nearer bookcases and approached him. She was human, and appeared to be in her mid-thirties. She smiled and extended a hand, helping him back to his feet.

It took him a moment or two to place her. "Dr. Lense?" Bumping into the woman who had narrowly beat him to the position of valedictorian of his Starfleet

Medical graduating class, here in his own personal memory cathedral, both unnerved and perplexed him.

Elizabeth Lense smiled. "Don't worry, Julian. It's only natural that you'd wonder why I'm here."

"So you're telepathic. No wonder you got ahead of me back in medical school."

She laughed, a pleasing, liquid sound. "I got ahead of you because even the best memories can hiccup once in a blue moon. Besides, I don't *need* to read your mind, Doctor. I'm only a figment *of* your mind."

He immediately felt foolish. "Of course. So why did my mind choose this moment to, ah, channel you?"

"Channel me? I'm not a ghost, either, Julian. I suppose you're thinking of me because of an accidental confluence of tangentially related information."

Of course. I remember. She's serving aboard the U.S.S. da Vinci *now. A ship named for the man who inspired me to build this place.*

Her smile widened disconcertingly. "One thing's for sure, Julian. You'll never confuse a preganglionic fiber with a postganglionic nerve ever again."

That had been the one exam question he had got wrong. That single error had cost him the privilege of giving his graduating class's valedictory address. That all-too-rare failure of his prodigious recall skills would have remained etched into his memory forever, Leonardo or no Leonardo.

He had to force himself to stay focused on his current problem. Dax was dying. An antidote existed, but if the symbiont didn't receive it within the next minute or two, then nine lifetimes would all be for naught.

Because I let myself get confused and distracted, Bashir raged at himself.

He shouldered his way into the room, brushing Lense

aside, and made his way to a particular three-meter-high bookshelf cut from dark, tropical hardwood.

When he reached it, he was surprised to find the book spines in noticeable disarray. It looked as though many of the volumes had been taken out, rifled quickly, and then tossed haphazardly back onto the shelves. More than a few were out of order, misfiled slightly to the left or to the right of their correct locations. Many looked tatty and shopworn.

He started when he felt Lense's hand on his shoulder. "Julian, please explain something to me," she said. "Why did you bother to come all the way here just to look up the fact that ten cc's of endomethalamine will counteract twenty cc's of isoboramine inside a Trill symbiont's vascular tract?"

Endomethalamine! He recognized the name of the correct counteragent as soon as he heard it. *Of course!*

"Doctor!" It was Krissten's voice.

The memory cathedral vanished like so much smoke, and Bashir was once again conscious of nothing but the medical bay's operating room, where Ezri lay, inert, barely breathing. Krissten and Juarez both stood staring at him, their faces portraits of worry.

Bashir felt the symbiont writhing and twitching in his hands.

"Doctor, are you all right?" Krissten said. The last time he'd heard her sound so fearful, the station had been under full-scale attack by the Jem'Hadar. "We need to get that counteragent into the symbiont."

Bashir nodded, his full attention once again focused on the crisis at hand. "The counteragent is . . ." For a harrowing moment the knowledge faded, then just as quickly snapped back into place. ". . . *endomethalamine.* Please administer ten cc's of endomethalamine,

Krissten. Directly into the symbiont's umbilical orifice."

Bashir held the thrashing symbiont steady while Krissten performed the injection. A moment later, the symbiont grew quiescent. Krissten used her tricorder to check its vital signs. Then she took charge of the symbiont as Juarez helped her place it into the medical transport pod, securing the box's seals and activating the biomonitors on its side. It took only a moment to ascertain that the symbiont was out of immediate danger.

No thanks to me.

Bashir suddenly recalled the question the *faux* Elizabeth Lense had asked him inside the memory cathedral. Why *hadn't* he simply asked the computer for the information he needed to save Dax? That clearly would have been the expedient solution. Perhaps he had become too used to his facile memory. Or had placed too much blind faith in it.

But he also wondered if something more fundamental was happening to him. If his judgment was failing along with his memory.

An even more alarming thought followed: *What if my entire intellect is disintegrating?*

With that fearful notion came a profound fatigue, rolling irresistibly over him like the fogs of Argelius II. And with that fatigue came a sad, certain knowledge. He now knew beyond all doubt that he hadn't escaped the bizarre, unpredictable influence of the alien artifact. He, too, had been aboard the *Sagan* when it had crossed the object's transdimensional wake. Just like Nog. Just like Ezri.

Ezri.

He crossed to her biobed, where she lay like some moribund princess from a fairy tale. But he knew that no kiss would be potent enough to rouse her. He took her hand, placing it between both of his. It felt cool and moist. He checked her vital signs, which were weak but holding steady for the moment.

He bent down and gently gave her that fairy-tale kiss. "Good-bye, my love," he whispered.

Her eyes fluttered open. She smiled at him.

"Ezri?"

Her voice was weak but steady. "Dax . . . is gone . . ."

He couldn't believe it. So weak, so close to death, there was no way she could have regained consciousness. Bashir noticed that Krissten had run over to the other side of the biobed to check Ezri's readings.

"Doctor, you have to look at this," said Krissten, a stunned expression on her face.

Bashir glanced up at the biobed monitors. Every indicator, from neurological to metabolic to cardiovascular to pulmonary, was up significantly. Impossibly, Ezri was getting stronger. She was returning to normal, as though she'd never been joined to a symbiont in the first place.

"The symbiont," Ezri said, her voice stronger, though her expression was desolate. "Julian, how is the symbiont?"

Bashir finally realized his mouth was hanging open. And his eyes were welling up with unshed tears. "The symbiont is fine," he said, his voice cracking like an adolescent's. "It's safe in the artificial environment. But you . . . Ezri, I think we may find a way to get you through this after all."

It's impossible, he told himself. Joined Trill hosts simply didn't recover after losing their symbionts.

She smiled up at him again, looking as tired as he felt. "This is the second time I've been at death's door since we came to the Gamma Quadrant, Julian. I think I'll wait until I'm strong enough to walk again before I actually step through it." Then she drifted off to sleep once more, her smile lingering.

Perhaps I found Vaughn's miracle after all, he thought, finally daring to believe it. After all, was Ezri's survival of the loss of her symbiont any more miraculous than the regeneration of Nog's leg? Or were such things really miracles? He found himself wondering abstractedly whether the alien artifact might really be a super-advanced medical facility, the product of brilliant, unfathomable alien minds.

Abruptly, his fatigue overtook him. He collapsed to the deck beside Ezri's biobed, visions of the ancient spaceborne artifact vying with Istanbul's Hagia Sophia for the attention of his unconscious mind's eye.

9

The passengers of the Bajoran ship-of-state *Li Nalas* were barely jostled during the hookup to Deep Space 9's docking ring. In the vessel's control room, the two pilots checked and double-checked switches and panels, making sure that the airlock seals were correctly aligned. In the center of the ship, a pair of young Bajoran assistants arranged the traveling bags for easy disembarkation.

First Minister Shakaar Edon and Second Minister Asarem Wadeen sat astern. Until moments ago, they had been meditating. Asarem had asked for silence, making the excuse that she wanted to prepare her mind for the coming day's events. Truthfully, she was still trying to figure out what Shakaar's motives were for forcing her to stonewall the peace talks with Cardassia. She had not been able to bring herself to discuss the matter with anyone, including her closest aides; Shakaar's reticence of late led her to believe that this was a political secret of which only the highest-ranking officials might be aware.

Asarem knew that Colonel Kira Nerys was aware of Shakaar's actions, since they had already discussed the matter aboard Deep Space 9 a few weeks earlier. According to Kira, Shakaar had almost gloated about the impasse to which he had brought the negotiations, an uncharacteristic action for someone who desired secrecy. What was to stop the colonel from revealing his political subterfuge? Asarem could only assume that Shakaar's power had kept Kira in check. The woman had already been cast out from the Bajoran faith—Attainted—and her military commission was the only power she had left. Shakaar could easily have that stripped from her as well, if she were to cross him, leaving her with nothing. Still, Kira was a deceptively strong woman. Her years in the Resistance, and the time she had spent fighting alongside Starfleet officers and Cardassian resistance fighters during the Dominion War had undoubtedly left her with more reserves of strength than Shakaar probably imagined.

He'd do well not to underestimate her.

As for herself, Asarem was trying to figure out how she was supposed to fit into Shakaar's plans, and how to insulate herself from any potential political fallout flowing from his peculiar actions. She had already received dozens of inquiries from other ministers as to why her stance on the Bajoran–Cardassian reconciliation had suddenly become so obdurate. Shakaar had put her in a very difficult political position, and she had to wonder to what end his actions with her were aimed. Was he trying to force her from the Chamber of Ministers? Perhaps he wanted to create a situation whereby she would be shamed and disgraced, and would remove herself from the levers of power as a consequence.

Despite these concerns, Asarem was excited to be docking aboard Deep Space 9. There was slightly less than a full day left before she and Shakaar were to officiate at the signing of the historic agreement heralding Bajor's formal entry into the United Federation of Planets. They had arrived earlier than most of the other Bajoran ministers and Federation diplomats; a few obscure details and legal loose ends remained to be discussed with Starfleet Fleet Admiral Leonard James Akaar and with the Andorian diplomat, Federation Councillor Charivretha zh'Thane.

Shakaar touched Asarem lightly on the hand. "You're not meditating, and yet you seem light-years away, Wadeen," he said.

"Hmmm, I guess I was," she said, managing a slight smile. "I have a lot to think about these days. Momentous events are upon us."

"They are indeed," Shakaar said, nodding. "I don't think that even in my wildest imaginings I could have foreseen that I would be among those to lead Bajor into an interstellar brotherhood."

"Nor could I," Asarem replied. "The Prophets work in strange and wonderful ways."

They both stood up, and Asarem smoothed the wrinkles from her robes. Shakaar stepped down from the slightly raised platform onto which their chairs were bolted and approached the hatchway leading to the airlock. The two assistants had their bags and stood waiting nearby. One of the pilots stepped toward him. Asarem knew that the man was unarmed in the traditional sense, but as pilot and bodyguard to the First Minister he had been trained in unarmed combat to such a degree that he was probably at least as effective as a platoon of phaser-toting protectors.

"To it, then," Shakaar said, smiling at those around him, and he depressed the button to open the door.

Asarem almost didn't notice the small silver box that Shakaar held in his other hand, but the glint of the airlock lights caught it. He had been carrying it with him for quite some time now. Perhaps it was a good luck charm, or a family heirloom that served to remind Shakaar of his ancestors.

But something about it vaguely unsettled her, though she couldn't say precisely why.

Stifling a yawn born of far too many late nights and early mornings, Kira Nerys stepped off the turbolift and onto the docking ring. Sergeant Gan Morr, apparently on his way back from servicing a spacecraft, saw her and smiled in acknowledgment. Kira returned the gesture, grateful once again that at least *some* of the Bajorans on board weren't treating her as though she had Perikian skin blight.

Approaching from one of the crossover bridges connecting the docking ring to the Habitat Ring, Lieutenant Ro Laren offered a wry smile of her own. "Late night, Colonel?"

"Always," Kira said as the pair began walking together. "I assume the preparations have been completed for all the diplomatic arrivals we're expecting today?"

Ro nodded, punching up data on a padd. "The guest quarters for our visiting dignitaries have been meticulously prepared. We're doing a final sweep for spying devices right now. We've already made sure that every last food replicator is in working order, and that the climate and atmospheric controls are all on species-appropriate settings. We've even turned down their sheets and put mints on their pillows."

Kira had no idea what Ro meant by that last comment, and the security chief obviously saw her perplexity. "Sorry," Ro said. "Earth custom. I learned about it back in my Starfleet Academy days." She offered a grin, and Kira gratefully accepted it, answering it with a smile of her own.

"Sounds as if you've got everything under control, Lieutenant, as usual." Kira had used Ro's title rather than her name, for the benefit of the two Bajoran security officers who trailed a few paces behind them.

"Thank you, Colonel," Ro said. "And of course, I've got all available security personnel pulling double shifts. There'll be no surprises during this ceremony if *I* have anything to say about it."

They reached docking port six just in time to see the display pad on the bulkhead change color, indicating that Shakaar's ship had docked. Kira keyed a command sequence into the control pad, and the massive, coglike door rolled to the side. Inside the docking-bay airlock stood Shakaar, Asarem, and two aides, one of whom Kira recognized as Sirsy, Shakaar's personal assistant. Also conspicuously present was a Bajoran man whom Kira immediately assumed to be a bodyguard, though he wore a pilot's orange flight suit.

"Ah, Colonel Kira, thank you for coming to greet us," Shakaar said, extending his hands.

Though she was sorely tempted to ignore Shakaar's gesture, Kira took the proffered hands. Her position as the station's commander was tenuous enough without offering insults to Bajor's highest political leader, however misguided his recent actions might be. She even managed to smile fractionally, if only for the benefit of everyone who stood by, watching and listening.

"First Minister, Second Minister, I hope that you had a safe and pleasant flight." She hoped that the ice in her tone was not too noticeable.

130

Shakaar withdrew his hands and clasped them together. Kira caught a fleeting glimmer in his eyes that told her he sensed her discomfiture in his presence— and that he either didn't give a damn about it or else positively enjoyed it. What was happening to the man she had once loved and followed into battle against the forces of the Cardassian Occupation? She knew well that there were some among her people for whom, sadly, the war they had fought all their lives would never be over. She had always thought of Shakaar as being beyond such vendettas. Could he be one of those unfortunates whose Occupation-inflicted wounds would never heal?

"The flight went without incident, Colonel," Asarem said, her tone somewhat tart. Kira wondered if Asarem had noticed her nonverbal exchange with Shakaar. She also wondered how hard the second minister was really working to persuade Shakaar to return to the negotiating table with the Cardassians. Kira realized, of course, that her assessment of Asarem might not be entirely fair. Like Kira, the second minister had a public persona to live up to. And Shakaar had always been difficult to persuade when his mind was made up. Just after the end of the Occupation, when he and a group of his fellow Dahkur Province farmers had defied orders to relinquish several government-owned soil reclamators, Shakaar had proved yet again to be one of the most doggedly stubborn men Kira had ever met. He had not only prevailed in that conflict, but had earned enough public sympathy to be elected Bajor's first minister.

Asarem continued, "Our passage from Bajor gave us both time to meditate on the historic nature of tomorrow's ceremonies, and what the coming changes will mean to Bajor. I'm certain you are as enthusiastic about this ceremony as we are, and that you share our feelings of happy fellowship."

Noticing a subtle tensing in Asarem's body language—and Ro's quizzical stare—Kira decided that the safest course of action was to keep things moving.

"Certainly, Second Minister. It *is* a momentous occasion." Gesturing toward Ro, Kira added, "You both know Lieutenant Ro Laren, Deep Space 9's head of security. She's also in charge of making sure that all the dignitaries attending the signing ceremony have a safe and enjoyable time."

Kira kept pace as the group followed Ro's lead into a turbolift. She saw the "pilot" conversing with Sergeant Etana Kol, who had gracefully insinuated herself into the group of aides behind the ministers, even as Ensign Charles Jimenez took point near the exit. As the lift made its way coreward, Ro began explaining to the ministers and their retinue where their quarters would be, what new security measures had been taken, and where the signing of the Federation entry document would take place.

As they entered the Promenade, Ro pointed in the direction of the Bajoran temple. "And of course, you both know your way to the temple," she said lightheartedly.

"Yes, *we* plan on going there to commune with the Prophets later this morning," Shakaar said. Kira avoided looking in his direction, but she knew that his comment had been directed toward her alone. Though this wasn't the first time he had rubbed her nose in her Attainder, it still stung. She decided she'd be damned if she'd give him the satisfaction of showing how deeply his words had cut her. *What is his problem these days?*

Kira recognized several of the Bajoran security officers in plainclothes, loitering about the Promenade. She also saw a larger than normal contingent of uniformed guards, both Bajoran and Starfleet. Ro really *had* beefed up security. Kira prayed it would all prove unnecessary in the end.

Passing Quark's Bar, Kira saw Taran'atar standing just inside the doorway, as if unsure whether or not he wanted to enter. He was standing so still that he might as well have been a statue guarding the entrance. She doubted Quark would allow him to remain perched there for long, scaring away his customers. On the other hand, many of Quark's regulars and others who frequented the Promenade seemed to be getting quite used to seeing a Jem'Hadar moving about—or standing statuelike—in their midst.

"In or out, Taran'atar," Kira heard from behind as the group neared a passageway leading to the guest quarters. It was Quark's unmistakable high-pitched voice. Ro half turned at the sound, and Kira thought she saw her cast a fond look in Quark's direction.

"In or out, Taran'atar," Quark shouted from the end of the bar. He might not even have noticed the Jem'Hadar, except that he had looked out into the Promenade to see the contingent of dignitaries walk by, along with Kira and Ro. And then, in the midst of a particularly salacious thought about the contours of Ro's uniform, he saw the giant creature standing to the side of the doorway, stock-still like some giant stone *slibut* staring down at the Sacred Marketplace from its perch atop the Tower of Commerce.

Taran'atar glanced in Quark's direction but did not move. Quark walked toward him, more comfortable with the gigantic, pebble-skinned humanoid since the Jem'Hadar had started buying time in the holosuites for his physical exercise. "Come on, Tarannie, I can't have you just hovering there in the doorway. You'll scare off the paying customers. Either in or out."

The Jem'Hadar lumbered in and took a seat, precariously balancing his body on one of the bar stools. *Morn's stool!* Quark rolled his eyes, glad for once that his best— and most talkative—customer had not yet come in for the day. He hated to think what would happen if Morn and Taran'atar got into a scuffle over the seating arrangements.

"Hey, Tarannie, you've just staked out Morn's regular stool. He isn't in yet, but you might want to know for future reference." Taran'atar gave him a blank look.

"I did not see his name on this stool," Taran'atar said. "I wasn't aware that he owned it. I thought *you* were the owner of this establishment."

"I *do* own the place. It's just that Morn doesn't like to sit anywhere else. You know, people have favorites." Taran'atar continued to stare at him in evident incomprehension, so Quark decided to let the matter drop, at least until Morn arrived. "What can I get you?"

"I wish to have the same drink you made for me last time I came here. The brown and white one."

Quark screwed up his face in distaste. "The root beer float? Ugh, I can't figure out what hew-mons see in that stuff, much less what *you* get out of it."

He nevertheless passed Taran'atar a large tankard of the frothy brown liquid, in which two lumps of vanilla ice cream floated. He watched in both wonderment and revulsion as Taran'atar lifted the noxious potion to his lips and downed it in a single swallow. After a nod from Taran'atar, Quark immediately set about filling a second tankard and handed it over.

Quark usually made it his policy never to question a client's tastes. But as Taran'atar started in on his fourth helping, Quark found he could no longer restrain himself. "Wouldn't you rather have a nice, slimy Slug-o-Cola instead?"

"No," Taran'atar said, in between quaffs, "I would not."

"Hmm. Well, you're sucking those things down like they're the last vials of ketracel-white in the whole quadrant."

Taran'atar paused, apparently contemplating his rapidly expanding collection of drinking vessels. Then he fixed his hard pale eyes on Quark. "I'm one of the very few of my kind who has never required the white."

Quark recalled the time, not so very long ago, when Dominion forces had controlled the station. Jem'Hadar soldiers could get pretty testy when their white didn't arrive on time. But they had never ordered root beer floats. Or anything else for that matter.

"There you go, then," Quark said. "Judging from the root beer habit my nephew Nog developed since joining Starfleet, maybe this stuff is just the Federation's version of the white."

"I've found that your root beer floats energize me. Are you telling me that this beverage also creates a chemical dependency?"

Quark wondered if he hadn't tweaked Taran'atar's nose a little too hard this time. Shaking his head, he said, "I'm only saying that you're drinking like a man who has a problem."

Taran'atar downed half of his fifth root beer float in one gulp, then turned to Quark, a foamy white mustache on his upper lip. "Perhaps I do. During my last holosuite exercise, I encountered something unexpected."

Quark tried not to stare at the ice cream that clung to the Jem'Hadar's upper lip. He couldn't imagine what Taran'atar might have encountered during his holo-battles that could possibly have surprised him. Those

331ultraviolent programs he used were pretty straightforward hack-and-slay scenarios.

"What do you mean, 'unexpected'?" Quark said, frowning. "Was there a glitch of some kind?" He hoped that Taran'atar wasn't ramming those sharpened *targ*-stickers of his into the imaging hardware again. And that another one of those holoprogrammer's "jack-in-the-box" subroutines hadn't popped up in the combat software.

"I'm not certain. During combat, a man appeared. A human. He was dressed in black, and had silver hair. He called me 'pallie.' "

Quark grinned. "Oh, that's just Vic. He's a Las Vegas entertainer."

"Curious. He told me that the noise from my combat scenario was disturbing others in an adjacent holosuite. I didn't think that was possible."

Quark chuckled. "It's not. Unless you've started jamming pointy things into the mechanisms again, there's no way even *you* could make *that* much noise."

Taran'atar looked as baffled as his inexpressive face would permit. "Then why did this Vic ask me to 'keep the noise down to a dull roar'?"

"Vic has probably taken an interest in you, and thinks you need to unwind a bit," Quark said with a grin.

"Unwind?"

Quark leaned toward the Jem'Hadar and whispered conspiratorially, "You probably strike Vic as a bit . . . tense."

"Then he's mistaken," Taran'atar said, a little too quickly. "But I am curious. I thought that all holographic characters were confined to particular programs or holosuites."

"Not this one. Vic's program is always on, and sometimes he crosses over into other programs."

Quark thought Taran'atar's expression had grown even stonier than usual, if that was possible. "Why is this Vic always left running? That seems inefficient and wasteful."

"It wasn't my idea," Quark said. "Blame my nephew."

Taran'atar now seemed truly astonished. "Nog is an engineer. Surely he knows that holograms are extremely energy intensive. Leaving them running perpetually is a frivolous use of the station's resources."

I'll make a Ferengi of you yet, big guy, Quark thought. Aloud, he said, "Not to mention expensive. But since Vic more or less saved Nog's life last year, I'm willing to cut him a little slack."

"For whom? Nog or Vic?"

Quark had to think about that for a moment. "You know, I'm not sure."

"How can a mere hologram save a man's life?" Taran'atar asked. Quark had never seen a Jem'Hadar exhibit such curiosity. Of course, Odo had ordered him to learn everything he could while living among Deep Space 9's diverse humanoid population. Quark wondered if Taran'atar was merely carrying out his people's genetically imprinted penchant for obedience to the Founders.

"Vic seems to be a great deal more than just another hologram," Quark said. "And he always comes up with just the right advice to help anyone with any problem. Just ask anybody who's ever visited him."

Taran'atar grunted. "A counselor."

"Not exactly. He's a lounge singer."

"He sings lounges? I'm not familiar with that musical form."

No wonder these guys lost the war. "He sings *in* a lounge, Tarannie. In a scenario set on ancient Earth."

"Are you saying that you believe this Vic to be *alive?*

That he has what the Bajorans call *pagh,* or what the humans term a soul?"

Quark hadn't expected the conversation to veer so abruptly from treacly Federation drinks to the hinterlands of quantum philosophy. "Whoa, there. I just pour the drinks around here. I make it my policy to leave the philosophizing to the people who leave their latinum behind."

The Jem'Hadar's next words appeared to be for his own benefit. "Do you believe a holographic entity can have a soul?"

Seeing how hard Taran'atar appeared to be struggling with the idea, Quark decided to step outside his usual conversational boundaries. "I dunno. Do *you* have one? Do *I?* In my experience, if the commodity can't be bought, sold, or rented, it's probably not even worth discussing."

Taran'atar downed the rest of his drink, in the process washing off half of the sticky ice cream smeared above his mouth. He stood, placing his final tankard on the counter beside its emptied brethren.

Taran'atar moved to depart, then turned back to the bar, tapping his finger on its smooth surface as he addressed Quark. "I have two requests to make of you, Quark."

Quark grinned, finally feeling that he had begun to connect with the dour Jem'Hadar on something approaching a personal level. "Name 'em."

"I would like to book some holosuite time today, to see this Vic. I wish to hear how he saved Nog's life."

"Done. Just as long as you're cleared out by twenty hundred tonight. And please try not to kill anything while you're in there."

Taran'atar nodded solemnly. "If nothing attacks me, I'll do as you ask."

Quark felt relieved to hear that. He wanted Vic's establishment to be in perfect working order tonight for his date with Ro. "What's your other request?"

The Jem'Hadar's eyes narrowed slightly. "Don't ever address me as 'Tarannie' again."

The Ferengi barkeep watched as the behemoth left his establishment, and only then noticed that his knees were quaking. *You try to be friendly to someone and what does it get you?*

He shook his head, then noticed a patron whose Alterian fizz was almost empty. He rushed over with another, the encounter with Taran'atar almost forgotten.

Almost.

By the afternoon, Ro Laren had ceased personally welcoming the Federation dignitaries aboard the station, allowing Starfleet Lieutenant Costello and some of the other junior officers to greet the arriving lower-echelon diplomats. Ro accompanied Kira to meet the higher-level guests. Several of these officials evidently knew of Ro's past run-ins with the Starfleet hierarchy, and her subsequent imprisonment, as well as the time she had spent fighting alongside the anti-Cardassian Maquis guerrillas. A few of the dignitaries, most notably the scowling martinet who represented Kostolain, hadn't tried very hard to disguise their disgust at having to be in her presence.

So this is the sort of abuse Kira has to deal with every day from her fellow Bajorans, Ro thought, her soul rendered desolate by the hours-long drumbeat of subtle disapproval. She wondered how much of it Kira had perceived, and to what extent the colonel was reining in her own reactions. But Ro didn't feel inclined to discuss it. All she wanted was to get away before she complicated her life even further by sending someone plunging over the Promenade railings.

She recalled the words of one of her Starfleet tactical training instructors. *Welcome to the future. It's where we're all going to spend the rest of our lives.*

As the afternoon wore on, and an opportunity to get away presented itself, she decided to spend at least a few minutes relaxing at Quark's. She fervently wished there was time to get gloriously, obstreperously drunk.

Perhaps a minute or two after she had taken a seat behind one of the place's more unobtrusive back tables, Frool, one of Quark's waiters, appeared as though by magic. The obsequious-mannered Ferengi set a tall glass of dark, steaming liquid onto the table before her.

"Thank you, but I didn't order this," she said. "And I'd really prefer to be left alone."

"It's a gift," said Frool.

Ro lifted the glass by its heat-resistant stem and sniffed its contents. *Hot Pyrellian ginger tea. Quark must have read my mind.*

It felt good to receive a kind gesture, however small. She smiled politely at Frool. "Sorry for snapping at you, Frool. Please pass my thanks along to your boss."

"Quark wasn't the one who sent this," Frool said, gesturing over his shoulder toward one of the tables in the far corner of the bar. Only then did Ro notice the strikingly handsome man who sat quietly in the shadows. Trill diplomatic aide Hiziki Gard smiled and raised his glass in Ro's direction. Gard was in charge of security for the Federation delegations, led by Trill Ambassador Seljin Gandres. When he'd first come aboard the station weeks ago, Gard had taken an immediate and thorough professional interest in the security measures Ro was planning for the coming Federation induction ceremonies—as well as an unmistakable extraprofessional interest in Ro herself.

Ro heard a querulous voice coming from a short distance behind her seat. "So what do you suppose *he* wants?"

"Gard and I are in the same line of work, Quark," Ro said as she lifted her own drink in Gard's direction, returning his salute. *At least for now. Who knows what I'll be doing a year from now?*

Quark looked suspicious. "He's a cop? A pity Odo never learned to drink like that. He'd have been a lot easier to deal with. I wonder why he's singling you out for attention."

"Maybe it's professional courtesy," Ro said with a shrug.

Quark took the seat beside Ro's while casting a withering glare in Gard's direction. "I'll believe that when he starts sending drinks over to Sergeant Shul or Sergeant Etana."

Though Gard was seated at a darkened table a good ten meters away, Ro could easily make out the pattern of Trill spots running down from his dark hairline into the high collar of his impeccably tailored, dun-colored civilian suit. She couldn't help but wonder how far down the markings went.

Ro took a careful sip of her tea, then said, "Jealousy doesn't become you, Quark."

"Jealousy? Why should I be jealous?" Quark said. "Unless you're planning on holding a private security briefing with Tall, Dark, and Joined over there tonight instead of partaking of the evening I've planned for us."

She recalled that tonight was to be her "second date" with Quark in the holosuites—and that *he* was in charge of setting the evening's agenda this time, since she had chosen their holographic milieu on the previous occasion. He had asked her to dress nicely, so she had high hopes that he wasn't merely trying to maneuver her into some cheap *oo-mox* trap.

"I wouldn't dream of missing it." She realized that she was actually looking forward to whatever Quark had planned this evening. Even though he could sometimes be crude and grabby, an evening with him was still a welcome escape from a reality that seemed to be growing grimmer by the hour. But her increasingly warm feelings toward Quark were no reason not to enjoy his obvious discomfiture at Gard's attentions. And now seemed like a good time to clear the air with the Trill security man.

As she made a beckoning gesture toward the smiling Gard, Quark's scowl deepened. "What are you doing?"

"Simply returning Mr. Gard's professional courtesy. See you tonight, Quark."

Quark rose, taking her blunt hint. "I've gotta go," he said, then vanished.

A moment later, Gard was sitting in Quark's former place. The Trill's smile was even more dazzling close up, his white teeth contrasting sharply with his dark goatee. "I'm not sure," Gard began, "but I get the sense your Ferengi friend doesn't like me very much."

Ro chuckled. "What gave it away, the frown, the loathing stare, or the bared teeth?"

"Ah. You've obviously had as many years of detective training as I've had."

"Don't mind Quark. He's just got a mild self-esteem problem."

Gard nodded knowingly, then took a quaff from his own glass. "I suppose being the last bastion of Ferengi capitalism can render a man's ego a little fragile."

Ro maintained a neutral expression as she sipped her tea, but she was nevertheless impressed; Gard had clearly done his homework regarding Quark. If his security arrangements were this thorough, then Ambassador Gandres ought to feel quite safe indeed.

"So," Ro said, "do you prefer being addressed as Hiziki or Gard?"

His dark eyes twinkled, and for a fleeting moment Ro regretted having already committed her evening to Quark. "My joined name is fine," he said, "except in professional situations. I find that when clients refer to me as 'Gard,' it only reminds them of what they hired me to do and keeps them ill at ease. I've heard *all* the puns and jokes, believe me. During more than one lifetime."

His breezy manner put Ro genuinely at ease. "You've had many previous hosts then?"

"Oh yes," he said, apparently very much at ease as well. "And I've worked in law enforcement or security during most of those lives. It seems that the Symbiosis Commission has either stereotyped me, or that the initiates themselves have."

She laughed slightly at that. "Most of my direct experience with joined Trills has been with Ezri Dax. If she weren't away on a Starfleet exploration mission in the Gamma Quadrant right now, I'd introduce you to her. Dax has had eight previous hosts, and they were a pretty diverse lot from what I hear."

Gard smiled again, and Ro saw a flash of recognition in his eyes. "Yes, I've met Dax. Her lives probably make mine seem quite dull by comparison."

"To boredom," Ro said, and they spontaneously clinked their glasses together before they each took another drink.

Ro set her glass down. "So how do you know Dax?"

Gard paused as a thoughtful expression crossed his face. At length, he said, "Let's just say that one of her earlier incarnations once ran into a spot of trouble with the law."

Ro's eyebrows rose, but the conversational lull that followed made it immediately clear that Gard was far too professional to tell her anything further. *My,* she thought. *Attractive* and *discreet.*

She decided to change the subject. "Thank you for the tea, by the way. Now what can I do for you? I don't imagine you came here intending to let a relative stranger interrogate you about your previous lives as a Trill cop."

"Oh, you're hardly a stranger to me, Lieutenant," he said. "I wouldn't be doing my job properly if I hadn't studied the files on everyone in attendance at this summit—or whoever was providing security for it. I know we've only spoken at a couple of general security briefings so far, but I've made a point of reading your rather checkered public record. I was particularly interested in your time with the Maquis, and your Starfleet mission to Garon II before that."

Eight of her fellow crew members from the *Wellington* had died on Garon II because she had disobeyed her commander's orders. Ro would never forget that day, nor the years she had spent imprisoned on Jaros II because of it. Nor, apparently, would anybody connected with the Federation ever tire of reminding her of it. The anger the senior dignitaries had stoked within her over the past few hours suddenly reignited, though she did her best to rein it in. Fistfights among the security providers would only endanger the diplomatic guests.

Her reply was stiff and formal. "If you've really researched me as much as you say, then you have to be aware that there were certain . . . extenuating circumstances on Garon II."

"Please, don't misunderstand me, Lieutenant," Gard

said, making a placating gesture. "I'm not criticizing your past performance. In fact, I rather admire most of the decisions you've made throughout your career, if not your luck. Mavericks aren't usually very popular with the top brass. But they know damned well they need people like us to get their dirty work done, don't they?"

Hiziki's reassuring words and gentle smile went a long way toward putting Ro at ease once again. "Not everyone sees it that way," she said, nodding.

"Which brings me to what's really on my mind. In reviewing the last six months or so of the goings-on aboard Deep Space 9—most specifically the rogue Jem'Hadar attack here about five months back—I have several concerns about the security for tomorrow's treaty signing, and for the subsequent celebratory events."

Now he's second-guessing my job performance. Ro was just about to spit out a curt response when Gard held a hand out, palm facing her, as if to gently silence her. "Please do not in any way misinterpret my concerns. I, too, resent it when bureaucrats intrude into my work. But I was hoping that, as fellow mavericks, we might review the security plans together. Perhaps I can be helpful to you in ways other than keeping Ambassador Gandres and the other delegates from wandering about the station and getting underfoot. After all, we both have junior staffers who can do *that.*"

Once again, Ro's anger dissipated. She was impressed. Gard was extremely smooth for a veteran cop. Perhaps all the time he had spent among diplomats— and the experiences of his past lives—had paid off. She realized that she might not only find his advice useful, but could also learn a thing or two about tact and persuasion from him as well. She had a feeling that such skills would be at least as valuable on Federationized Bajor as her Starfleet advanced tactical training.

"If you'd like, I can set up a formal security briefing for you first thing tomorrow morning," she said. "In my office at, say, oh six hundred."

"How about this evening? Over dinner?" His eyes glittered. Ro felt herself blushing slightly in spite of herself.

"Thank you for the offer, but I've already made dinner plans." Ro looked across the room and saw Quark, still glowering at Gard from the other side of the bar. Following Ro's eyes, Gard glanced toward Quark, then offered an understanding smile to Ro.

"Considering the caliber of Quark's dinner company, I think his ego is needlessly fragile." He rose to his feet, a small but provocative smile playing at his lips. "Oh six hundred tomorrow it is, then."

After Gard had left, Ro sank back into her chair. She realized that she was still blushing; it had been aeons since anyone had flirted with her so overtly—and so charmingly. Most of her earlier romances had been quick wartime dalliances with other freedom fighters. Her time among the Maquis had afforded few opportunities for true emotional sharing. With Jalik, Kyle, and even Dana, there had been time only for brief physical intimacies, vital affirmations of life that punctuated an endless series of bloody engagements with the Cardassians, and later, the Jem'Hadar.

After draining the last of her tea, Ro noticed that Quark was appraising her from across the bar, though no longer glowering. Clearly, that was an expression he was keeping in reserve for Gard. With no small amount of wonder, she reflected yet again on how much she was actually beginning to like the little scoundrel, even though she acknowledged that she still didn't entirely trust him. *Who would have seen* that *coming?*

But as she made her way back onto the Promenade, planning on visiting Hatrim Nabir's dress shop to prepare for her date with Quark, she found that Gard's bewitching smile still lingered in her thoughts.

10

Chief medical officer's personal log, stardate 53577.8

I woke up soaked in sweat, and as tired as though I'd just come off a double shift. I realized with a start that I was lying on one of the biobeds. Fewer things are more disconcerting to a ship's doctor than suddenly finding himself horizontal in his own medical bay.

But suddenly remembering that you recently almost killed three of your patients is far worse. Krissten noticed my agitation immediately and offered me a sedative to help me rest. I mustered up as much courage as I could and tried to reassure her that after being unconscious for the past several hours, what I needed most was to get back to work and try to get to the bottom of what had happened to all of us who had been aboard the Sagan. *I pressed her with questions about my patients, and she reassured me that Nog, the Dax symbiont, and my accidentally wounded alien patient were all doing well—and that Ezri had returned to duty on the bridge. Ezri was already on her way down to see me, apparently at least as worried about me as I was about her.*

As I began trying to calibrate the scanning equipment, Krissten noticed the unsteadiness of my hands and pitched in to help. Actually, she ended up handling the task essentially on her own. I was grateful for her help, but unsure how much of my own unsteadiness stemmed from simple fatigue and how much I could chalk up to my obviously deteriorating mind. I felt as though I'd stepped into a thick fog.

Over the course of perhaps an hour, I noticed that the mere act of thinking through technical problems was growing enormously wearying. As my fatigue mounted, I thought about the sedative Krissten had offered me and realized that Morpheus might as well be the Grim Reaper. If I risked going to sleep again before finding a solution, how much worse off would I be the next time I awoke?

"*Den D'Naali.*" The alien said, its vertically cleft mouth parts wrapping awkwardly around the sounds. Shar was surprised at the pure, almost crystalline quality of the synthetic voice issuing from Bowers's handheld universal translator unit. "*Den D'Naali bu kereve. Croi Ryek'ekbalabiozan'denlu bu Nyazen den. Enti Leyza.*"

Shar's antennae pitched forward in the alien's direction. Thanks to the ministrations of Dr. Bashir and Ensign Richter—to say nothing of several miniature antigrav units now strapped to various points around its body—the creature seemed healthy and strong—and apparently eager to communicate. Shar suddenly felt certain that they had finally broken the linguistic impasse which had so far thwarted all but the crudest attempts at communication. With Shar's certainty came a surge of unalloyed joy, the heady rush of imminent discovery. It reminded him of why he'd joined Starfleet in the first place.

Another realization startled him then: This was the first time he'd experienced this sensation since he'd learned of Thriss's suicide.

Shar turned to Bowers. "I believe we've just made a major breakthrough."

"You mean you *understood* that?" Bowers nodded toward the insectile alien, then resumed scowling at the translator in his hand.

Shar shook his head, his antennae bobbing. "Not a word of it. But we're finally hearing phonemes that humanoids can reproduce. We now have a starting point."

Shar knew well that language acquisition closely mirrored brain development. The brain of a preverbal humanoid child possessed twice the number of synaptic pathways as that of an adult, only to winnow out some connections while reinforcing others. As billions of neural circuits fell away, gradually collapsing a nearly infinite array of perceptual possibilities down to something more manageable, language emerged. Meaning coalesced as the still-growing brain pruned itself of excess capacity, honing and sharpening language and intellect in the process. In the absence of a clear linguistic key, Shar was becoming convinced that only a technological analog of this process could decrypt the aliens' puzzling language.

A thought flitted through his mind, unbidden and unwelcome: Would Thriss's death hone him in similar fashion, or would it merely leave him forever diminished and incomplete?

"Nearly a solid day of work," Bowers said. "And all we have to show for it so far is a few syllables of Gamma Quadrant baby babble. Not to mention megaquads of untranslatable alien *sehlat* scratches." He handed the translator over to Shar in a gesture of resignation.

Bowers's sentiments caused Shar to question, if only for a moment, his newfound certainty about their progress. How much of it was merely an attempt to cast off the crushing weight of grief that had lately settled upon his soul? Thriss was dead. Work was solace. Nevertheless, they *were* on the right track, Shar told himself. *We have to be.*

The mess hall doors slid open and John Candlewood stepped briskly into the room, holding yet another iteration of the reconfigured Pinker-Sato phonology module up to one of the room's overhead lights. He squinted for a moment at the translucent module's almost indiscernible filigree of isolinear microfibers, then nodded to Shar in apparent satisfaction.

"I think Cassini and T'rb got the replicator specs fine-tuned enough this time," Candlewood said as he handed the fingernail-sized chip to Shar, who accepted it with laconic thanks. "This one's loaded up with the main computer's latest quadrantwide cross-linguistic comparison algorithms. Let's hope this one doesn't overload the translation matrix."

Shar nodded, noting that the mess hall still smelled of ozone and burned insulation from the previous attempt to, as Bowers had put it at the time, "hot rod" the translator by means of a high-speed link to the *Defiant*'s main computer core. In the depths of that system, a sophisticated linguistic cross-matching program was currently busy comparing both the ancient text and the alien's every recorded utterance with all known Gamma Quadrant language groups; cross-correlating disparate samples of speech and writing; seeking syntactical and phonological relationships; and methodically winnowing out what amounted to cubic parsecs of coincidental linguistic chaff.

"I wish we could tear Senkowski and Permenter away from that alien engine room long enough to give this new chip a test-drive," Bowers said as Shar snapped the new Pinker-Sato module into the translator's haft. "After all the time they spent studying the hardware that translated the Vahni language, this assignment ought to be right up their street."

Candlewood cleared his throat, a look of friendly umbrage on his face. "I had a little bit to do with that, too, Sam—not that I'm trying to steal any credit from Nog's people. But we had a little more to work with in that situation. Even though the Vahni language was completely visual, it still had a far greater overlap with other known dialects than what we're working with here—and the Vahni already had their own translation equipment."

"Nog expects the alien ship's most urgent repairs to be finished within the hour," Shar said.

"The aliens will be able to ship out then," Bowers said, stroking his chin. "And I'll wager they'll insist on taking the last of our, um, guests with them when they do. I wish they'd given us access to something other than their engine room. It would be nice to know why they're here and what their fight with the other alien ship was all about."

"Perhaps our guest will be able to tell us soon," Shar said, nodding toward the alien, whose long and spindly body was splayed gingerly across two mess-hall chairs. "Though I don't doubt that his people will wish to be on their way as soon as possible. But as Mr. Candlewood has pointed out—"

"Call me John," Candlewood said.

Reminding himself once again of the human penchant for informality, Shar nodded and displayed his best synthetic smile. "As *John* has pointed out, Senkowski and Permenter wouldn't be likely to decipher this language any more quickly than we can."

"So we've got maybe an hour, tops, to do the impossible," Bowers said. "Otherwise, our new friend goes home without helping us puzzle out the alien text. And whatever it has to say about that Oort cloud artifact."

"We're lucky he's even still here," Candlewood said. "If his own medical bay hadn't been wrecked when his ship was attacked, he'd probably already be gone."

"And if we fail to return him by the time the aliens are ready to leave," Shar said, "we can't rule out a hostile reaction on their part."

"So we're back where we started," Candlewood said. "We may have a few phonemes, but we've still got no syntax or semantics. And no Rosetta stone to bail us out."

Nodding, Shar recalled what he'd read about the Rosetta stone at Starfleet Academy. That artifact, discovered nearly six centuries ago in the Terran town of Rashid, bore inscriptions of identical texts in Greek, Demotic, and Egyptian hieroglyphs. Only a prior knowledge of Demotic and Greek had allowed the stone's translators to comprehend the enigmatic Egyptian picture language. Without the Rosetta stone, those obscure

153

inscriptions might have remained unreadable, their authors' voices forever stilled.

Shar surmised that whatever Rosetta stone the Gamma Quadrant might hold had spread itself across whole sectors ages ago by the slow process of interstellar cultural and linguistic diffusion. It would take all the processing power the *Defiant*'s computer could muster to reconstruct those ancient language migration patterns—in effect sweeping up and reassembling the local Rosetta stone's billions of metaphorical shards.

"Display the alien text," Shar said.

Candlewood responded by giving the computer the appropriate command. A parade of large, cryptic characters, pictograms consisting of undulating lines, asymmetrical polygons, crosshatches, and intersecting and broken shapes, coalesced in the air above the table. There were no perceptible spaces between the symbols, nor anything resembling punctuation marks.

The alien's deep, oil-drop eyes watched the lockstep march of the pictograms without any evident recognition.

Bowers cast a doubtful glance at Shar. "Think we'll actually find out what he knows this time?"

"I believe," Shar said, activating the translator, "that we have only one way to find out for certain."

Shar discreetly angled the translator toward the alien, not eager to have his action mistaken for an attack. But the creature showed no sign of noticing, evidently engrossed in the parade of airborne text.

"Old, very, perceives me, self/ego," came the translator's melodious voice, the alien's speech-surrogate. "Perceives me not old very merely. Indeed, but is *oldoldold*."

Bowers startled Shar by suddenly launching into what appeared to be a brief victory dance. Candlewood grinned broadly, evidently expressing similar sentiments.

The text is not simply old, Shar thought, too intent on the unfolding mystery to join in his colleagues' jubilation. *The alien recognized it as* very *old.*

"Maybe it's his people's equivalent of the Book of Genesis," Candlewood said, his thoughts obviously moving along lines similar to Shar's.

But Bowers didn't look ready to celebrate just yet. "Remember, nobody here can read Genesis in the original Hebrew."

"Perhaps he only needs some clarification," Shar said, handing the translator off to Candlewood, then taking a padd from the table. He activated the padd's display, which began mirroring the holographic text that still flowed past the alien's rapt gaze. The padd tapped into the stream of data on syntax, phonology, and psycholinguistics now coursing back and forth between the translator and the main computer.

Parenthetical enclosures began to appear around certain regularly repeated groupings of symbols, isolating each such sequence inside an oval border. Shar recalled that the scholars who had interpreted the Rosetta stone's hieroglyphs had referred to such markings as cartouches—discrete words or phrases, rendered in a language that might as well have been devised light-years away from Egypt.

These groupings of characters, of course, were no revelation to Shar—or to anyone else in the room, for that matter. The repetition of certain symbol strings was one of the first discoveries made during the initial computer analyses of the alien text. But absent a lexicon of any sort, these recurring character groupings had been utterly devoid of meaning.

155

Now, thanks to the newly enhanced translator, they at least had a potential means of interpreting the alien's reactions to seeing those symbols.

Long minutes passed as the isolated strings of symbols continued scrolling past the alien's watchful eyes, one after another. The alien sat impassively, saying nothing further.

Bowers's wry comment finally broke the silence: "Looks like it's all Greek to him after all."

Shar's certainty was finally beginning to fade in earnest. He could see no sign of recognition whatsoever on the creature's face. Assuming, of course, that he was equipped to recognize such emotional cues in these beings, which he almost certainly wasn't.

Suddenly, the alien spoke up, loudly. *"Enti Leyza."*

The reconfigured translator, steeped as it currently was in quadrantwide linguistic comparisons, seemed to balk for a protracted moment. Shar typed a command into his padd, instructing it to display the translation of the alien's utterance as text.

"Run the display in reverse," Shar said, frowning at his recalcitrant padd. Candlewood moved the holographic text backward, very slowly.

"Enti Leyza!" The alien said as a particular cartouche hove back into view. He pointed toward it with a long, chitinous digit.

"Freeze it!" Shar said, then stared at the complex, symbol-strewn oval that was suddenly suspended motionless in midair.

"He recognizes that symbol," Candlewood whispered. "There's no doubt about that." Shar had to agree.

Bowers grinned. "Gentlemen, I think we may have just found our guide to the scenic spots of this part of the

Gamma Quadrant. Sacagawea, allow me to formally welcome you to the Corps of Discovery."

"Sacagawea?" Candlewood said, looking puzzled. Shar wasn't certain he placed the name either.

"In honor of the captain's enthusiasm for the Lewis and Clark expedition in ancient North America," Bowers said. Shar thought he sounded defensive.

"Until we can figure out what he actually calls himself," Candlewood said with a shrug, "I suppose it'll have to do."

Shar continued concentrating on the string of symbols, perhaps as intently as the alien was. The bristling shapes within the cartouche struck him as both comforting and disturbing—and somehow familiar.

Then he wondered if their ancient author might have been playing an onomatopoetic trick. Acting on a hunch, Shar instructed his padd to display, directly in front of the alien, a holographic image of the mysterious deep-space artifact the shuttlecraft *Sagan*'s crew had encountered in System GQ-12475's Oort cloud.

The resemblance between the cartouche symbols and the artifact's oddly shifting spires suddenly became obvious.

"Enti Leyza! Enti Leyza!" Shar thought he heard something akin to fear in the synthetic translator voice, though he immediately dismissed the notion as ridiculous.

Still, the alien appeared to be cowering before the image.

"Do we have an English equivalent for *Enti Leyza* yet?" Candlewood asked, fairly bouncing with eagerness.

Shar glanced down at his padd, then nodded. Two words flashed in alternation on the display, as though each was trying to elbow the other aside. Their starkly contradictory meanings made Shar's antennae rise straight upward.

"*Enti Leyza* translates either as 'cathedral,' " he said, "or 'anathema.' "

"Maybe it's both," Candlewood offered.

"Talk about your love-hate relationships," Bowers said. "To be honest, I've always been a bit ambivalent about organized religion myself. Maybe our guest here feels the same way."

"At any rate, we know he recognizes at least one of these symbols," Shar said, succumbing to the allure of a mystery that seemed on the verge of surrendering some of its secrets. "Perhaps his reaction demonstrates that this text is an archaic form of his own written language."

Candlewood made a subtle adjustment to the translator, then raised it as though in benediction. "Now that we're no longer forced to communicate entirely via charades and diagrams of the periodic table," he said, "let's just *ask* him."

His pulse thundering in his ears, Bashir lay on his back on the diagnostic table, seeing the twinkling lights of the resonance imaging equipment from an entirely unaccustomed angle. He kept his arms at his sides, just the way Krissten had asked, though he found it difficult to resist the urge to withdraw into himself by wrapping them tightly across his chest.

He experienced a brief interval of heart-clenching fear—"dentist-chair anxiety" was how he thought his father might have described it—between the moment when Krissten began keying the activation sequence into the control pad and the appearance of the dim lights of the submolecular scanner. The intersecting, moving beams bathed his body in an eerie orange glow.

He calmed as the scan progressed, then felt a renewed jolt of terror as he recalled having been subjected to a similar procedure, nearly three decades ago, by the illicit genengineers on Adigeon Prime. He closed his eyes as the scan continued, trying to banish the unaccountable sensation of soldier ants crawling deep beneath his skin.

A moment later he became aware of Ezri at his side, holding his hand. He smiled weakly at her, not eager to let on just how unnerved he felt. "Didn't hurt a bit."

Ezri grinned, her earlier pallor now only a fading memory. "I'd be pretty surprised if it did. Unless your body's individual molecules have suddenly developed their own nerve endings."

Bashir sat up and saw that Krissten was studying an adjacent computer terminal, where the results of the deep-tissue scan were already slowly scrolling up.

"I took the scan down past the DNA level this time," she said. "So we can do a cross-comparison with the scans we already made of Lieutenant Nog and Lieutenant Dax."

"And of my weirdly healthy yet still disembodied symbiont," Ezri said, gesturing toward a shelf across the room, where the Dax symbiont's medical transport pod sat. Bashir heard a brittleness in her voice, a sense of loss that Ezri appeared to be trying to conceal beneath a bantering façade.

Her other hand was still in his. He squeezed it, and she squeezed back hard, as though life itself depended on maintaining her grip. Meeting her beseeching gaze, he whispered, "We'll get to the bottom of this business, Ezri. I swear it."

"You always did have a fascination for lost causes, Julian," she said quietly. "But my body has rejected the symbiont. It no longer needs me. And apparently *I* no longer need *it*."

Bashir wasn't fooled by her flippant tone. He knew, of course, that Ezri had never wanted to be joined prior to the emergency that had brought Dax into her life, when the symbiont had been near death during its brief stay aboard her ship, the *U.S.S. Destiny*. But during the past eighteen months, Ezri's formerly neurotic personality had begun to flower, and Bashir attributed that fact largely to the influence of the Dax symbiont. He had watched, sometimes with alarm, sometimes with amusement, sometimes with satisfaction, as she had made continuous progress integrating her own personality with that of Dax and those of the symbiont's previous eight hosts. And he knew that having all those lives, memories, and talents summarily ripped from her psyche had to be a trauma of unspeakable proportions.

"It's not a lost cause just yet," he said, putting on his best confidence-instilling smile, though he wasn't sure he believed it himself. "We've seen neither hide nor hair of the Persian army yet. So we'll keep right on defending Thermopylae. That's a medical order."

His reference to the holosuite "hopeless battle" scenarios of which they had both become so fond lately succeeded in bringing a faint smile to her lips. "So we hold the mountain pass. Then back to Sparta, either with our shields or on them."

Bashir gently disengaged his hand from hers, rose, and crossed to Krissten and the medical display. He watched the chaotic rising and falling of the indicators.

And suddenly realized that he wasn't at all certain how to interpret them. He felt a surge of panic, then reminded himself that this wasn't the first time he'd seen peculiar readings. It would simply take a little time to figure them out.

Of course.

A deep frown creased Krissten's brow as she evaluated the display. "I just overlaid your quantum signature scan onto the ones we took from everybody else who was on the *Sagan*."

The readings didn't look right, but he couldn't quite say why. "There's something else there," he said.

"That's an overlay of the quantum resonance scans that Ensign Tenmei took of the *Sagan* itself."

"And your interpretation, Ensign?" Bashir said. Nothing was making sense.

"You can see it for yourself, Doctor," she said, raising an eyebrow at him. "Look at the way the aberrant quantum profiles line up on each and every one of these scans."

His heart raced. The lines still meant nothing to him. He wondered if this was what aphasia felt like.

"Of course," Bashir said, unable to find any other words. "But . . . I'd like to hear some independent confirmation." *What the hell is wrong with me?*

Krissten cleared her throat before speaking. "Julian, it seems pretty obvious that you, Nog, Ezri, and the symbiont are all exhibiting the very same weird quantum resonance pattern that Tenmei detected coming from the shuttle. And it's getting more pronounced hour by hour."

Bashir belatedly noticed that Ezri was standing beside him, also studying the indicators on the display. "So this has to be related to the shuttle's having passed through that alien artifact's interdimensional flux."

"I'm no science officer," Krissten said, "but it sure looks to me like your proverbial smoking gun. But that's not all."

Krissten touched the screen, which suddenly displayed two large, intertwined helical structures. Bashir immediately recognized it as a schematic representation of a strand of humanoid DNA. He was relieved to discover that he could still understand *something*.

"There's a progressive change going on in the DNA patterns of every one of you," Krissten said, sighing in frustration. "But I'll be damned if I can figure out *why* it's happening. Or what it's ultimately going to do to all of you."

"For starters," Bashir said, "it seems to have grown Nog a new leg. As well as given Ezri and the symbiont mutual independence."

"But what about *you*, Julian?" Ezri said, an edge of concern in her voice.

Krissten changed the display yet again, but Bashir couldn't bring himself to look directly at it. He could no longer deny what was happening to him. On some visceral level, he *knew* without needing any confirmation from the instruments.

"Progressive neurological degeneration," he said, studying the weave of the carpet near his right boot. It felt strangely liberating to voice aloud the thought he'd tried so hard to avoid for the past two days. "At the rate I'm declining, by tomorrow I'll probably no longer be able to function as this ship's chief medical officer."

"You don't know that," Ezri said.

"I can *feel* it, Ezri."

"I think we need to run some more tests," Krissten said, but Bashir couldn't hear any hope underlying her words. She knew he was right.

Fatigue once again crept up on him. His eyes ached, and when he spoke there was more acid in his words than he had intended. "Ensign, I've already been scanned down to the Planck scale."

"Yes, but—"

"Do you see a clear pattern of neural degeneration?" he said. "A systematic collapse of synaptic pathways?" In his mind's eye, he saw the windows of the Hagia Sophia, in which hundreds of small candles were slowly guttering and flickering out, one by one. The image chilled him to the marrow.

Krissten nodded silently, though with obvious reluctance.

"Then we already have the essential picture, at least in broad strokes. Call in Ensign Juarez and Lieutenant Candlewood. They'll be able to help you further interpret the data you've already collected. I want to know how long I have left." Feeling a sudden leaden weariness, he turned and strode toward the door and entered the corridor.

"Julian," Ezri said, dogging his heels.

He stopped and put his hands on her shoulders, in what he hoped was a reassuring gesture. "Ezri, I need to be alone. To rest."

"Well, it's good to hear you admit that every once in a while. But there's obviously more to it than that. So tell me." Her voice had none of the steel he'd become accustomed to over the last several months. She sounded every bit as frightened and vulnerable as he felt.

He decided that now wasn't an occasion that called for a stiff upper lip. "I believe I'm . . . *reverting,* Ezri. Regressing to what I was before Adigeon Prime."

Her eyes widened with sudden understanding. "Before you were genetically enhanced."

"I can't begin to explain it," he said, nodding. "But

somehow our encounter with the alien artifact has begun . . . *undoing* my genetic resequencing."

She seemed to mull that over for a moment before responding. "It sounds crazy, but it fits. Nog and I are reverting, too, if you think about it. He's become the two-legged Ferengi he used to be. I've been turned into the unjoined Trill I was before the *Destiny* brought me together with Dax. And you're becoming . . ." She trailed off.

Slow, plodding, uncoordinated, dumb *Jules Bashir,* he thought. *The little boy who was such a grave disappointment to his oh-so-doting, upwardly mobile parents.*

"Maybe this isn't such a great time to rest, Julian. If you're really slipping as fast as you think you are, then our best chance to find a cure might be sooner rather than—"

He cut her off. "Ezri, I don't know if I could find a cure for this even if I were at the top of my game."

She folded her arms before her, donning a smile that he sensed was purely for his benefit. "It's not like you to just give up, Julian. The Persian army still hasn't even shown up yet."

"I'm *not* giving up. I'm just trying to make you understand that the cure, if it exists, isn't going to come out of the medical bay. It's going to come from inside the alien artifact that caused all of this in the first place."

His mounting weariness was becoming acute, and she now seemed aware of it as well.

"All right, Julian," she said, seeming to draw on some inner reserve of strength. "Get some rest. I'll take what you've just told me straight to Commander Vaughn. If there's a cure anywhere aboard that artifact, I swear to you we'll find it."

He thanked her, then excused himself. Alone, he found himself momentarily lost on his way to the quarters he and Ezri shared, but quickly recovered and found his way.

Once the door was sealed behind him, he collapsed onto the narrow bunk and considered what lay ahead: a transformation from the educated, accomplished, nearly superhuman Julian Bashir to plain, slow, unmodified Jules.

Jules.

He had repudiated that name during his childhood, after his parents had, in effect, repudiated *him*—when they'd had his DNA illegally rewritten when he was only six years old. Whatever Jules might eventually have accomplished if left to his own devices had been rendered moot from that point on, forever after consigned to the shadow world of roads not taken. Inaccessible mirror universes.

After Adigeon Prime, the frustrating learning disabilities he'd suffered as Jules had slowly receded over the horizon of memory, banished to an obscure corner of some boarded-up cloakroom within his mental Hagia Sophia. Reborn, young Julian excelled intellectually, academically, and physically—but not spiritually. All too often he had felt like a created thing, an object designed to replace a child who hadn't measured up to his parents' lofty expectations.

Which, in a very real and undeniable sense, was exactly what he was.

He vividly recalled the day, three short years ago, when he had taken his parents to task over this. Facing the distinct possibility of dismissal from Starfleet because of his illegal genetic alterations, he had wished that Richard and Amsha Bashir had never taken him to Adigeon Prime, that they'd instead simply allowed nature to take its course with young Jules, for better or for worse.

That errant wish now appeared to be coming true—and the brutal reality of it horrified him. He realized now that it meant the loss of abilities and talents that he had come to take for granted over the better part of three decades. The loss of what he sometimes feared were the only things that gave him value as a human being.

The loss of *self.*

Bashir closed his eyes. But instead of sleep, he sought a cobbled street in Istanbul, where a flight of stone steps led him up to the front of the silver-domed Hagia Sophia. He stood for a moment just outside the main gallery of his memory cathedral, apprehensive about what might await him inside, but determined to survey the damage regardless.

He entered, expecting the series of chambers that curved around the dome's interior to be disordered, ransacked, essentially empty. Instead, he saw a party of white-smocked men and women, busily constructing walls with bricks and mortar. He smiled, uplifted for a moment by the hope that they were here to make repairs, that their presence was evidence that he was somehow recovering his faculties, that he was going to make a recovery without recourse to whatever inscrutable powers had deconstructed him in the first place.

Then his heart sank like a burned-out star abruptly collapsed by its own gravity. The white-smocked men and women weren't making repairs. They were walling off staircases, doorways, and vestibules. They ignored his screams, continuing their work as though he weren't even present.

Brick by brick, they were isolating him from a lifetime of memories—and systematically robbing him of every skill he'd ever come to take for granted.

Vaughn sat in the command chair, listening to the various busy sounds of the bridge consoles. He quietly mulled over what Ezri had just told him before she returned to the medical bay to assist Candlewood and Richter with their quantum-scan analyses. Clearly, the Oort cloud artifact—which, according to Shar, the aliens regarded as either a place of worship or as a chamber of horrors—held the solution to the puzzle of what had befallen the shuttlecraft *Sagan* and her crew.

And he was determined to get his hands on that solution, no matter the cost.

Vaughn rose and approached the science station, where Shar was intent on a scrolling display of the alien text. Many more of the symbols were now separated into groups by variously sized ovals, rather than running in an uninterrupted sequence. It certainly looked promising.

"Making any progress?" Vaughn said.

Shar lifted his eyes from the display only for a moment. "It's difficult to know for certain. I'm beginning to wonder if Ensign Cassini might have been a bit too optimistic about our chances of success."

"At least we're finally able to converse with our new friends," Vaughn said. He gestured toward the main viewer, where an image of the D'Naali ship hung suspended against the stygian darkness.

D'Naali. Vaughn turned the name over in his mind as his eyes swept the long, tapering lines of their vessel. Relief warred with frustration within him. On the one hand, it was a relief not to have to refer to the insectoid creatures solely as "the aliens" anymore. On the other,

167

Shar's initial translations of Sacagawea's speech had yet to shed any real light on the nature of the mysterious space artifact—or on the reason the D'Naali vessel had been chased and attacked.

The turbolift door slid open, and Vaughn turned toward the sound. Lieutenant Nog stepped onto the bridge, leaning heavily on a cane. His new left leg had grown considerably over the past day. At first glance, it was a perfect match for the right one and seemed to be getting stronger by the hour.

Vaughn still found it difficult not to glance at the new limb. "How did the last round of repairs go, Lieutenant?"

Nog smiled, obviously happy to be back in his element. "She's spaceworthy, just as long as no one else attacks her anytime soon. I told the D'Naali captain he can get under way whenever he needs to. Once we get Sacagawea back aboard his vessel, that is. I have to say, Shar's revamped translators really made the technical conversations go a lot more smoothly."

"Does that mean you were able to learn anything more about why the D'Naali were being chased out here?" Vaughn asked. "Our running into them so close to the alien artifact can't be a coincidence."

Nog shook his head. "They never did give us access to much of their ship, outside of the engine room and a few of the most heavily damaged portions of the hull. And whenever you ask them a direct question . . ." He trailed off.

"They're evasive?" Vaughn prompted.

"I'm not sure it's deliberate. The translators still haven't ironed out a lot of the wrinkles in their language. So the D'Naali are about as easy to understand as some of Morn's Lurian Postmodernist poetry."

Vaughn had heard some of Morn's poems shortly

after his initial arrival aboard Deep Space 9. The occasion had been an "open mike" night at Quark's; Vaughn recalled that he hadn't comprehended so much as a couplet of Morn's work. He made a mental note to recommend Shar for a promotion if he could coax just a little more performance out of the universal translator.

"Captain," Nog said, "if you don't need me up here at the moment, I'd like to get back to engineering. While Permenter and Senkowski and I have been off the ship, Merimark and Leishman have been a bit overworked." Vaughn watched as Nog looked down at his regrown limb yet again. Nog's smile made him appear more genuinely happy than Vaughn had ever seen him.

Tenmei was grinning in Nog's direction. "It's always best to stay on Merimark's good side," she said. "Especially if Leishman's hid the candy stash again."

It suddenly occurred to Vaughn that Nog could have saved time by making his report over the intercom. Of course, it wasn't every day that one's amputated leg grew back. Who could fault the lad for wanting to use it as much as possible?

"Dismissed," Vaughn said with a paternal smile, then watched as Nog exited.

He looked toward Bowers, who occupied the tactical console. "Please open a channel to the D'Naali ship, Mr. Bowers."

"Aye, Captain," Bowers said.

Moments later, a bug-visaged alien face appeared on the screen, its vertical mouth parts spread in what might have been a D'Naali smile. *"Grateful thanks of ours you have, humandefiantcaptain. Indebtedness, with thanks/beholden again reiterated/multiplied."*

"Not at all. We were happy to assist you."

"Anything in recompense/requital, we offer with

169

*gladness/joy to provide/make available. State the need/
request."*

Vaughn blinked while he parsed the translator's fractured grammar. Then he realized that the D'Naali commander was not only presenting his thanks, he was
offering to provide something of value in return for the
Defiant crew's labors.

He decided to seize the opportunity. "There is one
thing we'd like to ask of you."

"Denominate that one thing, I request."

"We need to survey a remote part of this solar system.
In the outer comet cloud. We could use a guide who is
familiar with the territory."

The D'Naali lapsed into what seemed a thoughtful
silence before he spoke again. *"Answer/result is
affirmative/positive. Ryek'ekbalabiozan'voslu now
dwells aboard your vessel."*

Vaughn realized that the other captain was referring
to the D'Naali whom Bowers had dubbed Sacagawea.

"We would be grateful if Sacagawea would act as our
guide," he said, glancing back toward Bowers, who now
looked somewhat embarrassed. Vaughn was aware, of
course, that the translators had been calibrated to render
the nickname into the D'Naali language. "If he is willing."

The D'Naali captain made a sweeping gesture with
one of its slender limbs. *"Unneeded it is to check.
Ryek'ekbalabiozan'voslu will be/is obligated to be your
guide. What time-interval is requested/required?"*

"A few solar days at the most," Vaughn said. "Then
we will return your crew member to you."

The D'Naali captain's head bobbed up and down.
*"Assent granted readily/with enthusiasm. After/follow-
ing five turnings-of-the-star, we will await/expect your*

return to this place/coordinates." And with that, he vanished, replaced by an exterior view of the D'Naali ship.

Vaughn returned to the captain's chair, sat, and looked at the conn station, where Tenmei was posted. Her dark eyes regarded him expectantly, and he could see that she had already laid in a course.

"Best speed to the alien artifact," Vaughn said.

The flight into the fringes of the system's Oort cloud, guided by the subspace beacon Nog had deployed during the *Sagan*'s close encounter, took less than ten minutes. Vaughn ordered Tenmei to bring the *Defiant* to a relative stop a mere one hundred kilometers from the coordinates where the *Sagan* had nearly been swept forever out of normal space by the enigmatic artifact's interdimensional effects.

In the center of the screen, an indistinct structure appeared, growing steadily in apparent size as Tenmei increased the viewer's magnification levels. At first, Vaughn thought it might be one of the countless dead, icy bodies that spangled this cold, remote region of the system. These objects were diffused throughout the Oort cloud, covering a volume of space so vast and dimly illuminated by this system's distant sun that any one icy body was scarcely distinguishable from any other.

But the object that was growing on the screen swiftly resolved itself into something else entirely. Its artificial nature was now clearly discernible, as it continued its stately, eternal tumble through the unfathomable interdimensional deeps. Its shape was constantly morphing as new, hitherto unseen facets rolled into view. Spires, arches, buttresses that evoked Gothic buildings appeared and vanished, each in their turn. Curving, swirling lines seemed to fall into existence, then straightened into right angles, contorting immediately afterward into shapes that no mind could fathom but which nevertheless bewitched the eyes.

The feeling of awe that had descended upon him when he'd first viewed a holographic image of the object returned tenfold. In spite of himself, Vaughn had to wonder if he was staring into the business end of another one of the universe's transcendent, inquiry-resistant mysteries. He recalled the peaceful, floating death-dream he'd experienced after touching a Linellian fluid effigy, a memory that remained green despite being nearly eight decades old. The artifact also brought to mind the life-changing epiphany he'd received from the Orb of Memory, when he had helped recover it from the derelict Cardassian freighter *Kamal* only a few months earlier. That encounter had forever altered the trajectory of his life, ultimately leading him to DS9, the *Defiant* . . . and finally out here, to confront the ragged edge of the human experience. In the presence of the weird alien construct, he could not help but recall his far more recent sojourn on the world of the Thoughtscape entity, which had forced him to confront the many mistakes he had made as Tenmei's absentee father. Over his almost eighty years of Starfleet service, he had witnessed enough inexplicable events to credit the notion that some things just might remain forever beyond human ken.

During the *Defiant*'s approach, the bridge's population had gradually increased. Vaughn glanced around the room and noted that Shar, Merimark, Gordimer, and science specialists T'rb and Kurt Hunter were all present. Along with Bowers, they stood totally still, staring owlishly at the geometrical contradiction that slowly

somersaulted end over end on the screen, a conglom-
eration of Platonic shapes viewed through a tumbling
kaleidoscope.

Vaughn's feelings of awe were being steadily mel-
lowed by an overtone of caution. He couldn't help but
recall Bowers' report on Sacagawea's obviously conflicted feelings toward the ancient edifice that now held
the entire bridge so spellbound.

Cathedral. Or anathema.

A hard determination rose within him to get at the
truth of it, no matter what it took. Cathedral. Anathema.
Either way, the artifact represented the only hope of reversing—or even understanding—whatever changes it
had wrought upon his first officer, chief medical officer,
and chief engineer.

His friends.

Vaughn saw that Tenmei was already running a series
of passive high-resolution scans on the object's interior.

"Anything, Ensign?" he said.

"Negative, Captain. It's a blank wall."

"We're going to have to work for it, then. Switch to
active mode." He turned to Shar and T'rb, who had already begun busying themselves at a pair of adjacent
consoles on the bridge's upper level. "The moment our
sensors turn up the smallest sign of internal activity, I
want to know about it."

"Standard sensors negative," T'rb said. "It's like the
thing isn't there."

Vaughn smiled. T'rb's off-the-cuff comment was almost literally true, since most of the artifact's mass lay
outside normal space.

"I'm picking up a graviton absorption signature,"
Shar said. He sounded almost triumphant, as though
he'd just proved a pet theory. "Evidently the object is

173

sweeping up energetic particles and carrying them into its own higher-dimensional spaces."

"What about positron tomography?" T'rb said to Shar.

"Already engaged." Shar frowned, his antennae and his gray eyes seeming to work in concert in an effort to bore a hole in his instrument display. "There," he said at length. "I'm reading a hollow space in the object's interior."

T'rb and Tenmei immediately tied their consoles in with Shar's. They quickly began nodding to each other, confirming Shar's discovery.

Then T'rb scowled at his readings. "The boundaries of the hollow space seem to be fluid. In motion."

"I see it, too," Shar said. "It must be a distortion effect caused by the object's being in multiple dimensions simultaneously."

"Or our sensors are just reading it wrong," T'rb said dryly.

Vaughn didn't like the sound of that. "Ensign Tenmei, can we beam an away team safely into the interior?"

Tenmei looked at her console again as though to double-check, then nodded. "I believe so, though I can't get a reading on the atmospheric composition, if any. And Chief Chao had better stay away from those shifting boundaries."

"I'll tell her to aim for the middle." Vaughn said, and turned back toward Shar. "Lieutenant ch'Thane, I want you to assemble an away team, with full environmental suits. Jury-rig an EV suit for Sacagawea and bring him along."

"Yes, sir," Shar said. "I request permission to lead the team as well."

"I don't think so, Lieutenant," Vaughn said with a gentle shake of the head. "I want to keep you on board. We still need a working translation of that alien text, and so far you're better grounded in it than anyone else."

The young Andorian's eyes flashed with an intensity Vaughn had never seen before. His aspect was half plea, half fulmination. "The computer and some ancillary equipment are handling the bulk of the work now, sir."

It wasn't like Shar to argue with him right on the bridge. Something was wrong. For some reason, the usually reticent science officer appeared to *need* to go.

"All right, Shar. You can come along. But I intend to lead the team myself. I want to keep a low profile, but I also want plenty of secur—"

"Incoming bogeys, Captain," Bowers said, his fingers suddenly moving at blinding speed across the tactical console.

Vaughn shifted instantly into his combat-imminent mode as everyone who had been standing about watching the screen scattered to various battle stations. "Are they coming from the artifact?"

"No, sir," Shar said from the science station, fully intent once again on his own console. "From the sunward direction."

"How many?" Vaughn wanted to know.

"Eleven," Bowers said. "No, thirteen ships. Closing fast, in a tight wedge formation. Configuration matches the hostiles we chased away from the D'Naali ship. And they're powering weapons."

Though his heart thudded heavily in his chest, Vaughn maintained a studied outward calm born of decades of practice. "Yellow Alert. We'll maintain a passive posture as long as possible, but I want you to

175

keep the shields and phaser banks warm, Mr. Bowers. And give me a tactical display."

The image of the mysterious alien edifice vanished, replaced instantly by a baker's dozen bulbous, blocky aggressor vessels, each of them very similar to the ship that had opened fire on the *Defiant* and the D'Naali earlier.

"Lead ship's range is three hundred thousand kilometers," Bowers said. "Closing fast."

"Hail them, Mr. Bowers."

The ships continued their inexorable approach. "One hundred and fifty thousand," Bowers reported.

Vaughn rose. "Any response?"

"Negative."

"Keep trying," Vaughn said. "And ready phasers."

Bowers: "Sixty thousand and closing."

"Aren't you going to raise shields, Captain?" Tenmei said. Vaughn heard the subtle *Are you nuts?* timbre that colored the phrase.

"Not yet. Be ready to fire on my command, Mr. Bowers. A shot across the lead ship's bow."

"Aye, Captain," Bowers said, showing no sign of apprehension.

Then, to Vaughn's immense surprise, the aggressor flotilla broke formation, with most of the ships tumbling rapidly away from the *Defiant*.

"They must have picked up our weapons signature," Tenmei said. "Maybe we scared them off."

"I wouldn't count on that, Ensign," Vaughn said.

Bowers consulted his console and quickly confirmed Vaughn's suspicions. "They've slipped around and behind the artifact. Now they're coming around toward our side of it and are taking up new positions between us and the object."

"Confirmed," Shar said.

Vaughn fumed silently. *Damn! Suckered me. They weren't planning to attack. They were trying to set up a blockade.*

Aloud, Vaughn said, "Hail them again, Shar."

Shar's antennae lofted in surprise. "Sir, *they* are hailing *us*."

"Put them on." *And let's hope the translator that's good for the goose is also good for the gander.*

The viewer image shifted again, this time revealing a dimly lit ship interior. A squat being that reminded Vaughn of nothing so much as a blotchy snowman draped in seaweed regarded him with an inhuman, unknowable expression.

This could only be a member of the species that Shar's enhanced translator had tentatively identified as Nyazen.

The translator spoke in a voice that evoked something halfway between wind chimes and highland pipes: *"Cathedral/anathema never you to be sullied/defiled by seekers-of-curiosity, such as we believe/intuit to be your motive/purpose/goal."*

He doesn't want us near the artifact. Either because it's holy, or because it's dangerous.

Vaughn spread his hands in what he hoped the Nyazen would take as a benign gesture, though he wasn't at all certain that the creature even *had* hands as such. "I understand that you don't wish to let strangers approach this . . . object. But it has brought harm to members of my crew. We believe that it also holds the key to undoing that harm."

"Believe you, we cannot. Your vessel, a D'Naali contains/shelters. Blood-foe/ancient-vow-to-destroy D'Naali represent/are/shall ever be. Trust with you not achievable/advisable, therefore." The Nyazen abruptly vanished

from the screen, replaced by the artifact, slowly tumbling through the yawning interdimensional gulfs.

It took Vaughn only a moment to gather the Nyazen's meaning. *His sensors have picked up Sacagawea's presence aboard the* Defiant.

Bowers spoke quickly, his voice half an octave higher than usual. "Energy readings spiking aboard all thirteen ships' weapons tubes."

"They're opening fire," Tenmei said.

It was no longer possible to read any ambiguity into the Nyazen fleet's motives. "Shields up, Mr. Bowers!" Vaughn said. "Lock and load."

"Well, you're certainly not one of my regular customers," Vic said, appearing mildly surprised. "What brings you to my establishment this fine afternoon?"

Taran'atar regarded the holographic human simulacrum stonily for a long moment before replying. Because his senses were attuned to energy fluctuations—such as those made by shrouded Jem'Hadar—he remained keenly aware of the twenty or so luminal demihumans who milled about the restaurant and dance floor of Vic Fontaine's lounge. Only one of these beings, a grayhaired humanoid who sat drinking alone at a small corner table, appeared to have any discernible substance. Taran'atar decided that he would do well to keep an eye on that one.

"I walked," Taran'atar said, turning his attention back to Vic. The tuxedoed human bared his teeth in what all humans and Vorta seemed to regard as a nonthreatening gesture. Taran'atar had never enjoyed looking at teeth, whether human or Vorta.

"And I thought Frank and Dean were the greatest straight men who ever played Vegas. They're not gonna be happy to hear about the competition, pallie."

Taran'atar wasn't at all certain what to make of the holo-human's remarks. "Are you saying I'm not welcome in this establishment?"

"I'll confess to preferring to see you in a tux," Vic said, indicating his own smart black-and-white ensemble before looking the Jem'Hadar's dark, featureless coverall up and down. "Or even a sportcoat. On the other hand, at least the getup you're wearing is black."

It had been many weeks since Taran'atar had given any thought to his apparel. "Colonel Kira ordered me to wear something other than my Dominion uniform. And it's the will of the Founder you call Odo that I obey the colonel's every order."

Vic's smile slanted very slightly to the side. "I had a feeling when you walked in here that you'd be the life of the party. So what can I do for you?"

Taran'atar suddenly realized that he wasn't certain exactly how to verbalize what was on his mind. At length, he said, "Many of the station's residents have come to value your advice."

Vic made a self-deprecating gesture with his shoulders. "I only tell them what I see. But it isn't always what they want to hear."

Taran'atar nodded. "Perhaps that's why so many of the humanoids have exhibited so much . . . faith in you."

"Whoa there. Faith is a concept I leave to the earring crowd, *capisce?* I'm only an entertainer."

"I've been told that your intervention prevented Nog's death."

Vic's eyebrows shot up and he seemed to be at an uncharacteristic loss for words, at least for the moment. After a pause he said, "Nog was pretty deep down in the dumps last year after losing his leg. He spent a lot of time here while he was recovering."

Taran'atar had not forgotten that it was Jem'Hadar who had been responsible for Nog's injuries. And shortly before his departure for the Gamma Quadrant, Nog had made it abundantly clear that *he* had not forgotten that fact either.

"I take that to mean that he was emotionally distressed after losing his limb in battle," Taran'atar said.

Vic nodded. "And how."

"Quark told me that you personally prevented Nog from dying."

"I only helped nudge him back into the real world. But Nog had to decide to do the living for himself. He learned to believe that things might get better for him out in the big bad universe if he'd just get out there and start participating in it again."

"So . . . Quark was merely being hyperbolic when he praised your abilities."

"I try not to think too much about what my reviewers say, pallie. Other people will believe whatever they want to believe, about me or anybody else. And that's probably the way things oughta be."

Taran'atar was growing increasingly bewildered. "You don't lay claim to any special psychotherapeutic talents. Yet others believe you possess those talents."

"Everybody has to have faith in something. For instance, you have faith that the Founders are gods, don't you?"

181

Taran'atar mulled that over momentarily. "No, I do not. Believing that the Founders are gods requires no faith on the part of a Jem'Hadar."

"Why's that?"

"Because the Founders *are* gods."

Vic shrugged again. "You ask a silly question—"

At that moment, Taran'atar became aware of some motion from the far corner table. The iron-haired humanoid he had noticed before had risen to his feet and was now walking in his direction. Taran'atar instantly noticed three things about the man: he was far taller and broader than he had appeared while seated; he was wearing an equally outsize black-and-white suit; and he was very definitely not a hologram.

"Have you two met?" Vic asked as the large man came to a halt within arm's reach. "I think you may have a fair amount in common."

Taran'atar faced the humanoid, and finally recognized him.

"This was the last place in the quadrant I expected to encounter a Jem'Hadar," the humanoid said, his expression neutral. But Taran'atar was relieved to note that the man made no effort to shake his hand, a human gesture that he still had not gotten used to.

"I didn't know that Capellans were interested in human popular culture," Taran'atar said. "You are Leonard James Akaar, fleet admiral, Starfleet. I did not recognize you right away because of your *tuck-see-doh*."

Akaar chuckled and raised a glass to his lips before responding. "I discovered long ago that human history and culture have much to recommend them. As they say on Earth, 'When in Rome, do as the Romans do.' Now tell me—what compels one of the soldiers of the Dominion to sample the historic pleasures of one of the Federation's founding worlds?"

"I'm not here in my capacity as a soldier. My current mission is one of peace. I've been instructed to learn all I can about the peoples of the Alpha Quadrant."

"Yes, I have been briefed about the mission on which Odo has sent you," Akaar said knowingly, then raised his glass toward Vic, who was listening attentively to the exchange. "You will find Vic to be quite a perspicacious host, Mr. Taran'atar. We do indeed have much in common, you and I. Though I confess to finding it somewhat strange that we both appear to be so at ease in one another's presence."

"I don't understand," Taran'atar said.

Akaar frowned. "You cannot be serious. Tell me—how many Jem'Hadar do you think I killed during the war?"

"I couldn't say," Taran'atar said, though there was no heat beneath his words. During war such things were to be expected. But now that the war was over, it was of no consequence.

"Tens of thousands," Akaar said. "Perhaps a hundred thousand or more. Sometimes I did it from the bridge of a starship, or from a starbase wardroom, or from Starfleet Headquarters. And I dispatched many of them at close quarters, sometimes with a hand phaser, and on other occasions with my triple-bladed *kligat*." Akaar fell silent, though he looked expectantly toward Taran'atar.

Vic winced as the tension appeared to escalate. "Fellas, please tell me you're not planning on trashing my place. The guys in the band are still jumpy from all those times Worf went berserk in here last year. And I'm not paying the bouncers enough to even *think* about going toe-to-toe with either one of you."

Then Akaar laughed, a low throaty sound. He placed

his right fist on the left side of his chest, then extended his palm outward toward Vic. "Be at peace, Vic. Like Mr. Taran'atar, I have come to this place with an open heart, and open hands."

"Your experiences during the Dominion War interest me," Taran'atar said. "But why tell me of the Jem'Hadar you've slain?"

"Because my aged ears overheard your discussion of faith, and it piqued my interest. Do you know why I have come here, Mr. Taran'atar?"

"To this lounge?"

"To this space station."

"You are one of the Federation dignitaries who will bear official witness to Bajor's entry into the Federation."

Akaar nodded. "An action that, in itself, is an act of faith. When a world joins the Federation, it is a most serious occasion. A time of both celebration and contemplation. Of faith."

Taran'atar recalled how carefully the Dominion's Vorta managers had worked to optimize the usage of each newly annexed planet's resources for the benefit of the Founders. But such things were merely prosaic facts of existence. They had been done with little ceremony or fanfare, other than the ordinary rituals and recitations that custom dictated surround the daily dispensations of ketracel-white.

"Again, I do not understand," Taran'atar said.

Akaar sighed, as though he had just failed to convey the intuitively obvious to a dull-witted child. Taran'atar felt his frustration rising at his failure to comprehend things that these Alpha Quadrant natives appeared to grasp so instinctively.

"I have faith," Akaar continued, "that the years of transformation which began after the Cardassian Occupation ended have prepared Bajor to integrate itself into our coalition of worlds. I have faith that an indissoluble bond will result between Bajor and Earth, Vulcan, Andor, and the scores of other Federation planets."

Something occurred to Taran'atar then. "I noticed that you did not number your own world among those others."

Akaar lifted a single ropy eyebrow. "Quite right. Capella has petitioned for Federation member status many times. But my countrymen are not yet ready, even after more than a century of civil war. They still have much to learn about the ways of peace."

"Interesting. Until seven years ago, Bajor was in a permanent state of military occupation and guerrilla war. And yet the Federation has agreed to admit Bajor before Capella. Does this not anger you?"

Akaar's eyes narrowed, and for a moment Taran'atar wondered if he would have to defend himself. But the admiral never moved. "If Bajor becomes a productive Federation member, it will bode well for other candidate worlds that have known the scourge of war during living memory. I have faith that Bajor's success will one day lead to the same for Capella. Perhaps not while I live. But someday."

Faith again. Taran'atar was beginning to find the concept most vexing. "But is not faith required only when no other factual basis exists for believing in a thing?"

Akaar downed the remainder of the contents of his glass, then fixed a steely eye on Taran'atar. "Precisely. Because we cannot know in advance what will happen, no matter how much we prepare. Consider Bajor again. There are some who believe that the Bajorans should not enter the Federation until after they make peace with their old enemies, the Cardassians, on their own. But there are many more who believe that Bajor is ready for membership now, and that peace with Cardassia will flow inevitably from her Federation allegiance. Both sides, however, are acting on faith."

Taran'atar found that his own curiosity had been piqued. "On which side have you placed *your* faith, Admiral?"

An enigmatic smile slowly spread across Akaar's face. "It is not my nature to advocate waiting over action. I believe Bajor to be more than ready for Federation membership, just as she is today. But no Capellan who hopes to live as long as I have believes that peace can *ever* be inevitable."

This last was the first straightforwardly sensible thing Taran'atar had heard the admiral say so far. And he also intuited that it gave him an opening to ask another question that had begun nagging at him.

"Why did you not ask me how many humans *I* slew during the war?" Taran'atar said quietly.

Akaar's expression suddenly grew dark, and Vic once again appeared worried. "Maybe we ought to steer clear of politics for the rest of the afternoon," the holographic host said.

Taran'atar wondered with some dismay whether he had once again trodden across one of the Alpha Quadrant's many indefinable social taboos. These humanoids seemed to hide them everywhere, like subspace antipersonnel mines.

He decided he could lose little by pressing on. "Perhaps it will ease your mind to know that I never entered the Alpha Quadrant during the war. I never fought against the Federation or its allies."

Akaar's glower was slowly replaced by a more thoughtful expression. He nodded. "Perhaps it will at that." Then, setting his empty glass on a passing waiter's tray, the fleet admiral made ready to leave.

Taran'atar perceived that an important opportunity was about to be lost forever. "May I ask you one final question, Admiral?"

Akaar paused, then assented with a sober nod.

"Would you have been as sanguine about my mission of peace had I slain many thousands of *your* people during the war?"

The question appeared to surprise the iron-haired Capellan. For a protracted moment he grappled with it. At length, he said, "I do not know for certain. But I have faith. Therefore I do not need to know for certain." And with that, Akaar bid adieu to both Vic and Taran'atar and was gone.

The Jem'Hadar stood mutely beside the crooner, who finally broke the contemplative silence by saying, "I hope that helped clear things up for you."

"I'm not sure," Taran'atar said.

"Have a seat, then, while you think about it. And let me order you something. Quark says you've got a soft spot for root beer floats."

Taran'atar favored Vic with an earnest nod. "He is correct." *And talkative.*

Returning the nod, Vic approached one of the cocktail waitresses, then paused to speak over his shoulder to Taran'atar. "Oh, by the way—sorry I accused you of being about to trash my lounge the way Worf did."

"Perhaps," Taran'atar said, "you should place more faith in people."

12

Gul Macet had piloted the shuttle from the *Trager* himself, aided by Norit, his most trusted young officer. Macet wasn't sure why he felt the need to flex his piloting muscles. Was it a desire to keep them sharp, or to show off a bit for Vedek Yevir's benefit? He suspected it was a bit of both.

He landed the shuttle in an open area amid the ruins of Lakarian City, near the coast of Cardassia Prime's largest continent, South Forbella. Dusk was approaching, and the descending sun cast long shadows across a horizon-to-horizon expanse of dusty wreckage. The city had once been numbered among the planet's most treasured leisure spots, boasting everything from fanciful entertainments for children to pleasures of a decidedly more adult nature. Their landing zone lay in the ruins of a wide section of what had once been Krendalee, a large amusement park, before it—and most of Lakarian City—had been razed during the waning hours of the

188

Dominion War. Because of the resource allocation decisions of Cardassia's provisional leadership, reconstruction of the city had not yet begun. Macet felt that this was a grave mistake. Cardassia's demoralized billions had become accustomed to living well prior to the coming of the Dominion; now more than ever, they needed the fantastical escape that Lakarian City represented.

Macet stepped out of the shuttle, followed by Norit, Yevir, and a pair of armed guards. The two protectors spread out, weapons drawn as they scouted the immediate area. Scans taken from orbit had shown seven Cardassian life signs in the area—which added up to two more than Cleric Ekosha had said would be in her party. Macet had his own suspicions regarding the identity of one of the surplus individuals, though the other remained a mystery.

Yevir wrinkled his nose further, his ridges collapsing in on themselves like a fan. "The air here is . . . acrid," he said.

"It's the smell of *trandagh* in the morning," Macet said, inhaling deeply. "Mixed, I suspect, with fallout composed mainly of pulverized buildingstone." They walked in silence through the rubble field for several moments before Macet continued. "I expect, Vedek Yevir, that many of your people would regard this tableau as a fitting recompense for the Occupation. After the Dominion War, it seems that we have been reduced to a far more abject level than even occupied Bajor experienced."

"You are certainly entitled to that opinion, Gul Macet," Yevir replied, his tone sharp enough to tell Macet that he had struck a sore spot.

"Please forgive me," Macet said quietly. "I didn't mean to trivialize the suffering we visited upon your people."

Yevir studied him for a moment, then nodded his acceptance of Macet's apology.

"Sir, six life signs approaching," Norit said, her portable scanner in her hand. She pointed toward a building—a theater of some kind—whose façade was scorched and crumbled. From the shadows to its side, a group of Cardassians approached them, led by a tall woman. She was regal, dressed in brocaded robes, her hair pulled back behind her head and then braided to cascade down her shoulders. Behind her were several men and women, each of them dressed in more utilitarian garb. Macet guessed that their pockets contained a multitude of small weapons, mostly of the edged, non-energy variety. One of the women was shorter and older than the rest; next to her was a fresh-faced lad who was still in his teens.

"Welcome to Lakarian City. Or what's left of it," the lead woman said sardonically. "You are Gul Macet."

Macet nodded his head slightly, then gestured toward the Bajoran beside him. "This is Vedek Yevir Linjarin." Pointing to his assistant, he introduced her as well. He waved his hand toward the rubble. "My other two men are scouting for any potentially threatening interlopers. You said there would be five in your party, and yet there are six?"

"My apologies, Macet," the woman said. She pointed to the boy, who Macet saw was gaping at him, his mouth forming a perfect O of incredulity. "When the young man heard that *you* were coming, he insisted on coming with us. He also said he'd always wanted to see Krendalee. Unfortunately, his father never managed to find the time to bring him here."

Something about the boy struck Macet as familiar. Something about the eyes, the forehead ridges. He couldn't quite put his finger on it. "Well, it's not much to look at now, is it?" he said to the lad.

The boy spat at him, the expectoration landing in the dust at Macet's feet. Then he turned and ran, heading toward a nearby copse of dead, shattered trees.

Macet smirked, then addressed the stout older woman who had been standing with the boy. "Well, that's a reaction I've gotten used to from Bajorans, but I rarely receive it from my own countrymen. Do you care to explain, *Cleric Ekosha?*"

The older woman looked surprised, and the taller woman began to speak, but she hadn't uttered more than a few syllables before the matron silenced her with a swift hand signal.

"How did you recognize me? We've never met."

"Years of military duty," Macet said. "And with all the clandestine skullduggery that's gone on during the last two wars . . . Let's just say I know a decoy when I see one, Ekosha." He nodded toward Yevir. "Now that we're all here, and have gotten the introductions out of the way, shall we get on with our business? Time is short. If we hope to bring our plan to fruition, we will have to move quickly."

The old woman nodded, and her decoy stepped back into the pack. "When you first contacted me, Macet, I was suspicious. The Oralian Way has been underground for so very long. Years of religious persecution against those who revere Oralius, and the First Hebitian Civilization of Cardassia, have made us all quite wary about whom we will agree to speak with candidly."

"My understanding is that the Oralian Way was legitimized recently," Yevir said.

A rueful smile spread across Ekosha's lined face. "There is a huge difference between legitimizing a religion and accepting it. Yes, it is no longer against Cardassian law to be an Oralian, but that does not mean that we are welcomed, or even tolerated. Even as our society rebuilds itself, the old-guard Cardassians—career politicians and military authorities, mainly—still take it upon themselves to try to keep us fearful and fragmented. Many of our churches have been mysteriously burned, and several of our more outspoken leaders have been beaten or have even disappeared in the dead of night. We decided to go underground again. Before we run out of martyrs to canonize."

"I assure you that our intentions here are far nobler than that, Cleric," Macet said, hoping she would believe him. If not, this entire venture would prove a colossal waste of time and effort.

"If I didn't already believe that on some level, Macet, I never would have agreed to meet with you," Ekosha said.

"Macet arranged this meeting at my request," Yevir said, stepping forward. "I am deeply troubled by the diplomatic impasse that now exists between Bajor and Cardassia. For both our planets to heal themselves, we need to let the oldest wounds heal first."

"I suspect those wounds will leave some rather livid scars," Ekosha said with a tiny sardonic smile.

"I suspect you're right," Yevir said, apparently unfazed by Ekosha's interruption. "Nevertheless, Bajor enters the Federation tomorrow. If we can establish peace between our two peoples *now*—before the Federation takes such matters out of our hands—think of the good it will accomplish. For both our peoples."

"And what of the benefits such a breakthrough would bring to both of *you?*" Ekosha asked, her eyes darting from Yevir to Macet and back again. "*You* want to be kai of Bajor, and if what I've heard is true, you're willing to suppress an offshoot religion if it helps you achieve that. *Macet* wants respect, and to finally emerge from the shadow of a man whom all of Bajor hates. Not to mention many Cardassians who haven't forgotten who began our world's slide into destruction."

Several troubling questions percolated up from the depths of Macet's soul at that moment. *Is she right? Have Yevir and I flattered ourselves into believing that we've come to forge peace between our respective worlds? Or has this all been an exercise in self-aggrandizement for us both?*

Yevir appeared to be grappling with similar notions. But unlike Macet, Yevir seemed to have a ready answer. "I swear to you, Cleric Ekosha, without reservation, without doubt, that I am acting solely in the interests of my people. To do that, I must also act in the best interests of yours."

Then Yevir did something that Macet didn't expect. Very deliberately, he removed his Bajoran earring and tossed it to the ground. Then he began stripping off his heavy clerical robes, setting them atop the earring in a careless pile. He stood in a plain white tunic and trousers, bereft of any badge of office. But what he had shed in clothing he more than made up for in simple dignity and courage. Until this moment, Macet had not been at all certain that Yevir possessed any such qualities.

"I don't deny that I might benefit personally from a last-minute rapprochement between Bajor and Cardassia. If the price of such a peace is that I throw all of that aside, then I will gladly do it.

"I come among you not as a candidate for kai, nor as a representative of any religion. I am here with one agenda only: to bring our peoples together without any force or coercion—even the benevolent kind that the Federation would surely bring.

"I ask only that you do the same thing. Forget about whether or not the Oralians will profit from emerging from your bunkers. Think instead about what's best for your *people*. You know as well as I do that without a just peace—arrived at freely—there will be war again between Bajor and Cardassia someday. If our two civilizations cannot reach out to one another without outside help, then old slights and injustices will fester on *both* sides. We can lance those boils and bring about a healing. But only if we act together *now*."

Yevir extended his hand toward the stout woman, who looked at it as though it might turn into a poisonous reptile at any moment. Macet had the sudden sense that the entire axis of history was revolving around this place and time. And that Yevir's words were absolutely right, whatever doubts Macet still harbored about his own motivations.

Macet felt a stab of regret at the sharp words he had hurled at Colonel Kira when he had confronted her about the intransigence of her world's political leaders. *A remarkable people, these Bajorans.*

Yevir's words had evidently struck a sonorous chord within the Oralian cleric. Ekosha extended both her hands and grasped Yevir's between them. "I am not so old as to imagine that even a masterstroke of peace will suddenly gain the Oralian Way the respect that is its due. Nor am I still so in love with living for its own sake that I am willing to hide underground forever."

Macet tried to put aside the jubilation that swelled within his chest. Like the master *kotra* player he was, he tried to anticipate the next move the fragile new alliance ought to make. But all he could come up with was yet another unsettling question, one that he didn't hesitate to ask aloud: "How do we broker a peace agreement when even our most accomplished diplomats have failed?"

Yevir answered without hesitation, a serene smile on his lips. "The Prophets will provide, Gul Macet."

"I think I may have a suggestion." A voice called out from the shadows surrounding a nearby pile of rubble. Sliding smoothly from the darkness was a middle-aged Cardassian man, his body lean and whip-strong, his black hair slicked back.

With wide eyes and a friendly demeanor, the man stepped toward Yevir and Macet. He extended his hand in an attempt to shake theirs. Macet knew that the newcomer had picked up the custom during the long years he had spent living among humans and Bajorans.

He greeted Macet first. "Gul Macet, always a pleasure. You're looking fit. And familiar. By the way, that boy with the atrocious manners is called Mekor. One of the children of Skrain Dukat. I believe he may have been expressing his sincere regret that his late father never found the time to take him here while the amusement park was still in operation."

The new arrival turned next to the half-dressed Bajoran. "Vedek Yevir, how good it is to finally meet you after having read so much about you. I must confess that I never expected to see a member of the Bajoran clergy in such a state of dishabille. At least, not since I left the haberdasher's trade. My name is Elim Garak. And I believe I may have the solution to our mutual problem."

13

"Evasive maneuvers!" Vaughn shouted just before the Nyazen flotilla opened fire.

But there were simply too many of them. The first salvo rocked the *Defiant* hard, and Vaughn gripped the arms of his command chair as the bridge pitched forward and the red emergency lights came on. T'rb sprawled headlong onto the deck, but regained his footing a moment later, evidently not seriously hurt.

"Bowers, engage cloaking device!" Vaughn said, loath to play this card so early in the game but seeing no viable alternative.

Bowers quickly entered one command, then another. He shook his head and regarded Vaughn grimly. "Cloak's off-line, Captain. Return fire?"

"Starting a war isn't one of our mission objectives, Lieutenant." Vaughn said with a stony scowl.

"Shields are down to forty-two percent," Bowers reported.

Shar righted his capsized chair and returned to his console. "All thirteen ships fired on us simultaneously with something resembling a compression disruptor," he said.

"We took at least seven direct hits," Bowers added.

A single compression disruptor would be no match for one of the *Defiant*'s pulse phaser cannons, and would pose no serious threat to her shields. But having to face more than a dozen Nyazen tubes simultaneously was quite another matter.

Vaughn acknowledged his science officer with a nod, then turned back to Bowers. "Damage report."

"There's been some buckling in the ablative armor," Bowers said. "And a minor hull breach on deck three, aft starboard. Force fields are holding. Nog and Celeste are already on damage-control detail."

"All weapons operational," Shar said, his antennae flattening forward in apparent belligerence.

"We still have warp and impulse power, Captain," Tenmei said, glancing at Vaughn significantly as if to say, *Now would be a good time to use a whole lot of both.*

Not yet, Vaughn told himself. *I haven't got what I came here for yet.*

"We're being hailed," Bowers said.

The Nyazen captain's indistinct oblong face suddenly reappeared on the bridge viewer. *"Withdraw/begone,"* he said, the venom behind his words belied only slightly by the translator's crystal-chime voice. *"Warning offered/given but once/this single instance."*

"We don't want to fight you," Vaughn said. "But we're prepared to defend ourselves."

Tenmei cast a brief *Oh, really?* glance over her shoulder at him. Then, for the Nyazen's benefit, she put on the face she always used just before Bowers trounced her on poker night.

But Vaughn ignored his daughter's quiet impertinence. "All we want is temporary access to the . . . cathedral." He rose and spread his hands before him. "Our need is urgent."

The turbolift door opened, and Vaughn saw Ezri enter the bridge. Though she still looked somewhat shaky, she was clearly no longer anywhere near death's door.

"Less than microscopic is concern of mine/ours for your need/desire," the Nyazen sang. *"You harbor/succor our enemy/blood-hated ones. None such may approach/loom upon cathedral/anathema."*

"The Nyazen are claiming ownership of the object," Ezri said, now standing almost directly behind the captain's chair. She didn't appear to be addressing anyone in particular. "And they don't want any D'Naali near it."

Great, Vaughn thought. *He wants to destroy us just because we've still got Sacagawea aboard.*

Vaughn tried to project calmness and reason as he regarded the bulbous alien on the screen. "There must be some way we can reach an agreement. Perhaps something we can trade—"

The Nyazen abruptly vanished, the communication apparently terminated at the other end.

"Their weapons are powering up again, Captain," Bowers said, anxiety evident beneath an enforced poker-night calm. Vaughn saw that he and Tenmei were both looking to him expectantly, each clearly ready to follow him through the gates of hell if need be.

"Sir?" Tenmei said as the moment stretched.

"Withdraw," Vaughn said. He chafed with frustration, but could see no alternative that would protect the lives of his crew, his D'Naali guest—and the Nyazen, with whom he had no quarrel other than their refusal to allow him access to the artifact. Perhaps later, and from a safer distance, the aliens could be persuaded to let him approach the object.

If not, he would have to bypass them somehow. And sort out the ethical proprieties later.

A gloom descended across the bridge. No one spoke for a seeming eternity as Tenmei quickly brought the *Defiant* about and put ten million kilometers between her and the Nyazen fleet.

"No sign of pursuit," Bowers said. "All thirteen of the Nyazen ships are maintaining their positions around the artifact."

"Keep station here," Vaughn instructed Tenmei. "Full stop."

"Full stop."

"A blockade," Ezri said. "They won't chase us, but they won't let us approach either."

"A blockade can't stop what it can't see," Vaughn said, then tapped his combadge. "Vaughn to Nog. How long until the cloak is back on-line?"

Nog's response sounded harried. "One of the mains is blown, and a whole bunch of EPS relays are down. We're looking at a few days, at least."

Vaughn turned that information over in his head. At the rate Bashir was declining, he surely didn't *have* a few days. "Then we'll have to find a short-term, work-around solution. Nog, I'm hereby putting you and Shar in charge of getting us close enough to the artifact to beam an away team over—without letting the Nyazen blow us out of the sky first. Use anybody you need, and bring me a plan in four hours."

Nog's response took a beat longer than Vaughn expected. "We'll get right on it. Nog out."

Vaughn saw that Shar was already on his way to the turbolift, leaving Ezri standing beside the empty science station. She stared at the console, touching its smooth surface tentatively, looking as though she'd never seen its like before. Now that she was suddenly shorn of the memories of Dax's previous hosts, Vaughn supposed that probably wasn't terribly far from the truth.

She's not the same woman I chose as my first officer, Vaughn thought, a lump of sorrow forming in his throat. He knew how badly Ezri Dax had wanted to expand her expertise beyond Ezri Tigan's counseling duties. He recalled how delighted she had been after he had sponsored her transition to a career track in command. Vaughn knew that if her current condition proved permanent, he would have to get a new exec. *That would destroy her.*

He was determined not to let it come to that. And he'd be damned if he'd take anything more away from her than she'd already lost, unless and until the safety of his ship and crew demanded it. He decided that what she really needed in the meantime was to keep busy and feel useful.

"Lieutenant D—" He stopped, cursing himself for his lapse. He began again in a quiet, almost apologetic tone. "Ezri, please give me an image of the alien artifact."

Ezri, having heard his false start, visibly stifled a wince as she began working the console.

The viewer before Vaughn began showing a recording of the artifact as it endlessly repeated its leisurely tumble across the adjacent dimensions. But this time it had an audio accompaniment. A series of weird, grinding, shrill-sweet musical tones stacked themselves into unearthly chords, gliding, jagged, stepwise melodies, and fading, colliding overtone-reverberations.

The music wasn't exactly Vaughn's cup of twig tea. But he decided that it wasn't entirely unpleasant either.

He glanced at Ezri, offering her what he hoped was a reassuring smile. "The music of the spheres, Lieutenant?"

"Sorry, Captain. This was something we noticed when we were surveying the Oort cloud in the *Sagan*. It comes from the subspace vibrations of the icy bodies nearest to the artifact. We translated those vibrations into sounds. I must have accidentally keyed the recording we made. I'll turn it off."

Vaughn raised a restraining hand. "No. Let it play."

With a sigh, he settled back into the command chair, idly watching the artifact as it slowly turned and morphed before his eyes. Though he couldn't say why, he had become more certain than ever before that the only hope of reversing whatever had been done to Ezri, Bashir, and Nog lay *inside* that object. Concealed. Mysterious. Perhaps even ultimately unknowable and ineffable, like the thoughts of a god. And the thing hovered tantalizingly beyond his reach, thanks to the vigilance of thirteen Nyazen blockade ships.

He wondered if the eerie celestial music was helping to inspire him to crack the artifact's mysteries—or if it merely sought to mock his helplessness.

Ezri left the bridge quietly, relieved to be away from its suddenly familiar-yet-alien environment. Surrounded by the cool competence of the bridge crew, she had felt as callow and awkward as though it were her first day out of the Academy.

At least I didn't fall to pieces right in front of Commander Vaughn, she thought, grateful for that small mercy. But it had been a near thing. She didn't want to know what would happen the next time someone inadvertently addressed her as "Lieutenant Dax." She wondered if she should ask everyone to start calling her Ezri.

But that wouldn't take her rank into account, nor the dignity of her job as the *Defiant*'s first officer. Lieutenant Tigan, then.

No. It was Lieutenant Dax. And I'm not Dax anymore. I ought to be busted back to ensign.

Ensign Ezri Tigan, late of the *U.S.S. Destiny*. An assistant ship's counselor still three months short of completing her psych training, and haunted by fading, ghostly dream memories. No, not memories, she corrected herself. *Memories* of memories. Ezri Tigan, suddenly dispossessed of the eight variegated lifetimes of accumulated expertise into which she had finally and thoroughly integrated her very sense of self, after more than a year of painstaking, determined effort.

At least Joran's memories will be gone, she told herself. *And Verad's, too. Those two killers will never bother me again.*

But she was also keenly aware that balanced against this slim benefit was the loss of Jadzia's drive and curiosity; the worldly wisdom of Lela, Audrid, and Curzon; the humor and scientific acumen of Tobin and Torias; Emony's exuberance and competitiveness; and her own sense of wholeness, which had lately become bound up in the lives of all the hosts that had preceded her, and the reassuring, cumulative gestalt they had formed within the core of her being.

As Quark might say, this was a lousy deal all around.

Ezri thought, not for the first time, that it was only a matter of time before Commander Vaughn realized that she was no longer fit to do the job he had assigned her. She would never again be fit for it. Not without Dax. The *Defiant*'s captain needed a rock-solid executive officer and second-in-command, not a struggling counselor. She knew on some visceral level, deeper than even the Dax symbiont had ever touched, that she was no longer worthy of the red uniform of command.

Over the past two days, she had repeatedly asked herself why Vaughn hadn't already removed her from active duty. Perhaps it was because he now considered her so ineffectual that formally relieving her simply wouldn't have served any useful purpose.

Her counseling training spoke up then: *You could simply ask him, Ezri.* But suppose Vaughn hadn't relieved her because he honestly still believed in her abilities. Would he continue to do so if she were to air her innermost doubts before him?

Ezri struggled to keep her face free of this internal argument as she passed several of her colleagues in the corridors. Crewman Rahim nodded to her as they passed. Lieutenant McCallum, crossing from another direction, didn't seem to pick up on her distress either, apparently intent on some urgent task elsewhere.

But Kaitlin Merimark stopped as Ezri brushed past and looked askance at the Trill. Kaitlin, who had seen her in the medical bay when she had been near death, obviously wanted to offer some words of comfort. But she just as obviously had no idea what to say.

Say anything, Ezri thought, *anything except "Lieutenant Dax."*

Ezri felt a surge of gratitude for Kaitlin's steadfast friendship. But she also knew she couldn't deal with comfort just now, any more than Kaitlin seemed to know how to give it.

She realized that she had arrived at her destination, the biochem lab. "It's my turn to watch over the slug," Ezri told Kaitlin, immediately aware of how flippant she sounded. She stepped quickly into the lab, sealing the door behind her before Kaitlin could respond.

After she'd dismissed M'Nok from his watch duty, she stood alone in the lab, appreciative of the solitude. In here, she would probably have no chance encounters with anyone, at least for the next few hours.

But she also knew she wasn't entirely alone. Dax was here as well, floating in some solitary universe of his own, thinking his unfathomable thoughts. Thoughts that had commingled so freely with her own for the past eighteen months. She approached the table on which the symbiont's artificial environment container sat and stared through the transparent viewport at the symbiont's dark, ridged surface. She placed a hand on the window. The creature didn't seem to notice her presence.

Ezri recalled her early trepidation about becoming joined. She had always regarded these sightless, silent life-forms as sinister parasites. And she truly never had wanted to be joined, a fact that she could scarcely believe now that her soul, in Dax's absence, felt as hollow as the Caves of Mak'ala back on Trill. Regardless, after her joining had become an irrevocable fact last year, she had worked like hell to make her symbiosis with Dax a successful one.

Now she could only wonder whether her old, prejoining persona was as lost to her as was Dax. Was there no way back even to the life she had lived before her encounter with the symbiont?

She realized then that not everybody in her life would regard her metamorphosis as a tragedy. Dr. Renhol from the Symbiosis Commission would no doubt be relieved to be freed from having to deal with her any further, shepherding the integration of her many personalities. And Mom would be positively thrilled. Yanas Tigan had never wanted to see her daughter, or either of her sons, joined in symbiosis in the first place. *It's so much easier to browbeat your children,* Ezri thought, *when they aren't also your elders.* Her brother Janel would get his sister back, albeit not quite in mint condition. And Norvo, the younger of her two brothers, would probably relate to her better now that she was no longer joined. *Once his prison term is finished,* she reminded herself.

And then there was Julian. Had she lost *him* as well? She knew that he had been in love with Jadzia Dax before he had begun sharing his life with Ezri Dax; Dax had been the common denominator in both of those relationships. Now, given Julian's cathedral-induced decline, was their current relationship a moot point?

There would be no way to know, she told herself—unless Vaughn could find a way to defeat the Nyazen blockade and search the interior of the alien artifact. Assuming, of course, that there were answers to be had there.

She quietly instructed the computer to play back the peculiar sounds Nog had recorded just before the first encounter with the artifact. The empty lab was immediately filled with the strains of the quasimusical cacophany. No longer filtered through Dax's sensibilities, it sounded different to her now than it had when she'd first heard it aboard the *Sagan.* It was almost agreeable. She thought of the *syn lara* compositions of Joran Belar, the twenty-third-century psychotic murderer who had briefly hosted the Dax symbiont, until Verjyl Gard had tracked him down and killed him. Ezri wondered if Joran's music in any way resembled these emergent, intertwining chords, melodies, and countermelodies.

Without the reassuring presence of the symbiont in her belly, she simply couldn't tell. All she knew was that it sounded alien, as ungraspable as the true shape of the interdimensional artifact itself.

Watching the leathery-skinned Dax symbiont as it floated in its purple nutrient bath, Ezri wondered if the creature was as distressed as she was over their current circumstances. Or was it relieved finally to be free of her, hoping perhaps for a more appropriate host-match once the *Defiant* returned it to Trill?

Feeling helpless and utterly alone, she wept as the bizarre nonmusic swelled and crashed all around her.

Nog set the celestial music at an agreeably bone-jarring volume. To his somewhat surprised satisfaction, Shar made no objection as the darkened lab came alive with sound.

In Nog's experience, the single place aboard the *Defiant* most conducive to thinking was the stellar cartography lab. Particularly when it was doing what it did best—displaying the universe in all its infinite scope and grandeur. The room was dark save for their softly glowing padds, the fixed, jeweled pinpoints of distant stars, the dimly reflective iceballs of the local Oort cloud, the haze of the distant galactic plane, which gleamed like latinum wherever it wasn't obscured by dark interstellar dust clouds—and the artifact.

In the middle distance, the alien construct continued its eternal tumble as the vibrational strains of several nearby icy bodies provided an eerie accompaniment. *It's guarding its secrets,* Nog thought as he watched holographic simulacra of the thirteen Nyazen ships that blockaded the object. Gently tapping his new left leg, Nog wondered if he and Shar could really do anything about that.

And just how badly he really *wanted* to do anything about that.

Nog was seated at a table large enough to accommodate both himself and Shar while they ate their hastily replicated dinners. Or rather, as they worked while simultaneously picking at their dinners. The table, chairs, and food trays were the only things mooring either of them to the solid world of decks and bulkheads and artificial gravity. Everywhere else around them, the Gamma Quadrant blazed and beckoned.

A padd cast an amber glow across Shar's pale blue features, turning them an almost Orion green as he stared intently at rows of figures. Nog noted that he appeared uninterested in his meal, something called *paella* that Shar had agreed to try on Bowers's recommendation. Nog saw that some of the dish's ingredients looked enough like the tube grubs on his own plate to be almost appealing.

Shar set the padd aside, his eyes now riveted on the alien artifact that floated above them.

"It's clearly a holy object to both the D'Naali and the Nyazen," Shar said in a tone that struck Nog as nearly reverent. It reminded him of the times during his childhood when his father had told him stories about the Divine Treasury.

"And the text you recovered has to be some sort of scripture," Shar continued.

"Scripture?"

"Sacred writings. A body of legend which may be based upon certain objectively true information. Or myth-driven ethical pronouncements, like the Ferengi Rules of Acquisition."

Nog scowled at that, then instructed the computer to turn the music down by a few decibels. "Translating the alien text is no longer our top priority. Let the computers handle that. We still have to find a way around the Nyazen blockade. And the captain wants our report in less than two hours. Let's meet with Senkowski and Leishman's teams one more time and go completely through it all again. There must have been something we missed on the first two tries."

Shar's eyes never wavered from the floating object. "Of course. Perhaps we can run another simulation on the idea of using the warp nacelles to extend the range of the transporter."

"We keep losing the transportee through signal attenuation," Nog said, shaking his head. "We need a different approach. I don't think brute force is going to work this time."

Whatever the solution was, it was bound to involve something subtle. Or perhaps several subtle somethings. A four-cushion bank shot on the dom-jot table, involving both luck and skill.

Shar nodded dreamily, his eyes still fixed on the artifact.

Nog had never seen his friend appear so . . . haunted. Or so quiet. He was used to Shar's reticence about discussing his personal life, of course, but his moody silence over the past several days was extreme, even for an Andorian.

Nog set his own padd down. "Shar, what's wrong?"

Shar sat mutely for a long time before speaking. "You are one of my most valued friends, Nog. I wonder if I have ever taken the time to tell you that before."

Nog wasn't sure what to say. "Thanks, Shar. The feeling's mutual. Now, what are you trying to tell me?"

"Just that the people in our lives are irreplaceable. Once they're gone, there are no more opportunities to repair our relationships with them. There are no second chances."

Nog was beginning to feel distinctly uncomfortable.

Clearly, something cataclysmic was going on in his friend's life. And just as clearly, Shar didn't know how to begin talking about it.

"Has something happened back home?" Nog asked quietly after ordering the computer to silence the background music.

Nog found Shar's sudden burst of brittle laughter surprising. He couldn't have been more shocked if his friend had suddenly sprouted a second head.

"*Tell me,* Shar," Nog said, after his friend had again subsided into silence. "Tell me what's happened."

Almost a minute elapsed before Shar spoke again. "It isn't easy. . . . We Andorians do not confide easily with one another, let alone with . . . outworlders."

"Ouch, Shar, I thought we had more in common than that. Aren't we *both* the sons of Very Influential People? And aren't we *both* always trying to keep that fact from swallowing us whole?"

Shar only nodded, looking miserable.

"So we're *both* outworlders," Nog said. "Anywhere we happen to be. No matter where you go, there you are."

Shar nodded again, but continued to remain silent.

"All right," Nog said. "I'll get confessional first, if that's what it's going to take to get you to talk."

Shar's antennae stood up quizzically, illuminated by the artifact's glow. "I have nothing to confess."

"Well, *I* do," Nog said, gesturing toward the artifact. "And do you know what I want to confess? I want to confess not being sure I'm really doing everything I possibly can to crack this mystery." He pushed his chair back and placed his new left leg on the tabletop with a loud *thunk.* His bowl of tube grubs arced onto the deck with an audible *splat,* but he ignored it.

Shar blinked in evident incomprehension, and Nog felt his frustrations begin to tear at their fetters.

"Don't you understand?" Nog said, pointing at his regenerated leg. "That alien thing hurt Dr. Bashir and Lieutenant Dax pretty badly. But *I* actually got some *good* luck out of it."

"That is fortunate for you," Shar said.

"No! It's terrible! If we reverse whatever that artifact did to the three of us who were on the *Sagan,* I'll probably go back to . . . the way I was *before.* Right after the Jem'Hadar took my leg at AR-558."

Shar's eyes widened with understanding. "Forgive me. I hadn't considered that."

Nog felt oddly relieved to finally begin articulating his thoughts on the matter. "I've had a tough time thinking about anything else."

"Perhaps," Shar said, steepling his fingers thoughtfully, "you could remain aboard the *Defiant* when we insert the away team onto the artifact. Dr. Bashir and Ezri could take the symbiont inside without you and seek a means of reversing their own conditions without altering yours."

"I already asked Sacagawea about that," Nog admitted, feeling a surge of shame. He wondered if he was reverting to type—becoming a stereotypical cowardly Ferengi, who'd always opt to hide rather than stand and fight. "As near as I can tell from his answer, everybody who was aboard the *Sagan* when we found the artifact is somehow linked. He says that if I don't go along, whatever Ezri and Dr. Bashir have lost will *stay* lost."

"Of course we have no objective proof that anything Sacagawea says is true," Shar said.

"Fair enough. But he's all we've got."

Shar's expression grew distant. "I have noticed that

you often seem to see the world in terms of things lost or things acquired."

"Ezri would probably call it a cultural predisposition," Nog said, pushing his chair back and withdrawing his new left leg from the table. He wasn't sure where his friend was going with this.

Shar nodded. "True enough. Perhaps it makes it difficult to recognize that the gains we make in life often come with certain losses built into them. That we are defined by our debits as much as by our credits."

Nog began suspecting that Shar's words were as much for Shar as for him. He smiled. "You'd make a *terrible* Ferengi."

Shar answered with a small wry smile of his own. "And your emotional transparency would not make you very popular on Andor."

Nog wondered if Shar was still trying to deflect attention from whatever secrets he was guarding. He decided that the time had come to confront the matter directly. "Okay. I've made *my* ugly confession. Now will you finally tell me what's been bothering *you?*"

Shar paused to gather his thoughts, then raised his gray eyes to Nog's. The science officer's jaw was set, as though he had just made a major decision. "When you first learned that you were going to lose your leg, and that the loss was to be permanent, how did it make you feel?"

Nog recognized Shar's primary evasive maneuver immediately. "Shar, why do you always answer a personal question with one of your own?"

"Please, Nog. Tell me how you felt."

Nog sighed. Sometimes Shar could be as stubborn as Uncle Quark. "All right. I felt . . . incomplete. It never occurred to me that I'd end up permanently scarred by the war."

211

Shar nodded, rocking quietly in his chair. Then, almost inaudibly, he said, "That is precisely how I feel, Nog. Incomplete. Permanently."

"I don't understand."

There was another pause. But this one was suffused with tension rather than evasion. Nog waited, sensing that a floodgate was about to open.

Finally, Shar said, "It's Thriss."

"One of your bondmates," Nog said, well aware that this was an extremely awkward conversational topic for Shar. A Jem'Hadar torturer would have had a tough time extracting such stuff from Shar.

"Yes. She came to the station with Dizhei and Anichent shortly before we left for the Gamma Quadrant. To try to persuade me to return to Andor with them, to marry. Instead, I left on the *Defiant*."

"I remember them. I just wasn't sure exactly why they wanted to see you."

Shar made a sound halfway between a chuckle and a cough. "Now you know."

Nog's throat went dry. "Something's happened since we left." Nog knew it had to be something terrible.

"Yes." Shar's eyes became as icy as one of the local comets. He dropped his padd on the table, rising to his feet and placing his hands behind his back as though unable to find any better use for them. "Thriss is dead, by her own hand. Our quad is sundered forever. I have no future. And I am solely to blame."

Shar's words struck Nog like a body blow. He knew he had never experienced anything remotely comparable to Shar's loss—even taking the battle at AR-558 into account. Nog knew that in spite of the loss of his leg, he could always marry and have children—and that he didn't need to be in any particular hurry to do it. But what little he'd studied about Andorian biology had made it clear that members of that species couldn't afford to live at such a leisurely pace. They had to contend with two extremely unforgiving biological constraints: four sexes and a narrow window of reproductive opportunity.

Nog quietly rose from his chair and approached Shar, following the curvature of the table until the two were less than a meter apart. He watched Shar's impassive face, well aware that he could offer no words that might assuage Shar's pain. All he had to offer was his presence.

Acting on a sudden impulse, he offered that presence, stepping toward Shar and drawing him into a gentle embrace. He felt Shar's body stiffen as though responding to an attack. Then the Andorian relaxed, evidently overcoming the violence that came so naturally to Andorians in dire emotional straits. Shar seemed to be accepting Nog's gesture as it was intended.

Seconds or perhaps minutes later, Nog disengaged himself and took a step back. *I want to help you through this. If only I had the words.*

As Nog took another silent step back, Shar broke the lengthening silence. "Nog?"

"Yes?"

"Watch where you're going. You're about to step into your tube grubs."

Still lying on the table, Shar's padd suddenly began emitting a rhythmic, repeating *bleep*. Nog felt a surge of gratitude for the interruption. Shar immediately got busy tapping at the padd's controls.

"The automated linguistics protocols seem to have finally translated a few large chunks of the alien text," he said, his voice still slightly quavering.

Nog thought Shar sounded apologetic for having even

raised the subject when the problem of the Nyazen blockade still remained unsolved. But Nog hadn't ordered Shar to ignore his computer alarms. And, though he didn't have time to think much about it at the moment, he had to admit that he was probably every bit as curious about the alien text as Shar was. Maybe the text could even shed some light on defeating the blockade. Nog allowed himself the faint hope that the text might contain just the lucky break he needed.

"Well? Any major mysteries solved?"

Shar's eyes were rapidly skimming back and forth across the padd, his face a mask of fascination. "Maybe you'd better see for yourself."

Chief medical officer's personal log, stardate 53578.6

Part of me knows that the size of the room isn't really changing. The quarters Ezri and I share are small—cozy, she would probably say—but I know that the bulkheads can't actually move.

Still, I'd be willing to swear that they do. When I lie on the bunk and close my eyes, I sometimes sense the ceiling dropping slowly toward me.

But I can live with it, at least for now. At least there's nobody here to witness what I'm becoming, except for the times when Ezri drops in to check on me. I smile and search for clever, reassuring things to say to her. There's still enough of me left in here to tell that she's anything but reassured. Just how clever my remaining words are I can't say. Nor can I understand how she can ever look at me the same way she used to. The Julian Bashir she loves simply isn't in here anymore. When the rest of whatever it is I've been my whole life finally finishes boiling off, what will be left for her to love?

Then there are what I've come to call my "red periods." When I was an intern, I once treated a severely autistic eight-year-old child. She didn't like to be touched, and if anything in her environment changed too quickly, she would succumb to fits of blind rage, lashing out with fists, feet, and teeth.

Now, at least some of the time, I think I understand how her world must have looked from the inside. Especially when I can't remember some simple thing. Some ridiculously common bit of knowledge, like a word with more than three syllables. Or the moment when I realized that I no longer could read, speak, or think in Latin. Or when I tried to ask the replicator for a cup of Darjeeling and instead just confused the computer. I can't even get the damned sonic shower working on the first try.

Thinking about things like preganglionic fibers or postganglionic nerves right now only makes me want to weep. Or smash something.

On the bulkhead beside the bunk are the words I etched this afternoon with one of the laser exoscalpels Ezri overlooked the last time she'd tried to rid our quarters of anything that might endanger me. My clumsy wall engraving occurred during one of those "red periods," and evidently involved my very last vestiges of Latin. I see that I'd been thoughtful enough at the time to carve an English translation as well. My own personal Rosetta stone, rendered in a hand that looks too childlike to be my own. In a few hours, it could be my epitaph as well.

"Vox et praeterea nihil."

"Voice and nothing more."

When I last closed my eyes to survey the progressive damage still going on inside my mind, it took longer than ever even to reach the outside of my memory cathedral. To get to the front steps, I had to step across an open pit filled with fragments of cobbles and concrete, apparently left behind by some massive piece of demolition equipment. An east-facing buttress was almost entirely gone, shattered by some force I couldn't even imagine.

Inside, the dome had begun letting in slivers of sunlight through several long cracks that weren't visible from the outside, as though some gigantic predatory bird had just raked its talons through the stonework and glass. Rubble lay everywhere, with books and papers scattered randomly against pieces of cracked, upended masonry and shattered bookcases. Tapestries lay twisted and soiled, discarded haphazardly across the floor. I started up the staircase leading to the upper-level library and paused on the fifth step from the bottom. It no longer squeaked.

If my memory processes had been functioning properly, that step would have squeaked automatically in response to the pressure of my mental foot.

Withdrawing from the staircase and walking through the main gallery, I saw that the dream corridor was completely bricked up. This had been the tunnel entrance leading to a twenty-second-century-vintage outbuilding where I kept my dreams in temporary storage until eventually filing them away permanently under the dome.

Everywhere else I looked, portals and entryways were similarly barred. Several slender, spidery creatures worked diligently to add to the chaos.

Each of them had Kukalaka's gumdrop eyes.

It seemed that there probably wasn't much more room left inside the Hagia Sophia than there was in my shrinking quarters. And I filled the tiny soundproofed space around me with screams.

14

As Quark dressed for the evening, his belly roiled with a curious mixture of anticipation and fear. The anticipation was easy enough to understand—Ro Laren was an extraordinarily attractive female. The fear was a little harder to fathom. After all, tonight wouldn't be the first time he and Ro had shared dinner together. But it *would* be the first time he had been the one to pick the evening's activities.

On the previous occasion, Ro had treated him to an evening of pointlessly strenuous windsurfing on a body of water called the Columbia River, which she had told him she'd visited during her Starfleet Academy days. No fun at all really, except for the company.

He set aside the tooth sharpener and inspected his tuxedoed reflection one last time. *What if she can't relate to this holosuite scenario at all?* he thought as he carefully smoothed his cummerbund and adjusted the knot on his black bow tie. *It's not as though she's some nostalgia-crazed hew-mon.*

As he made his way from his quarters onto the lightly populated Promenade, he tried to put his lingering misgivings aside. Whether or not Ro would appreciate Las Vegas might not matter any more than Quark's attitude toward windsurfing had.

Because if there was one being in the entire quadrant capable of putting Ro into a romantic frame of mind, it was Vic.

He entered the bar and crossed to the spiral staircase that led to the upper level and the holosuites. Behind the bar, Frool was doling out drinks to a pair of Rigelians and a Valerian while Morn appeared to be trying to regale them all with one of his innumerable traveler's tales. Quark walked quickly to avoid being drawn into the verbal melee. As he ascended, he glanced down toward the dabo wheel, where Broik was taking drink orders while Deputy Etana watched a hulking Nausicaan with obvious suspicion. Hetik, the aggressively profitable dabo boy Treir had hired, was doing an admirable job hustling the dabo customers—representatives of at least a half-dozen worlds—who had obviously been drawn to the gaming area by Treir's abundant charms. The tall Orion woman met Quark's gaze and regarded him with an unrestrained smirk. He wondered yet again what she had really said to Ro about their impending dinner engagement, then decided that it wasn't worth worrying about. *It's never too late to fire the staff,* Quark thought, quoting the 193rd Rule of Acquisition to himself. *Let's see how the evening goes first.*

There still was no sign of Ro, which concerned him. She was nothing if not punctual. Then he opened the holosuite door, where Julian Bashir's 1962 Las Vegas lounge scenario was perpetually up and running—except on those occasions when Vic himself voluntarily took his own program off-line. The band was tuning, perky cocktail waitresses were serving, and hew-mon alcoholic beverages of various sorts were flowing freely among the sparse but growing dinner crowd. Quark noted with considerable relief that Taran'atar apparently hadn't left the place in ruins after his visit a little earlier. It was important that everything go perfectly tonight.

Ro was already seated at a table not far from the stage, looking exquisite, if somewhat uncomfortable, in a black, off-the-shoulder evening gown. He had no idea whether she was as uneasy in this twentieth-century Earth scenario as he had been trying to control a holographic boat that seemed bent on tossing him overboard. But she didn't appear ready to bolt. At least not yet.

Which, Quark realized, had to be due to the reassuring presence of Vic Fontaine, who stood near Ro's table, an authentically archaic-looking stage microphone in his hand.

Acknowledging Quark's entrance with a knowing nod and a worldly smile, Vic turned toward the stage, where a trio of tuxedoed humans struck up an expert piano-bass-and-drums accompaniment as Vic began warbling a bouncy musical travelogue whose recurring refrain was "Let's Get Away From It All." Just before beginning his performance, Vic mentioned that an Earth singer named Sin-Ah-Trah had made the tune famous.

Quark took a seat across the small table from Ro, realizing that he'd already missed the opportunity to pull her chair out for her. But that was all right. If she could learn to feel as comfortable in this alien milieu as he had become over the past few months, then perhaps she would lower her shields voluntarily. Quark recalled how he had once regarded Vic's holographic establishment as unwelcome competition, until the upheavals of the Dominion War had taught him that ancient Las Vegas was really a refuge from troubles of every sort. A refuge that could be overused, as Nog had demonstrated during the months following the loss of his leg, but one that stood ready to offer solace at all times. *Twenty-six/seven, as some of the hew-mons around here like to say.*

As Vic concluded his number and took a bow before the applauding dinner crowd, Quark glanced at Ro, who seemed engrossed in the environment. *Good,* he thought.

Quark leaned forward and assayed his most non-threatening smile. "You got here a little early."

She nodded, a wry expression on her face. "I didn't think you'd mind. I'm less accessible here than I am in the security office. Besides, after the dress shop finished sewing me into this costume, I realized I wasn't exactly dressed for work."

"There's more to life than work," Quark said, grinning.

She favored him with a silent *that's-easy-for-you-to-say* glower.

Sensing that something else besides the demands of her job was bothering her, he decided to change the subject. "How do you like Las Vegas so far?"

"It's . . . interesting." Her tone was noncommittal and her brow remained furrowed as she gazed around the room. The earring dangling from her left ear gleamed enticingly in the room's subdued lighting.

Quark hadn't noticed that Vic had taken up a position alongside their table. *"Interesting,* doll-face?" the crooner said with an urbane smile.

Ro cast a quick glance over her shoulder as though convinced Vic had to be addressing someone else.

"No need for the double take, sweetheart," Vic said.

"I was just wondering when your beau here was going to get around to introducing us."

"I think maybe I need to have my universal translator checked," Ro said.

"This is 1962," Vic said, his smile disarming. "Here you'll have to pick up the lingo the old-fashioned way. By experience." He turned toward Quark while making a courtly gesture in Ro's direction. "So are you going to keep this vision you've found all to yourself?"

Quark realized he had been staring at Ro the entire time, drinking in her image. He shook himself as though from a dream. "Vic, meet Lieutenant Ro Laren, the station's chief of security. Ro, Vic Fontaine."

With the deftness of an expert stage magician, Vic somehow managed to take Ro's hand and raise it to his lips—without prompting her to throw him bodily across the neighboring table. *Charmed, I'm sure,* Quark thought, feeling all the satisfaction of a man entering the final-stage negotiations of a killer deal.

Until he noticed that Ro's forehead was still as wrinkled as her Bajoran nose.

Vic had obviously noticed as well. "If you don't mind my mentioning it, you seem a little distracted for someone who's here for a night on the town."

"So are you a touch telepath as well as a singer?" Ro asked, her frown persisting.

Vic laughed and shook his head. "I never work Harry Blackstone's side of the street. But I'd have to be a real Clyde to miss the fact that something's really eating you. A farmer could scrub his overalls on your corrugated but otherwise charming forehead. I think I'd better expedite the drinks. First round's on me."

"Quark, I thought you might try to seduce me," Ro

said with a wry smile. "But I never expected you to subject me to some sort of . . . covert counseling program."

Vic motioned to an improbably short-skirted waitress, who brought a small tray to the table, replete with a bottle on ice and a trio of champagne glasses. "It's flattering that you think of me as some sort of professional headshrinker," he said. "But I'm just a humble holographic student of the human—I mean the *humanoid*—heart."

Ro's eyebrows shot straight up, momentarily smoothing away the striations of worry. "You *know* you're a hologram?" she asked Vic.

Vic made an exaggerated bow. "Like a great man once said: 'Know thyself.' "

"Of all the holograms in all the hospitality venues in all the quadrant," Quark said, "Vic is unique."

Ro examined the bottle the waitress had set down before her. "Spring wine?"

Vic shook his head as he began filling the three glasses. "No can do. It's 1962, remember? I might be a self-aware hologram, but I'm also period specific. But Dom Pérignon isn't too shabby as a consolation prize."

Taking his lead from Vic, Quark raised his glass. Ro followed a moment later. "To the future," Vic said, then took a drink. Quark and Ro did likewise.

But Ro's dark expression returned almost immediately.

"Something wrong with the bubbly?" Vic asked.

Ro shook her head and regarded the contents of her glass, evidently transfixed by the continuous upward motion of its stream of perfectly uniform, nearly microscopic bubbles.

"Well, since the problem clearly can't be the company," Vic said in a bantering tone, "it has to be my toast."

Ro's contemplative scowl only deepened.

And Quark realized in a flash that Vic had, as usual, cut directly to the heart of the matter.

Vic seemed to realize it as well, and took that revelation as his cue to move on. "I'll leave you two lovebirds to your evening. Enjoy the show." Handing his barely touched champagne to a passing waitress, he was gone, moving cordially among the other tables as he made his way back to the stage.

Quark let the silence stretch for as long as he could stand it. Then he said, "It's still bothering you, isn't it?"

"What do you mean?"

"What we talked about before Shakaar made his big announcement. The future."

She nodded, looking bleak. "It'd help if you could convince me that there's even going to *be* a future."

Quark didn't like the sound of that. "What, did you just get wind of some new classified Starfleet crisis that's about to end the universe as we know it?"

She took another large swallow of champagne, her expression softening somewhat. She must have been warming up either to him or to the drink. "Things like that come and go. But the future is something else entirely. You're stuck with facing it every day the universe *doesn't* end."

Quark had to agree. He had already told her of his misgivings about trying to make a living in Bajoran territory after the Federation came in and introduced its cashless, abundance-based, replicator-driven economy. He felt all but certain that he was about to lose everything he'd built here over the past sixteen years.

He wondered if the incoming regime would deprive him of Ro as well. A determination rose within him to prevent that from happening, though he hadn't the faintest idea of how he might go about it.

It seemed hopeless on the face of it.

"So have you decided what you're going to do after the Federation comes in?" he asked, taking the liberty of refilling both their glasses.

"As a matter of fact," Ro said, throwing back a hefty quantity of the Dom Pérignon, "I think I've finally come to a decision."

On the stage, Vic and his ensemble launched into a rendition of a centuries-old Earth standard that repeatedly asked the question "Who Wants to Be a Millionaire?"—and continually presented "I don't" as the only acceptable answer. According to Vic, someone named Porter had written the song for a show called *High Society,* which apparently had starred this Sin-Ah-Trah person whom Vic seemed to regard so highly. But how a disdain for the acquisition of money equated with any so-called high society made absolutely no sense. Quark struggled to ignore the song's patently offensive lyrics, while Ro didn't seem to mind them. Or perhaps she hadn't even noticed, having lived among impecunious Starfleet hew-mons for as long as she had.

Quark watched her throughout Vic's performance, wondering if she intended to tell him what decision she'd made. He suspected it lay along lines similar to his own. "I suppose neither of us is considered a pillar of the community around here," he said. "And under the Federation, it's only going to get worse for us both. The new regime is never going to feel right for either one of us. Not as long as we're outsiders."

"It's been made pretty clear to me today that I can never wear a Starfleet uniform again," Ro said, as though talking to herself. "Not that I'd want to."

"But the Bajoran Militia is going to be part of Starfleet soon," Quark said. *Your choices look pretty much the same as mine. But where will yours take you?*

Ro took another drink and nodded. "Once the ministers sign those entry documents, home won't be a refuge from the Federation anymore. At least, not for me."

"And the Bajorans will become just like the hewmons," Quark said. "Flat broke, but too well fed to realize it."

"To outsiders," Ro said, raising her glass in an ironic toast. "So the next big question is, What do we do next?"

We?

Even as his despair about his personal financial prospects deepened, Quark allowed himself to nurture the hope that he was finally connecting with Ro on some level deeper than mere infatuation. But if she, too, was planning to leave the station, would he ever get the chance to capitalize on that?

Quark was suddenly terrified that the wrong word from him right now might drive her away from him forever. "Don't go," was all he could think of to say.

He realized a moment later that Vic had returned, his entrance evidently obscured by the gathering Dom Pérignon haze. "Let me guess," Quark said. "You heard everything we just said."

Vic grinned. "I heard enough, pallie, to make one thing as clear as where Goldwater stands on JFK: You two gloomy Guses are made for each other."

Ro's nearly empty drink slipped from her fingers and tipped over. She ignored the stain that was slowly spreading across the tablecloth. "Come again?"

"Listen, those ancient Chinese cats might have really been onto something when they decided to make 'danger' and 'opportunity' into the same word."

"I don't follow you," Quark said, wondering if his holosuite was beginning to malfunction. That would be damned inconvenient, with Nog over ninety thousand light-years away at the moment.

"Neither of you can see a way of making a go of it under the Federation flag," Vic said, looking first at Ro, then at Quark. "Which means that you're both going to have to get out of Dodge. Away from Starfleet. And away from a cashless Promenade."

"Right," Quark said. So far, Vic was only stating the obvious. Where was this leading?

"Dodge?" Ro said, obviously perplexed.

Vic sighed and shook his head in an exaggerated display of patience. "Okay, let me spell it out for you in great big letters, like the Sands' marquee: You two need to gallop off to the frontier and go into business together."

After a parting wink at a nonplussed Ro, Vic returned to the stage and began to sing "Fly Me to the Moon."

A moment later Quark realized that Vic was, yet again, uncannily right. He looked at Ro and saw the same realization beginning to dawn in her eyes as well.

"I think we need to talk," he said as he righted her glass and filled it again, emptying the bottle in the process.

Ro smiled. "Later," she said, and held out her hand to him. "Dance with me."

Quark felt a grin spreading across his face and took Laren's hand. They stepped onto the dance floor together.

Seated behind the large desk in the station commander's office, Kira didn't bother to look up from the security report she had been reading until after the door had hissed open and admitted her latest visitor.

She was surprised to see Colonel Lenaris Holem—no, she corrected herself, *General* Lenaris Holem—striding toward her desk.

The general's broad smile belied his mock-chiding tone. "Working this late is a bad habit, Colonel."

"Occupational hazard," she said, returning the smile. "I'm going to have a very busy day tomorrow." Tossing the padd aside, she rose from her chair in deference to Lenaris's superior rank.

His lips curled in a good-natured scowl. "Please. I don't think I'll ever get used to seeing colonels leaping to attention in my presence. Especially not *you*."

Kira felt her own smile increase in wattage. She had always genuinely liked the large, blunt-featured Militia officer. "Well, if you won't take a salute, then I hope you'll accept my congratulations on your promotion."

He touched the month-old general's pin on the collar of his gray uniform tunic, as though he thought a Vayan hornfly had just lit there. Kira knew that Lenaris had been promoted from colonel to general in recognition of his accomplishments as commander of the Lamnak fleet during the evacuation of Europa Nova, a non-Federation Earth colony whose population had been threatened by theta radiation a few months earlier. It also hadn't escaped her notice that she, the overall commander of that extremely complex mission, had received no promotions or commendations whatsoever.

So goes Militia politics, she thought. *For the Attainted.*

But she knew that Lenaris wasn't responsible for her shabby treatment, either at the hands of Yevir Linjarin's plurality in the Vedek Assembly, or from his sympathizers within the Bajoran Militia. She knew that both groups bore little love for her after her official excommunication from the mainstream of Bajor's religious life. Yet, on the eve of the planet's entry into the Federation, neither group seemed able to muster sufficient courage to fire her on purely religious grounds.

Still, Lenaris's promotion served as a depressing reminder to her of how far she had fallen in the eyes of so many influential Bajorans.

"What can I do for you?" she asked, gesturing toward the sofa in the meeting area of her office. She moved over to the replicator, from which she extracted two cups of alva nut tea, the general's favorite beverage. "And why didn't you let me know you were coming?"

"I didn't call ahead," said the general as he sat, "in case you already knew the answer to your first question. You might have found some convenient excuse not to see me."

She handed one of the two steaming mugs to Lenaris. "My door is always open to you, Holem. You know that."

"I do. And I'm grateful for it." He took a careful sip of the hot, fragrant liquid. Settling back into the sofa, he said, "You know, I nearly turned down this promotion. After Europa Nova, it felt like the High Command was deliberately snubbing you by offering these general's bars to me."

"Turning down a promotion wouldn't have made the Militia any nicer to me, Holem. Besides, you've earned it many times over."

He shrugged. "I don't know about that. But before I said anything foolish, I realized that I'd have a better chance of changing the attitudes of the old-guard brass as a general than I would have had as a colonel."

"Maybe," she said, eager to see where he was headed.

"And that brings me to the reason for my visit," he continued, gazing directly into her eyes over the top of his mug. "Ten days ago I decided to follow the path of Ohalu. I have committed my life to the tenets of Ohalu's Truthseekers, and to the Ohalavaru Way."

Kira nodded. She had heard the rumors of grumblings from certain highly placed Bajorans about Yevir's heavy-handedness. And that the authors of some of these complaints had, perhaps out of sheer frustration, thrown their support behind the Ohalavaru, the group whose formation Kira had apparently inspired by disseminating Ohalu's prophecies a few months back—an action that had led directly to her Attainder.

"It's not exactly a secret," Kira said. Beginning to wonder when the general intended to make his point, she sipped slowly at the contents of her mug.

"You should join us," Lenaris said.

Kira nearly spit her tea across the room. "What?!"

He appeared unmoved by her reaction. "It was your actions that catalyzed the Ohalavaru movement. And your Attainder that gave it drive and purpose."

Lenaris's reasoning sounded insane to Kira's ears. "My actions drove a wedge into the Bajoran faith."

He scowled. "That's Yevir and his cronies talking. I think Kira Nerys knows better. Besides, are you really prepared to spend years on your knees begging the forgiveness of Yevir and his toadies?"

She felt the hairs on the back of her neck rise. "I never asked for any forgiveness. I didn't do anything wrong."

"Exactly. I'm glad you're prepared to admit that you don't have to play their game. You have nothing to lose by joining us and throwing your public support behind Vedek Solis, our nominee for the kaiship."

Kira knew Solis well and liked him quite a lot. A week ago, she had been somewhat surprised by the news that Solis had become the nominal Ohalavaru leader. His sincerity and goodwill could never be called into question; he had always worked hard for the benefit of the Bajoran people, during and after the Cardassian Occupation. Kira would never forget the quarrel she had had with Odo more than a year earlier, after the constable had briefly detained Solis for conducting charitable fund-raising activities aboard the station without a permit. The vedek's actions had brought some quick, desperately needed relief to Bajoran flood victims. Like Odo, the man she had fallen in love with, Solis usually wasn't one to place the niceties of paperwork ahead of the urgent needs of people.

But she saw a huge flaw in the general's logic, and didn't hesitate to bring it up. "I'm Attainted. I'd be useless to you."

"Stop listening to the orthodoxy's propaganda," he said, military steel flashing behind his voice. "You obviously don't have a clear picture of how much general discontent there is on Bajor about your Attainder."

Or about how thoroughly I've fractured my people's faith, she thought, a bitter taste in her mouth.

"Attainted or not, you're considered a hero by many people," Lenaris continued. "A hero in war and a hero in peace. And now you can be a hero in a profound cultural struggle."

She felt anger warm her cheeks. "I never wanted to be anybody's hero. And I'm not going to be a religious symbol. That's Yevir's game."

He sighed. "Nerys, have you ever had the pleasure of meeting Li Nalas?"

"Of course I have," she said, frowning as she recalled the day the brave symbol of the resistance was murdered by other men bent on remaking Bajor in their own image. "You know that. We've both met him."

"So we both know that we sometimes aren't given a choice in these matters."

Kira was incredulous. "You're saying it's my *destiny* to support the Ohalavaru?"

"Call it what you will," he said, shrugging. "But we both know that your support would greatly influence whether or not Solis becomes the next kai. Unless you prefer to see Yevir in that position. Remember, he's a relatively young man. He could be kai for the rest of your life."

Kira couldn't dispute the general on most of these points. But it all still felt fundamentally wrong to her.

After taking a long, silent moment to compose her thoughts, she said, "I simply can't risk dividing Bajor any further. Especially not so close to Bajor's official entry into the Federation. Until Bajor's admission, the Emissary's work here is incomplete."

It was Lenaris's turn to appear incredulous. "The Emissary? Benjamin Sisko. Nerys, I have nothing but respect for your former commander, but he is part of the past. You should embrace the future instead."

"That's precisely what I'm trying to do, Holem. If the Ohalavaru would simply stand back, be objective, and try to look at the bigger political picture, they might be able to see that now isn't the best time to open up political rifts. Surely Vedek Solis can understand that."

"It was Vedek Solis who asked me to speak with you today."

Kira let out a weary sigh. "Has either of you considered the Bajor–Cardassia talks?"

"As little as possible," he said with another shrug. "What about them?"

"The talks are stalled at the moment. What chance will we have of restarting them if we're preoccupied with our own religious squabbles?"

Lenaris was clearly unmoved. "If the talks with Cardassia are stalled, then you can rest assured that the cause is Cardassian intransigence. Nothing that's happening on Bajor now or in the future will change that one way or the other."

232

But Kira knew better. She had already spoken at length about this very topic with Shakaar. And as far as she was concerned, the first minister could make a nice living conducting master classes in intransigence.

"General, I'd like you to speak to Solis for me," Kira said after another lengthy pause. "Ask him to be a little gentler in pushing the Ohalavaru agenda. At least until the current business with the Federation and Cardassia is resolved. There really is a bigger picture to consider here, Holem. Bigger than Solis. Bigger than Yevir. And certainly bigger than either of us."

Lenaris rose and set his empty cup on her desk. He looked sad, deflated. "You've changed, Nerys."

She bristled. "Yes. I've become a bit wiser about doing what's right for my people."

"You worry about dividing Bajor," he said with a bitter laugh. "But that sinoraptor's already jumped the fence. That happened the moment you uploaded Ohalu's suppressed prophecies onto the Bajoran comnet. The only question we ought to be asking now is how best to manage that division."

"I'll leave that to wiser heads than mine, thank you."

"*Whose* heads?" Lenaris walked over to the painting that hung on her wall, idly examining it for a moment before turning back to her. "Yevir's? Vedek Scio's? Vedek Eran's? The other hard-liners? This 'division' you're so frightened of might actually be the beginning of Bajor's future unity, Nerys. The start of a transformation into something with more vision than the current orthodoxy has. Something truer to the plans of the Prophets."

Kira's thoughts wandered back to the pivotal battles she had fought on behalf of the ancient Bajora after she had been thrown thirty millennia into her planet's past.

She hadn't hesitated to get involved then. But grappling in the same way with the future seemed an altogether different matter.

"Let history make those decisions," she said. "Not me."

His voice rose in both passion and volume. "Nerys, you *are* history. Wasn't it you who introduced us to Ohalu's truth after the vedeks tried to destroy it? Wasn't it you who created this 'division' in the first place?"

"I'm not proud of it. I just did what had to be done to let our people make up their own minds about their faith. To keep Yevir from short-circuiting those decisions by suppressing Ohalu's prophecies."

A triumphant smile spread slowly across the general's face. "You acted to defend prophecies which have turned out to be utterly, *perfectly* correct. Not just some of them. *All* of them, Nerys. Given those facts, how could Ohalu's writings be anything *but* the inspired words of the Prophets? And isn't your first duty to them?"

Kira couldn't avoid the ring of truth his words carried. How easy it would be to simply go along. To use the Ohalavaru as a weapon against Yevir and his ilk. But at what cost to Bajor's future? Other than her Orb experiences, she had never claimed to have any special knowledge of the minds of the Prophets. But surely such convulsions couldn't be part of their plan.

"No," she said quietly, her voice pitched almost in a whisper.

The general nodded, then took a different tack. "Do you think you might be more kindly disposed toward us if we were to convince the Vedek Assembly to reverse your Attainder?"

She decided that she had had just about enough of this. Friendship and rank would go just so far. "Why not

234

just tow all fourteen planets in the system into a straight line?" she said. "It would probably be easier. Besides, my religious status is something personal, between me and the Prophets and—"

"—and none of my damned business," he said with a chuckle, interrupting her. "Forgive me, Nerys. I over-reached myself."

The general moved toward the door, which opened for him. Then he turned around on the threshold and faced her. "It's clear to me now that you're not ready to come along with us on this. At least not just yet."

With that, he bid her a warm good-bye and departed. Alone in her office, Kira recalled how tenacious a fighter her old friend had been during the bad old days of the Occupation.

And she was absolutely certain that she hadn't heard the last of the Ohalavaru. Or of their agenda for Bajor.

15

Taking care to tread quietly, Ezri entered the quarters she shared with Julian. She wanted to look in on him once more before preparing for the tactical briefing.

"Hello, Julian."

He was sitting cross-legged on the bunk, his usually immaculate hair disheveled, his uniform jacket torn and askew, his eyes closed as though he had been deep in meditation. When they opened, she saw a momentary whirlpool of confusion in their brown depths.

Then he smiled at her.

She smiled back, relieved. She hadn't startled him this time. And he wasn't throwing things. Or screaming.

"You're quite pretty," he said, his voice sounding like a kilometer of gravel-strewn road. Her smile wavered as she looked into his eyes. Did he even recognize her?

Her gaze was drawn to the uneven lettering that Julian had evidently burned into the bulkhead during one

236

of her absences. Beside a few archaic Terran words was scrawled *Voice and nothing more.*

Was that how Julian saw himself during his lucid moments? Ezri found the idea difficult to understand. She had come to believe in his steady judgment, his rock-solid humanity, the way a mathematician accepts a geometrical axiom. She found the phrase Julian had carved to be a far better description of herself. Nothing but appearances, she thought. Pips on a uniform that's no longer even the right color.

She recalled her counseling training. "Impostor syndrome" was how the texts had described the feelings she was having. The irrational conviction that one's continued presence in a given job is somehow fraudulent. What frightened Ezri most about the notion was that it felt completely rational.

Because she knew it was the truth.

It was then that she noticed the laser scalpel on the beside table. The instrument lay discarded, apparently forgotten, atop a battered copy of a book titled *Alice in Wonderland,* a favorite from Julian's childhood. Ezri noticed then that the scalpel was still lit up and active. Not good. She realized that he must be stashing away some of his instruments. Or perhaps her own shortcomings had prevented her from finding and removing all the dangerous objects that were already in their quarters.

Some exec I am. I can't even keep the sharp objects away from the man I love.

Carefully meeting Julian's curiously childlike gaze, Ezri sat on the bunk beside him. Without calling attention to the gesture, she carefully picked up the scalpel and shut it off with a quiet flick of her thumb. She also took the dermal regenerator.

He noticed. "Those're mine," he said, scowling, his eyes hawklike.

Careful, she told herself. The last thing she wanted was to provoke him into another frustrated tantrum. She didn't want to be forced to have him sedated. What would be left of him after he woke up?

"It's all right, Julian," she said, trying to keep her tone pleasant without offering any condescension—that would be a sure way of setting him off. "You weren't planning on doing any surgery anytime soon, were you?"

Only then did she notice the small teddy bear that lay partially concealed by the chaotic bedclothes. The threadbare animal was missing an eye. She recognized Kukalaka, Julian's childhood teddy bear, which she had once been amused to discover that he still owned. Until now she hadn't realized that he had brought it along with him to the Gamma Quadrant.

Then she saw the crazy quilt of razor-thin, intersecting lines across the stuffed creature's abdomen. Obviously Julian had been using Kukalaka to practice whatever surgical skills he could still remember.

His eyes narrowed. "I'm a doctor. I need my instruments."

Julian's manner made her think of her brother Norvo. When they were little, he had announced that he was a dilithium miner. Norvo's face had had that same earnest expression.

"Yes, Julian. But doctors keep their instruments in the medical bay." She tucked the tools into a pouch on her jacket. "I'll take these there for you, while you stay here and get some rest."

"I don't *need* to rest." He pushed himself off the bed, reaching his feet with a stumble she'd never seen before. "I have to go to the medical bay, too."

"I don't think that's such a good idea, Julian."

He elbowed his way toward the door. In the room's tight confines, it was difficult to stay out of his way.

"There's a patient I need to see." The door whooshed open as he approached it. He made a dismissive gesture toward Kukalaka, who still lay on the bed. "A *real* patient. There's some . . . therapy I need to administer."

Sacagawea, she thought. He was talking about their D'Naali guide.

"Julian, you need to stay here. You're in no condition to care for a patient. Besides, Ensign Richter and Ensign Juarez can give the alien whatever therapy he might need."

He regarded her in silence for a lengthy moment, apparently about to explode in an emotional outburst. But when he finally spoke, his voice was surprisingly calm and gentle.

"You don't understand, Ezri. The therapy isn't for my patient. It's for me."

Ezri suddenly understood something: Whatever skills the artifact had taken from Julian, his courage and determination—his *emotional* intelligence—still remained with him, at least in some measure. And she knew that now wasn't the time to hide—or to surrender. Not while the alien artifact still held onto its secrets.

All he seemed to be asking for was some simple dignity. *Maybe,* she thought, *that's the only thing nobody can ever truly take from any of us.*

Tears stung her eyes as she forced aside all thought of her own loss. Simultaneously galvanized and shamed by Julian's courage, she arrived at a command decision.

"Let me walk with you to the medical bay, Julian." A moment later, they were moving together down the corridor.

And for at least a few fleeting minutes she felt far less like an impostor. She wished she could believe that the feeling would last.

Right ahead of Shar, Nog stepped onto the bridge. He relished the solid feel of his left leg as he put his weight on it. The new limb seemed every bit as strong as the other one. *Don't get too attached to it,* he reminded himself, then nearly laughed aloud at the absurdity of the notion.

Seated at the ops console, Ensign Tenmei glanced over her shoulder, acknowledging Nog and Shar with a smile and a nod. Commander Vaughn swiveled the command chair in their direction, an expectant expression on his face.

"Have you found a way around the blockade problem yet?"

Nog shook his head, feeling somewhat disappointed with himself. "Not quite, sir. We're still working on that."

"We did make another discovery, Captain," Shar said. "And we thought it best to bring it to your attention immediately. It concerns the alien text."

Vaughn's eyebrows rose. "You've translated it."

"Partially," Shar said, nodding. "I believe we've uncovered some of the artifact's history, or at least some sort of . . . origin myth."

"Go on," Vaughn said, stroking his silver beard thoughtfully.

"Apparently the Oort cloud artifact was once located on the surface of an inhabited planet," Shar said.

Bowers approached from the tactical station, his curiosity obviously piqued. "And where is this planet now?"

"Lots of places, as far as we can tell," Nog said. "And in lots of little pieces."

"The artifact's world of origin was apparently destroyed aeons ago," Shar said, "in some great, planetary-scale cataclysm."

"Caused by what?" Vaughn wanted to know.

"We think by the artifact itself," said Nog. "Whatever the artifact did released enough energy to send it way out here, to the outskirts of the system."

Vaughn gestured toward the main viewer, which continuously displayed the object's eternal tumble. "It's powerful enough to destroy an entire planet?"

"I don't think there's much that's beyond its capabilities," Shar said. "The text mentions a progenitor species, perhaps ancestral to both the D'Naali and the Nyazen, who constructed the artifact to 'reap the bounty of the many unseen realms.' "

Bowers frowned. " 'Unseen realms'?"

"Parallel universes, perhaps," Vaughn said. "Maybe it's some kind of interdimensional power collector."

"That's our best guess," Nog said. "We think it was designed to draw energy out of higher-dimensional spaces and the parallel universes adjacent to our own."

Bowers looked impressed. "I guess that would explain why parts of the thing are always bobbing in and out of normal space."

"And it might also explain," Tenmei said, "the weird quantum resonance patterns the *Sagan*'s been giving off. The shuttle must be carrying the fingerprints of some of those other universes."

Shar nodded, his expression dour. "And if the artifact *is* some sort of energy collection device, that might also account for the power-draining effect it had on the *Sagan*."

"So what do you suppose happened to the people who built this thing?" Vaughn asked, his eyes riveted to the artifact on the screen.

Bowers's brow wrinkled in thought. "And how did they manage to incorporate stuff into this text about what happened *after* their homeworld got blown to kingdom come?"

"That's been bothering me, too," Nog said. "From these translated fragments, it looks as though a number of people were aboard the artifact during the disaster. A few survivors evidently amended the text."

Shar glanced at his padd before weighing in on the matter. "Those survivors may have persisted for many generations, and might even be the remote ancestors of the D'Naali, the Nyazen, or both. Whatever really happened is shrouded in mythological language, so it's hard to be certain. But it appears that the attempt these beings made to mine the adjacent dimensions unleashed forces that literally ripped their homeworld apart."

"And the artifact itself survived because it was in the eye of the storm," Vaughn said.

Shar nodded. "Exactly."

"And the forces that destroyed the planet flung the object way out here," Nog said. The image of the powerful artifact caroming off billions of frozen planetesimals and icy Oort cloud fragments brought to mind a complicated bank shot on some cosmic dom-jot table.

Vaughn rose from the command chair. "Good work, gentlemen. Mr. Bowers, you have the bridge. Mr. Nog, I want you and your people to keep searching for a way around that blockade."

"Aye, sir," Nog found himself suppressing a sudden urge to smile. For some reason he couldn't quite articulate, he felt he was on the verge of a breakthrough. But he knew that a good engineer didn't discuss such things with his captain until *after* he'd taken the time to test them.

"Shar, I want you to come with me," Vaughn said on his way to the turbolift.

Shar's antennae rose in evident curiosity as he fell into step beside Vaughn. "Sir?"

"I want to know whether Sacagawea can shed some light on your translations," Vaughn said, throwing a backward glance toward the image of the artifact. "Maybe he can even help us use it to get inside that thing."

Striding into the medical bay a few paces ahead of Shar, Vaughn found the tableau that greeted him almost too painful to look at.

Julian Bashir was a mere shadow of himself, his hair mussed and beard stubble darkening his face. The doctor's dark eyes resembled those of a frightened child. In spite of it all, he persevered through what appeared to be an attempt to examine his D'Naali patient, who sat impassively on one of the biobeds. Ezri and Ensign Richter hovered close by, their faces masks of pained sympathy as the doctor moved haltingly, waving a medical tricorder before Sacagawea.

"You've taken good care of him, Julian," Ezri said, sounding awkward. "He seems . . . quite healthy now."

Vaughn cleared his throat, immediately drawing the attention of Ezri and Richter. "I'd like to speak to our guest for a moment."

Bashir turned toward Vaughn, staring at him without any apparent recognition. Vaughn found the idea of such a loss of self chilling in the extreme. Being over a century old, he sometimes wondered if senility would one day overcome him in much the same manner. It was difficult to imagine any worse fate.

"With your permission of course, Doctor," Vaughn said, keeping his eyes on Bashir rather than on either of the two women. Regardless of his current condition, this was still Bashir's medical bay; Vaughn wanted to be as solicitous of the doctor's dignity as possible, without drifting into condescension.

Quietly lowering his tricorder, Bashir nodded.

Vaughn approached the tall, willowy alien, who regarded him with unfathomable, fist-sized eyes. Shar looked on quietly, evidently content to observe.

"We need your assistance," Vaughn said.

As though mounted on gimbals, the alien's head swiveled closer to Vaughn. "Debt/obligation I have," it said, the universal translator rendering the words in incongruous bell peals. "With delight do I discharge same. What need/desire have you?"

"Your adversaries are preventing us from getting close to the . . . cathedral. We must find a way around that difficulty."

The creature's mouth parts moved laterally in what Vaughn thought might have been a smile. "Understand. You need/require interior access to the cathedral/anathema."

So far, Vaughn had had no luck in getting Sacagawea to explain why his people and the Nyazen were such bitter enemies. The creature either did not understand or was deliberately holding something back. Vaughn hoped he would make better progress pumping the alien for information about the artifact itself.

"Yes," Vaughn said.

Sacagawea pointed a long, branchlike finger toward Bashir first, then Ezri. "Access you desire/require because of this pair. Touched by the cathedral/anathema have they been both. Misaligned in their worldlines are they both as consequence/result. And both deteriorating/worsening steadily, per timeunit."

Remarkable, Vaughn thought as he parsed the alien's tortuous locutions. Ezri and Richter both stood by, saucer-eyed.

"How could it know that Julian and Ezri have been altered by their contact with the artifact?" Shar said, sounding nonplussed.

His own curiosity already moving at high warp, Vaughn wanted that question answered as well. But he also felt an irresistible desire to learn more about the artifact itself.

"The cathedral has a special meaning for your people, doesn't it?" Vaughn said. "And for the Nyazen as well."

"Source of all things is cathedral/anathema. Feared/revered by all D'Naali. Feared/revered by all Nyazen. But Nyazen wish exclusion. Desire/require cathedral/anathema for Nyazen only. This exclusion D'Naali cannot countenance/abide."

"Does *anybody* in the Gamma Quadrant know how to share?" Ezri said with a smile fit for the gallows.

Before Vaughn could respond, the medical bay's door slid open and Nog bounded into the room, his excitement palpable.

"Lieutenant?" Vaughn said.

"Sorry, sir. I hope I'm not interrupting anything critical."

"Never mind that. What's on your mind?"

Nog grinned. "I think I've finally found a way to get us around the Nyazen blockade."

Cutting off Vaughn's response, Sacagawea suddenly turned toward Nog. "Touched by the cathedral/anathema is *this* one as well. Worldlines as misaligned as the others."

Vaughn felt a serpent of apprehension beginning to turn in his gut. This creature had somehow identified everyone affected by the artifact, apparently by sight alone. "Nog," Vaughn said, "when you interviewed Sacagawea about the artifact earlier, did you tell him who had been aboard the *Sagan* during the survey mission?"

"Not exactly, sir," Nog said, looking embarrassed. "I mean, I did tell him that *I* was aboard, and that I wasn't alone. But I didn't tell him who was with me specifically."

"And what did he tell you?" Vaughn said.

"Not much that made sense. Mainly that everyone who was 'afflicted' had to go aboard the artifact together."

Vaughn turned his attention back to Sacagawea. "What do you mean by 'misaligned worldlines'?" He noticed that Shar had opened up a tricorder and was waving it in the direction of Ezri and Julian.

"Misaligned," Sacagawea said with what Vaughn thought sounded like a tinge of impatience. "Untethered. Adrift/lost midworlds. Is clear enough/sufficient, I judge."

Taking a step backward toward Shar and Nog, Vaughn shook his head in frustration. The alien's explanations were still about as clear as the Coal Sack Nebula.

Shar quickly scanned Nog, then shut the device down. "I think I understand at least part of what our guest is trying to tell us, Captain," he said. "Those peculiar quantum resonance patterns that each member of the shuttle crew is exhibiting seem to be growing steadily more extreme hour by hour."

Vaughn wasn't sure, but he thought he liked Sacagawea's explanation better. It, at least, had been somewhat poetic. "Explain."

Shar adopted a polite, not quite pedantic lecture-hall tone. "When a person's quantum resonance patterns drift far enough from normal, that person can become incompatible with the quantum signature of our universe. Imagine becoming 'unmoored' from our universe because of a quantum-level conflict. You would be hurled randomly into some alternate world."

Vaughn recalled some of the mission files he had read during his brief time aboard the *Enterprise* shortly before coming to DS9. About six years ago, a member of Jean-Luc Picard's crew had experienced something quite similar.

"Are the shuttle personnel showing any signs of . . . 'unmooring' anytime soon?"

Shar sighed, obviously frustrated by his paucity of hard information. "Not that I can tell. But as the effect progresses, who knows?"

Vaughn glanced briefly at Nog, who was shifting his weight anxiously from his old foot to his new one. He was clearly not enjoying the discussion, and seemed to be avoiding looking directly at either Ezri or Bashir.

Vaughn turned back to Shar. "Maybe those quantum signature readings show that something else is going on. Instead of being sent to some parallel world, maybe everyone affected is gradually transforming into some alternate self. For instance, a Julian Bashir whose genes were never resequenced." To Nog he said, "Like the one from the alternate universe that your father and uncle visited last year."

Ezri was nodding. "Or an Ezri Tigan who never joined with Dax."

"Or a Nog who listened to his uncle and went to business school instead of Starfleet Academy," Nog said, regarding his left leg with a wistful expression.

Shar pursed his lips as he considered the idea. "I'll grant that it's possible. But given the increasing flux in the quantum resonance readings, I can't rule out any sudden, permanent disappearances."

Vaughn sighed. "Lovely." Approaching Sacagawea again, he said, "How do we . . . realign these 'world-lines'?"

"Ingress to the cathedral/anathema," Sacagawea said. "Only inside may the four afflicted ones be resolved/re-stored. Only the four may enter. Others will be mis-aligned, ending badly."

Four?

"Hold it," Nog said, obviously having noticed the same discrepancy that had caught Vaughn's attention. "There were only *three* people aboard the *Sagan*."

Vaughn saw that Ezri was quietly shaking her head. She raised her hand and pointed across the room toward a gurney. On the gurney, the Dax symbiont's nutrient tank sat, evidently in preparation for a medical examination.

Four afflicted ones, Vaughn thought, understanding.

"Oh," Nog said.

"The four afflicted ones need/require ingress to cathedral/anathema," Sacagawea said. "While time per-sists/endures/lasts."

"Before it's too late," Vaughn whispered. Though he had nothing to go on other than the D'Naali's words and his own growing conviction, he felt more certain than ever that the key to everything lay somewhere within the artifact's enigmatic depths.

It's either there or nowhere.

"Okay," Ezri said. "Now we just have to get around that blockade."

"Option nonexistent," Sacagawea agreed, "to battle/ weapons discharge."

He's saying we have no alternative other than to fight. Vaughn was beginning to feel boxed in by circumstances. But he remained determined. A viable win-win scenario had to exist. He simply hadn't found it yet.

"Fighting's not our best option," he said at length. "Not with so many Nyazen tubes aimed right down our throats."

"Even if we *could* fight our way through the blockade," Ezri said, "what right would we have to do it? The Nyazen seem to be claiming the artifact, and they've already, ah, asked us to leave in no uncertain terms."

"That's not precisely how I see it, Lieutenant," Vaughn said, gently brushing her objection aside. "The jurisdictional issues seem to be in dispute here, at least from the D'Naali perspective. And since both the D'Naali and the Nyazen are spacefaring species, the Prime Directive doesn't apply."

Which means it falls to me to cut the Gordian knot.

"So what are you going to do?" Ezri said.

Vaughn knew without looking that everyone's eyes were upon him. He chose his words with great care before beginning to speak. "If I have to, I'll fight my way out of this and sort it all out with Starfleet later. But only *after* I've tried every other alternative."

Ezri and Ensign Richter both appeared relieved. Sacagawea was, as usual, unreadable, though Vaughn assumed that the alien was listening with a great deal more attentiveness than was apparent. Bashir merely looked bewildered, though he was clearly trying to appear brave—perhaps for Ezri's benefit.

Nog seemed fairly beside himself with the need to say something.

"I am not eager to belabor this point, Captain," Shar said, his features drawn and solemn. "But our alternatives are fairly limited. Fighting may become inevitable."

A brilliant, snaggle-toothed grin spread across Nog's face then. "Why fight over the front door," he said, "when you can just . . . sneak in through the back?"

Vaughn returned the grin as all heads, including Sacagawea's, turned expectantly toward the chief engineer.

16

Solis Tendren noticed right away that many of the vedeks were missing from this regularly scheduled meeting. The Vedek Assembly chamber was barely half full, and some of those in the room were ranjens, not vedeks. Most of the others had already departed for Deep Space 9 to witness the signing ceremony; many of the ministers were now on their way there as well.

Vedek Yevir, however, was conspicuous by his absence from either location. Bellis Nerani had a holonotarized document from Yevir, giving the vedek the right to act as the would-be kai's proxy during the Assembly's votes. Solis found it interesting that all of the other members of Yevir's inner circle were present; he knew that Bellis, Eran Dal, Frelan Syla, Scio Marses, Kyli Shon, and Sinchante Jin all sided with Yevir in virtually everything. They always voted the same way, a steadfast conservative bloc whose unified voice unwaveringly supported the strictest of orthodox positions.

This presented an unusual challenge to Solis. Each member of Yevir's cabal was a high-ranking vedek; frail Frelan was one of the oldest members of the Assembly, and she was fond of reminding the younger members that she had been a fixture in the clerical leadership hierarchy while they were still toddlers. Scio seemed malleable, willing to follow the prevailing beliefs of his fellows. Kyli was a thoughtful woman of middle years, who was willing at least to appear to consider divergent opinions, while Sinchante—also a middle-aged woman—was both pious and something of a zealot. Solis found Bellis to be noxious, a man with whom it was difficult to converse for any length of time, much less to debate on the Assembly floor. Shiny-pated Vedek Eran seemed the most open-minded of the lot, though Solis suspected that he had higher political ambitions than he let on.

Despite the lack of attendees—or perhaps because of it—the meeting had run longer than usual. Eran chaired the Assembly today, a role he had been taking on more and more often of late. They had discussed the effect that the Europani refugees were having on the Northwest Peninsula lands to which they had been temporarily relocated; the local water tables were falling, and food supplies were stretched to the limit. The matter was not yet a catastrophe, but was a cause for real concern.

Solis sighed. *Would that we had been as generous with those lands when those Skrreean farmers had asked to settle there seven years ago. Those lands would be supplying food and water in abundance by now.*

Next, Vedek Teetow had brought up some nonsense about a girl in his temple who claimed to have seen a vision of a Prophet in her flour-cakes; the Assembly had been ready to dismiss the topic out of hand until he also

claimed that she had—after experiencing the vision—
healed several people in her village who still suffered
from lingering war wounds. That spurred another
lengthy discussion about what to do with the apparently
gifted child.

Vedek Grenchen—an amiable man whom Solis always suspected had become a vedek because he loved
the pageantry and embroidered robes almost as much as
he did the Prophets—brought up the coming celebrations marking Bajor's entry into the Federation. Most of
the public parades and parties were scheduled to begin
approximately a month after the signing of the treaty, in
deference to those partaking of the abstemious rites of
the Bajoran Time of Cleansing. Grenchen felt that a new
annual holiday should be declared on Bajor, a symbolic
day on which the people could celebrate their role in the
greater fabric of the galaxy. Most of the vedeks seemed
to be in agreement with Grenchen, but the topic was
tabled until a full meeting of the Assembly could be
convened.

"Is there any final business before we adjourn?" Eran
asked, looking around the chamber to see if there were
any hands on the tables, which would signify a desire to
address the Assembly. Slowly but firmly, Solis put his
hands out. Eran saw him, and Solis saw a momentary
flash of hostility in his eyes. "Yes, Vedek Solis?"

Solis rose, gathering his robes around him. All eyes
turned to him, some with great suspicion. Since he had
publicly embraced the prophecies of Ohalu and announced his candidacy for kaiship, he found that his
presence among the Bajoran people had become an increasingly polarizing one; people were largely either
with him or against him, while but a few remained completely undecided. This held true with the vedeks as

well, and it was to those undecided clerics that he felt he had to appeal most carefully.

"We are now, as a people, looking to the future, and to what that future will bring," Solis said, looking each of the vedeks in the eyes in turn. "By joining the Federation, we are attuning ourselves to a presence in the galaxy greater than our own. Every sentient species on each of the planets within the Federation has a history, a tradition, a set of 'old ways.' Some of these have the potential for coming into great conflict with each other. There are people in the Federation who believe in a single god who created everything in the universe, who rules from a heaven above them. Others believe in a pantheon of gods and goddesses, each representative of an element of their lives. Others believe that there are *no* gods, that life itself is a cosmic happenstance. Still others believe that they may become gods themselves, if they work to perfect themselves during their lives.

"These are but a very few of the personal belief systems held by the peoples we will be joining within the Federation. That body is a diverse and ever-expanding construct, filled with people who are deeply religious as well as those who are indifferent, atheistic, or agnostic. We are about to become a people who side with *all* these others, whether pious, mystic, or empirical, peoples who share a common bond and goal of peace and exploration and growth."

Although a few vedeks were actively scowling at him, Solis saw several more nodding, even if barely. He continued. "Here on Bajor, the belief in our Prophets is what drives our people. And though we sometimes deny it, Bajor *is* ruled by its theocracy. The Chamber of Ministers is filled with Bajor's faithful, most of whom attend services conducted by some of us who are gathered here today. Even our planet's name is based upon our religious beliefs. If things had gone differently millennia ago, our people might be known as Perikians or Endtreeans. But we are *Bajorans*. Our faith *defines* us.

"But how do *we* define our *faith?* Does faith mean an unwavering, unquestioning belief in the doctrine of the Prophets? Or do we often question, often interpret what we believe the Will of the Prophets to be? How many of us saw the Occupation as the will of the Prophets, some horrifying test that we had to endure? How many of us saw it as a moment in time when the Prophets had abandoned us, or had chosen to punish us? And yet, even if we believed those things, we did not lose our faith; we merely interpreted events in ways that buoyed that faith.

"Most of us here today, even the ranjens, have experienced the power of the Prophets through the Orbs. The Orbs represent a tangible, tactile, physical proof that there is something beyond Bajor with a power greater than ours, a power to shape reality, to destroy, and to create.

"But we leave these Orb experiences with our own personal interpretations of what the Prophets are trying to tell us. Never have They handed us specific guidelines, and yet all too often, when we come away from the Orbs, our *interpretation* of our communion with the Prophets becomes Bajor's received wisdom. We use what we *feel* from the Prophets to guide our world. We act as the translators of Their wishes."

Solis paused for a moment, clearing his throat. He could see Bellis glaring at him, muttering under his mustache. He pressed on. "As we join the Federation, we combine with more than one hundred fifty other worlds, and hundreds of billions of people, all of whom have their own belief systems and faiths. We are not proselytizing to them about the Prophets because we recognize that their beliefs differ from ours. From their perspectives, their own beliefs are just as valid as our own. And truthfully, in this wonderful, vast galaxy of limitless possibilities, who among us can say that the gods of Andorians and Betazoids and humans are not as real as we know the Prophets to be?

"So now, in this time of joining and openness, the political and religious leaders of Bajor have many pressing concerns. We are standing at a physical and metaphysical crossroads, and we must choose which way to lead our people. Our animosity toward Cardassia may finally be at an end, but will we continue down the path of peace, or will we instead allow our grief and anger and Occupation-era grudges to block our way? And our faith in the Prophets is being questioned by those who propose that the prophecies contained in the Book of Ohalu should be given credence and legitimacy. Will we allow our people to question their beliefs, to question the Prophets, to emerge with their faith changed or renewed?"

Bellis stood, interrupting him. "We know that you lead this so-called Ohalavaru movement, Solis. Your liberal platitudes may have a place on the street, or in your own gatherings, but they are *heresy* in this hallowed place."

"Is your faith in the Prophets so fragile, Vedek Bellis, that you cannot hear the words of others whose opinions might diverge from your own?" Solis's voice remained firm, and he smiled beneficently at the vedeks arrayed about him in the semicircular chamber. Bellis sat down heavily, harumphing as he came to rest.

Solis continued. "I know one person whose faith in the Prophets is strong, perhaps as strong as any of ours . . . and certainly stronger than *some* of ours. Her *pagh* is incandescent, her actions always, *always* governed by her feelings for the Bajoran people. I have not always agreed with those actions over the years, and I know that many of you have had your squabbles with her as well. And yet, through it all, her belief and her faith and her intent have always been noble.

"Kira Nerys is one of the *best* of us. I am humbled to know her. And I don't find it at all surprising that the Emissary and his wife hold her in such high regard. Weeks ago, the wife of the Emissary all but cast Vedek Yevir out of her house, even as she welcomed Kira in her home to stay and recuperate from deep wounds. These are wounds which *we* have inflicted upon her, injuries to her standing among Bajorans, the military, and the faithful. We have Attainted her, cast her out of our faith."

Solis brought his hands together in front of himself, clasping them in a gesture of supplication. "This overly harsh sanction is an outrage that shocks the conscience of our world. It threatens to divide our people more than the words of Ohalu, which Kira liberated, ever could."

He paused, then delivered his final thoughts. "I *implore* you, my fellow Vedeks, to rescind the Attainder of Kira Nerys. I know that *she* has not lost faith in the Prophets. Please don't allow the people of Bajor to lose *their* faith in the Prophets—or in *us*—because of our unjustly punitive actions."

Solis sat down, suddenly weary. Around the chamber, he saw many contemplative faces. A few heads were bobbing up and down in agreement, while others shook in furious negation.

With a deep intake of breath, Vedek Eran called for a vote.

As Mika entered the room, she saw the Assembly's decision etched clearly on Solis's careworn face. The flickering candlelight reflected in the tears that rolled slowly down his cheeks.

"Uncle, you did your best," she said, crouching down near him. "All who heard your words were moved."

He snorted, wiping at his cheek. "Not moved enough, it seems. Nor necessarily in the right direction. I fear that my words may have deepened the divide."

"No," she said. When he looked away, she grasped his jaw in her hand, forcing him to look at her. *"No,"* she repeated, more emphatically. "You spoke eloquently and truthfully. *They* are the ones who have chosen to estrange those of us who question. If there truly is a divide, then it is the Vedek Assembly majority that has torn it wider."

He sniffed, and managed a weak smile. "At least the vote was a fraction closer this time."

She smiled too, and caressed his cheek with the back of her hand. "Yes, it was. And perhaps if the full Assembly had been present, you would have swayed more of them. But nowhere near enough, I fear. Vedeks can be a stubborn lot."

He made no argument with her gentle dig. "Some of the others will change their minds in time," he said, nodding. "After their fear of us subsides. After we have been in the Federation for a while and the majority finally realizes that Bajor has not fallen from its orbit because of our presence."

Mika's child toddled into the room through the open doorway and cooed, smiling and running over to throw his arms around Solis's legs.

Solis lifted the half-Cardassian child and hugged him back, looking over the boy's head into Mika's eyes. "I fear that by the time they change their minds, it will be too late. I won't let the matter drop, child. I will bring the colonel's cause up at the next Assembly session. And the one after that, and the one after that."

Mika shook her head. "That approach will take years. I owe Kira my life, and the life of my son. And we both owe Kira for preserving the prophecies of Ohalu. *Now* is the time to act directly. To do something decisive to let the vedeks and ministers know that the people are not willing to allow Kira to be cast aside."

Solis set the boy down and placed a hand on Mika's shoulder. "Please, don't do anything foolish. You have a child to consider now. Not to mention the rest of the Ohalavaru, who are in sore need of leaders."

"I believe that the Prophets have already decided whose actions are foolish." She scooped up her son, then kissed Solis on the forehead.

"Don't worry, uncle. What needs to be done will be done. I owe Kira and the Prophets no less."

Mika turned and walked out of the room, her retreating form casting long shadows across the candle-lit wall.

17

Chief medical officer's personal log, stardate 53579.0

I probably shouldn't be thinking of any of these recordings as "medical logs" anymore, since I can't call myself a doctor any longer. Not really. But I know that people trust doctors. They place a lot of faith in them, and faith can help people do whatever they have to get done. So if it will help Ezri and Nog and everybody else aboard this ship to get through whatever hell is coming, I'm willing to try to swallow this fear that makes me quake whenever I think about it. I'm willing to play along, and let everyone pretend I'm the wise, competent doctor, even though I might as well be little Jules stitching up poor Kukalaka's leg with sewing thread. I'm willing to keep at it, until the fear finally consumes me. Or whatever's left of me.

In the meantime, I'll be thankful that Saca-

gawea doesn't really need a doctor anymore. And I'll hope to God that nobody gets sick or injured and ends up really needing one.

After Nog had laid out the bare bones of his plan, then left the medical bay to prepare his detailed briefing for the senior staff, Ezri decided that she couldn't wait any longer to tell Commander Vaughn exactly what was on her mind. She began by asking to speak to him privately in his ready room. He nodded his assent, but his impassive face betrayed no emotion. Leaving Krissten to keep Julian occupied with another "examination" of their D'Naali guest, Ezri and Vaughn walked down the corridor in silence.

Once the ready room door had closed behind them, he turned to her, his face hard and determined.

"No," Vaughn said.

Surprised, Ezri took a quick step back. "Don't you want to hear what I have to say first?"

"It's not hard to guess what's on your mind. And before you make your request, I want you to know that the answer will be a firm 'no.' I will *not* relieve you of duty."

"Even though lifetimes of expertise have literally leaked right out of me."

"I need you as my first officer. Now more than ever, you've got to be my steady right hand."

Frustration and despair constricted Ezri's temples. It felt as though her spots were on too tight. "Sir, without Dax I'm no good to you. I can't contribute anything to the mission. I might even put it in danger."

Vaughn sat on the desk and stared up into a corner. His eyes seemed focused on something light-years away. As the silence stretched, she expected him to blow up at her, the way Benjamin Sisko had when she had tried to transfer from DS9 after her apparent failure to help Mr. Garak cope with his claustrophobia during the war. She'd been wrong then. But the circumstances had been very different.

That day, she'd still had Dax.

When Vaughn finally spoke, his voice was incongruously gentle. "You couldn't be more wrong, Lieutenant."

"But I can't help Nog and Shar get around the blockade," she said, taken aback by his softened demeanor.

He made a dismissive gesture, waving her protests away. "That matters a lot less than you'd think."

She scowled. "With all due respect, sir, we're not going to get past those Nyazen ships with kind wishes."

"Not entirely," he said with a chuckle. "Kind wishes and a duranium truncheon usually work better than kind wishes do all by themselves. But that's not what we're really talking about here."

"What *are* we talking about?"

"Your experiences. Not Dax's. *Yours*. The ones that you, Ezri Tigan, have had while wearing that command uniform. The expertise you've gathered over the last few months belongs to you at least as much as it does to Dax. And Dax didn't play any role at all in your Starfleet Academy training, or your career up until the end of your stint aboard the *Destiny*."

Ezri paused to consider his words. "I'll grant you that. But so much of what Ezri Dax was came from the other hosts, and *their* experiences."

"Which you found valuable, right?"

She was starting to think he was deliberately trying to goad her. "Of *course* I did. Joined Trills always integrate the personalities of the previous hosts into their symbioses. At least the healthy ones do. And they come to depend on them."

262

He folded his arms. "And why do you suppose that is, Lieutenant?"

"Because . . ." she stopped, finally understanding where this was leading. "Because each host brings something unique to the symbiosis."

He offered a paternal smile. *"Each* host. Not just Lela, or Audrid, or Curzon, or Jadzia. That list of unique worthies includes Ezri, too. The way I see it, the most critical part of a Trill joining isn't the slug in your belly—it's the walking, talking person who joins with it, nurtures it, and gives it the means to interact with the rest of the universe."

Shame wrestled with insecurity inside her. "I understand what you're saying, sir. And I appreciate it. But what if I still can't measure up without Dax? Let's face it, solving my problem is going to be a little harder than handing me some gadget I no longer know how to use and kidding everyone that I'm still able to pull my own weight around here. That might work for Julian at the moment, but—"

Vaughn stepped down hard on her words. "Julian needs to keep occupied for the sake of his *own* morale. *You* need to keep occupied for the sake of everybody else's."

She shook her head in confusion. "I'm not following you."

"We're talking about esprit de corps, Lieutenant. Morale. Specifically, that of Nog, Shar, Tenmei, T'rb, Cassini, Permenter, Hunter, Candlewood, Leishman, VanBuskirk, and whoever the hell else it'll take to finally get us inside that artifact. If you drop out of sight because of your own perceived shortcomings, how do you think that will affect *their* work?"

Ezri's mouth fell open. She hadn't considered that. And the fact that she hadn't considered that seemed to her a good argument in favor of removing her name from the active duty roster.

But she also understood that he was right.

"So you're staying put, Lieutenant," he continued, his gaze and voice hardening back into tempered steel. "That's a direct order. You *are* still capable of following orders, aren't you?"

Her despair began to abate as she came to a realization: Her ability to follow orders was perhaps the only thing about herself in which she still had any real confidence.

She offered him a small wry smile, sensing that Vaughn's gift for saying precisely the right thing at exactly the right time rivaled even that of Benjamin Sisko. Perhaps such bluntly honest and uncompromising counseling skills were one of the chief prerequisites for a career in command.

"Request permission to return to my post, Captain. I need to get ready for the blockade briefing."

Though Vaughn's craggy face remained hard, Ezri saw the warmth in his piercing blue eyes. At the same time, she felt tears of gratitude beginning to well up in her own.

"Permission granted, Lieutenant," he said. "Dismissed."

Barely an hour after he had left the medical bay with the essence of his novel blockade-busting plan percolating in his thoughts, Nog began to feel confident that his scheme might actually work. He only hoped that Commander Vaughn would have as much faith in the idea as he did.

He also found that concentrating on that hope helped him avoid dwelling on the consequences of success—consequences of which he was reminded every time he put his weight squarely on his regenerated left leg.

Regardless, when Vaughn scheduled a technical briefing for the senior staff at 0800 the next morning,

Nog felt that he was ready, his fears and misgivings notwithstanding.

Nog strode into the mess hall, where Vaughn, Ezri, and Shar were arranging themselves around the room's largest table. Also present was Dr. Bashir, who sat with his hands folded in his lap, conspicuously silent amid the low conversational murmur that filled the room. Though he was shaved and his hair was combed, he still had a hollow, haunted look about him that made Nog shiver inwardly. The doctor glanced occasionally toward Ezri, who was seated at his right, and at Sacagawea, who occupied a specially constructed chair on his left. The towering, slender alien seemed intensely curious, swiveling its great head in every direction as though taking great care to miss nothing. As he took a seat almost directly across the table from Sacagawea, Nog wondered how much of the proceedings the alien would understand—and exactly what Commander Vaughn believed their D'Naali guide could contribute to the briefing.

Seated near Tenmei, Shar, and science specialist T'rb, Bowers stared with obvious unease across the table at Sacagawea. Turning toward the head of the table, he addressed Vaughn. "Captain, are you sure it's appropriate for Sacagawea to attend this meeting?"

A look of sadness crossed Vaughn's features, then vanished behind the façade of command. "I do, Lieutenant. Our guest requires Dr. Bashir's constant attention." Vaughn looked significantly in Bowers's direction, and the tactical officer immediately seemed to grasp his meaning.

It's really the other way around, Nog realized a moment later. *Having the alien nearby must be keeping the doctor calm.* Trying not to stare, he watched as Bashir placed a hand on the table. It was impossible not to notice the hand's slight tremor. Or Ezri, as she placed her hand atop the doctor's while offering him chatty reassurances that soon, *very soon,* everything would be all right. He wondered if she was trying to be strong for them both, or if she was leaning on the doctor for support.

Once again, Nog felt a sensation of intense guilt welling up inside him. Two of his closest friends had been torn to pieces, maimed by the alien artifact. Perhaps forever. *I, on the other hand, get restored to perfect condition. At least until we get Sacagawea's "worldlines" untangled.*

"I said we're ready whenever you are, Lieutenant," Vaughn was saying, his impatient tone bringing Nog out of his reverie like a sudden Ferenginar cloudburst.

Nog felt like a cadet who'd turned up for inspection late and out of uniform. It took him a moment to gather his thoughts. "Yes, sir. I wanted to start by saying that Ensign ch'Thane has double-checked my figures, as have specialists T'rb, Hunter, and other members of the science and engineering teams involved." Nog was gratified to see that Shar and T'rb were both nodding. A wide smile bisected T'rb's cyan-hued Bolian features.

"And I'll give it an official thumbs-up from a tactical perspective," Bowers said. "At least, that's how it looks on the padd."

"Sounds chancy to me," Tenmei said, laying aside a padd that displayed some of Nog's numbers. "What you're essentially proposing is that we use a series of large Oort cloud bodies as relays for the *Defiant's* transporter."

"Actually," Nog said, "those frozen rocks will act as platforms for a series of self-replicating transporter relays, which we'll send out ahead of our away team. We'll beam the first one out to the nearest cometary body, and it will beam another relay out to the next body, and so on."

"It sounds too easy," Tenmei said. "There's got to be a huge power cost associated with doing something like this."

Shar nodded. "You're correct. The drain on the *Defiant*'s replicator systems will be enormous. Setting up the transporter relay system will burn out the central replicator waveguides."

"Meaning we'll be without replicator technology for the rest of the voyage," Nog said.

Vaughn appeared to take the news in stride. "It's a small price to pay if it means restoring our friends. Besides, the cargo bays are adequately stocked with field rations and spare parts. If the plan works, I'm sure that we're all prepared to 'rough it' until we're back home." He looked around the room, apparently looking for objections. There were none.

"The whole idea reminds me," Bowers said, "of the self-replicating mines Starfleet set up outside the wormhole during the war to discourage the Dominion from bringing reinforcements into the Alpha Quadrant."

Nog swelled with familial pride. Those mines had been conceived by his father, Rom, the year before he became the grand nagus of the Ferengi Alliance.

"That's partly where I got the idea," Nog said. "It's also a natural extension of something I was already researching when we took the *Sagan* into the Oort cloud in the first place. Originally, I thought that the crystal lattice structures of the cloud's comet fragments might be used as natural high-bandwidth enhancers for extending the range of our sensor beams. But when we almost collided with the alien artifact, we discovered that those crystalline bodies have another interesting property: Their subspace resonance patterns function like natural cloaking devices. Which is why we were almost right on top of the artifact before we even saw it."

Shar set aside the padd he'd been studying, his eyebrows and antennae raised in evident admiration of Nog's plan. "So this cloaking effect should prevent the Nyazen from detecting our away team's transporter beam as it moves from relay to relay through the Oort cloud."

"Possibly," Nog said. "It's a natural effect, so we can't count on it working perfectly. But it should cover our tracks well enough to let us slip our away team onto the artifact from extreme range. If we're lucky, the blockade ships will never even suspect what we're up to. And we only need to be within transporter range of the first relay station to do it. The other relay stations in the series will take care of the rest of the transport."

Tenmei looked skeptical. "As long as your figures aren't off. You've got to take into account all of the mutual motions and gravitational interactions of all the comets and planetesimals in that part of the Oort cloud."

"That was the hardest part," Nog said, nodding. "But everyone seems to agree that my numbers check out."

"I hope you're right," she said. "But we're not going to know for sure until a real live away team steps into harm's way."

"So the first big question is, Who gets to join this away team?" Bowers said.

"The original *Sagan* crew, of course," Vaughn said. "Ezri, the Dax symbiont, Nog, and Dr. Bashir."

Bowers frowned. "I have to point out that we have no idea what's inside that artifact. I'd feel more comfortable if some security or tactical personnel were going along. I'm volunteering, by the way."

"I appreciate that, but no," Vaughn said in a tone that

did not invite debate. "Only the shuttle crew will beam over. I'm not going to put more people at risk." Bowers subsided, though he still looked unhappy. Nog was mildly surprised to note that Vaughn had apparently taken to heart Sacagawea's warning that only the original *Sagan* crew should venture onto the artifact.

On the other hand, what choice does he have but to believe? What choice does any *of us have?*

"The next big question is," Ezri said, "Will it work?" Nog thought she sounded remarkably self-possessed. Still, his sensitive lobes detected a trace of well-concealed distress in her voice. He couldn't help but admire her toughness.

"I am confident that this is going to work," Nog said, his eyes locked with Ezri's. "And we can be ready to deploy the first self-replicating transporter relay after Shar and I finish programming the prototype. It'll take maybe three hours, tops."

"The procedure is actually somewhat simpler than the mathematics would make it appear," T'rb said.

"Unless you happen to be one of the people standing on the transporter pad," Ezri parried gently. "Nog's plan calls for the transporter relays to be beamed ahead of the away team by just a second or two. That's pretty slim timing."

"If we don't beam the relays out at essentially the same time as we send the away team," Shar pointed out, "the Nyazen ships are much likelier to discover what we're trying to do and launch an attack before we can carry off the mission."

"But it's risky," Ezri said. "The only test of the transporter relay series will be in actual use."

Shar nodded, conceding her point. "I admit that there is a . . . nonzero possibility that one of the relays might fail during operation, or that the transporter beam carrying either a relay or the away team might be diffracted or scattered by the internal crystalline structure of one of the Oort cloud bodies. Either of those eventualities, of course, would immediately kill the away team. Also, if any of our coordinate lock calculations contain errors—"

"Just how much of a 'nonzero possibility' are we talking about here?" Tenmei wanted to know.

Shar's antennae were nearly flat against his head. Nog knew he hated to be pinned down like that, with so many chaotic variables at play.

"If I were a betting man," Nog said, answering first, "I'd lay odds of seventeen or eighteen in twenty in favor of our surviving the process." *The riskier the road, the greater the profit.*

"I agree," Shar said.

Vaughn sat in silence, mulling it all over. He didn't look happy with the odds, as good as they were. For a moment, Nog feared that he was about to be sent back to the drawing board again. Vaughn appeared to be about to speak—

—when Nog realized all at once that he was *elsewhere*. He was outside, standing on a city street, a warm rain running down his face. He looked up into the darkening sky and saw the Tower of Commerce looming above him.

"Come along, Nog!" the scowling woman in front of him said. She was middle-aged, and nude in the old-guard fashion of Ferengi females. He recognized her with a start.

Prinadora!

He looked down at his clothing, and saw that drab green Ferengi street clothes had replaced his Starfleet uniform.

Starfleet. He laughed at himself for even entertaining

such a foolish hew-mon notion. Ever since his father's death at the hands of the Cardassians had forced him to leave Terok Nor, he had been so busy cleaning up his mother's financial messes that—

The *Defiant*'s mess hall suddenly returned, and almost everyone's face was a study in incredulity. Tenmei was opening up a tricorder.

"It wasn't a bad place at all," Bashir said, looking disoriented. "Not the way I expected."

"I was back on the *Destiny*," Ezri said, owl-eyed.

"What just happened?" Nog said, his voice a harsh whisper.

"The three of you," Bowers said, almost stammering, "you, Lieutenant, ah, Tigan, and Dr. Bashir—you all just . . . *vanished*."

Tenmei stood, carefully scanning the room with her tricorder. "For almost one second," she said, "your quantum signatures synced up with some other nearby parallel universes. It's another sign of your increasing quantum fluctuations. Fortunately you all snapped back to this reality as part of the oscillation. But there's no guarantee you'll be so lucky next time."

"Well," Vaughn said quietly. "We couldn't have asked for a better demonstration of the consequences of doing nothing."

"I don't know about anybody else here," Ezri said, "but I think I'd prefer the risk of scrambling my molecules to ending up in some random parallel universe. Or to the way I'm living right now, for that matter. I say we get on with it."

Nog couldn't see any better alternative either. "I have to agree."

Tenmei didn't look convinced. "And once you're aboard the artifact—what then?"

That question seemed to bring Ezri up short, at least for a moment. Nog realized then that he hadn't thought that far ahead himself. He looked across the table at the inscrutable alien, as though the answer might reveal itself in the creature's large, oil-black eyes.

"You will realign your worldlines," Sacagawea said with surprising clarity. "Restore yourselves, you will. Or in the attempt, perish/disperse."

No one spoke for almost another minute, and it was Commander Vaughn who finally broke the silence.

"There are times when we have to take certain things on faith. Considering our other alternatives—which consist of either doing nothing and losing the *Sagan* crew forever, or starting a fight with the Nyazen that we can't win—I'm forced to conclude that this is one of those times. Mr. Nog?"

"Sir?"

Vaughn stood up, signaling that the briefing was coming to an end. "I want you and Shar to see to whatever technical preparations remain to be made. Let's get busy."

Bashir startled everyone by choosing that moment to speak. His earnest brown eyes were trained on Sacagawea as he said, "Why would anyone worship a thing that can destroy entire worlds?"

That struck Nog as an excellent question, though he hadn't given the matter much thought before now. Sacagawea merely sat impassively, showing no overt evidence of having even understood the question.

"Many ancient Earth religions were built around some rather fearsome, angry gods," Vaughn said. He sat once again, keeping a weather eye on the doctor as he continued. "Maybe the D'Naali and the Nyazen have developed similar belief systems."

Ezri nodded in agreement. "That fits with everything we've seen so far. And it might explain their confusion about whether that artifact out there is a 'cathedral' or an 'anathema.' My guess is that they have a sort of love-hate relationship with whatever gods they worship."

Again, Sacagawea said nothing, though the creature was looking in Ezri's direction. The D'Naali either did not understand the drift of the discussion, or it was keeping its thoughts to itself.

Shar was scowling. "How much faith are *we* prepared to place in this alien religion?"

"Do we really have any other choice?" Vaughn said. Everyone rose, most of them clearly anxious to see Nog's calculations finally put to some practical use.

"So the Kukalakans worship monsters," Bashir said to Ezri in a plaintive, almost singsong voice. She took his hand again. "I wonder if any of them will be waiting for us inside the cathedral."

Ezri's reply was quiet, but not quiet enough to elude Nog's sensitive Ferengi hearing. "I'll be right beside you, Julian. And there aren't *really* any monsters."

Images of Taran'atar, Kitana'klan, and the Jem'Hadar hordes who took his leg at AR-558 sprang without warning to Nog's mind. He wasn't at all certain he agreed with Ezri's reassurances.

Bashir didn't look completely convinced either. But Nog saw no sign of panic on the doctor's face. Despite his obviously stressed, diminished state, Bashir still seemed prepared to face whatever terrors awaited them all within the alien structure.

As Vaughn adjourned the meeting and dispatched everyone to their various tasks, Nog resolved that he could do no less. With Shar at his side, he walked briskly toward transporter bay one.

And tried very hard with every step not to think about his left leg.

Chief medical officer's personal log, stardate 53580.3

While we were sitting in the place where Ezri and I eat, and where the captain sometimes calls meetings, I went away. There was a flash of light, and I was . . . gone. Sam Bowers says it wasn't just a dream this time. He says we were actually off the ship, someplace else, for a second or two.

Sam says that Ezri and Nog went away, too. But they didn't seem very happy about wherever it was they went. Nobody seems to want to talk about it much, so I'm telling the computer about it instead of worrying my friends with this. They already seem to have plenty to worry about.

It seems like I spent years in the place I vanished into during those few moments Sam said I was gone. It was as though I'd stepped into a whole different life for myself. I was still Julian Bashir—maybe nothing that doesn't outright kill me can take that away—but I wasn't the same Julian Bashir everybody here knows. I wasn't a doctor, but I didn't seem to mind that. My days were filled with plenty of interesting things to do and a great many wonderful people to speak with. I was living on Earth, where everything anyone needs pops out of replicators. Lack of professional credentials isn't really a big issue in the heartland of the Federation the way it is in other places, after all. It was an alternate world, and I lived in it as an alternate Julian Bashir, although everybody there called me Jules, including my wife—who was also the mother of our two very happy, very healthy children, a boy of six and a girl of three.

It's funny. I haven't let anybody call me Jules since I first found out about my genetic enhancements as a teenager. That was when I started insisting that everyone call me Julian. From that time forward, I'd thought of Jules as dead, and never expected to hear from him again. But running into Jules again wasn't the most unexpected thing about my little trip. The biggest surprise was discovering that Jules seemed to be a fairly happy man with a lot of friends and family who cared about him.

I can't help but wonder which of us is better off, Jules or Julian. If I really am reverting into Jules, maybe I ought to stay this way.

18

Vedek Yevir had never paid much attention to his distaste for confinement, but he noticed that it had become unnaturally heightened ever since his visit to the crypts at the ancient city of B'hala months ago. Now, sealed into a bulky radiation suit and skulking about in the dust-choked streets and dim corridors of ruined Cardassia City's Munda'ar Sector, he was becoming keenly aware of his burgeoning feelings of claustrophobia.

The entire group had come to the shattered core of this vast, secret storage facility. Garak explained to them that the building had formerly been maintained by the Obsidian Order, Cardassia's powerful and deadly secret police. Nondescript from the outside, the squat gray building had apparently escaped obliteration during the Jem'Hadar bombing spree of the Dominion War's final blood-soaked hours—but not by much. Still, Yevir was surprised at the extent to which the building, holed and broken though it was, remained intact and standing, given the utterly pulverized condition of the surrounding structures.

Most of the members of the Oralian Way who had come along had remained above, standing guard throughout the facility, alert for the inopportune appearance of any of the Way's domestic political enemies. Only four of the combined group—Yevir, Macet, Garak, and Cleric Ekosha—had ventured into the subbasements. Yevir was quite surprised that the stout older woman was able to keep pace with the men, then reminded himself that neither he nor the two Cardassians were likely to be more than a decade and a half younger than she was.

Now the foursome was rappelling into the very bowels of the cracked and blasted structure—cautiously. Transporters were useless in this area, owing to the residual hard radiation levels, and not even Garak claimed to know for certain precisely what lay below them. The wrist- and belt-lights they all wore provided some illumination, but a dust-caked darkness seemed to close around them as they descended deeper. Every now and then, a fist-sized creature would come flying at them, apparently drawn by their lights—and obviously well adapted to radiation. Yevir hoped that the animals' predatory-looking teeth couldn't pierce their radiation suits, and that nothing larger awaited them further below. "They can't smell us through these suits, can they?" he finally asked, after the sixth flapping creature dove past them.

"The *utoxa?* No, they can't smell you," Garak said, from the other side of Macet. "There could be some *scottril* down there, though, and they'll be able to smell us easily, radiation suits notwithstanding. But phasers can stop them. *Usually.* If we see *them* before they see *us.*"

Yevir hoped that the Cardassian was smiling behind his face shield, but he couldn't tell for certain. *Prophets, protect me. You have not led me this far to allow me to fall to my death, or be eaten by a* scottril. *Whatever that might be.* His prayer comforted him slightly. Enough to get his feet and hands moving again.

"The pattern of destruction seems to intensify as we descend," Ekosha said, wonder and concern in her voice. "Are you certain anything could have survived this?"

"We have little more to proceed on than the word of Elim Garak, and our faith," Macet said in a wry tone.

"I'm not at all certain whether to be wounded or flattered, Macet," Garak responded. "But I must say I find your display of faith encouraging. There might be a place for you in the Oralian Way after all—if only you weren't quite so ugly."

Yevir heard Macet and Ekosha laugh, an incongruous sound filtering through their masks and the echoing darkness. Garak checked something on a wall panel, and a few meters below them several doors slid open. "We're nearly there," Garak said. "Drop down to the next level and I believe we will have arrived."

Once all four of them had disengaged from their climbing ropes, they took stock of the room around them. There were numerous computer banks and monitors, all powered down but glowing with the dim light Yevir recognized as a still-functional emergency power source; evidently the radiation levels here were not so severe as up above. Three heavily armed Cardassian guards lay dead, their decomposing bodies scattered around the room, phaser burns visible precisely at the most efficient kill points.

As Garak powered up the computers, punching a number of buttons, it dawned on Yevir that DS9's former tailor knew the system a little too well. He had clearly been here before. Had this been one of his previous postings, or had he been to this place more recently?

To their right, a few dim hallway lights came on, and a wall of interlaced metal bars shrank back into the walls. Down the hall, Yevir could see another dead guard near what was most likely the frame for a force-field barrier. It, too, was powered down. Finally, a giant metal door clanked partially open, spilling light from the chamber within.

"Ah. Here we are," Garak said.

Yevir moved forward first, passing the inactive security devices, stepping over the dead guard, and stopped at the door. He found he had to yank hard on the massive portal. The door slowly swung wide and the brilliance beyond it washed over him like a mighty river. As his eyes slowly adjusted, he finally began to see what lay within the vast, brightly lit chamber.

His faith rewarded, Yevir was filled with a rapture more intense than any joy he had ever known . . .

19

Chief medical officer's personal log, stardate 53580.5

Ezri tells me that all of us who were aboard the shuttle are about to go inside the big building we found floating out in space. Once we're inside, we might be able to find a way to fix what's wrong with me, and put Dax and Ezri back together.

I ask her whether this means Nog will go back to having to live with one leg. She won't answer me. I tell her that I don't see why Nog should have to lose his leg again, that it isn't fair. Why can't he stay home, on the Defiant, *while Ezri and I go? I can feel my heart thumping fast, and I'm afraid.*

Ezri's trying to hide it, but I can tell that she's afraid, too. And I want her not to be afraid so much that I pretend very hard that I'm not afraid.

Then I start thinking about Nog's leg again. I

*can remember having to cut it off the first time,
and the memory quickly makes me feel like crying.*

*I force myself not to cry because I don't want
her to be afraid. Because there's nothing worse
than being afraid.*

Shar made a final check of the readings on his bridge
science console, noting yet again that his calculations
remained in agreement with those of Nog, Candlewood,
T'rb, and the other science and engineering specialists.
The complex motions of the icy Oort cloud objects now
appeared to be a completely known quantity. The element of random chance had been reduced to as small
a margin as possible—excluding, of course, the inevitable, minuscule quantum-level variances and mea-
surement resolution errors that could always arise,
causing one transporter relay's signal to go awry, missing the next relay in the chain and thereby irrecoverably
scattering the away team's matter stream.

But he knew he could do nothing about any of those
things. Such risks became irreducible at some level, beyond the ken of either brain or computer.

Shar rose and turned toward Vaughn, who sat in the
captain's chair, an anxious glint in his eye.

"Is everything ready, Mr. ch'Thane?"

Shar hesitated a beat before answering. "Aye, Captain. Chief Chao has confirmed that the first self-
replicating transporter relay is already in place and
operational on the first Oort cloud body."

"You don't sound very confident, Ensign." Vaughn's
eyes narrowed.

"I'm sorry if I sound equivocal, sir. But as good as the
numbers look, we are still operating on the very margins
of what is possible. What we are about to attempt may

MICHAEL A. MARTIN AND ANDY MANGELS

work perfectly, or it may not. We still stand a good ten percent chance of losing everyone in the transporter beam. We have to face that."

"Ten percent," Vaughn said, frowning as he stroked his beard. "Versus the certainty of losing them if we don't move ahead with Nog's plan."

Sitting behind the conn station, Tenmei displayed a look of anxiety that clearly mirrored Vaughn's. Glancing at her chronometer, she said, "If we wait much longer, the cosmic rubber band will snap again and toss them into some other universe. Judging from the hourly increase in the quantum signature flux, it'll probably be permanent the next time it happens."

"Obviously," Shar said through clenched teeth. He was growing weary of having the obvious pointed out to him—or perhaps he was simply growing weary. "But I would still feel more comfortable if we were to beam some inanimate objects in and out of the . . . cathedral." He addressed his next words to Vaughn alone. "*Before* we attempt it on living people. Sir."

"Couldn't we use the first transporter relay to just replicate the entire series of relays needed to get the away team inside?" Tenmei asked. "That would be a good deal less risky than timing things so that the transporter relays materialize just ahead of the away team's transporter beam."

Vaughn looked thoughtful for a long moment, then shook his head. "If the Nyazen were to detect any use of the transporter too close to the cathedral, they'd most likely attack us right away. Then we'd never get a second opportunity to try to beam the away team in." The commander's gaze increased to an intensity that reminded Shar of his *zhavey*. "Give me your scientific appraisal, Ensign. In light of present circumstances, do the risks of proceeding appear acceptable to you?"

Shar knew well that the universe issued no guarantees, other than the eventual certainty of entropy and death. Nor did it care what became of starships, their clever engineers, or their intrepid crews.

Or the lives of three souls, now cast adrift. A trio of faces haunted him even now, weeping, glowering, raging. But these faces weren't those of Nog, Bashir, or Ezri. They belonged to Dizhei and Anichent.

And Thriss.

"Well, Ensign?" Vaughn said, an edge of impatience in his voice. Shar noticed that every pair of eyes on the bridge was trained on him.

"I can see no alternative, sir," Shar said. "We should proceed. With your permission, I'd like to assist Chief Chao and Lieutenant Bowers in transporter bay one."

Nodding, Vaughn said, "Granted."

As he entered the turbolift, Shar reflected on how little assistance he could actually offer at this point. The beam-out parameters were already set. The die had been cast. The operation would either save his friends or kill them. But at least he would have the opportunity first to bid them all farewell.

A privilege that Thriss had denied him.

Bowers felt his palms grow sweaty as he and Chief Jeannette Chao prepped the transporter console. Three of his colleagues—his *friends*—would shortly step onto the transporter pads and cast their fates to the whims of matter-stream physics that he didn't even pretend to understand.

Give me a life-or-death tactical situation involving photon torpedoes over this *any day.*

He watched quietly as Shar and an environmental-suited Nog entered the room, carrying between them the artificial-environment tank in which the Dax symbiont floated. Silently, they mounted the transporter platform and placed the bulky container onto one of the pads before stepping back down toward the console. Nog and Shar immediately began double-checking the settings Bowers had just entered, too preoccupied even to exchange greetings with him. Bowers didn't take it as an insult.

Ezri walked in with Dr. Bashir trudging beside her, both of them already clad in their EV suits, carrying their helmets at their sides. Ezri looked fairly anxious, which was to be expected. But the expression on the doctor's face gave Bowers pause. Though his eyes were huge and fearful, Bowers thought he could see a bedrock of courage in them as well.

Either he's made out of some pretty stern stuff, or he's not smart enough anymore to understand the danger he's about to step into. Still, Bowers wondered if Ezri was the one drawing emotional strength from Bashir, rather than the reverse.

Suddenly Bowers's vision was overcome by an intense assault. His eyes blinked furiously, but he could see nothing but white for several seconds. "What the hell was *that?*" he shouted, his vision slowly returning.

Still blinking through tearing eyes, Bowers could see Chao shaking her head as if to clear it. Shar had his tricorder out and was slowly turning in a semicircle as he scanned. "That appeared to be another quantum effect," he said, his antennae probing forward. "It was a sudden release of photons from other-dimensional space, caused by the shuttle crew's rapidly oscillating quantum signatures."

"I went someplace else again," Ezri said, evidently

unwilling to supply any details. She rubbed at her eyes with a thumb and forefinger.

"Me, too," Nog said, sounding anxious.

Bashir was silent, looking more bewildered than fearful.

"According to the ship's combadge monitors, you all vanished for almost one-point-five seconds," Shar said.

"I'll take that flash of light to mean that we've come to the end of our, um, dimensional tether," Nog said, his dazzled eyes still blinking rapidly. He patted the phaser on the side of his EV suit, evidently to reassure himself that it was still there. "We'd better get to the pads. *Now.*"

Ezri paused long enough to check her own phaser, then gingerly escorted Bashir onto the platform, helping him don his helmet and then putting on her own. She and Nog took turns checking the seals on all three EV suits. Then they took their places on pads flanking Dax's container, with Ezri standing beside Bashir. After Nog took a moment to confirm that the subspace transponder mounted on the symbiont's transport pod was operating, he signaled to Chief Chao that the away team was ready.

"Good luck," Shar said from beside the console. To Bowers's ear, it sounded more like a farewell.

Taking a deep breath, Chao energized the transporter. "Confirm activation of first transporter relay," she said. "It's transmitting its signal, beaming a second relay to the next Oort-cloud body in the sequence."

"Beam us out," Ezri said.

"Godspeed," Bowers whispered as the beam engulfed the four shapes on the platform.

Vaughn clutched the arms of the captain's chair so tightly that his fingers had grown numb. On the viewer before him was spread a velvet-black sky, bejeweled with countless points of light. In the left foreground drifted a computer-enhanced image of an icy, potato-shaped cometary body. To its right was a tactical image of the alien cathedral.

"The transporter beam's away," said Tenmei from the conn console, her voice businesslike and rock-steady.

"Passive scans confirm the beam has struck the first cometary body in the sequence," said T'rb, leaning forward over the science console. "The first transporter relay has redirected the beam precisely toward the next body in the line. And the away team's beam is right behind it."

For a seeming eternity, T'rb gave a running commentary as each new transporter relay appeared on a comet body closer to the artifact's position, followed in each instance a moment later by the arrival and retransmission of the away team's transporter beam. Reduced to a coherent stream of energetic particles, the *Sagan*'s crew was slowly working its way in an indirect, caroming zigzag pattern across a gulf of trackless space some ten million kilometers wide. With more than a little awe, Vaughn calculated that Nog and Shar had increased the transporter's range by a factor of about twenty-five.

"How's the signal attenuation, T'rb?" said John Candlewood from a secondary upper-bridge science console.

"Acceptable," T'rb said, his voice and manner bereft of their usual jocularity. "So far."

Moments later, Candlewood announced that the away team had just cleared the final relay—and that their transporter beam had finally reached the alien cathedral.

"Awaiting the combadge signals confirming beam-in, Captain," Ensign Merimark said from the tactical station. Vaughn knew that the same relay network that had sent the away team would also carry their combadge signals after the materialization had been completed.

Long moments elapsed, time slowly piling up in drifts around Vaughn. What had surely been half a minute or less since the beam-out had begun seemed to be taking hours. *We can't have failed. We can't have come this far only to scatter their molecules across the outskirts of some gods-forsaken Gamma Quadrant system.*

"Anything, Mr. Merimark?" Vaughn said, his voice scarcely above a whisper. The relief tactical officer turned in her seat to face him with a stricken expression, her hand on her earpiece.

"Nothing yet, sir. I—"

A strident klaxon interrupted her, in concert with the urgent flashing of an alarm indicator on her comm panel.

Merimark's smile was triumphant. "Confirming receipt of four tight-beam subspace blips, Captain." The bridge was suddenly awash in the sound of applause, and T'rb gave out an enthusiastic war whoop.

They're aboard the cathedral. Vaughn slumped backward in his chair, just for a moment. A tremendous weight had just fallen from his shoulders, though he knew that the mission was still far from complete.

"All right, people," Vaughn said as order quickly restored itself. "We still have the problem of recovering the away team once they signal that they're ready to leave."

If they can signal when they need an evac. And a great deal else can still go wrong between now and then.

"Mr. T'rb," Vaughn said, leaning forward and facing the science station. "Have the Nyazen blockade ships detected the away team's signals?"

After glancing quickly at the science panel, T'rb shook his head. "No, sir. Given the subspace vibrations of these Oort cloud bodies, it should have been pretty hard to distinguish them from the galactic subspace background noise—unless you happen to be listening for them, the way we were. It's highly unlikely that anybody else would even recognize them for what they were."

"It's also highly unlikely that three Starfleet officers would be yanked toward umpty-million parallel dimensions by an ancient alien construct," Vaughn said. Sometimes these brilliant science-specialist types needed to be reminded of the dangers of overconfidence.

"Aye, Captain," T'rb said, sounding chastened.

Addressing the entire bridge crew, Vaughn said, "Maintain yellow alert, but keep our shields down for the moment. Watch those Nyazen ships for any hostile moves. If they so much as dump their waste overboard, I want to know about it." He punched a button on the arm of his chair. "Vaughn to transporter bay one."

"Bowers here, Captain."

"Maintain a constant transporter lock on the away team."

"Not a problem, sir, unless we have to change our position in a hurry. But we can't maintain the lock if we're forced to move out of transporter range of the first relay unit."

"Let's hope it doesn't come to that. Vaughn out."

Merimark spoke up in alarmed tones. "Four of the Nyazen blockade ships have broken away from the main group, Captain. The Nyazen flagship is leading them. They're approaching us at high impulse speeds, close to warp one. They'll be on top of us in thirty seconds. And they're powering up their compression disruptors."

"Our shields can probably handle a simultaneous barrage from four of them, Captain," Tenmei said. "For a while, at least. But extensive combat maneuvering might break the transporter lock."

"The flagship is hailing us on subspace bands," Merimark said.

"On screen," Vaughn said.

The starscape fluttered for a fraction of a second, to be replaced almost instantly by a view of the bridge of the Nyazen flagship. It was a collection of blocky shapes whose functions were obscure. In the foreground stood—or perhaps sat—a blotchy, off-white figure, visible only from the shoulders up. An inarticulate bellow issued from the creature's oval mouth, and its whiplike limbs twirled in apparent outrage.

"Firing of weapons at the cathedral/anathema is not acceptable practice," shouted the Nyazen commander, its voice rendered into incongruously mellow, bell-like sounds by the universal translator. *"Withdraw from this system presently, or face decompression/discorporation."*

So they did *detect the transporter beam,* Vaughn thought, wondering if they possessed transporter technology themselves. Judging from their instant assumption of an attack, he concluded that they probably did not. But he also knew that he was in no position to tell the Nyazen the whole truth—not unless he wanted to provoke an angry reprisal by beings determined to protect their sacred object from outsiders.

Vaughn raised his hands in what he hoped his counterpart would see as a gesture of peace. "I assure you, we fired *no* weapons at the cathedral."

"Lies/prevarications," the alien said. *"Energy beams directed into cathedral/anathema originated on* your *vessel. Withdraw!"* The creature's image vanished.

"The Nyazen commander has closed the channel," Merimark said. "And they're opening fire!"

"Red alert! Evasive maneuvers!" Eight decades of

training and experience immediately shifted Vaughn from peacemaker to warrior.

Tenmei hastily tapped commands into her board, and the bridge shook fairly hard a moment later. Warning klaxons blared.

"Two direct hits on our forward shields," Merimark said. "But they're holding. Return fire?"

"Not yet. Mr. Bowers, how's the transporter lock?"

Bowers's voice came through the intercom, an agitated edge underlying it. "We're doing our best to maintain it, Captain. But we won't be able to keep it up much longer unless things settle down in a hurry."

"Understood."

"More of the Nyazen vessels are heading our way, Captain," Merimark said.

The bridge rocked again, more roughly this time; the viewer flared with a painful brightness, a half second ahead of the automatic light filters. "At least five direct hits, fore and amidships," Merimark said, one hand hovering over the weapons controls as she struggled to evade further hostile fire. "Shields down to eighty-two percent. Return fire?"

"No," Vaughn said. "Just stay ahead of them."

A deep rumbling sound briefly drowned out everything else, until Vaughn heard Merimark's shout rise above it. "Aft shields are down! Ablative shielding's taking some damage as well."

The tumult and noise faded somewhat, though Tenmei still worked frantically to evade the hostile fleet, obviously paying particular attention to safeguarding the newly vulnerable stern section. The lights failed, replaced seconds later with red-tinted emergency illumination. An overhead conduit ruptured in response to another salvo, and ozone-tinged vapors filled the bridge. Vaughn coughed, trying to focus past his discomfort.

The comm system resounded again with Bowers's voice. This time, he sounded distraught. "Captain, we've lost the transporter lock. There's no way we can get the away team back at the moment."

"Sir, if we don't return fire, the away team won't have a ship to come back to," Tenmei said, her words pitched low, evidently solely for Vaughn's consumption.

His daughter's comment annoyed him, but he couldn't deny that she was right. With no way to recover the away team—at least for now—there was simply no longer any point in putting the *Defiant* at risk.

Vaughn's thoughts strayed to the four brave souls who had only moments ago leaped into the complete unknown. They had trusted him. Necessary or not, sounding the retreat now felt like a craven act of betrayal.

But his command instincts were too deeply ingrained to make any other choice possible.

"Withdraw into the system's interior," he said, his own reluctance a palpable force within his breast. "Pull back another ten million klicks sunward."

Tenmei didn't hesitate. "Aye, sir."

"Maybe they'll let us go," Vaughn said as Tenmei brought the *Defiant* to a relative stop approximately .07 astronomical units closer to System GQ-12475's distant, pale star. "Just like last time."

Merimark placed a new tactical display up on the viewer, with icons showing the *Defiant*'s position, as well as those of the rest of the Nyazen blockade fleet.

"No such luck," she said, no humor in her tone. "I think they meant what they said about wanting us out of the system."

Nine of the hostiles were in hot pursuit of the *Defiant*, and were rapidly closing to weapons range.

Vaughn breathed a silent curse.

The away team members would have to be on their own for the foreseeable future. *Or perhaps even longer.*

20

His voice carried out over the crowd of faithful; even unamplified, it was strong, gentle, and almost melodious. The temple was full of worshipers at this special late-night service, and Vedek Capril was moved to see so many in attendance.

Mixed into the crowd were dozens of Bajoran dignitaries, politicians, entertainers, and other members of the clergy. As he sermonized, Capril couldn't help but feel some pride that he had more vedeks in his flock tonight than in almost any past service he had ever attended, much less one that he had administered.

But Capril wasn't so prideful to think that they had come to hear him in particular. Attendance was inordinately high because of the ceremonies tomorrow, during which Bajor would formally join the Federation. He had tailored his sermon carefully, speaking of unity and community, and of the need for peace and understanding as the Bajoran people were welcomed into the larger family of the universe.

"Bajor is poised at a precipice, metaphorically speaking," Capril said, "but that need not frighten her faithful. Instead, we should look out from that cliff, surveying the beauteous lands and myriad new treasures that await our exploration. The will of the Prophets has brought us to this point in our history, a time when Bajor has gained innumerable friends and allies. We must—we will— embrace the glorious future that the Prophets have laid out for us."

As Capril concluded his peroration, a rustle of motion among the congregation caught his eye. The worshipers were beginning to make ready to leave. Then a young man, perhaps in his mid-twenties, strode purposely toward Capril's lectern. A heartbeat later, the young man had turned to face the milling worshipers. Before Capril could gather his thoughts, the man removed his earring and ceremoniously dropped it to the floor.

"For Kira Nerys," the young man intoned. Then he stood quietly beside the lectern, his eyes closed as though in prayer or meditation.

Capril was beside himself with surprise, as were most of the worshipers, each of whom sat or stood about in stunned silence. But before Capril could make a move to remonstrate with the man, another supplicant, this one a middle-aged woman, stood and walked toward the lectern. Like the young man, she turned to the congregation, solemnly doffed her earring, and said, "For Kira Nerys." Her voice was aimed for the back of the temple. Like the young man beside whom she stood, the woman immediately lapsed into silence. Now a third supplicant, a young woman, stood and repeated the behavior of the first two.

Ohalavaru, Capril thought. He was rapidly growing

irritated, though it occurred to him that these people could have caused far more disruption had they not waited until the close of temple services to undertake their little demonstration.

But this was still unacceptable behavior within the hallowed walls of a Bajoran shrine.

"For Kira Nerys." Yet another Bajoran rose to remove an earring, and stood beside the growing cluster of Ohalavaru. Two more. Then another. "For Kira Nerys." Several more people joined the group.

Voices were rising in consternation throughout the chamber. Looking out across the congregation of perhaps sixty or so lay people and vedeks, Capril saw that he was far from alone in his vexation.

"For Kira Nerys." This time it was a woman, barely old enough to have completed her schooling. Her robes were brightly colored, trimmed with various brocades from over a dozen Bajoran regions. Like the others beside her, she stood still—passive, yet at the same time resolute.

Capril shot a worried look at several of the other vedeks. He was grateful to see a scowling Vedek Sinchante muttering something to one of the ranjens near the back of the shrine, who quickly scurried out of the temple. *I hope she's sent them to summon security.* Struggling to master his own rising anger, Capril waved his hands outward, as if to sweep all disruptive influences to the edges of the temple.

Three more Ohalavaru joined their fellows, making more than a dozen. "For Kira Nerys." Capril saw that one of these, a pale, dark-haired woman, held a gray-skinned, half-Cardassian baby. The woman looked somehow familiar.

Before he could speak again, the mother's voice rang out across the temple, echoing over the heads of the congregation. "We are the Ohalavaru, and we do this in the name of Kira Nerys, the *Truthgiver.*" Like her fellows, she removed her earring and dropped it to the floor.

A Bajoran man, his scowl articulating his disdain for the Ohalavaru, stood and pushed one of the Ohalavaru women away from Capril's lectern, toward the door. She nearly fell, then recovered her footing, clearly determined not to be moved. Several of the angrier worshipers were beginning to insist—loudly—that the Ohalavaru leave the shrine. And a handful of these had made it plain that they would take the matter into their own hands should the heretics refuse to go voluntarily.

Since the end of the Occupation, Capril had had nothing to do with violence of any kind. *I must gain control over this situation,* he thought, knowing that a general melee could erupt at any moment. While the heretics were clearly outnumbered, violence of any sort in the temple was unthinkable, regardless of the provocation; if it were to occur now, it could also generate sympathy for the Ohalavaru. Though Capril knew that something decisive had to be done, his feet seemed to have become rooted to the floor.

Desperate, Capril shouted over the rising tumult. His voice reverberated loudly from the vaulted temple ceilings. "Children of the Prophets! Violence here will solve *nothing!* Turn your passions toward the *Prophets, not* toward these intruders!"

Capril saw First Minister Shakaar and Second Minister Asarem in the back of the hall, gesturing to several security officers. To his discomfort, he realized that one of the incoming officers was Ro Laren, the woman who purposely wore her earring on the wrong ear, in the manner of the now thankfully extinct Pah-wraith cult. He wondered momentarily whose side she would take as she and her deputies dispersed through the increasingly agitated crowd.

Ro and Sergeant Etana were having quick cups of *raktajino* near the front door of Quark's when Ro's combadge chimed, followed a second later by the voice of Corporal Hava. *"All available officers, report to the shrine. It sounds like there's a confrontation of some sort brewing there."*

In the shrine?

Ro got up so quickly that the *raktajino* spilled on her hand and onto the table. She shot a quick guilty glance toward one of the dabo girls who had heard Hava's message. Shaking the scalding liquid from her right hand, Ro slapped her combadge with her left. "Ro here. Etana and I are on the way. What's going on?"

Of course, by the time Hava's voice filtered back, explaining that temple service was being disrupted, Ro and Etana were already approaching the shrine's entrance, and sounds of the tumult within were already becoming audible. Several Bajorans and non-Bajorans had already begun crowding toward the door.

As a squad of six other officers joined Ro and Etana, First Minister Shakaar and Second Minister Asarem and their entourage approached them from just inside the temple. Ro could hear shouting inside, and thought she heard Kira's name being spoken.

"What's the problem, Minister?" Ro asked.

"The renegade followers of Ohalu are treating us to a little demonstration," Asarem said, her voice trembling with anger. "At the behest of your commanding officer, evidently."

Before Ro could ask Asarem to explain her puzzling comment, Shakaar spoke up, pointing into the sanctuary. "I want those people arrested. Drag them out of here and make an example of them." Although his words were harsh, Ro didn't sense the same roiling passion behind them that she observed in Asarem and several of the ranjens who stood nearby.

"If we arrest them within the temple, there could be violence, Minister," Ro said. "And you also run the risk of turning them into political heroes."

"Of course *you* would argue that," said Vedek Bellis, his jowls wobbling angrily as he pushed his way toward them through those assembled nearby. *"You're* hardly fit to deal with a crisis in *our* temple."

Ro glanced quickly at Etana, her eyes narrowing. During her days with the Maquis, Ro might have dropped the obnoxious vedek with a knee to the groin. But she was well aware that tactics of a very different sort were necessary here. Etana rolled her eyes, clearly trying to mask her disgust at the vedek's sentiments.

Ro turned to the assembled deputies, who now numbered over a dozen. "First, let's make sure nobody gets hurt. Escort the protesters out in the most expedient manner possible, and order them to disperse. If they refuse, take them to holding cells so I can explain station regs to them. And don't forget that you're in a holy place." That last comment, though spoken to her deputies, was intended as a backhanded jab at the still-huffing Bellis.

Ensign Jimenez trailed Ro as she made her way up the center aisle. Several of the assembled worshipers moved aside, allowing them to reach the group of Ohalavaru, all of whom had linked arms. They were apparently meditating or praying, their eyes closed as though maintaining some sort of vigil. Ro placed her hand gently on the back of the nearest protester, a middle-aged woman.

"Ma'am, please come with me," Ro said loudly, so she could be heard over the angry shouts of the crowd. She ignored her, prompting Ro to try again, more firmly. "Ma'am, you are committing a crime by willfully disturbing this shrine. I must ask you to leave *now,* or we will be forced to remove you."

The woman continued to behave as though Ro weren't even there. Ro glanced at Jimenez, who had maneuvered himself to the woman's opposite side. His hand was on his phaser, and he looked to Ro for a nod. She wasn't ready to give it; at least, not yet. Ro looked around the room and saw that the situation was the same with most of the other deputies. None of the Ohalavaru would leave voluntarily, or even acknowledge the presence of the officers. The mood of the congregation, which obviously interpreted the Ohalavaru's actions as disrespectful, was growing increasingly ugly. Several of the worshipers were beginning to raise their voices, demanding that the Ohalavaru leave. Vedek Capril merely glowered at them from behind the lectern.

The protesters clearly had no intention of moving anytime soon. *Damn,* Ro thought. The last thing she wanted to do was get rough with these people. Particularly inside a place that so many Bajorans—if not Ro herself—considered hallowed ground.

Ro raised her voice again, inflecting it with military steel. "Those of you who are disturbing this shrine must leave *now.* You are committing a criminal act, and if you do not leave voluntarily, we will take you into custody. Please, gather up your earrings and walk out of the temple. This has been your *final* warning."

Her words did indeed produce a reaction, but only among the regular worshipers, many of whom seemed to be calming down. Some of the faithful appeared content to allow Ro and her people to handle matters, while others continued shouting their demands that the Ohalavaru depart.

Ro sighed. The protesters had left her only one option. "You leave us *no choice* but to take you into custody. Deputies?" Ro nodded to the ocher-uniformed men and women who began reaching toward the protesters.

But as each officer laid hands on his respective Bajoran sectarian, the Ohalavaru abruptly began chanting. "For Kira Nerys, the Truthgiver," they said as one, though none of them offered any resistance to the deputies who restrained them. "For Kira Nerys, the Truthgiver."

"That's *enough!*"

Ro recognized the voice instantly, though she had never before heard it raised to such a stentorian volume. She turned toward the speaker, who stood silhouetted in the shrine's Promenade doorway.

Kira Nerys. Being Attainted, the colonel was obviously taking great care not to cross the shrine's threshold.

"That's enough," Kira repeated, once it became clear that she had succeeded in gaining the attention of everyone in the room. The chanting had stopped. "You Ohalavaru have made your point. I'm asking you to exit the shrine *now* with our security staff. I ask that you all move in a quiet and orderly fashion."

Several of the Ohalavaru looked toward a dark-haired woman who held a squirming toddler in her arms. The woman nodded her assent, and the Ohalavaru responded by scooping up their earrings and filing toward the exit. Unbidden, the security officers followed, keeping a safe distance from the protesters, but staying close enough to protect them should any of the frustrated orthodox Bajorans follow and lash out.

As each of the Ohalavaru passed Kira, Shakaar, and Asarem, they reached out to touch the colonel—no doubt to thank her for exposing them to Ohalu's prophecies—but she remained impassive, neither acknowledging nor flinching from them. Ro also saw that Kira still had not set a foot within the boundaries of the shrine. *She's still obeying those pompous-ass vedeks who Attainted her.*

Ro turned and in a low voice apologized to Vedek Capril for the intrusion. He brusquely accepted her words, then glared across the room toward Kira. Ro knew that Capril had been on pleasant terms with Nerys in the past; had her Attainder changed that, or had the Ohalavaru demonstration merely rattled him?

Following the last of her officers out of the shrine, Ro strode over to First Minister Shakaar. "I'll leave a detachment of guards posted nearby in case of any further disturbances, Minister," she said.

He nodded, one eyebrow cocked as he watched the officers herding the Ohalavaru through the Promenade toward the security office and the adjacent holding cells. "I hope that this will be the *only* trouble they'll make here in the coming days."

"Perhaps if they weren't aboard the same station as their *leader,*" said Vedek Bellis, his baleful gaze cast upon Kira.

"I don't believe that Colonel Kira has either endorsed or allied herself with the Ohalavaru, Vedek Bellis," Shakaar said. He put a hand on the rotund man's shoulder, half turning him back toward the temple interior, and beckoned to Asarem. "Come, let's renew our devotion to the Prophets and Their Word."

Ro couldn't help but wonder if Shakaar had just gone out of his way to remind Kira that she wasn't permitted inside.

Asarem nodded almost imperceptibly. Apparently avoiding eye contact with either Kira or Ro, she turned back toward the temple to join Shakaar and Bellis. Ro saw Kira hesitate for a moment, then spin on her heel and walk briskly away from the shrine entrance. Ro could see that Kira's jaw was clenched so tightly that she could have bitten through hull metal without any trouble.

Deputy Etana approached Ro with a padd. "All sixteen of the Ohalavaru have been taken into custody, Lieutenant. We kept the mother and her child together. They're all cooperating fully with us. From the way they're acting now, you'd never guess they did anything wrong."

"In *their* minds, they *didn't*," Ro said, looking over the names on the padd. More information was being added remotely, from the officers working at the security office, and it continuously scrolled onto the tiny display. None of the names belonged to known felons, though one of them seemed familiar: Cerin Mika. Pointing to the name, she gave the padd back to Etana. "Pull any files we have on all of these people, but I want you to pay particular attention to hers. Then send them on their way unless their files give us any further reason to hold them."

Catching the attention of the nearby Sergeant Shul, Ro pointed back to the shrine. "Shul, I want you and three others to take the first shift watching the temple. Tomorrow is going to be complicated enough without more surprises around here."

After Shul acknowledged her order and peeled away, Ro turned back to Etana and put her hand on the woman's shoulder. "I need to go and . . . brief the colonel on a few things, Kol," she said, using Etana's familiar name. "You're in charge here." Ro looked at her chronometer and saw that one day had segued into the next just ten minutes ago. She sighed profusely. "Not a very auspicious beginning for this eve of peace, is it?"

Etana smiled warmly and patted Ro's hand. "We'll get through it, Laren. Go take care of the colonel."

I've got to tell her, Ro thought as she approached the sliding doors to Kira's office. As the doors whisked open, she saw Kira sitting with most of the illumination off, the distant stars shining brilliantly through the office window. Kira appeared to be meditating, or perhaps praying. *Good for her. The damned vedeks can't do anything about* that.

"Colonel," Ro said softly. "Are you all right?"

"Yes," Kira said. Then just as quickly, *"No."*

"I'm glad you showed up when you did," Ro said. "You saved us from what could have been a very . . . distressing scene. It seems that the Ohalavaru are pretty intent on getting you reinstated into the Bajoran faith."

"Huhn," Kira said, half chuckling. "So I've heard. Did you know that there were similar demonstrations in shrines in every province on Bajor? There were only a handful of Ohalavaru in each place. All of them stripped their earrings off. Because of me."

"I hadn't heard," Ro said. "Was anyone hurt?"

"Thankfully, no. There were some scuffles and shouting matches, but everything seems to have been resolved peacefully. For now, at least."

"I'm not sure I should say this, Colonel, but maybe you should be glad that you have the support of so many passionate people. It says good things about you. And about your decision not to let the Vedek Assembly suppress the Ohalu text."

"Good things?" Kira placed a hand to her bare right ear as though unconsciously feeling for a phantom limb. *"What* good? I've unleashed a horrifying division on the

303

people of Bajor. I'm responsible for who knows how many believers losing their faith! Maybe Vedek Yevir was right about me all along. Maybe what I did was rash and unthinking and *stupid*. Maybe I've only *begun* to reap the condemnation I'm due."

Ro felt profoundly sad that Kira apparently couldn't recognize how much she meant to so many. "You did what I would never have had the courage to do, Nerys," she said, using Kira's given name for the first time. "You, with all your faith in the Prophets and Their Will, you still did what was right." Kira stared back at her, and even in the near darkness, Ro sensed that she was listening intently.

"Haven't you considered the dichotomy of the Ohalavaru's actions tonight?" Ro asked. "The teachings of Ohalu tell them that the Prophets may not be everything they have been taught. So why, when they're rejecting the most basic tenets of that religion, would the Ohalavaru stage a planetwide protest, which has the apparent goal of forcing the Vedek Assembly to take you back into the fold?"

"I . . . I don't know," Kira said plainly.

"Well, I haven't talked to any of them directly yet, but I think I know what their answer is going to be. You were punished because you gave them a choice. Before you uploaded the prophecies of Ohalu, they had only two options: join up with the faithful, or become outcast agnostics like me. But now they have another path to follow, one that seems to offer them some concrete possibilities for the future. And don't think that their timing wasn't influenced by the upcoming signing. Bajor's entry into the Federation will offer its people even more freedom. New belief systems, new technologies, new interspecies interactions . . ."

"I'm still not sure I understand where you're going with this, Ro."

"It seems to me that what the Ohalavaru are saying, in maybe too roundabout a way, is that *you* deserve a choice as well. Attainted or not, you still choose to follow the Prophets. The church has cast you out. But your dissemination of Ohalu's teachings wasn't a reflection on your faith in the Prophets, or based on a desire to lead anybody astray. The Ohalavaru are telling all of Bajor that if you choose to follow the Prophets—if that's where your *pagh* takes you—then you have every right to do just that."

Kira sat in silence, staring at her. Ro was suddenly aware that she was still standing beside the desk, talking down to her commander almost as though she were a recalcitrant child. She sat down in a nearby chair and placed a finger on her nose ridge, massaging it for a moment.

"I'm sorry, Colonel. I didn't mean to lecture you."

"No, that's all right," Kira said, putting out a hand as if to deflect any further apologies. "I hadn't considered that before." She sighed heavily. "There's just so much going on."

Ro swallowed hard, bracing herself for what she had to say next. "I'm afraid I've got something else to tell you. I know this isn't going to make you any happier, but there's not likely to be a better moment, and time is running out." Kira sighed again, and Ro continued, determined to unburden herself. "Shortly after the Federation ceremony, I'll be leaving my post as Deep Space 9's chief of security. I'll also resign my commission in the Bajoran Militia."

"What? *Why?*" Kira leaned forward, and Ro could see the shock blossoming on her face, as though she'd just been slapped.

"It's something I've been afraid to consider fully until

305

recently, but I just can't put this off any longer. I've struggled with this decision, believe me. You know about my history with Starfleet. With Bajor joining the Federation, I . . ." She paused to compose herself, afraid that her voice might crack. "I'll *never* have a place in the coming new order. I'd rather bow out now, gracefully, than put you or Commander Vaughn or anyone else out trying to justify my presence around here."

Kira paused briefly before responding. "I can't say I blame you, Laren. At the moment, I'm tempted to join you." She smiled grimly. "What do you plan to do?"

Ro sighed. Now wasn't the time to bring up the ventures she and Quark had been discussing. "I've started looking into some . . . other opportunities. It's a big galaxy. There are lots of things to do in it."

"I'm going to fight to get you to stay," Kira said, a trace of forced mirth in her voice. "You know that, don't you?"

"Won't do any good," Ro said, standing. "I'll stay on board through the official changeover, to get my replacement ready. But after that, I'll be moving on."

Feeling her emotions beginning to surge, and her lip trembling, Ro turned and left the office without saying another word.

Alone in her office, Kira Nerys glanced down at the drawer into which she had consigned Benjamin Sisko's baseball months earlier. Then she turned her gaze toward the bucket which she kept on one of the low shelves beside the desk. She was reminded forcefully of the two people in all the universe whose advice she could most use now.

A rage had been simmering within her ever since she had begun discussing the peace talks with Shakaar. Now the feeling moved within her like a tropical storm lashing at the Jo'kala coast. Still seated in her chair, she raised her legs until her boots made contact with the desk's heavy wooden framework. Kicking out, she up-ended the desk, which made a very satisfying crash onto the floor. The force of her kick sent her chair flying backward into the bookcase. She rose to her feet, struggling to bring herself back under some semblance of control.

What have I done to Bajor? Kira thought, surveying the wreckage of her office. She looked out the window at the stars, sending a silent prayer toward the wormhole—the Celestial Temple of the Prophets. *What have I done to the faith You have sustained me with?*

Unbidden, a familiar line of ancient prophecy sprang into her mind: *When the children have wept all, anew will shine the twilight of their destiny.*

Stretching out a hand to touch the spaceward window, Kira suddenly began to weep. Convulsive sobs racked her body, and her tears spilled unheeded into the silent darkness.

21

The transporter beam chilled Ezri to the bone, as though the inky emptiness of space had reached through the matter stream to steal every calorie of heat from her body. But the sensation passed almost as quickly as it had begun.

Ezri stood in a chamber lit only by several small sconces, each of which stood about two meters off the ground and a few body-lengths apart. Rough-hewn granite walls trailed off into the stygian darkness. The air was warm and stale, though it moved in a steady breeze across her skin. Strange, discordant music reverberated in the distance, at the edge of audibility. Though it sounded vaguely familiar, she couldn't quite place it.

Ezri realized then that her environmental suit was gone, as was her phaser. She found that she now wore a nondescript, lightweight jumpsuit. She carried a hard hat in her left hand. The gravel on the cavern floor crunched beneath her heavy boots. *Work clothes,* she thought as she paused momentarily to examine her new wardrobe. Running a hand through her hair, she noted that it was longer, and cut differently than before she had beamed over. Donning the hard hat, she made a complete turn, investigating what she could see of her surroundings in the dim illumination.

What is this place? And where are the others?

Noticing that she still had her wrist lamps, she raised and activated them. A ribbon of brilliance cleaved the darkness, revealing a craggy, gray-hued ceiling several meters overhead. The irregular passage and its chaotic tumbles of rocks and gravel seemed somehow familiar. It also struck her as odd to find such a place within the confines of the clean, deliberate geometries of the alien artifact.

Her wrist lamp held high, Ezri took a deep breath and began walking into the darkness. She called out, first to Julian and then to Nog, her voice reverberating to infinity and back, the aural equivalent of an endless series of funhouse mirrors.

There was no response. She was alone, with no company other than the thunder of her own pulse, the rhythmic crunch of her boot heels, and the distant peals of the weird almost-music.

She was startled by a voice that suddenly spoke from behind her. "Ezri."

Ezri spun toward the sound, stepping quickly back to give herself some maneuvering room in case the owner of the voice intended to make trouble.

To her surprise, Ezri found herself facing her mother. Who *was* trouble, she reflected, almost by definition.

"You *can't* be here," Ezri said, realizing that she had unconsciously arranged her body into a combat-crouch straight out of one of her Starfleet Academy hand-to-hand training classes. *Guess I don't need Dax for every-thing.*

"That's really what this is about, isn't it?" said Yanas Tigan, a smile stretching her skin taut. A condescending smile, Ezri thought. Typical.

"Excuse me?" Ezri said, scowling.

Yanas adopted the tone of a put-upon teacher address-ing a willfully obtuse student. "About your relationship with Dax."

"When did I mention Dax to you, Mother?"

"Oh, please. If you can accept that I'm here with you all the way out in the Gamma Quadrant, then why would you be surprised that I can also hear your thoughts?"

Fair enough, Ezri decided. But this being obviously *couldn't* be her mother. It had to be some sort of mani-festation of the artifact. But why would whatever in-telligence guided this place select her mother as a communications channel?

The Yanas-thing smiled. "I'm sorry that Starfleet didn't work out for you the way you thought it would. But I can't pretend not to be glad that you've come back to New Sydney to help me keep the minerals flowing out of here on schedule."

New Sydney? So that's why this place seems so famil-iar. I've come back home to the pergium mines in the Sappora System.

All at once Ezri began recalling things, including what seemed to be more than one version of the last few years of her life. Conflicting recollections tumbled onto one another, overlapping like palimpsests: Brinner Finok, and the brief fling they had shared aboard the *Destiny;* the horrors of the Dominion War, which had taken Brinner from her; the cataclysmic arrival of Dax in her life; her deepening romantic relationship with Julian—

—and her withdrawal from Starfleet Academy, only weeks before graduation.

Her ignominious return home, with all prospects of a Starfleet career dashed by the irresistible force that was her mother.

Yanas was scowling at her, obviously still following the drift of her thoughts. "That's not fair, Ezri. You came home because you understood where your real responsibilities lay. Unless you believe that what happened to Norvo and Janel was somehow *my* fault."

Ezri suddenly felt ashamed. "Of course not, Mother." She recalled vividly how she had agonized over the decision about dropping out of the Academy. But after the cave-in that had killed both of her brothers—and had dealt the family business a crippling blow—Ezri had made the only choice possible.

I couldn't let her run the pergium-mining business all alone. She needed *me.*

Yanas's smile broadened, but it contained little warmth. "Such a dutiful daughter. I can understand why you didn't know where you were, by the way. You always did make it a point to get down into the mines as little as possible."

Ezri's belly spasmed slightly, then settled down. She placed her hand on her abdomen. Where Dax had once been, she thought. She scowled at the obvious untrustworthiness of her own memories.

Who the hell is Dax?

"Nobody now," Yanas said casually. "I think Dax was a symbiont who died just after its host got killed during the Dominion War. But that's not your concern anymore."

It never was, Ezri thought, feeling desolate without quite knowing why.

"Right again. Now I need you to get back to the accounting office and catch up on the books. Those quota reports aren't going to write themselves, you know."

Quota reports. The idea made her insides squirm in revulsion. She wondered if becoming joined to one of those ageless Trill brain-vampires, as frightening as the notion had always struck her, could really be any worse than giving over the entirety of one's single, finite lifetime to mining contracts, shipping manifests, and pergium futures.

I've been joined, all right, Ezri thought. *To stacks of padds and mountains of paperwork.*

She heard another pair of footsteps behind her and turned quickly toward the sound.

The man who regarded her was tall, thin, and dour-looking. Humanoid, with the brow wrinkles common to many of New Sydney's residents. He, too, wore mining attire. She saw a steely glint in his eyes that she recognized.

And hated, without quite remembering why.

"Thadeo Bokar," Ezri said, taking a step backward. She was beginning to remember still more.

Bokar grinned, displaying even rows of immaculate white teeth. "I've come to discuss your recent equipment orders, Miss Tigan. I think you'd do well to consider making a few . . . additional purchases."

Ezri struggled to master a rush of anger. "Why, Bokar? To pay off the Orion Syndicate so we won't have any more mysterious cave-ins down here?"

Bokar made an unconvincing show of sympathy. "It must have been terrible, losing both your brothers like that. So sudden and tragic. Makes you appreciate what you still have all the more. And, I would hope, eager to do whatever it takes to hold onto it."

Ezri glanced back toward Yanas, who was glaring accusingly at her.

"What's he saying, Ezri? Did you make some sort of deal with the Orion Syndicate? I knew we had some cash-flow problems after the Ferengi opened those mines on Timor II, but I never thought you'd stoop to . . ." She trailed off into silence, which was filled only by the weird quasi-music that still reverberated through the stony corridor.

Ezri looked at Yanas, an inchoate apology on her lips. But the naggingly familiar music stopped her.

Because she recognized it now, and remembered where she'd been when she'd first heard it.

It had been aboard the *Sagan,* during the survey of System GQ-12475's Oort cloud. Just before the initial encounter with the alien artifact—the cathedral, or anathema, into which she had just transported. With Nog. And Julian.

And Dax.

Ezri experienced another rush of conflicting memory—and realized that she had nothing to apologize for. She hadn't gotten the family business into bed with the Orion Syndicate. *Janel* had done that.

But Janel was dead. Had *been* dead for years.

Misaligned in their worldlines. Sacagawea's wind-chime voice spoke inside her head, from some spectral interior world. *Untethered. Adrift/lost midworlds.*

Janel isn't dead, Ezri told herself, shaking her head as though stunned by a physical blow. *Norvo isn't dead either. Not in* my *world. They're the ones who stayed behind with Mother, and the Orion Syndicate didn't begin leaning on them until years later.* Meanwhile, Ezri had finished up at Starfleet Academy, then had shipped out on the *Destiny.*

Ezri had left home, and had stayed away. She had resisted the all too frequent squalls of withering maternal criticism that had kept both her brothers on such short tethers for so many years. She hadn't allowed herself to be moved by Yanas's levers of guilt and duty and obligation the way Norvo and Janel had.

It came to Ezri then why the cathedral had confronted her with this simulacrum of Yanas Tigan: It was an external representation of her need to separate herself from the infinitude of Ezri Tigans whose lives weren't hers. It was her touchstone for avoiding taking a path traveled only by some phantom-Ezri in some other hypothetical reality.

This artifact-generated creature had to be the key to avoiding becoming "unmoored," as Shar had put it, from the life she knew, washed away in a torrent of might-have-beens. *She's got to be my ticket to fixing those tangled "worldlines" Sacagawea kept talking about.*

Ezri noticed then that Bokar was still talking. "There is a bright side to your little brother's passing, though," Bokar was saying, facing Ezri. "Some of those paintings of his are finally fetching some decent prices. It's too bad that nobody appreciates artists while they're still alive."

Ezri could feel something moving within her. Shifting. Something at the core of her being was changing, awakening. She had her own life to lead, and now she was determined to take it back. Sacagawea's translator-filtered voice rang in her mind: *Misaligned in their worldlines.*

She reached up and doffed her hat, tossing it to the ground. She touched her hair again, noting without surprise that it had returned to the severe, short style that she'd adopted shortly after her joining.

On the *Destiny*.

As a Starfleet officer.

Just before she'd been posted to DS9.

Yanas was confronting her again, as though she hadn't heard Bokar's cruel words about her late son.

Mom never was a great one for listening, Ezri thought. Eavesdropping, perhaps, but not *listening*.

"So what are you planning to do?" Yanas said, clearly still attuned to Ezri's thoughts. The older woman's tone was harsh, obviously calculated to demoralize. To reassert control. "Will you go back to chasing those Starfleet daydreams again? You need to learn to accept life as it comes, Ezri."

True enough, Ezri thought, recalling Nog's dire warning about how little time remained before the "untethering" became permanent. *The only question is,* Which *life?*

"Listen to your mother, Miss Tigan," Bokar said, his lips inclined in a contemptuous smirk.

And in that instant, Ezri made a decision. *A command decision,* she thought with some satisfaction. Advancing quickly on Bokar, she treated him to a pair of quick rabbit punches to the face, followed by a hard abdominal jab. The gangster's unconscious form thumped hard against the stone floor. She was gratified to note that he was no longer smirking.

"Problem solved, Mother. At least for now. This time it's *your* turn to clean up the long-term mess."

Ezri noticed then that a Starfleet combadge was attached to the left side of her jumpsuit. Had it been there all along, waiting for her to sever her ties to all her might-have-been lives?

She tapped the combadge. *"Defiant,* if you can hear me, beam me back. Now."

Her stomach lurched. Whatever changes were going on within her mind and body seemed to be accelerating. Nausea rose within her, and she felt her knees turning to water. Abruptly, another realization came.

It's the symbiont. I feel weak because my body needs the symbiont again.

It came to her then that she must have succeeded in "realigning her worldline." That was the good news. The bad news was that without Dax she would probably be dead within a few short hours.

Yanas's face was a mask of incredulity. Defiance wasn't something she encountered very often, whether from employees or from offspring.

"You can't just leave, Ezri. Why would you return to the life you had before? You never wanted to be joined in the first place."

"I'm just following your own advice, Mother. Accepting life as it comes." *Or as it* came.

"But I need you *here!*"

"Hire a damned bookkeeper," Ezri said, her consciousness beginning to ebb. She felt as though she were falling over a precipice into one of the open pergium shafts. A voice from her combadge spoke, perhaps in acknowledgment of her signal. But she couldn't be sure.

Ezri saw another shape appear, as if out of nowhere, at her mother's side. Janel smiled in Ezri's direction. "I'll take over from here, Zee."

"I still hate your hair," Ezri heard Yanas say a moment before darkness closed in around her.

The colorful tunic Moogie had given him for his Attainment Ceremony was already thoroughly soaked with sweat. Nog had already forgotten how he'd gotten here. Wherever *here* was. He only knew that his pursuers had killed a lot of people. Kellin, Larkin, Vargas. Countless others. They all lay in the dust, some blown apart, others sliced to gory slivers. All Nog could think of was running, and staying ahead of their killers.

Uncle Quark's voice sprang into his mind unbidden:

Maybe you'll grow up to be a real Ferengi after all. Not like your father.

Clutching his phaser tightly, he ignored the daggers of pain that lanced his side and kept moving as quickly as the absurd terrain permitted. Thanks to the semidarkness and the profusion of tall, irregularly shaped rock formations that seemed to cover every square meter of this Chin'toka hellhole, he couldn't see them coming. But his sensitive hearing counted dozens of pounding footfalls, all coming toward him. Unvarying in their rhythm, their approach as inexorable as death itself.

He knew he was getting winded. He was also grimly aware that his pursuers never got tired. Sooner or later the Jem'Hadar would catch up with him, and there was nothing he could do to prevent it. He would have to stop, stand his ground, and fight them. Fight the most relentless, implacable, nightmarish foes he'd ever imagined.

The still-green memory of how they'd shot him during the battle for control of the Dominion's AR-558 communications array—forcing Dr. Bashir to amputate his leg—sent a jolt of terror through his lobes and down his spine. He paused beside a large outcropping, the dusty air making him cough and wheeze as he struggled to catch his breath.

Sudden confusion struck him as he looked down at his two perfectly good, utterly normal legs. *When did the Jem'Hadar shoot me in the leg?* The recollection had the quality of a fading dream. He clearly remembered a time six years ago, when Captain Sisko and his Uncle Quark had briefly fallen into Jem'Hadar hands. Nog and his now-missing best friend Jake Sisko had done their best to mount a rescue. Luckily, Uncle Quark's dignity had been the only thing seriously wounded that day.

Still, Nog couldn't shake a strange mental image, half memory and half premonition, of wearing a Starfleet uniform. Of serving aboard starships. Of having fought alongside some of the bravest people he'd ever known, in this desolate place. *Chin'toka,* he somehow knew.

Before he could consider the matter further, an enormous humanoid shape flung itself toward him from behind one of the larger rocks. Without thinking, Nog leveled his phaser and fired with the ease of long practice.

Repulsed by the phaser's blunt impact, the Jem'Hadar fell backward against the unyielding bedrock, so much dead weight. Nog wanted to look away, but discovered he couldn't. He squinted in the shadows at the supine corpse's pebble-textured face.

Nog recognized it. He wasn't sure how, but he knew that he'd seen this particular Jem'Hadar's face before, many times. He remembered that he hadn't enjoyed the experience. It made no sense, but this sensation of quasi-memory felt more profoundly real than even his evanescent, dreamlike recollections of Starfleet.

He considered the reassuring heft of the phaser in his hand. Starfleet issue, he decided, not at all certain how he knew that fact either. Perhaps he *had* been in Starfleet. Maybe that was why using this thing had come so naturally to him. And perhaps it also explained why he recognized this strange place, where some shadow-Nog had lost a leg in some all but forgotten Dominion War battle.

Maybe I've been hurt. Lost my memory.
Misaligned.
In.
The.
World.
Lines.

Sacagawea's translator-mediated voice, like a *glebbening* rainstorm made of latinum slips, came back to him. And he remembered. He was in the cathedral now. Or the anathema.

He had beamed inside the alien artifact.

He tried to reassure himself that everything he was experiencing in here was probably not objectively real. It had to be the artifact acting on his mind. Or his own mind trying to come to terms with an infinite number of alternate Nogs across an infinite number of parallel worlds.

So why do I think I'm in the Chin'toka System, of all places?

The footfalls were much closer now. His pursuers would be on top of him soon. Nog started to throw himself into motion once again, responding to Ferengi instincts honed by untold aeons of evolution.

He stopped. Maybe running wasn't the way to fix Sacagawea's worldlines, he thought. He heard his uncle's voice again, pleading with him to flee, the way any sensible Ferengi would. *They're going to take your leg again. Unless you run. On your two good legs.*

The Jem'Hadar footfalls continued growing louder as a new thought chilled him: Was losing his leg the only way to remained "tethered," to borrow Sacagawea's word, to the correct universe? Or perhaps it was the price of restoring Ezri, Dax, and Dr. Bashir to their normal condition. He was an engineer. He knew that nature was, in its own way, an excellent model of the Ferengi way of life. It always balanced the books, and it never gave anything away without eventually demanding payment. Usually with interest.

He looked down at his left leg again, and thought of his absent friends.

Then he smiled. *So be it.*

The sound of his own pulse nearly drowning out the rising din of the approaching Jem'Hadar, Nog planted his feet in the dust and raised his phaser toward his still-concealed pursuers.

"Sorry, Uncle," he said out loud, his voice sounding flat in the stale, stagnant air. "It looks like my running days are over. In more ways than one."

Another Jem'Hadar appeared from behind the same outcropping that had produced the first. A second and a third followed hard on his heels. Nog fired and fired again. Three times. Five times. Still more Jem'Hadar filed into view from behind the rocks, moving closer, contemptuous of the death Nog dispensed. Corpses fell in twisted heaps, and still more Jem'Hadar leaped over them, approaching faster than Nog could kill them. The press of hostile flesh was now only a few meters away, and every soldier in the line wore the same face.

The face of the first Jem'Hadar to fall.

Taran'atar's face.

Nog continued firing. But they kept coming, surrounding him, every countenance overflowing with the brute savagery he'd always known lay just beneath Taran'atar's veneer of civility.

The phaser in his hand suddenly stopped firing. Out of power. *Great.*

To Nog's astonishment, the columns of Jem'Hadar abruptly halted their advance. Except for the cacophonous strains of distant music, utter silence engulfed the world.

A lone, black-clad Jem'Hadar soldier stepped forward, continuing his deliberate approach until he stood within arm's reach. The creature towered forbiddingly over Nog, who felt his guts turn to parboiled gree worms. He concentrated on the barely audible music in an effort to master his fear. He wished fervently that

Captain Sisko had agreed to sponsor his application to Starfleet Academy more than four years ago. If that had happened, then he'd know how to handle himself now.

Confused, overlapping memories assailed him. Sisko *had* sponsored him. He'd made it into the Academy. He'd served in a cadet unit called Omega Squadron, under the grandson of a famous Starfleet commodore. By graduation he'd already visited and seen more strange places than he could count, from Cardassia Prime to Talos IV. Perhaps more than any other Ferengi that had ever lived.

Then Nog recognized the ethereal sounds that were drifting across the dismal landscape: He'd first heard them aboard the *Sagan,* just before the artifact had first appeared. Its entwining, random-numerical melodies reminded him of the physical unreality of this place and helped him to suppress his overpowering urge to flee. And its steady pulse reminded him that the clock was still ticking inevitably toward the interdimensional "untethering" that Sacagawea had described—and which he had already previewed aboard the *Defiant* on more than one occasion.

Somehow, Nog managed to hold his ground. When he spoke, his voice shook. "All right, Taran'atar. Get on with it."

Then, to Nog's immense surprise, an unexpected equanimity descended upon him. Right after they'd discovered the artifact, Ezri had tried to tell him that he needed to clear the air between himself and Taran'atar. He wondered if that's what he was about to do, consciously or not. Maybe it explained why the artifact had recreated AR-558's killing ground.

Taran'atar took a step back, raised his bloodied *kar'-takin,* and swung the blade into Nog's left leg, just below the knee. Whether real or imaginary, the pain utterly convinced Nog. He collapsed to the dust, screaming.

As though disconnected from his own body, Nog watched as Taran'atar reached down and picked up the severed leg as though it were some hard-won battle trophy. The Jem'Hadar smiled enigmatically as he tucked the limb behind his back, along with his gore-spattered blade. Then he tossed a small metallic object into the dust beside Nog.

Nog saw that it was a Starfleet combadge. He picked it up. He felt light-headed, unable to speak, conscious of little besides his own blood, which was rapidly soaking the desiccated ground. With trembling fingers, he activated the little device's homing beacon, uncertain as to whether it could reach the *Defiant*. Or if it was working, or if it was even real.

The world turned sideways, the way it had the time he'd unwisely tried to match Vic Fontaine's drummer drink for drink. "I'll be seeing you," he thought he heard Taran'atar say in an incongruously clear tenor voice, "in all the old familiar places."

And just before consciousness fled him, Nog realized that he could probably deal with that.

All at once, Dax became aware that something in its environment had changed. The blind and deaf creature was well acquainted with the curious tingling sensation of being disassembled and reconstituted by a transporter beam—even harrowing, rather rough beamings such as the one it had just experienced. But this current feeling of sudden change was subtly different.

Dax still enjoyed the same euphoric freedom of gentle, aqueous suspension it had been experiencing for the past day or so, ever since its abrupt removal from Ezri Tigan's body. What was different and perplexing was where the symbiont now found itself floating. It made no sense, but there could be no denying the water's distinctive salinity and mineral factors. Even the limited sensorium of a symbiont could never mistake this particular place for any other.

Mak'ala. Somehow, I have been brought home, all the way from the hinterlands of the Gamma Quadrant.

With that recognition came an ominous tingle of dread. Dax had never enjoyed spending extended periods here. The symbiont had always taken great care to prearrange as brief a recuperation interval here as possible while between hosts. Floating in the complex network of caves for too long had always brought on a curious, and admittedly irrational, feeling of vulnerability.

After returning to the pools briefly following the death of Lela, the first Dax host, the symbiont had dreamed of predators—eyeless creatures who trolled the caves until their hyperolfactory abilities guided them unerringly to some unsuspecting symbiont. Then these inescapable horrors of unhinged jaws and serrated teeth would pounce. Scores of lifetimes would end, suddenly and ignominiously, in some brute's foul gullet—

Stop it, *Dax told itself.* Such things did not exist. The humanoid Trills who tended the pools had seen to that long ago.

Yet the apprehension lingered.

Dax wished there had been an opportunity to arrange a new joining before being disassociated from Ezri Tigan. But the separation had come without any warning. How long would the Symbiosis Commission take to assign a new host? Not long, Dax trusted. The Commission knew that Dax's lifetimes of experience were too valuable to the Federation to be allowed to languish for long.

Dax wished Ezri well. It had no desire to see her come to harm because of the sudden collapse of their joining. And it appreciated all the painstaking, after-the-fact preparation Ezri had done to accommodate their ad hoc *symbiosis, once it had become a necessary and unalterable* fait accompli. *But the encounter with the alien artifact had caused that symbiosis to fail, or had at least catalyzed its failure. That aborted joining was now part of Dax's lengthy past, and was likely to remain so. And although it shamed Dax to admit it, being free of Ezri's sometimes disorderly thought processes was a real relief. The portion of Dax that recalled Audrid's love of peaceful walks in the woods exulted in this newfound freedom.*

Dax reached out into its liquid environment with its limited physical senses, probing around itself with insubstantial electrolyte filaments. It perceived immediately that other symbionts were in the pool, which was as expected. Willing itself forward, Dax probed to the pool's boundaries, sensed the limits of its rocky walls in every direction. It was a finite, though by no means cramped, space. But Dax knew that this would be the extent of its universe until its next joining. The wider, less confining worlds beyond were far more inviting.

The symbiont sensed that a narrow passage lay in its path, seeming to beckon. The notion of entering such a restrictive space raised the wise apprehension of Audrid and Lela. But the inquisitive natures of Tobin and Jadzia immediately overruled this initial cautious impulse. Dax undulated forward, eager to encounter whatever lay ahead.

Entering the constricted passage, the symbiont began picking up speed, reacquainting itself with Emony's love of kinesthetic motion. The narrow channel soon widened again, and Dax found itself delighting in the freedom of yet another large underground pool, this one seeming to stretch into infinity. Reaching out with its limited senso-rium, Dax detected other shapes floating in the distance.

But they weren't symbionts. Tobin's fear rose as the shapes approached, but the battle-tempered courage of Curzon and Jadzia deftly parried it.

The shapes grew larger and more complex. While they weren't limbless symbionts, neither were they razor-toothed predators. Feeling relieved, Dax quickly ascertained that they had arms and legs, heads and tor-sos. They were humanoids, all of them as naked as sym-bionts. There were nine of them, all swimming about him, and all apparently emotionally agitated, judging from their movements. The rhythmic flailing of their limbs set up chaotic, overlapping waves throughout the pool, vibrations that reminded Dax of the celestial music produced by the Oort cloud bodies near the alien artifact. Dax probed at the faces of each of the hu-manoids with gentle, bioelectrical fingers.

Moving from one face to the next, Dax recognized each and every one of the humanoids. Though it knew this was impossible, Dax also knew that their identities were unmistakable.

"You've known about what's coming for the past cen-tury," Audrid said, somehow speaking directly into the symbiont's mind. She was obviously completely unmind-ful of the absurdity—no, the utter impossibility*—of her presence here.*

"It's more like the past century and a quarter," Torias said, floating beside her.

"But it still hasn't done anything about it." This came from Lela.

"All those years," Torias said. "All those lifetimes. And you spent most of them assing around the galaxy."

"Why haven't you at least tried *to warn anyone,*

Dax?" Emony said, her words dripping with bitter accusation.

Dax felt genuine confusion. I don't know what any of you are talking about.

"Perhaps you don't." This voice belonged to Joran Belar, a man whose sense of aesthetics had been matched only by his psychotic bloodlust. Dax had been well rid of that joining, late in the previous century.

You're the last person I'd expect to encounter, *Dax said.* Here or anywhere else.

"You see what you want to see, Dax," Joran said. "You always were a master of repressing whatever parts of yourself you'd rather not face."

"It's pure denial," Ezri said, using her best counselor-to-patient tones.

"Why have you been holding back?" Tobin said.

Holding back? Holding back what?

Jadzia spoke up. "Your nightmares, Dax."

Dax recalled the post-Lela visions of slashing jaws, and the terror and the helplessness that had always accompanied them.

And it remembered something else as well. Something that Dax hadn't considered since Audrid's lifetime—something it never wanted to consider. The part of Dax that was Ezri wondered, just for a moment, if its persistent apprehension regarding the pools was indeed somehow bound up with the events of that horrible day so long ago. If it bore any relationship to the tenebrous, obscene nightmare that had swallowed poor Jayvin Vod whole and had riven Audrid's life and family for so many years . . .

Then Verad's cold rage welled up from deep within. How dare his old hosts dredge such things up? My nightmares are my own affair.

"You couldn't be more wrong," Curzon said. *"Soon, half the galaxy will be* living *your nightmares."*

"Unless you rejoin with Ezri," Audrid said. *"And warn everyone."*

Why Ezri?

"Because we're both aboard the Defiant," Ezri said, her anger palpable. *"Look, I don't like this joining thing any better than you do. But we're a long way from home. And we can't afford to wait until a better match turns up."*

But your thoughts are so . . . jumbled. Disorganized. Unsubtle. I am better off without you.

"Ibid and op. cit. *what I just said, slug,"* Ezri said. *"But I'm willing to take one for the team if you are."*

Tobin laughed, but without any evident humor. " *'Unsubtle thoughts' ought to be an asset this time, Dax. It seems to me that too much subtlety is what created our mutual problem in the first place."*

"Or at least allowed it to remain hidden for so long," added Curzon. *"Perhaps past the point where it can ever be dealt with. But we gain nothing by waiting."*

"You know what you have to do, Dax," Audrid said. And with that, all nine of them broke away, swimming in leisurely fashion back into the depths, dwindling and finally vanishing entirely from Dax's sensorium.

Lost in troubled thought, Dax failed to notice the approach of a multitude of other shapes until they were very close. This time, there were dozens. More naked humanoids, none of whose faces Dax recognized. Among them were many Trills of both sexes, as well as members of various non-Trill species. From what little it could glean of their specific morphologies, Dax concluded that humans, Vulcans, Andorians, Tellarites, Rigelians, Orions, Ferengi, Romulans, Klingons, and even Vorta, and Jem'Hadar were among the bizarre *press of flesh. There were also scores of others, from inside and outside the Federation. Members, allies, and enemies, as well as species Dax did not immediately recognize.*

And all of them were dead, their bodies shredded and torn by forces Dax had seen on only one previous occasion, long ago. It could scarcely bear to think about it.

A body stirred among the corpses, then swam rapidly toward the symbiont. Dax wondered briefly if its predatory nightmare had finally returned for a day of reckoning.

Then he recognized the approaching being as Ezri Tigan. She had returned.

"So how about it, slug?" she said.

Acceding to the rational impulses of Curzon and Jadzia, Dax came to the decision that it knew could be put off no longer. The time for concealment is past. We will confront the old lies directly. Together.

Ezri's answering smile was lost in a spray of bubbles as the universe suddenly turned inside out.

22

Ro Laren couldn't recall a time when she'd been more tired and on edge, at least since she had left the Maquis. Just as in those days, sleep came in brief snatches, and the rest of her time in bed had been spent pondering her future, her evolving relationship with Quark, the religious schism on Bajor, the political rift between Bajor and Cardassia, the upcoming Federation signing, the health of Dizhei and Anichent, the whereabouts of the missing Jake Sisko, the flirtations of Hiziki Gard, and the effect she knew her announcement had had on Kira Nerys. Small wonder that slumber did not come easily.

Still, knowing that today's proceedings were probably the most significant events she would ever witness, Ro found her body buzzing with energy. She made sure to press her back-up dress tunic, in case the one she was already wearing got stained or damaged. She even carefully styled her hair and applied a modicum of makeup, something she was generally loath to do.

Her morning had so far consisted of three security meetings. The first was the private briefing, held in her security office, that she had promised Hiziki Gard, who somehow managed to be charming despite the horrendous earliness of the hour. The next meeting was held in the wardroom, where she gave a final briefing to almost all of the guards and deputies serving on the station; those who were on duty and could not attend the meeting were given earpieces and a holofeed to enable them to follow the presentation. Sergeants Shul and Etana were tremendously helpful, and she knew she'd be able to rely on them implicitly.

Ro's third meeting—also held in the wardroom—was with the various security contingents and representatives from the visiting dignitaries. As she surveyed the room, she saw the true diversity of the Federation and its allies; present were Vulcans, a pair of Bynars, two burly Klingons, a jovial-looking Bolian woman, a transparent-skulled Gallamite man, a voluminous female Denobulan, two diplomats from Skorr—and the ever-attentive Gard. Ro was surprised that no Cardassians were in attendance, but given the current impasse in the peace negotiations between her world and theirs, perhaps they were deliberately maintaining a low profile.

The representatives had asked a wide variety of questions, all aimed at safeguarding their respective delegates to the signing. Several of them were concerned about the previous evening's disturbance in the Bajoran shrine, but Ro explained clearly that the Ohalavaru had been making a religious statement, and that they had expressed no interest whatsoever in interrupting the proceedings today. Most of them, in fact, had already left the station, since there had been little justification for keeping them in custody.

Gard had asked more probing questions, reviewing the capabilities of Ro's security scanners, the types of weapons being screened, making sure that all personnel were alert for changelings or shrouded Jem'Hadar, and inquiring about the readiness and training of Ro's deputies. Ro might have taken umbrage at some of the questions had they come from anyone else, but since she knew of Gard's police background, she felt relatively at ease with his highly specific interrogation.

After being assured that the station's shields would be up throughout the ceremony as an added precaution, most of the visiting security teams seemed satisfied with Ro's elaborate measures. Even the Klingons grumbled only slightly, mainly at having to leave their *bat'leths, d'k tahgs,* and other bladed weapons in their quarters. Ro made a point of going out of her way to prepare each security contingent not to overreact at the sight of Taran'atar. She wondered if the war-weary peoples of the Alpha Quadrant would ever learn to be at ease in the presence of a Jem'Hadar soldier, however benign his current mission.

"Are there any further questions?" Ro asked, winding up the morning's final security briefing. Seeing none, she was about to adjourn the meeting and release everyone, when she saw Etana reenter the room, an unreadable expression on her face. The deputy made a subtle hand gesture, part of a set of prearranged signals which were well known to every member of Ro's regular staff. Ro acknowledged Etana with a small nod. *Something big is happening, but no lives are in danger.*

"Thank you all for your attention and your help in making this historic event go smoothly and safely for all involved," Ro said, adjourning the meeting. Etana quickly approached her as the wardroom emptied, and

331

they partially turned their backs to the people still leaving.

"The *Trager* has just returned without calling ahead," Etana said quietly. "*Vedek Yevir* is aboard. He and Gul Macet are awfully excited about something, but they won't tell us what it's all about yet."

Ro sighed heavily. The last thing she needed right now was another complication.

23

I know this place, Julian thought a moment after the transporter beam released him. And he felt some genuine surprise that this should be so, given everything else he knew he'd forgotten.

Clad only in paper slippers and one of the loose, robe-like garments he recognized from his childhood doctor visits, he stood alone on the shattered stone steps that led to the entrance of the Hagia Sophia. But sixth-century Istanbul's grandest cathedral was much smaller than it had been during his last visit. Its gleaming dome was far shallower than he remembered it, and now lay many meters closer to the sun-baked street. The structure gave the impression of a scale model, its entire physical footprint now scarcely larger than a Starfleet runabout.

Shrunken down, just like me.

Julian gazed around at the tumble of block buildings flanking the ancient cobblestone streets. Except for the faint echoes of some distant, semimusical noise, the city was utterly still. No people at all were in evidence, not Ezri, Nog, or anyone else. This realization made the small hairs on his neck stand up like vigilant soldiers.

At least Ezri was right about the monsters, he thought, seizing the notion for whatever small comfort it provided.

Perhaps, he thought, his friends had already gone inside the cathedral. That was where they'd said we were all going, after all. Into the cathedral. He knew that they had come here with him in search of healing. And this place was where he kept every cure and remedy he had ever studied.

Whatever he had not yet forgotten was either here, or nowhere.

Julian had to crouch to get through the door to the gallery at the cathedral's perimeter. Once inside, he bumped his head painfully on the ceiling when he tried to stand up straight. The great gallery was cleared of the rubble he recalled from his previous visit, and it was as empty of people as the surrounding city. But the gallery was now only a narrow corridor, lined with makeshift walls of bricks and plywood. The low ceiling forced him to walk stooped over as he made his way toward the now-tiny staircase—

—which he now saw led up to a library doorway so small that not even Kukalaka would have been able to wriggle through it. *There's no help here,* Julian thought, looking back over his shoulder at the way he had come. He saw that the door through which he had entered was now impossibly small as well.

Panic electrified him. *Trapped!*

He turned his head toward where he remembered a large external window ought to be. It was boarded up, but the wood didn't look very strong. Curling into a fetal position on the marble floor, Julian braced his back against a gallery wall and pushed his feet against the wood with all his strength. He heard the building itself groan, as though its ancient bricks and mortar were actively struggling against him.

The wooden barrier suddenly gave way in a shower of chips and flinders, and his own momentum launched him like a missile through the window frame—

—and into a large, white, brightly lit chamber. He looked up and saw three people, two human women and a dour-faced Vulcan male, sitting behind a long table, gazing at him in expectation. All of them wore blue Starfleet uniforms.

"Well, *Mister* Bashir?" the Vulcan said. He sounded impatient, and not very much fun. "Which is it? A preganglionic fiber, or a postganglionic nerve?"

Starfleet Medical School, he thought, recalling a particular variety of panic he thought he'd locked safely away years ago. *The oral exams.*

"I . . . I'm afraid I don't know . . . I can't recall the answer to that, sir."

One of the women, a brassy redhead with bright cherry-colored lipstick, glared at him as she pressed a large red button on the side of the table. "Another defective," she said, her voice dripping with contempt. "He needs to be placed with the others."

A pair of burly, white-clad hospital orderlies were suddenly flanking him, as though the woman had conjured them from thin air. They took his arms in a firm grasp, lifting him between them so that his feet couldn't touch the ground. Before he could protest, they had whisked him out of the room and into a long, sterile-looking white corridor.

"This way, sir," said the one on his right. Julian saw

that the man's collar bore stitching in the shape of three letters: *DEE*.

"We've got the perfect place for you," said the other one. *DUM* was stenciled onto his collar.

They came to a stop before a small, open room whose broad entryway crackled with the telltale blue glow of a security force field. Four people stood, sat, or reclined in the chamber. As the orderlies placed Bashir on his feet and set about lowering the force field, one of the figures in the cell, a black-clad, goateed young man, leaped up onto a table. Atop his head was a wide-brimmed top hat. Tucked into the hatband was a large card bearing the inscription *IN THIS STYLE 10/6*. He regarded Julian in nervous silence, his eyes brimming with suspicion, his body bowstring-taut.

Julian knew he'd seen the hat before, as well as the lettering on the orderlies' collars. He supposed he'd seen both images, and perhaps some of the other oddities he'd encountered here, in the illustrations from some beloved children's book whose title he could no longer recall.

The man in the hat, however, he recognized immediately.

"So who's the new plebe, hmmm?" said the goateed man, his words spilling out like rapid-fire projectiles. "This is a private club, hmmm? We're not accepting pledges at the moment. Try us again in a few months, hmmm?"

"Take it easy, Jack," said one of the orderlies, standing in the entryway, the force field now down. Turning to address the other three people in the room, he said, "I want you all to meet Jules. You and he will be seeing a lot of each other from now on."

"I'm *not* Jules," Bashir said to the orderlies, who did

not appear interested in responding. "My name is Julian."

"Hi," said a rotund, sixtyish male with a fringe of wild white hair who stood in the center of the room. He was smiling beatifically and holding a bottle whose neck bore a tag emblazoned with the words *DRINK ME*.

"I'm Patrick," he said to Bashir. "Don't mind Jack here. They say he's antisocial." Patrick punctuated the last word by turning the first two fingers of both hands into pantomime quotation marks. "But Jack's not like me. Or Lauren." He gestured toward a corner divan on which a young, dark-haired woman was sprawled in a languorous pose.

"Charmed," said the woman, her body's contours concealed very little by her tight-fitting scarlet jumpsuit. She smiled up at Julian with a predatory glint in her eyes that made Julian blanch. A silver tea service was arranged on a table beside the divan, and she sat up and began filling a quartet of delicate porcelain cups. "Welcome to our little tea party."

"I don't belong here," Julian said to the orderly nearest him, stammering as he groped for the right words. "These people are having . . . unintended side effects. From . . . from their genetic, ah, resequencing."

The orderly smiled condescendingly. "That's right, Jules. Just as *you* are. Or have you already forgotten why you've come here?"

Then Julian noticed the silent, sandy-haired young woman who sat alone on a straight-backed chair in the opposite corner. Her eyes were vacant, set in a delicately structured face as pale as a classical marble statue. *Sarina Douglas,* Julian thought, recalling how someone who looked very much like him had once helped her regain the ability to speak and interact with the world. The romance that they had almost shared now seemed dreamlike, as though it were a memory that belonged to someone else.

Sarina abruptly lifted her eyes and looked around the cell. "I wasn't asleep," she said, smiling broadly though her voice was hoarse and weak. "I heard every word you fellows were saying." Then she locked her gaze with Julian's. "I'm so glad you've decided to join us, Jules."

"Get in, Jules," said the smiling orderly.

"Now," said the other one, who was scowling dangerously.

"No," Julian said. He took a step back.

"You're one of *us* now, Jules," Lauren said. Jack and Patrick grinned.

"No!" Julian screamed, backing away from the open cell. The two orderlies approached him. Both were scowling now, their thick biceps rippling beneath their short sleeves. The larger and meaner of the two grabbed for him. Julian twisted to the side without thinking, allowing the big man to overbalance himself and plunge hard onto the tile floor.

Before Julian could move farther, the second orderly had clasped him from behind in a bear hug, holding him fast as the first man began to regain his feet. Julian struggled, but simply didn't have enough power or leverage to break free.

Suddenly, the orderly's weight shifted, and the big man sank to his knees, releasing his grip. Julian pushed himself free, fell to the floor, and rolled into a crouch.

Jack gave out a long, ululating war whoop, his arms and legs wrapped around the orderly's back and shoulders. Though the big man struggled to dislodge his rider, the wiry patient held on with the tenacity of a Tiberian bat.

The force field is still down, Julian realized as he regained his feet. *The lunatics are out of the asylum.*

He pounded away down the corridor at a flat-out run, a tumult of voices falling away behind him, but there was no immediate pursuit. After several minutes of running, the corridor widened into another room. It was a comfortably appointed lounge, where a man and a woman sat side by side on a low sofa, each of them reading silently. And studiously ignoring one another.

They were much younger than the way he remembered them, so much so that he almost failed to recognize them as Richard and Amsha Bashir, his parents. So intent were they on their respective reading material—Father pored over what appeared to be a blueprint of some sort, while Mother studied an old-fashioned hardcover thriller—that they both failed to notice his entrance. *Not at all unusual, really.* A bitter smile came to his lips. *Some things never change.*

"Hello, Mother," Julian said. "Father."

Father looked up from his blueprint and offered Julian an uneasy smile. "Ah, there you are, Jules."

Mother matched Father's wan smile. "We were beginning to think you were lost."

Julian said nothing. *I am lost,* he thought, until he began recognizing some of the details of the room's appointments. The corner chair, upholstered in a scaly gray leather made from the hide of some genetically altered beast. A bas-relief on the wall depicting one of the local eight-legged riding animals. Those details had been among the earliest trophies he'd placed in the Hagia Sophia.

I'm in the waiting room. On Adigeon Prime.

"Why have you brought me here again?" Julian said, glaring at his father.

A scowl creased Father's swarthy features. "Because it's necessary, Jules."

"Because I turned out so dumb, you mean."

Mother adopted a sad, long-suffering expression. "Because we want you to have a chance to lead a happy, fulfilled life, Jules. And once the procedures are done, that's exactly what you'll have."

Julian struggled against his growing confusion. "We already did this once, Father. When I was six."

Father rose to his feet, his scowl deepening. "I'd never know it from looking at you now, Jules."

"Stop calling me that," Julian said, an arc of rage sparking across some gap in his soul. "I'm *Julian* now. I've *been* Julian ever since I came to understand what you'd done to me here."

Mother rose and approached Julian, taking both of his hands, holding their palms upward. *"Are* you?"

"Am I *what?"*

"Are you really the same Julian we brought home from Adigeon Prime?"

Julian looked down at his hands, encircled by hers, and studied them. They were the hands of a grown man, rather than those of a six-year-old child. In a rush, he realized that he could no longer remember having come to Adigeon Prime as a child.

Because he had never been here.

Because he had never undergone the "procedures."

Because he was now the grown man who young, ungenengineered Jules Bashir would have become, had he been left alone, unaltered.

Father eyed the chronometer on his wrist with evident impatience. "Get ready, Jules. The doctors will be coming to examine you any minute now."

Julian thought about that for a long, silent interval.

Perhaps he was being offered a way to recover everything he had lost. Everything that the alien cathedral had taken from him. Or perhaps not.

Procedures. They think I'm nothing without their precious procedures. And maybe they're right.

Mother held his hands more tightly. Julian saw great tears of disappointment pooling in her eyes. "We only want what's best for you, Jules. We love you so much—"

He shook her hands away. "You obviously don't love me the way I am *now*," he said, taking a backward step and nearly tripping over his own feet in the process. He felt slow and awkward as well as stupid.

A door across the room opened, and Richard Bashir turned toward the sound, blocking Julian's view momentarily. Then he turned back, smiling. "The doctors are ready to see you now, Jules."

Julian's breath caught in his throat when he saw that the two burly orderlies he had just eluded were standing in the open doorway, menacing glares fixed on their faces, fists as big as cured hams planted on their hips.

Limbs flailing, Julian ran from the room the same way he'd entered.

The air shaft was cold and filthy, but at least he was out of sight. Safe, if only for the moment. His hands shaking, Julian peered through the ventilation grill at the white corridor several meters below. Nobody seemed to be searching for him. He had no idea how long he'd lain in the cramped conduit, and wondered how much longer he could continue to hide. Or if he even should.

Maybe those men only wanted to make me smart, the way Mother and Father said. He wondered how he could ever hope to recover what he'd lost if he remained too frightened to take a chance and let them try.

341

He recalled how doctors had always frightened him during his childhood, until he'd understood that they were only trying to help him. The death of that poor little girl back on Invernia II, which he had witnessed at the tender age of ten, had occurred because an ion storm had prevented anybody from reaching a doctor in time—and because nobody had known that a local herb could have saved her from the fever that took her life. That sad incident had made him want to become a doctor, a notion that had already been in the back of his mind ever since five-year-old Jules had begun stitching up Kukalaka's wounds.

That memory hadn't been taken from him, he realized. He tried to recall exactly what it was that had been hunting down and killing his memories, but couldn't. All he could come up with was the vague impression that his memories had been somehow related to a church of some sort.

Footfalls echoed loudly in the corridor below, startling Julian into clunking his head into the side of the air shaft. Ignoring the sharp pain, he looked through the grillwork again to see who was coming. The footfalls crescendoed, and a moment later the two large orderlies walked by directly beneath Julian's vantage point. They were escorting a small figure who appeared to be a patient. He was a frail boy who couldn't have been older than six. Julian could hear him crying; one of the orderlies appeared to be muttering bland reassurances to the child.

Julian's heart leaped into his throat when the boy looked up at one of the men, turning his tear-streaked face ceilingward, his eyes bright and alert. The child bore little resemblance to the dull, vacant creature Julian had expected to see. But there was no mistaking his identity.

The weeping, terrified patient was young Jules Bashir. And he was about to undergo, Julian was certain, the "procedures" his parents had arranged.

A short while later, Julian clambered down from the stifling air duct into another corridor, which turned out, thankfully, to be empty. Hearing approaching footfalls, he flattened himself against the wall. Julian knew he had an important task to perform here, but couldn't quite recall what it was. Trying to think in terms of plans and objectives was proving utterly frustrating.

But there wasn't time to think as the footfalls grew near. The orderlies, their young charge between them, passed Julian along a perpendicular corridor. He heaved a sigh of relief as they went by without noticing him, then quietly shadowed them through several turns. Luckily, they never turned to look behind them, and the sounds of their passage covered whatever noise Julian's pursuit was making.

Peering from around a corner, Julian watched as the two large men shepherded young Jules through a door to what appeared to be some sort of lab or infirmary. Moments later, the two men emerged again into the corridor—this time without the child—and walked away, taking no notice of Julian as they disappeared around another bend in the hallway.

Responding intuitively to some vague ghost of a memory, Julian saw that this had to be the place. *The place where the doctors changed me.*

He moved quietly to the unlocked door, pushed it open, and stepped into the room.

The boy sat in a too-large, swept-back chair. His slight body all but lost in his bulky hospital gown, the child's slippered feet dangled several centimeters off the sterile floor. His small hands were in his lap, clutching at one another as though each were competing for the protection of the other. Little Jules was facing in Julian's direction, while a trio of graceful, birdlike Adigeons—evidently doctors or surgeons—handled hypos and tricorders, their white-smocked backs to the door, apparently oblivious to Julian's presence. The boy, though he clearly had noticed Julian's entrance immediately, said nothing. He made no sign that might serve to alert the Adigeons.

Clever child.

Julian stood in silence, studying the boy's dusky eyes—the same eyes that once studied him from the other side of his father's old-fashioned looking glass—for what seemed like minutes, seeking some justification there for his parents' fervid desire to remold and remake him. The child's eyes, though betraying a hard edge of fear, nevertheless smoldered with something irrepressible. This boy seemed to be anything but the afflicted alter ego his parents had assured him that he was so much better off without. Young Jules bore scant resemblance to the cautionary specter that had followed him ever since the day when fifteen-year-old Julian Subatoi Bashir had learned the far-reaching extent of the genetic enhancements his parents had secured for him on Adigeon Prime. The child looked more like the bright if slightly learning-disabled doppelganger who sometimes stalked Julian's dreams like the ghost of a murdered twin.

Despite the accelerating deterioration of his own intellect and perceptions, Julian knew that he could believe in one simple, objective truth about young Jules simply by meeting his gaze—somebody was in there, a tenacious soul stoking an inner fire.

A pointed question suddenly jolted him: Would his

parents' well-intentioned interference douse those fires?

Julian fell out of his reverie when he noticed that one of the three Adigeons had turned to him. The creature glared at him, its feathery neck ruff rising in agitation. "How did you get in here?"

The other two Adigeons turned to him as well. "Don't worry, Doctor," said a second one. "Don't you recognize him? He's the mature version of the youngling we're treating."

"I see," said the first Adigeon, scouring Julian from top to bottom with one of its side-mounted, lidless eyes. "Well, we certainly do seem to have made a botch of things, haven't we?"

"I'll call the large humans back in to remove him," said the third physician. "If he interferes with these procedures, even accidentally, who knows what will happen to this child as it matures?"

Who knows? Julian thought, wondering whether he would have fallen so far had he never been forced to climb so high in the first place. Still, what these doctors wanted sounded like what he should want as well. As though it were the whole point of his having come to this place. He wished he could remember more than that.

And that the boy's pleading eyes didn't make the whole endeavor feel so completely *wrong*.

Young Jules sat, watching in silence. But Julian sensed that the boy wasn't simply staring vacantly. He seemed to be paying very close attention to the tableau before him. Discordant music played quietly in the background, echoing down some distant corridor.

The first Adigeon approached Julian until he could smell the creature's cool breath. Its aroma was an incongruous mixture of buttered popcorn, peppermint, and Tarkalean tea. "You're not supposed to be here," it said.

His arm suddenly tremulous, Julian pointed to the boy—the person he had once been, so long ago. And without being certain why, he came to an utterly visceral decision.

"You're not supposed to be here," the Adigeon repeated, raising one of its taloned hands threateningly.

"Neither is he," Julian said, and then rushed the delicate alien, bowling him over into the other two Adigeons. Surprised, they collapsed in a heap of flapping limbs. Julian knew they wouldn't stay down long. He only had seconds.

He moved quickly to young Jules, whose eyes had widened in either fright or awe, or perhaps both. The child offered no resistance when Julian took his hand, pulled him to his feet, and marched him through the laboratory door.

They stopped for a moment in the corridor, regarding one another appraisingly. "Thank you," Jules said. Julian grinned down at the boy. *Thank* me, he thought. And then they ran together down the corridor.

Past the orderlies, who gave chase but swiftly fell behind, waving lollipops in the air in their impotent rage.

Past a very surprised Richard and Amsha Bashir, whose confused, angry shouts died away as they sprinted across the waiting room, knocking over a potted plant from which sprays of royal red, heart-shaped flowers spilled.

Past the astonished-looking members of the Starfleet Medical oral examination jury. The Vulcan's mouth made an O of surprise as Jack's top hat fell from his head.

Julian felt a stitch in his side and stopped to catch his breath. Jules came to a halt beside him, standing in companionable silence. Julian looked up. The Adigeon Prime hospital was gone. Seemingly kilometers above their heads, the wildly intersecting interdimensional

geometries of the alien artifact soared, appearing somehow inside out.

*Because I've been inside the thing all along. All of us
from the* Sagan *have been inside it.*

He could feel that everything he hadn't been able to
remember was flooding back to him. He stared up into
the artifact's ever-shifting skyscape of counterintuitively
constructed beams, braces, and spires as he felt his body
and mind surge with every genetically enhanced talent
he'd feared had been lost forever. Turning his eyes back
to young Jules, Julian regarded the child for a long moment before speaking.

But he was completely at a loss as to why.

"My God," he said. "What have I just done?" Unearthly
crystalline sounds, like those he'd first heard aboard the
Sagan, began reverberating gently in the middle distance.
Or perhaps they were coming from light-years away.

The boy smiled. "You finally recognized me."

"I think you mean I rescued you. And it was a stupid
thing for me to do, considering that it should have made
whatever the artifact did to me permanent."

"No," Jules said with a solemn shake of his head. "It
was the act of a simple but decent man."

"But I prevented you from . . . having the 'procedures.' Where does that leave me?"

"You've merely cut a tether to an unhealthy part of
your past," Jules said, then pointed straight up. Julian's
neck and eyes followed the gesture. "Consider your
love-hate relationship with me resolved."

The gilded dome of the Hagia Sophia now arced ma-
jestically over their heads. The discordant yet not unpleasant music swelled through the basilica in long,
reverberating strains. The cathedral's gallery stretched
out to a remote vanishing point, restored to its full sixth-

century splendor. Every painting, every tapestry, every sculpture appeared to be back in its appointed place and repaired to its original condition.

My memory cathedral.

Relief vied with incomprehension. "How?"

Jules beamed at him. "You'll have to find your own answers, Julian," the boy said as he began walking. Julian quickly followed, easily keeping pace as Jules moved through the gallery.

Julian felt a rush of gratitude for the inexplicable return of his mental acuity as one possible answer immediately presented itself. *Making my peace with Jules must have snapped me loose from all the other quantum realities. All those other worlds in which Mother and Father never brought me to Adigeon Prime.*

Jules nodded, as though he were privy to Julian's innermost thoughts. *Of course,* Julian thought, *how could he* not *be?*

"That's undoubtedly part of it," the boy said, coming to a stop beside the staircase leading to the main library. "But not the biggest part."

"So you're saying that I'm missing the point about what happened here," Julian said as he walked a short distance up the staircase. He put all his weight on the fifth step, and it made a satisfying squeaking sound in response. Just as it was supposed to.

"Yup," the boy said.

He looked down the staircase toward Jules. "This doesn't make sense. How could this place 'realign my worldline' when I actively prevented the procedures that would have turned *you* into *me?*"

Without saying a word, Jules strode toward a large stained-glass window that loomed nearby. Julian abandoned the staircase and followed the boy, noting that both of their reflections were clearly visible in the glass. Julian realized then that he was clad once again in a Starfleet duty uniform—complete with a combadge—and wondered idly what had become of the environmental suit he'd been wearing when the away team had beamed into the cathedral.

The child smiled up at Julian. "Let me give you a hint, then. Every decision you made in here was without the benefit of Adigeon Prime genetic engineering."

"I wasn't given much choice about that."

"Exactly," Jules said. "But in spite of that, you displayed courage and compassion. And not just here. Back aboard the *Defiant* as well." Then the child approached him, as though seeking a brotherly embrace.

Julian put his arms around the child—and was surprised to feel the youngster's volume seeming to diminish. Looking toward their reflected images, he watched in shock as the child's body grew insubstantial, literally melting into his own before vanishing, wraithlike.

Except for the image of the boy's smile, which seemed to linger on the glass a moment longer before it, too, disappeared.

In that instant, Julian came to an epiphanic understanding of his unexpected rapprochement with his long-vanished alter ego. For the first time in his life, he saw that there was no difference, at the core, between Jules and himself.

Jules never left me. He's been with me all my life. And Adigeon Prime never changed that.

Julian looked up, taking in the vista that stretched into infinity above his head. The Hagia Sophia's central dome had given way to the mind-bending internal geometries of the alien cathedral. A Wonderland, Julian thought, recalling a beloved bit of verse from his childhood.

> *Ever drifting down the stream*
> *Lingering in the golden gleam*
> *Life, what is it but a dream?*

The combadge on his chest began speaking, but he paid scant attention to it. Instead, he continued staring up into the infinite, exultant. *Himself* once again. Whole and complete. He wondered if this was how Kira had felt during her now-forbidden communions with Bajor's enigmatic gods. The volume of the ambient quasi-music rose to an almost cacophonous level, utterly drowning out the sounds of the combadge, but Julian found he didn't mind it at all.

Some measureless interval later, a coruscating shaft of light enfolded him. And the cathedral splintered around him, breaking into jagged shards like the memory of a dream.

24

Vedek Yevir could scarcely stop himself from blurting out the truth. First Minister Shakaar and Second Minister Asarem stared at him from the *Trager*'s main viewscreen. Shakaar seemed almost unable to control his anger as his words hissed through clenched teeth.

"Have you taken complete leave of your senses, Yevir? The reconciliation talks with Cardassia are stalemated, and any maverick action on your part can only result in a great loss of standing for you among both the Vedek Assembly and *the Chamber of Ministers."*

When Shakaar paused for breath, Yevir interrupted him. "As I said, First Minister, what I will be presenting today will likely change everything. Forever and for the better. My standing with either chamber of the Bajoran Great Assembly is as nothing compared to that. Please join me on the Promenade in ten minutes." He punched a button on the Cardassian console, and the viewscreen went blank, cutting off the tirade that was obviously coming.

Yevir smiled to himself. It wasn't like him to be so abrupt with Shakaar—doing so certainly wasn't politically advantageous—but the elation that he was feeling far outweighed his concern over any potential consequences. *The Prophets are indeed guiding me. They could not have sent a clearer sign.*

Immediately after contacting the other vedeks who constituted his inner circle, Yevir rose. He led the way as the group disembarked from the *Trager*, though Gul Macet and Cleric Ekosha trailed him by only a step or two. Several lower-level Oralian Way functionaries—rectorates—guided four small antigrav sleds through the docking ring passageway.

Vedeks Eran, Scio, Kyli, Bellis, Frelan, and Sinchante all crowded the hall in front of him, their aides and several guards moving behind them. Yevir saw that each of his compatriots' eyes were bright, their smiles wide. He grinned in response and gestured past them. "I assume we'll have an audience?" he asked.

"Most definitely, Linjarin," Frelan said. "Word has spread throughout the station. Everyone is buzzing with anticipation of your announcement."

Yevir nodded and continued past the others as they parted to allow him a path through the center of the corridor. He cast a quick glance over his shoulder, pleased to note that the others had fallen into procession behind the sled bearers.

As they made their way onto the habitat ring, Yevir saw that Frelan had not exaggerated. The station was already lavishly decorated for the signing ceremony, with Bajoran flags, ornate Old Bajoran tapestries, and UFP banners all suspended from the tall ceiling. But what was most impressive were the large numbers of people crowded onto the Promenade. Representatives of dozens of races, as well as hundreds of Bajorans and humans, milled about. Yevir looked up and saw Shakaar and Asarem on the Promenade's upper level, glaring down at him from over the railing. Nearby stood Trill Ambassador Seljin Gandres, who was chatting amiably with Bajor's supreme magistrate, Hegel Ytrin, who looked resplendent in her dark judicial robes.

Yevir mounted a small riser nearby, a prop intended for use during the many Bajoran cultural festivities planned for the evening's celebrations. He couldn't see any amplification devices, but the past few years of administering at temple had given him a more than adequately audible public-speaking voice. He reached into the pocket of his robe, touched the cold object within, then withdrew his hand and raised his arms to the assembled throng.

"Greetings to all who have assembled here on this historic day," he said loudly as the crowd settled down. "Today's ceremonies will mark the entry of Bajor into a larger realm, a galaxy full of undreamed-of possibilities.

"For many long decades we were a world under siege, and even as we continue the long process of rebuilding our homes and farms and cities, we must also rebuild our hearts and our trust. Nowhere has this trust been more fragile than in our relationship with Cardassia. Once our sworn enemies, they have now petitioned to become our friends."

Yevir saw that he had the complete attention of everyone on the Promenade. He also noted that Colonel Kira and other members of her staff stood on the upper level, watching him. Vedek Solis, he observed, was beside the colonel.

He continued, "Over the past several months, First Minister Shakaar and Second Minister Asarem have worked with Cardassian Ambassador Natima Lang to draw up a blueprint for a lasting peace between our world's political leaders and the Ghemor government on Cardassia. Unfortunately, those plans have stalled of late. Without extraordinary efforts by extragovernmental entities—specifically, the clergy of two great civilizations and the ordinary citizens from whom their moral authority flows—Bajor's joyous Federation Day might also sound the death knell for any chance of an honest, unmediated peace between Bajor and Cardassia. But I have recently learned that the people of Bajor and Cardassia aren't about to permit that to happen."

Yevir reached into his pocket, pulled out the jevonite statue, and held it up for all to see. During his speech he'd searched the crowd for Mika and her child, but failed to pick them out; despite the folly of her belief in Ohalu, he regretted that she would not be able to share in this moment.

"Kasidy Yates, the wife of the Emissary, recently gave me this statue, which was unearthed from the ruins of the lost city of B'hala. It is many thousands of years old, made during a time long before any star travel was possible in the sector which encompasses both Bajor and Cardassia. Yet this statue is composed of jevonite, a mineral previously had been found nowhere else *except* Cardassia. The figure's face is carved to represent both Bajoran and Cardassian features.

"How can this be possible? I have asked myself this question repeatedly. Ages before Bajor and Cardassia were known to have crossed paths, a statue depicting a union between our two peoples was brought to Bajor. I can come to but one conclusion: For this to have happened so long ago, for it to have been discovered *now,* for the wife of the Emissary to give it to me during our time of greatest change . . . clearly, these things all show the guiding hand of the Prophets."

Yevir motioned to the vedeks behind him. "The peace-loving, ordinary people of two worlds have begun to bring about the rapprochement that their leaders have yet to accomplish. Some say that politics is the art of the possible, and that may be so. But to conceive and bring about a reality which has been characterized by many as *impossible* requires *faith*. When intergovernmental diplomacy and negotiation fail to bring about what *must* come about, then it is time for people of faith to step into the breach." He fixed his eyes on Shakaar and Asarem for a moment, then returned his gaze to the crowd.

"To ensure the future of both our worlds, I have joined my voice to those of a small but influential group of Bajoran vedeks and Cardassian clerics. Cleric Ekosha leads Cardassia's Oralian Way, the largest denomination of the faithful who wish to build a trusting mutual relationship with Bajor. During the last several hours, she and many key members of the Oralian hierarchy have already provisionally agreed to an exchange of spiritual ambassadors—Bajoran vedeks and prylars and Cardassian clerics and rectorates who will go to their former enemy's respective homeworlds as part of an ongoing grassroots effort to build a sincere, uncoerced, and enduring peace. Many of the details remain to be worked out, to be sure. Perhaps because faith is our mutual stock-in-trade, Cleric Ekosha and I both have tremendous confidence that this plan will tie our two worlds together in amity and generosity—and make any future wars between our two civilizations as unthinkable as those age-old conflicts that pitted the ancient Bajora against the Perikians, the Lerrit, the Endtree, and so many of our other ancient forebears."

Yevir turned toward the Oralian rectorates, who responded by moving forward and repositioning the four antigrav sleds. Each Oralian knelt beside one of the sleds and grasped the cloths that covered the objects supported by the floating devices. The vedeks and Ekosha stepped forward, smiling in anticipation. Gul Macet hung back a bit, behind the others, though he remained prominently visible to all.

"As these negotiations began, Cleric Ekosha impressed me with her clear understanding that building trust was paramount, particularly with so many of Bajor's Occupation-inflicted wounds still livid and unhealed. Ekosha and others therefore sought to bring us tangible proof of their sincerity. So together we combed Cardassia's ruins, hoping to recover at least one of Bajor's most significant spiritual artifacts, the Tears of the Prophets. Imagine my astonishment when a journey into a demolished Cardassian city yielded *all four* of the missing Orbs!"

At Yevir's prearranged signal, the rectorates bowed their heads and pulled the cloth coverings away, revealing four ornately carved arks. The vedeks behind Yevir surged forward. Frelan reached toward one of the arks, then fainted dead away. Luckily, Eran caught her, supporting her frail body with one trembling arm. Sinchante's jaw dropped as though captured by a neutron star.

Concurrently, faithful Bajorans throughout the Promenade began reacting in a variety of ways. A few fainted just as Frelan had. Many began to pray. Others lifted their arms and cheered. Some began to chant or sing or hug those next to them, Bajoran or not. Yevir lifted his eyes to witness the effect his unexpected unveiling was having on Shakaar and Asarem, and was delighted to see astonishment etched across their features.

Yevir spoke again, his voice clear and resonant. "Because peace is too important to be thwarted by failures of leadership, the people of two worlds have taken direct action of their own. This is no mere stunt or gesture; it is real. Children of the Prophets, on this joyous inaugural Federation Day, Cardassia returns to you the Orb of Truth, the Orb of Destiny, the Orb of Souls, and the Orb of Unity. It is my fervent hope that we will keep these four precepts in our minds and in our hearts as we face Bajor's new future. As long as our faith remains strong, there is no goal the Will of the Prophets cannot achieve. Including the creation of peace between Bajor and Cardassia, and a repudiation of war as complete as the banishment of the Pah-wraiths."

Yevir turned and opened his arms to Ekosha, and the two embraced.

The Prophets have truly blessed us all.

Standing on the Promenade's upper level, Vedek Solis placed his trembling hand on Kira Nerys's shoulder. She turned to him, shock reflected on her face as much as he imagined it showed on his. He enfolded her in his arms for a moment, his robes cloaking her as she held tightly to him. He didn't need to touch her ear to feel her *pagh;* it radiated from her brightly enough that even nonbelievers should have been able to perceive it.

He smoothed her hair, speaking in low tones so that only she could hear. "Yevir is obviously capable of doing good. No matter what the Prophets are to Bajor, gods or teachers, his actions *have* been guided by a higher power. But I also believe that power has as much faith in *you*, Nerys, as you have in *it*."

She embraced him even more tightly, and he heard her recite what he recognized as a prophecy from one of the sacred texts: *"When the children have wept all, anew will shine the twilight of their destiny."* Then she grew silent, and he felt her begin to sob. Solis gently patted her back, taking care that his robes shielded her from anyone else's view. The colonel's feelings about her faith did not deserve to be scrutinized in public.

Shakaar paced the room, which had been emptied of all personnel. Yevir's announcement had stunned him and had created a sensation throughout Deep Space 9, as well as all across Bajor. He could no longer stand to watch the reports on the secular or religious comnets, though they scrolled quietly across viewscreens set up on work tables near the windows.

Stalking over to the replicator, he angrily ordered a *reqilof,* but after taking one sip of the drink, he flung it and its container across the room. *Curse Yevir and his little diplomatic coup!* Shakaar moved to his desk and pressed a tiny button, opening a drawer. He pulled out a small silver box and stared at his reflection on its gleaming surface. Stroking the hasps that kept the box closed, he willfully changed his thinking. *What can I do to turn this situation to our advantage?*

The door chimed, interrupting his thoughts, and he quickly placed the silver box back into the drawer. He looked at the security monitor mounted near the door and saw that Asarem stood outside. "Come in," he said.

The door slid open and she moved into the room, worry evident in her eyes. "Edon, I don't mean to intrude, but we really should confer about how these latest developments might affect today's signing ceremony." Voicing an apparent afterthought, she asked, "Are you all right?"

He slumped into a couch, unconcerned about wrinkling his simple yet formal suit. "Why wouldn't I be all right? Just because one of our top religious leaders has done the very thing *we* would not, and has struck a very public deal with the people who were once our greatest enemies?"

She took a seat across from him, and he realized that his tone was alarming her. He softened his voice and smiled. "Of course I'm ecstatic to have the Tears of the Prophets returned. Their significance to the people of Bajor is immeasurable. And perhaps we can use Yevir's maverick actions to our political, as well as spiritual, advantage. Certainly, presenting a publicly supportive face will prove to all in the Federation just how well Bajor's religious and secular authorities can work together. Everyone should be convinced of how very advanced and peace-loving the Bajoran people truly are—despite the depredations they've suffered for so many decades at the hands of their Cardassian oppressors."

Asarem looked perplexed for a moment, but she smiled wanly. "I agree. To that end, let me also inform you that I have received a communiqué from Cardassia Prime. In the wake of Vedek Yevir's surprising achievement, Ambassador Natima Lang is eager to resume high-level talks between Cardassia and Bajor."

Shakaar snorted. "I expected as much."

Asarem appeared ready to ask a question, but then her expression changed, as though she had decided against it. "Would you like me to schedule a time to restart the negotiations with Lang? It will certainly help us to take advantage of the surprising good fortune and good faith brought by Yevir and Cleric Ekosha."

Shakaar waved his hand dismissively, and his traditionally calm demeanor returned, seeming to settle over him like a cloak. "No. We have other things to prepare for right now. Our biggest responsibility to the people of Bajor lies in the signing ceremony this afternoon. There will be plenty of time to deal with Lang and the Cardassians . . . especially once the Federation takes over responsibility for such things. With the UFP leading the charge, any negotiation can't help but be a lot more favorable for us."

Asarem's brow wrinkled, but she nodded slowly nonetheless. Her lukewarm reaction made Shakaar consider giving her a glimpse into his desk drawer.

Asarem exited the dignitary suite a few minutes later. Two guards fell into step behind her, but neither of them spoke to her.

She wasn't sure where she was going, nor with whom she should speak. Something had been nagging at her for weeks now, and this latest meeting with Shakaar only further crystallized her feelings. *Something is different about Shakaar. It isn't like him to be so angry and vindictive—even toward the Cardassians he used to fight during the Resistance.* She was no longer sure that his agenda and hers matched.

At a time when the coming days should have filled her with hope, Asarem could feel only unease.

What does Shakaar really intend for Bajor's future?

25

After Chief Chao had finished diverting auxiliary power to the targeting circuits, Shar attempted once again to reestablish the transporter lock on the away team as the deck beneath him shuddered and rolled.

"Nothing," Chao said. "I'm resetting the targeting scanner and reinitializing the transporter relays. Let's try this again."

Standing behind Shar and the transporter chief, Bowers breathed a quiet curse when this latest attempt to lock onto the away team failed as well. "Any more combadge signals from the artifact?"

"Negative," Shar said, shaking his head, his antennae curling backward. "But they've only been inside for a few minutes. I'm not even certain that time flows at the same rate inside the artifact as it does in normal space."

"Resetting again," Chao said, clearly not intending to give up anytime soon. "This would be a lot easier if we could bypass the relay network and bring the *Defiant* right up close to that artifact."

The ship rumbled and shook yet again under the Nyazen onslaught. "That doesn't strike me as particularly likely at the moment," Shar said, trying very hard not to think about the fact that three of his friends and colleagues might never be recovered. And as with Thriss, their deaths would weigh heavily on his soul.

But he knew he had no time or energy to spare on such self-recriminations. *We're in a combat situation now.* Turning toward Bowers, he said, "We have to get to the bridge." Even in his own ears, his voice sounded hoarse, pained.

Bowers's combadge spoke before either of them managed to get into motion. *"Medical bay to security!"* Ensign Richter's voice played a note of controlled panic.

"Bowers here. Go ahead, Krissten."

"The alien—Sacagawea—has just gotten into a highly agitated state. Maybe the fighting out there has spooked him, but I don't want to take any chances."

"I'm on my way," Bowers said, drawing his phaser, already at a run. Shar followed him out into the corridor and within moments the pair came bounding into the medical bay, where Lieutenant McCallum had also just arrived, phaser in hand. Bowers signaled with a quick shake of his head, and the lanky security officer stood ready to back him up.

Ensign Richter held a large hypospray in front of her. She had backed a few meters away from Sacagawea, who stood in the center of the chamber, gesticulating wildly with his spindly, insectile limbs. "Nothing is to fear now/presently," the D'Naali was saying, repeating the phrase like a mantra. "Help/assistance is inbound/coming. Soonfastsoon."

Shar felt an odd tingling in his antennae, a sensation he'd felt only in the immediate proximity of either a shrouded Jem'Hadar soldier—

—or a powerful subspace transmitter.

His curiosity fully roused, Shar approached the tall, willowy being, raising a hand in the direction of Bowers and McCallum to silence their protests. Sacagawea was immediately calmed, either by the science officer's mere presence or by his utter lack of fear.

"Are you saying that D'Naali ships are coming to assist us against the Nyazen?" Shar said, speaking slowly and distinctly so as not to overtax the universal translator. The ship shook and pitched again as yet another Nyazen salvo grappled with the *Defiant*'s shielding.

"Affirm/aver this to be so," said the creature.

Yes, Shar thought, glancing back at Bowers, whose eyes were beginning to narrow with suspicion. McCallum merely stood by, holding his phaser and looking bewildered.

"I would like to know why," the tactical officer said to the D'Naali, "you seem so sure about that."

Shar tapped his combadge. "Ensign ch'Thane to Commander Vaughn."

"Vaughn here," came the curt response. *"We're a bit busy at the moment, Ensign."* The ship shook yet again, as though to underscore the commander's words.

Shar winced inwardly, recalling his *zhavey*'s frequent tongue-lashings over far more trivial matters. "I don't think this can wait, sir."

"Then make it good, Mister."

* * *

After listening to Shar's bare-bones report, Vaughn ordered Tenmei to fall back another twenty million kilometers sunward. Undeterred, the Nyazen flotilla continued its dogged pursuit.

"They're rapidly closing to weapons range again," Merimark said from the tactical station, her tone losing a bit of its customary professional detachment. "Pulse phaser cannons are still off-line from the last salvos."

"Propulsion?" Vaughn asked.

"Warp and impulse both available," Merimark reported. "As long as we don't take any more damage, that is. Ensign VanBuskirk reports that the last hits effectively wiped out the cloaking-device repairs that were in progress."

Vaughn wasn't surprised. A working cloaking device would have been far too much to ask for. "Look sharp, Ensign Merimark. Ensign Tenmei, I want you to be ready to warp us out of this system on my order."

Tenmei cast a quizzical glance over her shoulder. "Sir?"

"That's only as a last resort, Ensign. I'm *not* abandoning our away team while there's an alternative."

"Captain, we can't survive another sustained, simultaneous assault from all nine ships," Tenmei observed with a frown.

Vaughn smiled humorlessly, recalling the discovery Shar had just related to him. "Somehow I don't think we'll have to."

"I've got several more incoming bogeys on the long-range scanners, sir," Merimark reported.

Vaughn hoped that was good news. "How many?"

"Eleven. No, twelve. They've just dropped out of low warp speed. Quickly closing on our position."

Stroking his beard, Vaughn grunted in acknowledgment. "Let me see them." An instant later, several long, gracefully tapered vessels appeared on the viewer.

D'Naali, Vaughn thought, picking out a particular ship from the group. Its distinctive pattern of hull scorches positively identified it as the vessel from which Sacagawea had come.

He heard the turbolift doors whoosh open behind him, and turned his chair toward the sound. Shar and Bowers stepped onto the bridge, flanking Sacagawea. The tall, insectile alien adopted a slouched-over, splayed-legged stance to accommodate the bridge's relatively low ceiling.

"Keep a close eye on him, Mr. Bowers," Vaughn said.

"The D'Naali are powering up their weapons," Merimark reported, her tone wary.

A split second later the bridge viewer showed bright bluish pulses of energy issuing from the prows of several of the newly arrived vessels. But the *Defiant* wasn't their target. The bursts struck the bulbous hulls of the lead Nyazen ships, who promptly returned fire. *Compression disruptors again,* Vaughn observed silently. *Relatively low-power stuff, on both sides.*

The battle unfolded quickly, and was decidedly one-sided. Although the weaponry of both sides was essentially equivalent, the newly arrived D'Naali fleet was stronger in both numbers and, apparently, in energy reserves.

"The Nyazen are breaking off," Tenmei reported. "Most of them are now on a direct heading for the alien cathedral. Several of the D'Naali are pursuing."

"Sometimes the cavalry really *does* come riding over the hill in the proverbial nick," Bowers said, still standing vigilantly beside Sacagawea and Shar.

Vaughn turned his chair toward the tactical station. "Hail the D'Naali flagship, Ensign Merimark."

Merimark was already listening intently to something on her earpiece. "Sir, the lead vessel is already hailing *us*."

A moment later the buglike face of a D'Naali commander appeared on the viewer. Vaughn wasn't absolutely certain this was the same being with whom he had spoken previously. They all looked remarkably similar, and Vaughn was willing to bet that they harbored precisely the same notion about humans.

"Thanking us not required/needful," the alien began. *"But your help/assistance we could accept/use in the now/futuretime."*

"How can we assist you?"

"Most impressed/astonished were we to discover/learn of your mattermover, with which your crew/people came/went to/from our vessel—and later/subsequently gained cathedral/anathema ingress."

Vaughn's initial impulse was one of anger, but he reined it in, reminding himself that these beings weren't human, or even humanoid. He had to make allowances for their culture, particularly in view of the difficulties that still existed in simply communicating with them. Nevertheless, Shar's report that Sacagawea had somehow informed his people of the beam-in to the cathedral was obviously right on the money.

Vaughn made a slashing gesture toward Merimark, who responded by cutting the audio channel. The alien commander's face remained on the screen as Vaughn turned toward Bowers and Shar. "How did Sacagawea report to his people, gentlemen? I presume he was searched and scanned for transmitters when he first came aboard."

"He was, sir," Bowers said, obviously at a loss. "We didn't find anything."

"We obviously missed *something*," Vaughn said,

wondering how the universal translator might mangle the D'Naali word for "spy."

"I stumbled across this inadvertently only a few minutes ago, Captain," Shar said, gesturing toward his antennae. "The D'Naali evidently possess an internal electromagnetic organ that enables them to communicate nonverbally on the lower-energy subspace bands. We never detected it because no one thought to monitor the long-wavelength channels."

Vaughn couldn't conceal his surprise. "You're saying they're . . . subspace telepaths?"

"Essentially," Shar said, nodding toward the alien visage on the screen. "And as such, they probably aren't being deterred by interrupting our audio feed."

Damn! Of course. The D'Naali commander is hearing everything we're saying—through Sacagawea. Vaughn gestured toward Merimark, who immediately restored the audio link with the D'Naali ship.

"Hear/perceive me enabled?" the alien captain was saying. *"Relieved/gratified am I that hearing/audition/reception is restored."*

"I can hear you quite well," Vaughn said, coming to a decision. Whether the D'Naali had intended to commit espionage aboard the *Defiant* or not, there was no reason to allow it to continue. "We thank you for allowing Sacagawea to act as our guide."

"Ryek'ekbalabiozan'voslu assures/attests that his timeinterval aboard/within your vessel has been enjoyable/profitable/instructive."

Vaughn smiled at the alien commander, whose casual mention of communications with Sacagawea made it appear that the D'Naali had no treacherous intentions. "We are prepared to beam him back to you any time. Now, if you wish."

The D'Naali commander made a gesture resembling a shrug. *"Not urgency, Ryek'ekbalabiozan'voslu's return/recovery. Far more interest/desire in matters other/different. Now/presently, we need/require use of your mattermover device/machine. And your new scheme/plan for enhancing/increasing its capability/power. Such machine/method we D'Naali could put to virtuous/appropriate use."*

They want to use our transporter? Vaughn bit back a curse at the deficiencies of the universal translator. Aloud, he said, *"What use?"*

The D'Naali blinked several times before replying, as though it had just heard an unutterably stupid question. *"With it, we too/as well may ingress/enter cathedral/anathema, just as Ryek'ekbalabiozan'voslu informs/reports that you have done/accomplished. With your mattermover, we can resolve/finish cathedral/anathema. For now, and for evermore/eternity."*

At last Vaughn felt he was beginning to understand the nature of the obscure conflict between the D'Naali and the Nyazen. His initial anger, sparked by Sacagawea's covert conversations with his commander, began smoldering again.

"You want to beam weapons into the cathedral," Vaughn said. "Those Nyazen ships aren't trying to prevent you from *worshiping* the thing—they're trying to keep you from *destroying* it."

"The Nyazen worship/revere the power/puissance of the cathedral/anathema," the D'Naali captain said. *"Its reach spans realms/worlds/universes. It is a sacred/terrible thing to them. It is a sacred/terrible thing to us— the selfsame sacred/terrible thing which shattered/destroyed our innersystem ancient/ancestral homeworld, longlonglong ago. An ancient evil/desolator,*

which scattered both lineages to the outervoids un-counted timeoutofmind ages/aeons past."

Beginning to believe that something more sinister than a language barrier was responsible for the apparent obfuscation on the part of the D'Naali, Vaughn suddenly had a chilling thought. If their sole purpose all along had been to destroy the cathedral, they might be inclined to say anything to achieve that objective—even if it jeopardized the *Defiant.* Turning away from the viewer, Vaughn crossed to Sacagawea. Had the alien not stood more than a head taller, they would have been standing nose to nose.

"We've sent members of our crew inside the cathedral because *you* told us that their . . . afflictions could be cured only there," Vaughn said evenly. "I sincerely hope you were telling us the whole truth about that."

Sacagawea shrank away from Vaughn, clearly intimidated. The creature's long, graceful fingers played idly with the small antigrav units harnessed to its appendages, as though suddenly aware of its extreme vulnerability aboard the *Defiant.* "No prevarications/lies I told," it said. "All this D'Naali-being has stated about/concerning afflicted ones is correct/true/sincere. The anathema's power/puissance is/remains your afflicted ones' sole/final hope."

Vaughn backed away from Sacagawea, not interested in appearing belligerent before its commander. Facing the viewer again, he said, "Your conflict with the Nyazen is none of my business. Our involvement was strictly in the interests of preventing any needless deaths."

"Our thanks/gratitude you have earned for this," the D'Naali commander said. *"Many D'Naali live/endure because of you."*

Vaughn smiled. "I'd like you to return the favor. Before you resume your fight with the Nyazen over the fate of your . . . anathema, we ask that you assist us in gaining access to it. Just long enough to locate and rescue our people. Then we'll be on our way."

The D'Naali commander seemed to consider Vaughn's proposal for a protracted moment before saying, *"Counteroffer/proposal. Afterward/following, you will give/send us your mattermover device/machine. We will then use it to resolve/finish the cathedral/anathema."*

"I can't do that," Vaughn replied without hesitation. Because both of these civilizations were warp capable, however marginally, the noninterference protections of the Prime Directive did not strictly apply. But the thought of radically disrupting the delicate, aeons-old balance of power that had obviously evolved between these two peoples didn't sit well with him.

The alien commander made a sound that evoked an image of a rusty iron gate. Vaughn interpreted it as a self-satisfied laugh. *"Damaged/strained is your vessel. Much/greatly drained/depleted are your energies/capabilities. Refusal is no option/poor choice."*

"Don't underestimate us," Vaughn said, realizing that his earlier unfavorable appraisal of the D'Naali's motivations now seemed precisely on the mark. "And don't think you'll impress us by making threats. Especially while one of your own people is still aboard my vessel."

"You will surrender/relinquish your hostage/prisoner," the D'Naali captain said.

"Primed/ready am I to die as a prisoner/hostage," Sacagawea responded, folding his long limbs about himself in what Vaughn interpreted as an elaborate display of D'Naali dignity. Clearly, the alien was preparing to die.

Not on my ship.

Vaughn turned toward the tactical station. "Ensign

Merimark, inform transporter chief Chao that our 'guest' will be beaming back to his ship immediately. Straight from the bridge."

"Respectfully, Captain, are you sure that's wise?" Bowers said, his wary eyes on Sacagawea. He and Shar had backed several paces away from the creature.

"Damn sure," Vaughn said, his glare spelling out plainly that there would be no further debate. "We can still run if we have to."

Vaughn faced the alien leader again as Sacagawea disappeared in a blaze of sparkling light. "Whatever you may believe about us, D'Naali, we're not hostage-takers."

The alien commander's mouth parts moved in a manner that Vaughn could only interpret as a grin. *Defend/ protect your ship, then.*

"Tenmei, make your best speed toward the alien artifact."

"Aye, sir." Her hands worked the console with the virtuosity of a concert pianist.

Vaughn saw a flash of blue light originate at the D'Naali flagship's prow just as the entire fleet fell away into the distance.

Relieving Merimark at tactical, Bowers said, "The D'Naali vessels are pursuing. But they won't be able to catch up to us."

"Unless we *stop*," Tenmei said from the conn. Over her shoulder, she flashed Vaughn a mock-questioning look.

Vaughn favored her with a good-natured scowl as he seated himself in the command chair. "We will, Ensign. At the Nyazen blockade fleet. And let's hope that the defenders are a little more reasonable than the destroyers."

* * *

"Keeping station at one hundred thousand klicks from the artifact, Captain," Tenmei said.

"No sign of weapons activity," said Bowers. "But the blockade ships have scanned us. They seem more curious than hostile."

"Perhaps they saw their adversaries firing on us," Shar said from the main science console.

My enemy's enemy is my friend, Vaughn thought. He sat in the command chair, absorbing and considering the constant reports coming from each member of his bridge crew.

"The Nyazen flagship is finally answering our hails," Hunter said.

The round, blotchy, whitish face that appeared on the viewer struck Vaughn as a study in astonishment, though he knew he was anthropomorphizing an alien being. On the other hand, perhaps the Nyazen captain simply couldn't believe Vaughn's audacity in approaching with a request to parley after having been driven away so recently by the massed forces of thirteen Nyazen blockade ships.

"You wish/desire to aid/assist us against the D'Naali destroyers?"

Who are going to arrive in force any second. "As I said," Vaughn continued, using his most patient, persuasive tones, "members of my crew are inside the cathedral at this very moment. They seek cures to the maladies that the cathedral caused."

"Not possible/believable. We prevented/averted your approach to cathedral/anathema."

Vaughn sighed. "You detected the energy beam we directed at the cathedral, did you not?"

"Detected, we did, your weapon," the Nyazen commander growled. *"Ineffectual/inconsequential it was."*

"It did no damage because it wasn't a weapon." *Time*

to roll the dice, Vaughn thought, pausing. "It was a material transmission device."

As inscrutable as the alien had been up until now, Vaughn could tell instantly that he had finally piqued his counterpart's interest. He continued his effort at persuasion: "Your sensors must have detected the approach of the D'Naali fleet by now. So here's my proposal: We will help you defend the cathedral against them—*if* you will allow us to approach it and render assistance to our officers."

"You could/might use your mattercaster to deliver weapons to/within cathedral/anathema."

Vaughn took a deep breath to keep from raising his voice. "We could have done that *before.* We *didn't.*"

The Nyazen commander was clearly turning that fact over in his mind.

Bowers spoke up. "Twelve D'Naali ships are dropping out of warp, Captain. Almost right on top of the blockade."

"Red alert!" Vaughn said, and alarm klaxons began blaring. He signaled to Bowers to turn them down.

"Incoming fire!" Bowers said. Tenmei reacted swiftly, turning the stronger starboard shields toward the massed fire of four of the arriving vessels. The deck pitched, and Vaughn held tightly to the arms of his chair.

Over the next few seconds, several more salvos struck the *Defiant*'s shields, including one that apparently got all the way through to the ablative hull armor before burning itself out. Then the attacks immediately trailed off as the Nyazen fleet began opening fire on their opposite numbers.

Vaughn watched as the viewer split its view; in addition to the face of the indecisive Nyazen commander, it also presented a tableau of two fairly evenly matched fleets bringing all their tubes to bear against one another. And in the unfathomable space beyond the warring spacefleets—one committed to destroying a much-feared anathema, another acting to defend its most sacred cathedral—the inexplicable spaceborne artifact continued its heedless, eternal tumble across the dimensions.

The Nyazen captain had evidently seen enough. *"This one agrees/assents,"* it said, then vanished from the screen.

Vaughn smiled a canny gambler's smile. "You heard the man, Tenmei. Bring us into transporter range. Shar, start scanning the thing's interior for our people. Leishman, get those phasers up and running."

The battle had been at a near stalemate from the beginning. But thanks to Tenmei's skillful flying, some inspired jury-rigging by Celeste, Leishman, and Van Buskirk—not to mention Bowers's pinpoint targeting—two of the *Defiant*'s four pulse phaser cannons very quickly encouraged a critical handful of the D'Naali ships to withdraw to a safer distance. Vaughn was relieved to note that all it had taken to accomplish this was several shots across the bow.

Watching the massed Nyazen forces chase away the remainder of the D'Naali flotilla, Vaughn considered the difficulties that still lay ahead. *Once our common threat is gone, the Nyazen are certain to turn on us.*

Shar spoke up from the primary science console. "Captain! I believe I've made sensor contact with our away team."

Bowers turned to Vaughn, displaying a look of delighted surprise. "I'm receiving combadge signals from inside the artifact. They're the prearranged evac signals,

374

sir. They're very weak, and extremely red-shifted, as though moving away from us at great speed."

"They could be temporally distorted by the artifact," Shar said. "There's no way to tell how long they've been transmitting."

Vaughn was beside himself, but kept his emotions in check. "How many signals are you getting?"

"Two," Bowers said, intent on both his earpiece and a complex wave-form display on his instrument panel. "No, three. And one subspace transponder."

Dax's transport pod. Vaughn grinned. It was about time for some good luck. *Where better than a cathedral to go looking for a miracle?*

"Good work, people." Vaughn hit the intercom. "Vaughn to transporter bay one. Chief Chao, I want you to lock onto the away team. Shar and Hunter will feed you the coordinates."

Chao took a moment to respond. *"Sir? That last hit seems to have overloaded the entire transporter system. I can't get a lock, either from here or with the secondary system."*

"Half the Nyazen blockade fleet is coming about in our direction," Bowers said, not sounding a bit surprised. "Weapons powering up."

"Shields?" Vaughn asked.

Bowers shook his head. "They're still in pretty rough shape, sir."

"We've still got warp power," Tenmei said. "I can get us clear of these guys so fast they'll think they're hallucinating."

So much for miracles. At my age, I ought to know better.

Vaughn summarily banished that train of thought. "We've also got an away team to rescue."

"And no working transporters," Tenmei reminded him.

Vaughn stared into the screen at the approaching ships. It had been a long time since he had recalled his rather unhappy Starfleet Academy Kobayashi Maru test so vividly. *So it's come to this.*

"We don't have much time," Tenmei said. "Should I take us out, sir?"

Shar abruptly sat bolt upright in his seat, as though he'd just received a sizable electrical shock.

Vaughn raised an eyebrow. "Lieutenant?"

"We still have *one* working transporter," Shar said, frantically entering commands into his console.

Tenmei scowled at the science officer. "Jeannette said the secondary bay was down as well."

Vaughn suddenly realized what Shar meant: the *Sagan*. "Do it. Fast."

Shar nodded. "Remotely engaging the *Sagan*'s transporter system."

"Tenmei, lower the shields and keep them off our backs for at least a few more seconds. Then get us the hell out of here on Shar's mark. Maximum warp."

Tenmei flashed Vaughn her best *I-love-a-challenge* smirk. "I'll do my best, Captain."

As she refocused her attention on her console, Vaughn smiled gently. He expected no less from his only daughter.

Krissten received only a scant moment's notice from the bridge before the away team members began materializing, one by one, in a great sprawl across the center of the medical bay floor.

The first to appear was Ezri, her skin looking as pale as death through the helmet of her environmental suit. An instant later, the transport pod containing the Dax symbiont shimmered into existence beside her; its liquid interior sloshed audibly, as though the small creature within had become greatly agitated. Ensign Juarez's quick tricorder scan immediately revealed the reason for Ezri's frightening pallor: Her body was rapidly shutting down because of the absence of the symbiont, which, luckily enough, appeared healthy. As she carefully laser-scalpeled the EV suit from Ezri's body, Krissten breathed a silent prayer that host and symbiont could be reunited before the Trill woman expired.

But before either nurse could begin hoisting Ezri's limp form onto a biobed, a second humanoid figure materialized on the floor: Nog, lying unconscious, his environmental suit's left leg conspicuously flattened, folded, and empty. Krissten could see no punctures, blood, or other signs of trauma. But the regenerated leg was nonetheless gone, as though it had never been.

Through his helmet, she could see that Nog was *smiling.*

"I've never seen anything like this before," Juarez said, apparently thinking out loud. "Whatever that weird object out there did to them seems to have just *un*-happened."

The ship suddenly rocked, then settled down. *Under attack again, no doubt,* Krissten thought as she and Juarez concentrated on moving Ezri very carefully onto one of the biobeds. Nog seemed stable enough for the moment. But even a mere medical technician could see that Ezri was dying.

Where's Dr. Bashir?

Juarez monitored Ezri's vital signs, shaking his head grimly. "We can't wait for Julian to return. We've got to get the symbiont back into Ezri's body *now.*"

"I agree," Krissten said, swinging open the lid to Dax's box. "Um, any idea how we go about doing that?" Assisting Bashir in removing the symbiont was one thing. Reversing the procedure without even a real surgeon's supervision was quite another matter.

Krissten looked to Ezri's chalk-white face, irrationally hoping to find guidance there. *I'm not trained for this procedure, Ezri. Neither of us is. We can only guess at it.*

Krissten looked up and studied the biobed readouts. Every indicator on the panel was steadily plunging. Several bio-alarms pertaining to blood pressure, respiration, and major organ functions had begun sounding shrilly. Hot tears of frustration rose in Krissten's eyes, but she forestalled them with an exercise of pure will. There was far too much at stake right now to allow herself to fall apart. Determined to put forth her best effort, she turned back toward the symbiont's transport pod—

—and collided with Julian Bashir, who must have just materialized behind her, the noise of his beam-in drowned out by the numerous medical alarms. She hadn't even heard him remove the helmet from his EV suit. He caught her in his arms, steadying her before releasing her. She stared for a moment into his dark eyes.

He was *in* there. Restored. She smiled up at him, and this time she didn't try to fight the tears.

She saw Bashir looking past her, first at Ezri, then at her bio-readings. He blanched when he saw how near death she was, but only for a split second. From then on, he was in full-on trauma-team mode.

"Ensign Juarez," he said, glancing at the insensate figure sprawled on the floor. "Please see to Lieutenant Nog." Falling back on her training, Krissten reached for her flame-colored trauma smock and began prepping Ezri for surgery. Meanwhile, Bashir stripped off his environmental suit and donned sterile surgical garb with preternatural speed. Once properly suited up, he reached into the open transport pod and gently lifted out the dripping-wet, russet-colored symbiont.

"Exoscalpel," he said.

Krissten handed him the instrument. "Sir?" she said.

He paused in his labors for only a moment. "Yes?"

"It's good to have you back."

26

Two hundred and fourteen, Joseph Sisko thought, updating his tally as he carefully made his way down the antebellum mansion's polished hardwood staircase. *One-hundred and twenty-three.*

Keeping track of the numbers had become a daily ritual, one that Joseph observed every morning as soon as he realized he was awake. He had become religious about it from the beginning; it had given him something to focus on other than the procession of new aches and ailments that each new day brought. No matter that carrying the ever-increasing weight of those days threatened to crush his frail bones. He *had* to count the days, dragging them with him wherever he went.

Two hundred and fourteen. One hundred and twenty-three. The first figure represented the number of days that had elapsed since his only son, Benjamin Lafayette

Sisko, had disappeared into that damned alien hellhole near Bajor.

The second marked the span of days since Benjamin's only son—Joseph's beloved grandson, Jake—had gone into the wormhole after his father, only to be swallowed up without a trace as well.

Passing through the broad atrium and into the kitchen, Joseph contemplated the sunlight that streamed in through the French windows, and yet brought him no joy. The August day—was it August already?—was already shaping up to be hot and muggy, but would surely be easier to face after he'd had his morning cup of coffee. He glanced up at the old-fashioned analog clock hanging above the range. Twelve fifty-five.

Afternoon coffee, then. He shrugged, then set about grinding the beans, ignoring the cold, persistent ache in his fingers, his neck, his shoulders. His soul. Morning. Noon. Night. What was the damned difference?

He paused as the water boiled and the coffee brewed, looking around the kitchen. Nothing of any consequence had changed here in years. On the far wall, above the sink, hung a framed photograph of the façade of his restaurant. The building that housed Sisko's Creole Kitchen for the past quarter-century had been a landmark in New Orleans' French Quarter for more than two hundred years. For Joseph, working in his kitchen among his loyal staff—serving a daily procession of new and regular customers—had always provided refuge from life's troubles. During later years, marked by heart trouble and too-frequent entreaties from employees, friends, and customers that he slow down, he found in the charming old building a comforting reminder of easier times, when Judith and Ben were still children. In those days, he'd never heard of shapeshifters or the Dominion, and never had cause to consider the casual damage that Starfleet could inflict on ordinary people who were just trying to make lives for themselves.

I raised you to be a chef, Ben. For all the good it did me.

On the shelf beside the sink lay an upended plastic bottle, its cap askew. The heart medicine. Joseph had been planning on getting the prescription refilled for the better part of a week now, but it hadn't seemed all that urgent. Somewhere in the back of his brain, he heard Ben's voice rising in wrath: *Damn it, Dad! Ask somebody on your staff to help you. Can't you cooperate just one time?*

The glare from the early-afternoon sun revealed the thickening patina of dust that covered the picture's glass frame. He reached up to touch Ben's inscription of one of Joseph's own favorite aphorisms: *"Worry and doubt are the greatest enemies of a great chef."* His finger came away streaked with a paste of old dirt and cooking grease. Searching his memories, he found he couldn't recall the last time he'd given this place a really good cleaning. Perhaps this, too, simply didn't matter all that much anymore.

A few minutes later, Joseph stood before the kitchen sink, holding a mug of hot, strong coffee in his hand. The hand trembled sharply, and a copious splash of near-boiling liquid forced him to place the cup on the counter. Cursing, he plunged his scalded hand beneath a stream of cold water—and glimpsed his own reflection in one of the metal pans he'd left on the drying rack.

He shut the water off, staring at the gaunt image he'd been trying so hard to avoid seeing in the bathroom mirror over the past few months. He wondered when exactly he had decided to stop shaving, but couldn't recall. And when had his hair gone so completely white?

Joseph lifted the pan and stuffed it haphazardly into one of the kitchen's lower cabinets. The motion seemed to have displaced several other objects located farther back on the shelf; he ignored the sounds of tumbling crockery.

The house stood silent again, except for the thready beat of his own heart and the hum of the wall clock that tirelessly measured out his remaining hours and days.

Was I supposed to do something today? He picked up his coffee, more carefully this time, and considered the coming evening without any real enthusiasm. The dinner crowd would arrive tonight, just as it always had, first in dribs and drabs, and later in waves. It would be just another night, indistinguishable from the years of nights on either side of it.

Enough of this. He set his half-full cup aside and pulled his thin cotton robe tightly around his narrow frame. Opening the blinds above the kitchen sink, he looked out into the vegetable garden. The sight immediately jogged his memory, bringing the day's agenda to the front of his thoughts. Walking to the back door, he slipped his feet into the work boots he'd left on the mat. Grabbing the gardening gloves from the peg beside the door, he ventured outside.

Jays and yellowhammers sang through the green canopy of longleaf pines and cypresses as Joseph deliberately picked his way down the narrow stone steps, wary of falling. Soon he was approaching the neat, green rows that had called to him from the kitchen window. Looking closely, he could see that all was not well in the garden today. Ropy, hairy strands of grape-scented kudzu vine had wormed their way through the neatly manicured rows of squash, cayenne peppers, and new potatoes, like some implacable Jem'Hadar road-building project. *We can send starships to the ends of the galaxy. But we still can't do a blessed thing about these damned weeds.*

There was something oddly reassuring about that.

Donning his gloves, he knelt on aching knees, pausing as his heart began to race disconcertingly. Minutes later, after he was satisfied that the worst of the discomfort had passed, he thrust his gnarled fingers into the black earth and got to work.

Gabrielle Vicente let herself into the house with the emergency key that Judith Sisko had surreptitiously given her during her visit last Easter. That day, Mr. Sisko's daughter had asked every member of the Creole Kitchen's staff—out of earshot of her father, of course—to keep a particularly close eye on Joseph. Gabrielle had been among the first to notice the old man's gradual deterioration since he had learned of his son's disappearance last Thanksgiving. Then, some four months later, when his grandson Jake had also gone missing, Mr. Sisko's decline had grown precipitous.

She stepped into the foyer, fearing the worst. "Mr. Sisko?"

There was no reply. Other than the clicking of her flat shoes on the ancient hardwood floor, the house was as silent as a tomb. The thought made her wince, and she banished it.

She continued calling out as she made her way through the large living room and entered the kitchen. A cup of coffee sat on the countertop beside the sink. She touched it, noting that it was still warm.

She heaved a sigh of relief.

Then she raised her eyes to the kitchen window and looked out across the vegetable garden.

Joseph Sisko lay sprawled in the dirt, silent and unmoving.

27

Captain's Log, stardate 53581.0

The Defiant *has finally passed the apex of its mission of exploration in the Gamma Quadrant. As we loop past the mysterious alien artifact—whose precise status as either a cathedral or a religious anathema I leave for better minds than mine to determine—our new heading will take us beyond System GQ-12475, bringing the Gamma Quadrant mouth of the wormhole ever nearer. At last we are homeward bound.*

But our investigations of this still largely unknown quarter of the galaxy are far from finished; the Defiant's *new trajectory will carry us through dozens of sectors into which no Alpha Quadrant humanoid has ever ventured before. The wonders and terrors of these past weeks haven't blunted the desire of the crew to see what lies over the next hill, and the one after that. The feeling of anticipa-*

tion I sense from everyone aboard remains nothing short of exhilarating. Even—or perhaps especially—among those whose lives were most profoundly affected by our encounter with the alien cathedral: the Defiant's first officer, Lieutenant Ezri Dax; chief medical officer Julian Bashir; and Lieutenant Nog, my chief engineer.

The readings, measurements, and holorecordings the crew has taken of the cathedral ought to keep the Federation's best physicists and architects—and maybe even the psychiatrists as well— busy for decades, if not longer. I find myself almost wishing it were possible to tow the thing home— until I stop to consider the havoc the artifact wrought among my crew.

Since sovereign jurisdiction over the object has been claimed by both the D'Naali and the Nyazen—two local sentient species who have for millennia used armed spacefleets to enforce their conflicting claims—it is my judgment that any further visitation by Starfleet personnel would be inappropriate. Certainly, neither group wants us around, at least at present. Perhaps one day the D'Naali and the Nyazen will reach an accord and invite us to investigate the object further. But until that time, my official recommendation to Starfleet Command and the Federation Council is to enforce a strict hands-off policy. And gods help any other alien crew that should happen to blunder into it.

Julian Bashir stood on the *Defiant*'s bridge as Vaughn finished recording his log entry. On the viewer, a recorded image of the alien artifact hovered, its infinitely shifting, eye-deceiving surfaces still stubbornly guarding its secrets.

Most of them, anyway.

Across the bridge, Nog paced back and forth before the engineering console, examining data on a padd he held and periodically comparing them to the console's readouts. He was no doubt doing his best to evaluate and expedite the repairs made necessary throughout the ship by the weapons of the Nyazen and D'Naali fleets. Although it had been only hours since Bashir had reattached the engineer's biosynthetic left leg, Nog was already moving about with a surprising degree of confidence, refusing to use the cane he'd been offered in the medical bay. He had yet to speak in any great detail about his personal experiences inside the artifact, at least to Bashir. But judging from the spring in Nog's step, it was hard to tell that the events of the last couple of days had ever happened.

You have to look into his eyes to see that, Bashir thought, feeling a surge of sympathy for his young friend's renewed physical loss, as well as a twinge of guilt. *Ezri and I obviously got the better part of whatever bargains we struck with the multiverse. At least we're both whole.*

The turbolift doors slid open, and Bowers strode onto the bridge, right beside Ezri.

Ezri *Dax* once again, now that the symbiont had been restored to her. It had been a near thing, so weakened had Ezri become because of her lengthy separation from the symbiont. But once Bashir had realized that the alien artifact had somehow restored his talents, he had become immovably determined to save the woman he loved. Of course, her own subjective experiences inside the artifact—to say nothing of her tenacious hold on life—might have contributed at least as much to her survival as had his and Krissten's efforts.

Dax smiled brilliantly at Bashir as she handed a padd to Vaughn, who was sitting in the command chair, gazing abstractedly at the floating space construct's haunting image.

"Ship's status report," she said, every inch the spit-and-polish executive officer. When he didn't respond immediately, she added, "Sir?"

Vaughn took another moment to accept the proffered report. "Excuse me, Lieutenant. That object lends itself to woolgathering."

She nodded, gazing out into infinity with Vaughn. "I know what you mean. You ought to see it from the *inside.*"

"I can't tell you how badly I'd like an opportunity to do just that. As horrific as some of what you've told me sounds, the opportunity to confront one's alternate selves—to take shortcuts onto the roads not taken—well, it's hard not to find certain aspects of that compelling."

As Vaughn spoke, Bashir saw the commander's blue eyes fill with some unaccustomed emotion—regret, perhaps?—as they strayed toward Ensign Tenmei, who busied herself at the conn station. It was no secret that Prynn was Vaughn's daughter and that, until fairly recently, a great deal of familial tension had existed between the two. But these weren't matters one could simply ask one's commanding officer about.

Bashir decided to broach something less sensitive. Gesturing toward the mysterious object on the viewer, he said, "Permission to speak freely, sir?"

Setting Ezri's padd aside, Vaughn turned the captain's chair in Bashir's direction, "Always," he said, though his expression had grown guarded.

"Sir, I couldn't help but notice that you left something rather significant out of your log entry just now."

The commander raised an inquisitive eyebrow. "Oh?"

"Yes, sir. I'm speaking of our interference in the conflict between the D'Naali and the Nyazen."

"Interference?" Vaughn repeated, steepling his fingers in front of his salt-and-pepper beard and arching an eyebrow. "Defined how?"

"By our direct participation in combat against the D'Naali," Bashir said, glancing quickly toward Shar at the science station, who appeared to be listening attentively to this exchange. While Bashir had been reattaching Nog's biosynthetic limb, Shar had visited the medical bay, where he had brought them both up to speed on almost everything that had transpired during the away team's foray into the artifact.

"We *did* prevent the D'Naali from blowing the object up," Bashir continued.

The commander chuckled, shaking his head. "Not at all. From what I observed, the Nyazen didn't get particularly vigilant about guarding the cathedral until after *we* arrived. I think that's because the D'Naali never truly had the ability to do any real damage in the first place. If they'd had that kind of power, then they would have found a way to destroy the cathedral thousands of years ago. One side would surely have wiped the other out long before now. The D'Naali themselves probably never believed they'd get the upper hand in their ancient little war—until Sacagawea informed them of our plan to use relays to beam an away team into the cathedral."

Bashir allowed a tiny smile to tug at the corner of his mouth. "We *did* fire a few shots their way, sir."

Vaughn matched the smile. "They seemed in need of

a little . . . demonstration of our sincerity, Doctor. But remember: we never actually scored a hit. The balance of forces between the Nyazen and the D'Naali remains intact. And we recovered you and the rest of the away team."

Bashir found he couldn't fault Vaughn's reasoning, and some subtle shift in the commander's demeanor told him it might not be such a good idea to try. Instead, he merely nodded and glanced in Nog's direction; he noticed that Nog, too, had been listening with interest—and seemed eager to make his own contribution to the discussion.

Vaughn had evidently noticed the same thing. "Yes, Lieutenant?"

Looking down at his inanimate leg, Nog said, "Sir, there's still one main question about the, um, cathedral that nobody's been able to answer yet—even with the translation of the alien text."

"And that is?"

"What's it *for?*" Nog said, an overtone of pain in his voice.

Bowers spoke up, his arms folded as he leaned against the bulkhead beside the tactical station. "The text gave us a pretty fair idea of why the thing's builders made it. They wanted to tap into unlimited power, but they couldn't control it, and they lost their homeworld because of it."

"That's not what I'm talking about," Nog said, shaking his head. "What I want to know is . . . what is the thing *now?* What exactly has it *become* during the half-billion years since it was built? And *why?*"

Ezri bit her lip, evidently considering Nog's questions carefully before attempting to answer them. "For starters, whatever intelligence still drives the thing is strongly telepathic. And it appeared to use issues and problems each of us was already struggling with as the tether connecting us to our alternate selves in those other universes."

Shar chose that moment to break his silence. "As far as the 'why' part of the question goes, I'd attribute a lot of it to the phenomenon of emergent properties. Because of its original function as an interdimensional energy tap, the object has always connected with and searched through many parallel universes and alternate dimensions. Therefore its ability to allow people to address alternate versions of themselves may be purely accidental—an emergent outgrowth of its original purpose, abetted by the object's built-in multidimensional physical topography."

Bowers flashed Shar a *that's-sure-easy-for-you-to-say* look before responding. "You're saying you think that thing's just . . . an *accident?*"

"Precisely. Just as the universe itself may be."

Looking at Shar, Vaughn nodded sagely. "That makes perfect sense, Ensign. Still, the existence of a miraculous cathedral could be interpreted to imply the existence of a miraculous cathedral builder. And, by extension, some sort of Grand Plan. Those with great faith rarely believe that anything happens entirely by accident." Bashir saw the commander turn his expectant gaze upon him, as though anticipating a debate.

But once again, he merely nodded. Prior to his own experiences inside the object—no, the cathedral—Bashir would have been inclined to dismiss its mystical ramifications out of hand.

Now he wasn't quite so certain.

Tenmei finally transferred her attention from her console and spoke to the room. "I'm hearing the word 'cathedral' bandied about so often here that I'm beginning to think some of you have developed genuine . . . religious feelings toward this artifact."

"Would that be such a terrible thing?" Vaughn said, a vaguely paternal smile playing on his lips.

"Not necessarily. Look, I don't mean to criticize anybody's private beliefs, but isn't it just possible that everyone's subjective experiences inside that thing were just . . . manifestations of the subconscious, like dreams?"

"I certainly hope so," Ezri said almost inaudibly. Bashir wanted to ask her what she meant, but the bridge seemed the wrong place to pry into the matter.

"What little we know about the away team's experiences does bear some resemblance," Shar said, "to the neurologically created 'ghosts' that some people report seeing during so-called near-death experiences. These 'cathedral experiences,' so to speak, may merely have been subconscious surrogates for whatever objective process severed each person's ties to the other alternate quantum dimensions."

Bashir was surprised at how ambivalent he felt about that. Ezri said nothing, but looked doubtful.

Vaughn resumed staring directly into the infinite, as rendered on the viewer. "Perhaps we'll never understand the extent of the object's capabilities. Rather like the riddle of existence itself."

Hence the need for faith, Bashir thought, mildly surprised to find himself so sanguine about the notion. *At least on certain occasions.*

Aloud, he said, "There was a time when my inquiries into imponderables like this would have been limited solely to the cold equations of science. But ever since the cathedral brought me face to face with . . . my*self,* I have to wonder whether those equations, by themselves, can ever be sufficient again."

"Maybe there's more to the universe than that," Vaughn said, nodding. "More than we can see or measure."

The entire bridge crew subsided into a thoughtful silence, with the exception of Shar, who was wordlessly keying something into a padd.

Bashir smiled as he watched the science officer work. No mystical experience, it seemed, could ever entirely displace those comforting, cold equations. But it was nice to have more than one thing to believe in.

From his seat at the bridge's main science station, Shar watched and listened, semidetached from his friends and colleagues as they debated the purpose behind the alien artifact—as though its *having* a purpose were some immutable, foreordained law of nature.

Why is it that most humans can't simply accept the universe as the cold, uncaring place that it really is?

Still, he thought he was finally beginning to understand the human religious impulse, at least on a certain visceral, reflexive level. How tempting it must be to believe that the artifact is some sort of divinely created holy object. Based on what the away team had reported so far, it might even conceivably provide a gateway into some parallel universe in which Thriss still lived. A place in which he and his bondmates would all survive, ameliorating Andor's bleak future by contributing that most precious of all gifts—a child.

A child who will now never come to be.

Eager for the solace of work, Shar reached for a padd, keying in commands with fingers stained indigo with blood not his own.

28

"Everything's going smoothly," Ro said under her breath.

"So far," Kira responded. "Let's hope we've already seen the last of today's surprises."

Ro nodded and scanned the crowds once again. The grand meeting hall adjacent to the Promenade had been transformed into a sumptuous gallery of Bajoran art and culture, including facsimiles of beautifully calligraphed musical scores drafted two centuries ago by the Boldaric Masters, as well as those of the incomparable modern composer Tor Jolan; reproductions of the paintings and tapestries of Vedek Topeka, along with some of the graphic artworks of the late Tora Ziyal; and even a live flute-recorder performance by the renowned Bajoran musician Varani.

All the attendees were dressed in their finest regalia. Treir stood chatting with a middle-level male Federation diplomat, who was clearly trying to negotiate something; sipping daintily at an outsize glass of something bubbly, the statuesque Orion woman managed to look beautiful as well as completely in charge of the encounter. With the addition of Taran'atar, who was keeping a low profile in a corner, the room even had its Gamma Quadrant delegate. Ro wondered briefly if Vaughn and the crew of the *Defiant* had made enough allies during their exploration mission so that future diplomatic events aboard the station would see even more Gamma Quadrant species represented.

As Kira moved to speak with Councillor zh'Thane, Ro saw General Lenaris standing nearby with Cerin Mika, the Ohalavaru woman who had been the *de facto* leader at last night's demonstration. Ro stepped over toward them, a gentle smile on her lips. "General. Mika. Are you enjoying the event so far?"

"A little too much pomp for an old warhorse like me, Ro, but I suppose I can stand it for one day," Lenaris said.

"I'm grateful you and your staff released us in time to attend the festivities," Mika said.

Ro cocked an eyebrow and said, "I'm sure our decision won't sit well with certain vedeks. It would probably be best if you steered clear of the most unhappy-looking ones today." She hesitated a moment, and decided that diplomacy needed to take a backseat to safety. "As we discussed before, I trust there won't be any . . . interruptions of today's ceremonies?"

"Certainly not," Mika said. "We made our point last night, and we will continue to press the Vedek Assembly in the future. But today is not a day to air religious differences or questions of faith."

"Glad to hear it," Ro said, patting Mika on the shoulder. She saw a familiar face grinning at her from across the room. Hiziki Gard. Excusing herself, Ro crossed over to him.

"You look . . . quite dashing," Ro said. She meant it. Gard was wearing tight trousers with piping down the sides, and a wrapped shirt with loose sleeves. A brocade sash belted the shirt at his waist. The colors of his clothes complemented his dark eyes and Trill markings.

"Thank you, Ro." He bowed and kissed her hand, then straightened and grinned at her again. "And you look as beautiful as a woman *could* in a dress Militia uniform."

Her smile was lopsided. "Thanks. I think."

They chatted a moment, and Ro became aware that she was being watched closely by someone. Scanning the crowd, she finally settled on who it was. Quark.

Excusing herself from Gard, Ro went over to Quark. He was holding a bottle of some kind of Orion wine, but the expression on his face was more sour than anything that liquid could have inspired. And he didn't appear to have been drinking. "Hello, Quark."

"Him again?" Quark gestured toward Gard with his head.

She sighed. "He and I are both working here, Quark."

"So am I." Quark said, baring his pointed teeth. "What's that got to do with anything? I just don't like him, that's all."

"Okay, so he's flirting with me. Are you going to react that way with *anyone* who pays the least little bit of attention to me?"

"No, it's not that," Quark replied, looking her in the eyes. "There's something . . . He makes me nervous."

I'll bet he does. Because you think I'm attracted to him. And I am attracted to him, dammit!

"I promise I'll keep an eye on him," Ro said, then realized her faux pas. "The same way I'm keeping an eye on everyone here. Including *you*." She brushed her fingertips across his ear, and Quark's expression almost immediately changed to one of delight. "Now, let me do my job, and I'll let you get that wine delivered to wherever it's going."

Ro gazed after Quark as he scurried away. Jealousy seemed so out of character for Quark. Maybe he really *was* falling for her. And she had to admit that he was growing on her as well.

". . . this truly auspicious day, the United Federation of Planets welcomes Bajor as its newest member!" Standing at the head of the lengthy table, Admiral Leonard James Akaar unfurled a long paper document. Kira knew that the parchment was merely decorative and ceremonial, intended for display at the Chamber of Ministers or some public museum; the actual document would be signed using a simple padd.

Kira hadn't had an opportunity to spend much time with Akaar today, but she knew that he was an old friend of Elias Vaughn. *Emphasis on old,* she thought with an inner smile. At 109 years, Akaar had lived longer than almost anyone present except for some of the Vulcans and—if you counted their multiple lives—most of the joined Trills. He wore his years lightly, though, cutting an almost regal figure in a heavily decorated fleet admiral's dress uniform. His dark eyes were sharp and alert, set into a deeply lined but vigorous face.

Despite the trials of the previous months, today's recovery of the Orbs and the signing ceremony for Bajor filled Kira's heart with a renewed sense of hope. Perhaps the future was not so bleak as she had imagined. She had endured so much already during her brief life; to see both of today's epoch-making events— to be a part of them—was incredible, to say the least.

Lost in her reverie, Kira had paid little attention to Shakaar's words as he droned on. She could barely bring herself to look at him, to say nothing of Vedek Yevir and his political-clerical cronies.

Glancing elsewhere, Kira saw that Gul Macet and Cleric Ekosha were watching the proceedings attentively. As her gaze continued slowly traveling through the room, she locked eyes with Taran'atar for a moment, then Matthias, then Quark, then Ro. Ro grinned, gesturing with a nod of the head, directing Kira to focus her attention back to the head of the ceremonial table.

Shakaar had stopped speaking, and was now rubbing his thumbs with ink on a small ceremonial blotter on the podium in front of him.

Akaar laid the parchment down on the table, smoothing it with his large, callused hands.

Out of the corner of her eye, Kira saw an impeccably dressed Hiziki Gard snap his arm down, as if trying to awaken it.

And then something tumbled into his hand, sliding out from under his sleeve.

Gard raised his arm and prongs snapped out from the object in his hand. A projectile shot forward from between them.

Shakaar raised his inked thumbs.

Kira started to shout a warning.

Two side blades snapped open on the projectile as it sped toward its target.

People began to turn toward Kira as the sound of her cry reached them.

The projectile tore into Shakaar's neck, its serrated blades cutting cleanly to the sides, its pointed center puncturing the first minister's throat. Shakaar's head toppled backward, impossibly far.

Scarcely conscious of her movements, Kira vaulted onto the table and was sliding toward the assassin, yelling for security. Time seemed to stand still as if suspended in amber. Kira noticed that Ro and several guards had drawn their phasers and were sprinting forward as well. Shakaar's body slumped forward onto the table, his lifeblood spilling out onto the ceremonial Federation document.

Security guards reacted swiftly, pushing Minister Asarem to the floor. Admiral Akaar reached into his uniform jacket, but if he had secreted one of his Capellan throwing knives there, he lacked the clear shot he needed to use it on the assassin.

Kira's eyes sought out the man who had attacked Shakaar. Hiziki Gard shot a grim smile in Ro's direction and then shimmered out of existence. Picked up by someone's transporter beam.

In the seconds it took Kira to reach the spot where he had stood, the assassin had made good his escape.

The room had erupted into a cacophony of screams and shouts. Ro yelled into her combadge to lock down the habitat and docking rings and to intercept all active transporter beams.

Kira moved quickly to the head of the table, dodging a screaming Asarem and the much more composed Councillor zh'Thane. Slapping her combadge as she sprinted, she yelled, "Emergency transport! Two to the Infirmary from this signal!"

Kira reached Shakaar as the transporter beam took hold of them both. But she already knew beyond doubt that the wounds were mortal.

Shakaar Edon was dead.

**CONTINUED IN
MISSION: GAMMA, BOOK FOUR
LESSER EVIL**

ABOUT THE AUTHORS

Michael A. Martin, whose short fiction has appeared in *The Magazine of Fantasy & Science Fiction,* is co-author of *Star Trek: The Next Generation, Section 31—Rogue* and *Roswell: Skeletons in the Closet* (both with Andy Mangels). Martin was the regular co-writer (also with Andy Mangels) of Marvel Comics' monthly *Star Trek: Deep Space Nine* comic-book series, and has generated heaps of copy for Atlas Editions' *Star Trek Universe* subscription card series. He has written for *Star Trek Monthly, Dreamwatch,* Grolier Books, Wildstorm, Platinum Studios, and Gareth Stevens, Inc., for whom he has penned several *Almanac of the States* nonfiction books. *Cathedral* is the second *Star Trek* novel to bear his name. Martin and Mangels currently have several other collaborative projects in the works, including two *Star Trek* novels involving the crew of the *U.S.S. Excelsior* and a *Starfleet Corps of Engineers* e-book. When not hunkered over a keyboard in his windowless basement, Martin reads voraciously, plots the revolution, and plays with his two wee bairns, James and William; he lives in Portland, Oregon, with his wife, Jennifer J. Dottery, their aforementioned children, and a mortgage of galactic proportions.

* * *

Andy Mangels is the co-author of *Star Trek: The Next Generation, Section 31—Rogue,* the upcoming *Roswell: Skeletons in the Closet,* and several future *Star Trek* book projects. Flying solo, he is the author of the upcoming *Animation on DVD: The Ultimate Guide,* as well as the best-selling book *Star Wars: The Essential Guide to Characters,* plus *Beyond Mulder & Scully: The Mysterious Characters of The X-Files* and *From Scream to Dawson's Creek: The Phenomenal Career of Kevin Williamson.*

Mangels has written for *The Hollywood Reporter, The Advocate, Just Out, Cinescape, Gauntlet, Dreamwatch, Sci-Fi Universe, SFX, Anime Invasion, Outweek, Frontiers, Portland Mercury, Comics Buyer's Guide,* and scores of other entertainment and lifestyle magazines. He has also written licensed material based on properties by Lucasfilm, Paramount, New Line Cinema, Universal Studios, Warner Bros., Microsoft, Abrams-Gentile, and Platinum Studios. His comic-book work has been seen from DC Comics, Marvel Comics, Dark Horse, Wildstorm, Image, Innovation, WaRP Graphics, Topps, and others, and he was the editor of the award-winning *Gay Comics* anthology for eight years.

In what little spare time he has, he likes to country dance and collect uniforms and Wonder Woman memorabilia. He lives in Portland, Oregon, with his longtime partner, Don Hood.

Visit his website at www.andymangels.com

Look for STAR TREK fiction from Pocket Books

#5 • *Fallen Heroes* • Dafydd ab Hugh

#6 • *Betrayal* • Lois Tilton

#7 • *Warchild* • Esther Friesner

#8 • *Antimatter* • John Vornholt

#9 • *Proud Helios* • Melissa Scott

#10 • *Valhalla* • Nathan Archer

#11 • *Devil in the Sky* • Greg Cox & John Gregory Betancourt

#12 • *The Laertian Gamble* • Robert Sheckley

#13 • *Station Rage* • Diane Carey

#14 • *The Long Night* • Dean Wesley Smith & Kristine Kathryn Rusch

#15 • *Objective: Bajor* • John Peel

#16 • *Invasion!* #3: *Time's Enemy* • L.A. Graf

#17 • *The Heart of the Warrior* • John Gregory Betancourt

#18 • *Saratoga* • Michael Jan Friedman

#19 • *The Tempest* • Susan Wright

#20 • *Wrath of the Prophets* • David, Friedman & Greenberger

#21 • *Trial by Error* • Mark Garland

#22 • *Vengeance* • Dafydd ab Hugh

#23 • *The 34th Rule* • Armin Shimerman & David R. George III

#24-26 • *Rebels* • Dafydd ab Hugh

    #24 • *The Conquered*

    #25 • *The Courageous*

    #26 • *The Liberated*

Books set after the series

    The Lives of Dax • Marco Palmieri, ed.

    Millennium Omnibus • Judith and Garfield Reeves-Stevens

        #1 • *The Fall of Terok Nor*

        #2 • *The War of the Prophets*

        #3 • *Inferno*

    A Stitch in Time • Andrew J. Robinson

    Avatar, Book One • S.D. Perry

    Avatar, Book Two • S.D. Perry

    Section 31: Abyss • David Weddle & Jeffrey Lang

    Gateways #4: Demons of Air and Darkness • Keith R.A. DeCandido

    Gateways #7: What Lay Beyond: "Horn and Ivory" • Keith R.A. DeCandido

    Mission: Gamma

        #1 • *Twilight* • David R. George III

        #2 • *This Gray Spirit* • Heather Jarman

        #3 • *Cathedral* • Michael A. Martin & Andy Mangels

Star Trek: Voyager®

    Mosaic • Jeri Taylor

    Pathways • Jeri Taylor

    Captain Proton: Defender of the Earth • D.W. "Prof" Smith

Novelizations

 Caretaker • L.A. Graf
 Flashback • Diane Carey
 Day of Honor • Michael Jan Friedman
 Equinox • Diane Carey
 Endgame • Diane Carey & Christie Golden

 #1 • *Caretaker* • L.A. Graf
 #2 • *The Escape* • Dean Wesley Smith & Kristine Kathryn Rusch
 #3 • *Ragnarok* • Nathan Archer
 #4 • *Violations* • Susan Wright
 #5 • *Incident at Arbuk* • John Gregory Betancourt
 #6 • *The Murdered Sun* • Christie Golden
 #7 • *Ghost of a Chance* • Mark A. Garland & Charles G. McGraw
 #8 • *Cybersong* • S.N. Lewitt
 #9 • *Invasion!* #4: *The Final Fury* • Dafydd ab Hugh
 #10 • *Bless the Beasts* • Karen Haber
 #11 • *The Garden* • Melissa Scott
 #12 • *Chrysalis* • David Niall Wilson
 #13 • *The Black Shore* • Greg Cox
 #14 • *Marooned* • Christie Golden
 #15 • *Echoes* • Dean Wesley Smith, Kristine Kathryn Rusch &
  Nina Kiriki Hoffman
 #16 • *Seven of Nine* • Christie Golden
 #17 • *Death of a Neutron Star* • Eric Kotani
 #18 • *Battle Lines* • Dave Galanter & Greg Brodeur
 #19-21 • *Dark Matters* • Christie Golden
  #19 • *Cloak and Dagger*
  #20 • *Ghost Dance*
  #21 • *Shadow of Heaven*

Enterprise®

Broken Bow • Diane Carey
By the Book • Dean Wesley Smith & Kristine Kathryn Rusch

Star Trek®: New Frontier

New Frontier #1-4 Collector's Edition • Peter David
 #1 • *House of Cards*
 #2 • *Into the Void*
 #3 • *The Two-Front War*
 #4 • *End Game*
#5 • *Martyr* • Peter David
#6 • *Fire on High* • Peter David

Star Trek®: Invasion!

#1 • *First Strike* • Diane Carey
#2 • *The Soldiers of Fear* • Dean Wesley Smith & Kristine Kathryn Rusch
#3 • *Time's Enemy* • L.A. Graf
#4 • *The Final Fury* • Dafydd ab Hugh
Invasion! Omnibus • various

Star Trek®: Day of Honor

#1 • *Ancient Blood* • Diane Carey
#2 • *Armageddon Sky* • L.A. Graf
#3 • *Her Klingon Soul* • Michael Jan Friedman
#4 • *Treaty's Law* • Dean Wesley Smith & Kristine Kathryn Rusch
The Television Episode • Michael Jan Friedman
Day of Honor Omnibus • various

Star Trek®: The Captain's Table

#1 • *War Dragons* • L.A. Graf
#2 • *Dujonian's Hoard* • Michael Jan Friedman
#3 • *The Mist* • Dean Wesley Smith & Kristine Kathryn Rusch
#4 • *Fire Ship* • Diane Carey
#5 • *Once Burned* • Peter David
#6 • *Where Sea Meets Sky* • Jerry Oltion
The Captain's Table Omnibus • various

Star Trek®: The Dominion War

#1 • *Behind Enemy Lines* • John Vornholt
#2 • *Call to Arms...* • Diane Carey
#3 • *Tunnel Through the Stars* • John Vornholt
#4 • *...Sacrifice of Angels* • Diane Carey

Star Trek®: Section 31™

Rogue • Andy Mangels & Michael A. Martin
Shadow • Dean Wesley Smith & Kristine Kathryn Rusch
Cloak • S.D. Perry
Abyss • David Weddle & Jeffrey Lang

Star Trek®: Gateways

#1 • *One Small Step* • Susan Wright
#2 • *Chainmail* • Diane Carey
#3 • *Doors Into Chaos* • Robert Greenberger
#4 • *Demons of Air and Darkness* • Keith R.A. DeCandido

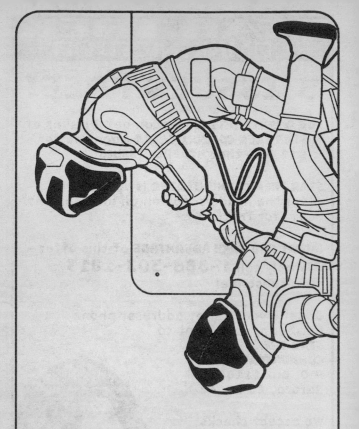

STAR TREK®
THE STARFLEET
SURVIVAL GUIDE
AVAILABLE NOW... FOR THOSE
WHO PLAN AHEAD.

STSG

STAR TREK
SECTION 31

BASHIR
Never heard of it.

SLOAN
We keep a low profile....
We search out and identify
potential dangers to the
Federation.

BASHIR
And Starfleet sanctions
what you're doing?

SLOAN
We're an autonomous
department.

BASHIR
Authorized by whom?

SLOAN
Section Thirty-One was
part of the original
Starfleet Charter.

BASHIR
That was two hundred years
ago. Are you telling me
you've been on your own
ever since? Without specific
orders? Accountable to
nobody but yourselves?

SLOAN
You make it sound so
ominous.

BASHIR
Isn't it?

No law. No conscience. No stopping them.
A four book, all <u>Star Trek</u> series beginning in June.

Excerpt adapted from *Star Trek: Deep Space Nine*
"Inquisition" written by Bradley Thompson & David Weddle.

Picard comes face to face with a man
who may be his most dangerous
adversary yet...
and a surprisingly personal nemesis.

STAR TREK
nemesis

novelization by
J. M. Dillard

screenplay by
John Logan

story by
John Logan & Rick Berman
& Brent Spiner

Star Trek: The Next Generation®
created by Gene Roddenberry

THIS NOVEMBER!

HEME